The Gravediggers Series 1

Blood Feud:
A PUNK ROCK VAMPIRE STORY

MATTHEW R. MILLER

The Book's Savant Talent

Content Editing by Leoneh Charmell

Cover Art by Elvins Acurero

Interior Design by Avril Acurero

https://thebookssavant.com

SECOND EDITION

Disclaimer: This is a work of fiction. Names, characters, places, and incidents either are the product of the author's imagination or are used fictitiously. Any resemblance to actual persons, living or dead, events, or locales is entirely coincidental.

INDEX

CHAPTER 1

A BOY GOES TO WAR

West Virginia
January 7, 1865
U.S. Civil War

It's hard enough being a seven-foot-tall teenager without also having to dodge flying musket balls. Asa Harmon McCoy was finding this out the hard way. Like so many Civil War soldiers, Asa was just a teenager when he had left home to fight for the Union against the Confederacy. Also, like so many soldiers in all wars, he had held a glorified view of it until the bullets had started flying, and then he had instantly realized it was hell on earth. So, he thought it was a little ridiculous that he found himself on a battlefield, holding a musket and wearing a grey uniform, looking across at the enemy—a bunch of boys just like him, just as scared and just as awkward.

He was supposed to shoot and kill them, but he really didn't want to do that. After all, they were fellow Americans, and even some of his own family were fighting for the Confederacy. What if he accidentally killed family? Could he ever forgive himself?

In any case, Sergeant Tapnik was shouting at everyone to shoot, so he couldn't just stand there doing nothing. He loaded his musket and pointed it in the general direction of an enemy troop, who was also loading his musket frantically. The poor boy looked about thirteen years old, barely old enough to even function without his mother. The enemy saw Asa aiming at him, and a look of panic and terror washed onto his face as he realized what was happening—Asa just couldn't do it.

He fired the bullet into the ground in front of the poor boy. When the boy understood what Asa had done, he smiled, nodded, and mouthed the words, "Thank you."

Other boys were not so lucky.

In the middle of the battlefield, between the two warring sides, lay the young casualties of war. Just boys that had been cut down in the flower of their youths – many were dead, already becoming stiff and pale, and the ones who were wounded were screaming. They screamed for help, screamed for their friends, screamed for their mommies to save them… but no one could save them while the battle still raged. Some of them were missing arms or legs, or had gaping, bloody holes in their bodies in places where holes should never be. One of them even had a hole in his skull, the result of a leaden musket ball that had cracked it open without killing him, and his grey brains were visible. Another was trying to hold his intestines inside of the gaping maw in his stomach.

There is nothing glorious about war, thought Asa and every other kid there.

As the sun began to set, the shots started to slow until nightfall brought an end to that day's fighting with an implied ceasefire.

Both sides returned to their camp to eat and drink, and the medics tried in vain to heal the wounded. As the campfires crackled, the boys sat around in companies; some boys wrote letters to their mothers, others smoked tobacco out of corncob pipes, and some began to tell ghost stories for entertainment. One of the older boys in Asa's company, a boy of maybe seventeen years, had grown up right near the battlefield, and he began to tell them of a local legend.

"When I was growin' up here, my grandpappy used to tell us stories 'bout the forest. One of them stories was about a creature that's been livin' here since before us, even before the Injuns, before man was here. Now there's plenty of creatures out there, some good, some bad. Some of 'em are ghosts, some of 'em are Wendigos, and some of 'em are the angry spirits of people've died in violence."

Several of them glanced out at the battlefield—they could still hear some of the last surviving boys screaming like babies. It was too dangerous to help them, so they were going to simply be left to die in agony. The boy continued.

"Grandpappy said there's one creature out there that's the worst of 'em all. He said there ain't no name for it. Even the Injuns ain't got a name for it. They feared it and avoided it, since they thought givin' it a name'd give it power. Cherokees, Shawnee, Tutelo, Saponi — they all told tales of the demon."

"What kind of spirit, Jake?" asked a boy of about twelve, whose voice had not even changed yet.

"A dark, dark spirit. Black. The blackest black you ever seen."

As the campfire's smoke curled up into the dark canopy of pine trees, the boys scooted a little closer to one another.

"Yep, blacker'n black," Jake went on. "It's bad, too—wicked bad. Real evil, boys. 'Cuz it don't just haint you, don't just scare you. Now the Wendigo, it'll bite you and make you wanna eat other people. But this one, the one without a name, it drinks yer blood. It drinks it all down, 'til you die from bein' drained of all yer blood."

The boys gasped.

"And that ain't it! When it drinks yer blood, you die, but you come back. You come back like one of 'em, like the dark thing. An' then *you* start cravin' the blood of other people, an' *you* start killin' 'em, and makin' 'em like you until everyone in a village is a monster. It's so bad, so evil, that it can't go out in the day, 'cuz the sun'll burn it all up. It can't go near nothin' Christian, 'cuz it'll scare it away. It's like a dead person what's come back as a monster."

Some of the younger boys had begun to turn their heads anxiously to look into the forest around them.

"Aw, that's just a legend, Jake!" said Asa confidently.

Jake answered, "Well, Asa, maybe it is, and maybe it ain't. You know the Injuns know this forest lots better'n us, and they say it's true. But who knows?"

The group of boys puffed on their pipes in silence, pondering the tale that Jake had just told them. The pine forest around them was silent, too silent; no animals scurried or called out. A scream came from the Confederate camp across the field.

"What was that?" asked Asa.

"Some poor bastard gettin' his leg amputated, I'll bet," said Jake.

Another shriek sounded across the field, then another.

"That's lots of amputations!" said one boy.

"Wait," said Asa. "Hush. Just listen."

The screams increased until dozens of Confederate men were crying out in mortal terror. Soon, it wounded like the whole damn Confederate Army was yelling for mercy, and then, in a matter of seconds, the screams ended.

"Somethin' ain't right, there," noted Jake.

The trees around the Union camp began to shiver like there was a strong breeze, quivering in the way that only pine trees do, and the boys were looking around nervously like prairie dogs. Asa looked across the camp at another campfire, around which some other boys were sitting, and pangs of fear gripped his stomach as he saw a raven-black figure seem to sweep between him and the fire. It was tall, and seemed to hover inches off the ground as it passed back into the forest.

Asa was not the only boy to notice them, as several others in his company frantically looked around from campfire to campfire. The dark figures were everywhere at once, moving at impossible speeds.

They began to pounce upon the soldiers, ripping them apart, pulling off heads, tearing open chests worse than any musket ball ever could. The screams of dread and pain were like those that had come from the Confederate side, each one cut short as one of the horrors killed some poor boy, then bent down to his neck and began audibly guzzling and slurping his blood. The gurgling blood was like a forest stream, but thick and viscous rather than sprite and bubbly. The entire encampment was being torn apart by the creatures, and Asa fainted from fear.

He must have remained unconscious for an entire day, for when he came to, it was evening again, and he was in the same place. He could no longer move his tongue around his desiccated mouth, and his nostrils were on fire and bleeding. His neck was too stiff to even think of turning, and he ached with a sick hunger and thirst.

Death seemed like the best option, and he would have chosen that, were it not for the thought of his beloved mother, waiting for him at home. She likely would receive news soon of the battle and the number of casualties, and if he did not return home, she would be heartbroken. The thought of that pained his heart and soul to a depth never before reached by any of life's troubles.

He would have cried, but there was not enough liquid left in his husk.

Moving was next to impossible, but he began by scratching his fingers in the dirt and then swaying his forearm slowly, then his upper arm, and then his other limbs, until he had broken the seal of stiffness. Over the course of ten minutes, Asa suffered searing bursts of pain in his joints and muscles, but finally managed to bear a convincing resemblance to standing upright. Hobbling through the gory remains of the Union camp, he found some water and food rations.

Asa turned in the direction of his home and began heading back.

In a while, he began to see familiar surroundings on the road. He was about one hour's walk from his home, and that thought warmed him with great cheer, even though the night was falling fast. He limped yet still picked up his pace, the hearth-warmth tugging at his heartstrings as if real, fleshy arms, warming his spirit so that even the bloody gashes and cuts about his body felt like mere caresses. His salivary glands tingled the way they did before a big feast, and he fantasized about the warm, savory flavors that he would enjoy that night.

"Well, well, well. What do we have here, boys?" A youthful, twangy voice rang out from the side of the path, and before he had time to even register it, he saw six or seven Confederates emerging from the brush, grinning like cats who had cornered their mouse.

"Oh, hell," muttered Asa.

"Boys, I think I see me a Yankee here. Ain't you a Yankee, man?"

"I just want to get home," Asa pleaded. "Please, I was almost killed in the battle. Please just let me pass."

"Please just let me pass," mocked the leader of the gang in an effeminate voice. "You're a Yankee."

Asa remained silent, squinting his eyes in a desperate plea for mercy when recognition swept across the leader's face.

"Well damn, boys! Look at who we got here! If it ain't none other than one Asa McCoy!"

"That's a McCoy?" asked one of the boys incredulously. "McCoy! Your clan's been our neighbors for years, and you went and turned against us in the war. Why would you do a thing like that?"

"I... look, this war has us all messed up," begged Asa. "Now boys, your family and mine's known each other for too long to let this war divide us like this. Every man makes his choices."

"And every man must live with the consequences," answered the leader as he swaggered toward Asa with a pistol in his hand. "Whaddya say, boys? A little extra-judicial justice? We are at war, to be sure, and this 'un here's the enemy, ain't he?"

The other Confederate boys laughed and nodded, one calling out, "Damn right, Lucius, and ain't we commanded to kill the enemy?"

"That we are, Titus," answered Lucius while cocking back the pistol's hammer. "Why, I reckon it'd be treason to let the enemy live." The boys chuckled again.

"Finish him, Lucius! Think of all them boys he must've killed from our side!" called out a boy in the back of the group.

"Oh, no, oh please now, Lucius," begged Asa. "Please just let me go home. Consider it a favor from family to family. I got my poor mother waiting for me at home. Please don't kill me."

Asa, exhausted to the point of shaking, fell to his knees in supplication, only causing the Confederates to laugh at him and Lucius to put the pistol to his temple.

"Say goodbye to this world, McCoy. He who lives by the sword shall die by the…"

Lucius' words were cut off by a black figure rushing out of the forest at the speed of a bullet. It tore Lucius' head off, then went and did the same to every one of his horrified companions before they could even scream in fear. Asa watched for a second time as the creature tore into their necks and slurped their blood. Too tired to move, he had no choice but to watch in a combination of fascination and disgust. After feeding, however, the creature turned toward him.

It was like a person in its shape, but under a black cloak and hood that looked as if they were made out of the very night and the fabric of the universe. The face was invisible behind the blackness, save two glowing, red dots that must have been the thing's eyes.

Well, that was apparently enough to endow young Asa with superhuman strength, for he stood up and began to run away from the thing as if he were fresh from a good night's sleep. Lucky was he that, even in his state of panic and terror, he managed to run in the direction of his home, and once he came to that knowledge, he ran like the wind, adrenaline masking all of the battle wounds and agonies.

He ran for a time that seemed like forever but was, in reality, a couple of minutes, until the thick, dark forest surrounding him gave way to a faint, yellow glow, a glow which expanded like the iris of an eye until he could see, through the trees, his homestead!

Muttering thanks to God, Jesus, Buddha, Zoroaster, and any other deity he could think of, he burst out of the forest onto his very own property. God help him, he could see his mother through the parlor window, sitting at a desk, writing a letter (perhaps to him?)!

He slowed his run to a trot, catching his breath—he was in the clear, and only steps remained between himself and his home. Any pain and coldness in his body were instantly replaced with warm feelings of ecstasy and anticipation. To hug his mother, to taste hot, well-seasoned meat, to sleep in a soft, pillowy bed — these had been but fantasies a few days ago, but now, they were being fulfilled.

A noise, a shuffle of leaves, a clattering of branches: poor Asa sensed and knew it before he turned to look. In this living world, the last thing he saw was that sickening pair of red eyes beneath the black hood and the dark shape rushing at him.

CHAPTER 2

THE PUNKS BREAK DOWN

West Virginia
Modern Day

"**S**top spitting on the floor of my van, prick!" screamed *Scary* Mary Gambino over the blast of The Ramones' *I Wanna Be Sedated*. In return, Paul *Junk* Roy spat again, the ruddy tobacco juice pooling into a nauseating glob on the driver's floormat underneath his combat boots.

"Shit! What kind of hick hillbilly punk chews tobacco anyway?" yelled Scary Mary.

Paul Junk spat a little more through the gap in his two front teeth and grinned. "We're in West fucking Virginia now, Scary! Yeehaw! Might as well be a hillbilly! Don't you wanna fit in?"

"You think we fit in anywhere?" asked *Gutter* Gill LeBlanc from the back seat of the trashed 1964 Volkswagen Microbus, which was rusted, wobbly, and covered with punk band stickers. "Isn't that rather the point?" he continued in a baritone, affected half-British accent. "I swear, Paul, it's like you don't even understand the punk philosophy. We're anti-authoritarian, anti-conformity. Christ." He shook his head depressingly while Paul just shrugged his shoulders.

"Oh, for fuck's sake," replied Mary, acquiescing and cranking up the music even louder, if that were possible. The eardrum-puncturing, glass-shattering volume of The Ramones almost covered up the earthshaking, contrabass snores of *Mucky* Matt Moulin, who was curled up in the back floor space, managing almost supernaturally to sleep peacefully despite the utter chaos in the van.

Blitzkrieg Pop came on next, and Junk shouted out the chorus, replacing "Blitzkrieg pop" with "Hillybilly poon." Scary Mary furrowed her brows.

"Oh my God, you are so stupid, Junk. Jesus."

He sang louder and laughed maniacally.

"And slow the fuck down! I don't have insurance on this van. If we get pulled over by some hick cop, he'll probably put us in jail."

Junk pressed the accelerator and sped up.

"Why do I even fucking try?" asked Mary.

"The girl has a point," chimed in Gutter Gill. "You know the law enforcement in these small, rural villages tend to be rather mistrusting of outsiders, much less a punk band from New Orleans. We are, doubtless, like aliens to them."

"You're a fucking alien, bitch!" yelled Junk, bellowing with self-indulgent laughter. Gutter just looked down and shook his head again. Mucky Matt, against all laws of nature, slept on.

The narrow state highway they were on, flanked by an impenetrable wall of pine trees, rose and fell like waves as it passed over the Allegheny foothills. The tough little Volkswagen four-banger protested and whined with each rise and crest, but with every slope, the cool Fall wind passed over the angry cylinders and calmed them down. The little Hitlermobile only had so much life left in it, however, and at the peak of the next foothill, the engine cut out, also silencing The Ramones and waking up Mucky Matt, who promptly and unceremoniously asked, "Where the fuck are we, and what the fuck is happening?"

"Well, Matt," replied Scary Mary, "it seems like Junk doesn't know how to drive a fucking van, and now it broke down."

"Me?" demanded Paul amidst a fit of giggling. "Shit, Mary, don't blame me 'cuz you can't maintain a fucking van."

"Just pull over, Paul. Pull right over. I know something about engines. Stop yelling too. I have a headache," added Gill.

Paul shrugged, spat a big loogie, then pulled the steering wheel to the right, causing the van to silently coast farther than they would have imagined it could have, having no functioning engine. In fact, it coasted right into the dusty parking lot of the countriest country store that any of the four ridiculous city slickers had ever seen.

The wooden building—perhaps *shack* was a better term—was dilapidated or in the process of dilapidating. A rusted, tin sign hung slanted, proudly presenting the text: *Ushaville General Store*. A large, slatted wooden porch creaked rhythmically to the beat of splintery old rocking chairs, ensconced upon which were a sundry range of hillbilly stereotypes. Some chewed tobacco, some picked the banjo, some played gin rummy, and some just stared out at the forest like they were sedated. A missing tooth here, a patch of hair there—these old men might have been on the front of a demented postcard: *Missing You in West Virginia!* As if enjoying the chaos, the Microbus glided to a smooth, silent stop right in front of the porch. A hubcap came loose and rolled up onto the porch. The banjo music ceased.

For at least two excruciating, awkward, horrifying minutes of total silence, as if the forest creatures themselves were in awe of this mighty clash of cultures, the four rockers, and the four locals stared at one other, each slightly terrified yet insanely curious. Mohawk-to-mullet, piercing-to-stubble, guitar-to-banjo, leather-to-flannel, the punk-to-hillbilly standoff was finally broken when a local sitting on a rocking chair offered, in a nervous and cracking voice, "Can—can I help you boys... uh... ladies and gents, and—well, can I help you?"

Gill rolled his eyes in exasperation and decided to answer for the group. "Van broke down. Can I just use your parking lot for a little while? I have some tools. I think I can fix it."

Well, the concept of working on engines in parking lots turned out to be the one uniting factor between the two groups. The man nodded, stood up, and walked toward the Volkswagen, stopping at the edge of the shadow created by the porch's awning.

"Welcome to Ushaville. I'm Red, and this is my store. We aim to be hospitable 'round here, so y'uns just use our parking lot as long as you need, you hear? And if you're hungry or thirsty, we got barbecue and cold drinks inside the store."

"Got any beer?" shouted Paul from the driver's seat.

"Beer? It's not even noon, son."

Paul nodded, laughed, and spat through his dental gap. "Yeah, buddy, that's the point!"

"I, well, sure we got beer," answered Red. "We sure do, if you're given to drinkin' in the morning. Meet me inside, and I'll check you out."

"Yeehaw!" yelled Paul. "You hear that, Matt? They got beer! Let's go, mate."

Matt, eyes looking drowsy still, followed Paul into the store as Red took his tools to Gill timidly, wondering if this particular human species was apt to attack without provocation. He stared a little too long at Gill's nose piercing, prompting Gill to ask, "You like it? I could give you one. I have a license."

Red's eyes grew wide, and he stammered, "Uh, no, no! That's alright. Thanky though. My nose'll stay how the good Lord made it. Let's have a look at that engine."

As Gill lifted the rear engine cover, Red seemed to realize his mistake in leaving the store unattended. He huffed and stammered, made some excuse, then ran toward the store, but it was too late.

As soon as Paul and Matt had entered the store, they had begun stuffing cigarettes, chips, lighters, and sundry bobbles into their boots, underwear, and jackets. As Red huffed his fat belly inside, the derelicts began examining the beer choices a bit too innocently.

"Got anything besides this watery crap?" yelled Paul across the store as Red eyed them both suspiciously.

"Sorry, but it's all we got. We ain't got fancy stuff here, but we manage to get along all the same."

"Yeah. Alright," replied Paul. "Matt, grab a few cases. I'll get some more."

They plopped six cases of Natural Light onto the sales counter and whipped out a few crinkled, filthy, torn old twenty-dollar bills. Red rang them up, his lips pursed and eyebrows furrowed. He looked up at Paul.

"You're a tall feller!"

Paul grinned and spat on the floor. Red just continued to stare.

"You want to ask something, bud? Just ask. It's alright," said Matt.

Red smiled weakly and answered, "Well, I guess I was wonderin' what a group of—what are you, rock and rollers?" Paul stifled a chuckle. "What are you doin' here in the middle of bumfuck nowhere? I was born here. That's my excuse. But there can't be much for a group of young'uns here, can they?"

"Young'uns? Jesus," muttered Paul under his breath.

"We're on our way to a gig."

Red shook his head.

"A show. You know? We're playing a rock concert in Charleston. We're a band, The Gravediggers. This was supposed to be a shortcut," explained Matt.

"A short cut? Hell, I'm not sure we're a shortcut to anywhere out here. We're plumb in the middle of a giant forest. Sorry to tell y'uns, but you're a hell of a long way from Charleston. What you want to do is get that there van of yours fixed up and head back the other way. Nothing for y'uns in Ushaville, I promise you that."

11

As Red gave them their change, he eyed their bulging jackets, filled with stolen items, and their torn jeans. Paul hissed at him like a goat, and Red jumped back.

"Thanks for the beer, man."

A crowd of rednecks had gathered around Gill and the van, watching him turn the wrench here and there. He yelled, "Shit!" causing the crowd of locals to jump back.

"Relax, guys. I'm harmless, mostly. I think we're screwed, though. The carb's dead. Got a car shop in town?"

By this time, Red, Paul, and Matt had returned outside. Red shook his head.

"I think y'uns need to call someone to pick you up. We're just a tiny little settlement, not much here to help you."

The locals all stole furtive glances at one another.

"Not a single fucking person in your town has an auto shop?" demanded Paul.

"Look, son, I've been more than accommodatin' to you bunch. No need to talk to us like that!" huffed Red.

"Paul, calm down. Christ," interjected Scary Mary. "Sorry, Mister Red. He's just an asshole. Look, we appreciate your help. The thing is, we're stuck. We don't know anyone in West Virginia. We're from New Orleans, and everyone we know is there."

At the mention of the Crescent City, the locals seemed to pay more careful attention to Mary's words.

"New'arlins, you say?" asked Billy *Mack* McCoy, the banjoist. "We know somethin' 'bout that city," he said, chuckling.

"That's enough, Billy," snapped Red. "These folks don't want to hear your life story. They need to be gettin' along, though. It's gettin' close to noon."

While ignoring Red, Paul was studying the store and squinting his eyes like he was trying to remember something. He looked the wooden shack up and down, then focused on the sign. Under the *Ushaville General Store* title were the words, *Red McCoy, Owner*. Then it clicked in his drunken mind.

"McCoy? Red McCoy? Like the Hatfield and McCoy feud?" he asked loudly.

Red frowned at him but replied, "Yes, Sir. That's us. Ushaville's the center of the area where the famous feud began. This side of town's us McCoys, and east side of town's all Hatfields."

"Oh shit!" added Mary, who had doubled over in laughter. "Seriously? The Hatfield-McCoy feud? Holy crap, we really are in the boonies! Please, oh please tell me, Red, that the feud isn't still going on?"

Mary, Paul, Gill, and Matt watched Red in anticipation, hardly believing this.

Red seemed a little embarrassed but replied, "Well, if you want the truth, then yes. Ushaville never really recovered. It's not like in Charleston, where the whole thing is a tourist attraction. Here, bad blood spills into the next generation's veins. It's a matter of family honor. You'd have to be from here to understand."

Mary lost it, doing a spit take with her beer.

"Well, holy hell. The Hatfield-McCoy fucking feud continues, and we managed to find it!" The band laughed heartily, but the rednecks did not seem too jovial about it.

"You wouldn't understand!" yelled Joey McCoy. "It's a long, private history. There's lots more to it than meets the eye!"

"Easy, Joey," spoke Red. "You four'd better watch your manners. It's you stuck out in the middle of nowhere with no help, not us."

The euphemized threat dampened the laughter, and Gill stepped in to try to help: "Alright, sorry, Red. Look, we're just some stupid punks from New Orleans. We don't mean harm, alright? I apologize on behalf of my idiot bandmates. It's been a long trip, and they are just slightly losing their minds, which were not too great, to begin with. Please, there must be some place in your town to get our van fixed. It needs a new carburetor or at least a rebuild. We're not rich, as you can see, but I can pay for at least that and a hotel room for the night. Please, Red. I am sorry for our behavior. It goes with the lifestyle, but inside, we're harmless."

"Speak for yourself, fag!" yelled the drunken Paul Junk, with a gratuitous spit of tobacco juice through his gap.

"Shut up for now, Paul. Seriously, we're in deep shit here, especially if you keep insulting these gentlemen. Now, Red, please be reasonable," pleaded Gill.

"Sorry, son, but there ain't nothin' we can do for you. Ushaville's no place for strangers. You can sleep in your van, and tomorrow I'll take a look at the carb myself. I might have a spare one, and if not, I can fix it no matter what. Now, y'uns is free to use the store bathroom and the parking lot, and you can buy all you want from the store, but just don't cause trouble, got it? We're just peaceful folks here."

"Come on, Red!" said Matt, now fully awake thanks to chugging three beers. "There's gotta at least be a hotel here! I don't mind sleeping in the damn van, but we're stuck here forever without some help. Is it about your stupid feud? Is that why you won't help us? We don't care, man. None of our business, right? Just give us a place to sleep and a way to fix our van, and come tomorrow, you'll never see us again.

"I told y'uns, it just ain't—" Red was interrupted by the loud hum of a motorcycle engine. A vintage Triumph Bonneville rounded the road's corner, then pulled into the parking lot.

Turning off the engine and resting the bike on its kickstand, a man stepped off. Wearing black jeans, a black leather jacket, dark sunglasses, and a black scarf tied around his head, he must have been seven feet tall or more. The opposite of a bodybuilder, he was wraith-thin, like an animated scarecrow: positively terrifying. All talk ceased, and a viscous silence enveloped everyone. No birds chirped; no breeze blew.

Leaving his sunglasses on his face, the wispy-tall man surveyed the scene. In a controlled baritone voice, a voice that practiced meek subduction but hinted at a great force below, he said: "Red McCoy? What is going on here?"

Red, removing his hat and looking down, answered in a trembling voice, "Nothing, Sir... just... we have some visitors, Sir."

"Visitors?" The man looked toward the band. Paul whispered, "Holy hell, he looks like Joey Ramone!" Mary kicked his foot to shut him up.

"Where are you from, visitors, and how did you stumble upon Ushaville?"

The four were, frankly, too intimidated to answer, but Gill decided to be the adult in the group of overgrown adolescents: "We're from New Orleans. We're traveling to Charleston, and our van broke down right here at this store."

The tall man took a few steps toward them, still wearing his dark sunglasses. He seemed to think for a moment, then said, "And I assume that Red McCoy has shown you four strangers hospitality?"

"He told us to bugger off, basically," interjected Paul from behind Gill.

The man slowly turned and looked directly at Red, who, if he were not pissing his pants now, would surely crap them later.

"Is this so, Red McCoy? Strangers come into our town, and you insult them? Is that how we have taught you to act?"

Red whimpered, "I... but, Sir, I didn't want them to..."

"That's enough, Red McCoy," interrupted the man calmly, and Red became ghostly silent.

"Forgive my... friends, travelers. How often we forget the old ways of hospitality that our ancestors taught us in this town. You are most welcome to stay in our hotel. I will see that your van is repaired, and I will have you back on the road tomorrow. Until then, you are free to enjoy our town. Micky McCoy," and he then nodded toward a rather rough-looking fellow in overalls on the porch, "will drive you into town. All I ask is that you do not disturb the peace, and I also strongly urge you not to venture into the east side of the town. Welcome to Ushaville."

In utter silence among them all, the willow of a man strode back to his Triumph in barely two steps, mounted it, and started the engine. The bike hummed a buzzing song. Nature returned to life. Without looking back, he calmly rode back the way he had come.

CHAPTER 3

JEAN-PIERRE DE LA FRESNIÈRE

Father Jean-Pierre de la Fresnière always became a bit nervous when the bishop showed up unannounced at the office of the St. Louis Cathedral in Jackson Square, New Orleans. It was not so much that Jean-Pierre worried that the bishop would chastise him for sipping wine during the day; after all, the bishop was a known inebriate, although it was certainly never spoken of in priestly circles. Jean-Pierre smoked cigars, too. Again, the bishop did not care. No, the individual trappings of hedonism did not move the bishop. Not much did. In his 80 years, he had seen enough priests of all types to simply stop caring.

Did any particular priest fulfill his duties? Did he offer mass? Give the Eucharist? Visit the sick? Did he help give to the poor? Was his doctrine sound enough to not arouse the sniffing around of the Vatican? Then that was a good priest, as far as the bishop was concerned.

No, Father Jean-Pierre hated the bishop's sudden visits simply because he, though a priest, was losing his faith. It was more than that, in fact. He was slipping down, not only into the pits of agnosticism and—dare he even mumble the word?—atheism, but even more so, into becoming overall pissed off at God and the Church. Oh, Mother Church, who promises succor then slaps her children in the face! What good was he, a priest? Why did he even continue to live? To chant some Latin here and there? To give wine to those already drunk on delusion? To visit the sick with empty promises of prayer and healing, only to watch them wither and die anyway? Was he not merely a glorified public speaker with the ultimate bully pulpit?

Jean-Pierre had recently been thinking often of his past. Though he was only 45 years old, he had lived a wealthy, wild, and profligate youth as the son of a very successful international merchant. His father, though often emotionally unavailable, had nonetheless shown Jan-Pierre the world. Then, when he himself had come of age and received his trust fund, he himself had traveled the world. After graduating Oxford, there were Paris, London, Berlin, Beijing, Manila, Lima, New York, Tokyo—he had played his fleshly folly in these and more, wanting for nothing yet unfulfilled. Wine, women, song, and expensive baubles: these had seemed, at that time, to make him a sort of god. When he had grown bored with one situation, he had merely moved somewhere else. Of course, this lifestyle had made him the happiest man in the world for a decade or so. Then, as with most young men who live in that manner, he had become his own Faust: overly educated but miserable, a Bacchanalian in ennui.

One night, in a drunken and drug-addled stupor, he had somehow found a Bible and had thumbed through it. A few parables later, and he had seen a light burst forth from the ceiling and a voice booming out, claiming to be God, telling him to become a Catholic priest. The experience had seemed quite real to him, though his mother, a fundamentalist Protestant, had insisted that it was merely an effect of the drugs and booze. Against her warnings, he had joined the seminary and had never looked back. He had replaced his wild life with a life of piety and faith, and had quickly become a rising star among priests. His sermons had tugged at the heartstrings, and his care for the poor and suffering had been legendary. That had lasted for a decade.

He had shared with his Confessor, Father Martin Peter, who was also a close, personal friend, about his loss of faith. The priest had tried several times to provoke Jean-Pierre into revealing the event or moment that had changed his faith for the worse. Still, Jean-Pierre had remained coy, only indicating that he had witnessed something on a mission trip to Colombia, something so terrible that it had forced him to reassess his faith, not only in a good and loving God, but any god at all.

"Maybe I'll tell you about what happened down in Bogota one day, Martin. Right now, I need to try to cling to the last hanging rope of faith and of the Church that I can find," he had told Father Martin, and Father Martin, being wise beyond his years, had let it rest at that.

That had left Father Jean-Pierre de la Fresnière in a state of tension when performing his priestly duties—wanting to do them with enthusiasm and genuine faith, but being tormented by that seed of doubt that had been planted by the unspeakable thing that he had seen in Bogota.

So, Jean-Pierre despised the bishop's visits, precisely because the tension under which he lived could not go on forever. Rubber bands eventually tear. Bubbles pop. Smoke dissipates. It was only a matter of time before Jean-Pierre tore as well, and each visit by the bishop served only to remind him that he was living on the clock. Each doctrinal discussion saddened him. A brilliant hermeneuticist, did he even matter without faith?

So, when the bishop and Father Peter knocked on his office door one atypically cold, foggy morning in January, Father Jean-Pierre simply released a defeated sigh and opened it. The two visitors smiled and stepped inside the admittedly richly-appointed office. Oaken panels for walls, exotic rugs for flooring, and a library to make the Vatican envious—Jean-Pierre enjoyed his scholarly time. He offered seats and hot tea to the two.

"Jean-Pierre," said the bishop, "I do hope we are not inconveniencing you. I was in the area and thought that Father Martin and I would spend the afternoon in the Quarter. Naturally, we could not do so without visiting you. I trust things have been well?"

"Well enough, Bishop. Nothing new or sudden, as you might imagine."

"Father Peter was telling me," continued the bishop, "about the recent spate of murders here in the French Quarter. As you might know, I've been in Rome for the past couple of months, so this is news to me. Terrible, isn't it?"

Jean-Pierre had almost forgotten about the killings that he had read about in the *Times-Picayune*. So far, there had been three within a period of a few months. In each case, a body had been found decapitated in some narrow alley or another, but exsanguination was the principal cause of death. His mind had been so self-absorbed, so attendant to his crisis of faith, that he realized he had been selfish in ignoring the outside world. After all, hadn't serving others been one of his primary joys in the priesthood? Had he grown so calloused as to ignore murder?

"It is, Bishop. Apparently, they were very violent murders, too. Can it be anything but a serial killer?" Father Peter frowned and furrowed his brows. He knew Jean-Pierre well enough to sense the doubt in his voice. The bishop remained oblivious.

"I suppose so. Such evil in this world, Fathers. Such evil. We need God's grace more than ever. Please stay safe, Father Jean-Pierre; you know how the Quarter can get at night," advised the bishop. "It's almost like Victorian London with Jack the Ripper around."

"A sobering thought, Bishop!" exclaimed Father Peter. "Jean-Pierre is a homebody anyway; it's hard to find him away from his books on any given night."

Jean-Pierre chuckled. "Well, that's true. In any case, Bishop, I have the statistics you were asking about."

They conducted their business and the bishop left the two priests and friends alone. The rosy sun began its nightly descent, and like every night, the French Quarter started to metamorphosize from its loud, gaudy, colorful, touristy day persona into its true self: dark, cloistered, daring, dangerous, and mysterious. People began walking the streets and alleys. They filled the myriad bars and restaurants, the clinking of glasses mingling with the chinking of silverware and the buzzing murmur and sibilation of conversation.

"What's new, Jean-Pierre?" asked Father Peter. "We haven't spoken in a couple of weeks."

Jean-Pierre produced a bottle of 16-year-old Lagavulin, poured them each a finger's dram, and sat back pensively. "Off the record, Martin, I'm falling down the rabbit hole of doubt. I'm still struggling against the waves, though. I'm just not sure what I need to either push me under into agnosticism, or lift me back up into my belief."

"Sometimes God knows. Sometimes we're swallowed by a whale and taken under. Remember, though, that Jonah came back," offered Father Peter.

"Why does it have to be through the whale's body, Martin? Why can't God just give me a clear sign, a message? Why won't he just show me that it's all real, that there's an ultimate point to it all? Take these murder victims. What was the point? What lesson or message could God possibly have wanted to give to anyone? Just for once, how about a good, positive, clear message?"

"Because, without the belly of the whale, my friend, we never are truly stripped down to our bare essence. Without the struggle, we never become authentic; we never tear away the masks and crawl before God, naked and hopeless. It's really the only way that he can lift us back up," replied Father Peter.

The two men sat in silence for a few minutes, in the silence that only two true friends can endure without wriggling in uncomfortable anticipation and awkwardness.

"What happened in Colombia, Jean-Pierre?" asked Father Peter softly.

"Why do you ask right now?"

"Call it a hunch, but I have long sensed that, whatever horrible thing you saw that night, was the seed that was planted that is growing into the flower of doubt. Something must have happened that made you question everything you thought you knew about the world, about God."

"You're not wrong, Martin," admitted Jean-Pierre. "One day, I'll tell you what I witnessed."

"How about next confession?"

Jean-Pierre considered this and replied, "Possibly, Martin. Possibly. I suppose I have to talk about it eventually."

"It will only help you with your crisis of faith, you know."

Jean-Pierre nodded. They finished their scotch, chatted a bit, and then Jean-Pierre walked Father Peter to his car and saw him off.

Re-entering his office, the priest poured himself another rather stiff glass of Lagavulin. He pulled out a volume of the writings of Saint Jerome, hoping for some guidance from the ancient. The first line he saw read, "When the stomach is full, it is easy to talk of fasting." Jean-Pierre chuckled and read on into the night.

Around midnight, as the tickling fingers of sleep were about to gently pull his eyelids closed, a piercing shriek from Pirates Alley, right next to his office, broke the still of the night. Jumping hurriedly out of his leather reading chair, he peeked through the peephole in the sturdy door that led to the alley. He spied a woman lying on the ground, unmoving.

After calling the police, he hesitantly opened the door. Cautious, he looked around to make sure no one else was near, then knelt next to the woman. He tried to feel for a pulse, but as soon as he touched her neck area, her head rolled off of her body. She had been decapitated.

He gasped and said a quick prayer for her soul. Noticeably absent was the pool of blood, which surely should have accompanied such a violent act. The police arrived, took a statement from Jean-Pierre, and went about removing the body and processing the crime scene.

"Father, I'm Detective Pace Barillo, NOPD," said a short, rotund, and haggard man of a certain age. He looked like he had a troubled and long-distance relationship with his bed. "Let's go over what happened again."

Jean-Pierre repeated his account, then asked, "It's the serial killer again, isn't it, detective?"

"Well, it certainly looks like the other cases, but we have to investigate it first to make a conclusion. Did you notice anything in particular really strange about this crime scene?"

"Yes, detective. There's no blood! How is that even possible?"

"Weird as hell, Father, isn't it? Like the other ones. This guy seems like some sort of weirdo into blood rituals or something. You know anything about Satanists in the area, Father?"

"I know that there are many young people around here," answered Jean-Pierre, "who like to seem edgy and dark, and claim to practice something like Satanism, but it's mostly just a lifestyle, not the real thing."

"But you know, Father, that we have lots of people into Voodoo, Hoodoo, and Santeria in New Orleans," added Barillo.

"We do," admitted Jean-Pierre, "but those are just religions. It's mostly a myth that they do anything even close to this. The most blood you might see in those ceremonies is from a chicken."

The detective jotted down some notes and nodded. "Well, thanks for the info, Father. I'll be in touch if I need anything else."

"Anytime, detective. But should I be worried? This happened right outside of my office. It's very disturbing, as you can imagine."

"Alright, we'll put a uniform to patrol around the church for a few days. Good enough?"

"Thanks, detective."

Pensive, Jean-Pierre sat back in his chair after the police left and looked at the clock. It was already two in the morning, but how could he sleep after such horror? He leaned back comfortably into the plush cushions and closed his eyes. He could not shake the vision of that poor woman's head rolling off. Such violence! Such aggression! Such needless terror! That sort of murder was neither random nor impulsive. It was the work of a monster, of a man who had a goal and a fantasy.

A flash of memories sliced into his mind in an instant.

A sweaty jungle. Dark nightfall. A small village. Lit torches. Confusion, fear. There is a girl on the ground of maybe fourteen years old. She is filthy, bloody, smeared in her own vomit. Her clothes are almost completely ripped off. Standing above her is another priest. Jean-Pierre hears a forceful, baritone voice. Latin. Rites. It is an exorcism. The girl writhes and wails.

Every couple of minutes, her voice is replaced by a guttural, grating, animalistic growl—it is too deep and loud and amplified to be proceeding from her little teenage lungs and throat. She is tied down on a bamboo mat. The priest's brave voice continues without success.

Jean-Pierre can hear little sprinkles of fear and doubt entering into his cadence, and soon, he sounds exhausted and weak.

*The demon laughs and looks at Jean-Pierre, "**Vamos, padre. ¿No lo quieres intentar?**" Jean-Pierre ignores it and continues to pray along with the exorcist. Nothing is working. The girl growls and breaks through her fetters. She leaps up with superhuman speed upon the exorcist and knocks him to the ground. Among his high-pitched shrieks and pleas, she bites into his throat and rips out his larynx. She guzzles his blood as Jean-Pierre watches, too paralyzed by fear and terror to move.*

The people of the village scream and cry, but they can do nothing. From among the crowd steps a man. He is not from the village and is dressed like someone from the city, from Bogota. He carefully but fearlessly grabs the girl's shoulders and turns her over.

He has a sharpened wooden stick in his hand, and the girl sees it. For the first time, her mocking, demonic face shows fear.

The man plunges the stick into her chest, into her heart.

Her eyes grow wide, and her mouth is agape. She falls to the ground, and her flesh disintegrates, leaving only her bones, which then blacken and wither. There is total silence in the village.

Jean-Pierre jumped back into the present. Since the incident, he had never remembered or envisioned the entire thing. Yes, he had twisted in his sweaty sheets in the night with dreamy flashes of blood here or screams there. That, however, was the first time that he had relived the entire experience. Now, he remembered. He remembered the entire wicked ordeal.

He lay back again in the chair and began to fall asleep, trying to suck energy from the remaining few early-morning hours. As he drifted into a troubled, dreamless slumber, he remembered the words of the man from Bogota who had killed the girl: *"Father, this kind does not respond to exorcism. It is not a possession. It is another creature entirely, and the only way to stop it is to kill it."*

When Jean-Pierre woke up the next morning, he immediately called Father Martin Peter.

"Martin, I remembered. I remembered everything. God, it was terrible. I need a confession."

"Come over, Jean-Pierre. We can do it now."

CHAPTER 4

PROFESSOR MILLER'S MOVE

"**W**ell, it's much cheaper, for one, and it's actually a quaint little town, sort of an Old World feel, which really surprised me."

Professor Sager Miller, a specialist in the Maya civilization at the university in Glenville, was on the telephone with his colleague and girlfriend, Research Assistant Xiaoqing Yan.

"I know… I know… but it's really not that far from the university if you take the interstate as far as you can. Then there's this old highway, but the traffic is light, so you can speed. What? Oh, maybe an hour from campus tops. I mean, I drove farther than that at my last job. Definitely! I should finish moving and arranging everything by tomorrow. I'll see what sort of groceries I can find here, then cook dinner for us. Hopefully, they have a wine shop too. Okay, yeah, bye."

One benefit of being a rather renowned scholar in a rather limited field at a rather small and rural university, was the luxuries the university afforded him when possible, such as movers to move all of his belongings so that he did not have to lift a finger.

The small but attractive row-house he had chosen was on a lovely little cobblestoned lane just off of the town's main street. One thing that had attracted Sager to Ushaville was the distinctly European style of its design, which seemed rare in West Virginia. Lining the main street were rows of brick buildings with shops on the lower floor and living quarters above, with rather delicate details—a tower room here, a gargoyle there, a carved flourish here, an elegant dormer window there.

It was as if the founders of this little town had arrived directly from Europe, and with money at that. The entire Appalachian area had, in fact, been settled by the Scottish people, but most of them had been poor. Ushaville must have been a special case, and Sager determined to read through its history when he found the time. After all, such a charming little town surely had a museum or historical society.

The movers finished in the afternoon, so Sager tipped them and then decided to walk around the town. Unlike so many American towns that were built after the invention of the automobile and thus are not suitable for pedestrians, Ushaville was older. It had been set up in a distinctly compact manner to facilitate walking.

He strolled along his tree-lined lane and then onto the main street, named *Unter den Linden* Street. Sager was surprised at reading something in German and decided that wealthy German settlers must have founded the town—it would explain the name, the architectural style, and the general cleanliness and order to the layout.

The street was populated with pedestrians of all sorts. Still, Sager immediately noticed what felt so uncanny about them: any wore black or dark grey clothing, walked with their heads mostly down, and generally gave an affect of being a bit withdrawn. So sharp was the contrast between the cheery, comforting European-style buildings and the grim people, that it was almost comical. Once in a while, a person or two would walk by with a more normal appearance, but they were few overall. That being so, the town was replete with businesses, restaurants, cafés, and even bars.

As Sager strolled, he noted that one particular building stood out from the rest. It was not hard to spot The Fairie Realm Café, as its bright, almost-Caribbean colors and hanging trinkets and baubles seemed to clash with the more conservative and darker colors found on the surrounding buildings. Inside, it was indeed like a fairyland. The booths were made from large tree trunks that formed seats then continued upwards, twirling into the ceiling. Colors on the walls whirled and merged into dreamy patterns, and little twists and nooks and corners gave the impression of a never-ending space. The central bar was an oval island in the middle of the café, and above it hung multicolored lights, colorful pieces of glass, and other such decorations that reflected rainbows all around the room. The walls were all covered with various knick-knacks, as well as little paintings and sketches of fairies.

More than the interior design, the atmosphere itself emanated a feeling of warmth, safety, and lulling contentment: almost a drunkenness, a palpable effect that was entirely unexpected and striking. Sager wanted to stay there forever, to explore its little spaces and read every book in its wall library, to drink every creation it served. In a word, the café was *enamoring* in its entirety. He approached the center bar to see their menu, and a girl stood up as if she had been doing work below.

"Hi! Welcome to The Fairie Realm! What can I get for you today?"

She was tall and thin but shapely, with hair so blonde that it almost seemed snow-white. Her face was beautifully chiseled into defined angles and planes, but not so much that it was sharp. Her eyes were deep blue like a lake in Switzerland, and when she smiled, Sager felt himself become relaxed, warm, and happy. It was not so much that he was attracted to her beauty personally, but simply that such a beautiful creature existed. Did she even have the right to be in this ugly world, so lovely as she was?

He stammered something, and she simply smiled and replied, "You look like someone who can appreciate a very fine Chinese tea. Have you ever had *Pu'er* tea from Yunnan Province?"

Composing himself, he said, "How did you know I like tea? *Pu'er* is my favorite."

"Oh, I just felt it," she answered. "We have some very high-grade, aged *Pu'er*. Please have a seat somewhere, and I'll take it to you."

She smiled again and turned away to begin working on his tea. He felt euphoric and dreamy at the same time, and it was as if he had floated to a table and wafted down into the comfortable, plush chair like a leaf delicately falling from a tree, swinging lightly from side to side like a gentle pendulum. A couple of minutes later, the girl brought his tea over.

"My name's Titania. You can just call me over if you would like anything else. Enjoy!" She half-smiled knowingly, as if she held some secret about him that even he did not know, then spun around like a ballet dancer and walked (drifted?) back to the central bar.

Liking this café immensely, Sager relaxed and thought that he had made a good choice of a town to live in. Aside from the weird attitude of many of the people, it was generally a lovely and quaint place. Perhaps he had misread the people? Maybe it was a local cultural feature. After all, he was originally from New Orleans, and people there tended to be very relaxed, happy, talkative, and often drunk. *I should give them another chance*, he thought. *Titania is delightful, after all.*

He sipped his tea and savored the rich, earthy, subtle flavors. A bit of a connoisseur of Chinese tea, Sager could tell that it was of very high quality. As if reading his mind, Titania said, "Don't worry. It's not too expensive!" He chuckled.

He heard the chime of the bell above the entrance door to the café, so he casually looked up, gasped, and stared. A girl was walking inside, and she was the most beautiful creature he had ever seen. He felt enchanted by the stark, almost unnatural contrast between her black hair and pale skin—hair that was so raven that it nearly bled into a funerary purple, and such delicate, blanched skin that she appeared to be a Geisha doll, created artificially for the pleasure of others rather than as her own, sentient being. It was as if Sager were staring directly into one of the wondrous mysteries of the universe, so jarring was this contrast. She appeared to be Asian, or maybe not—her almond eyes melted downward onto her wide cheeks, and her tiny, convex nose tilted outward at the slightest upward angle.

He quickly glanced away, but he could feel his face flush with blood. Titania looked at him and winked, humiliating him even more.

There was a free table near Sager's, and the mysterious girl sat there facing him. She ordered coffee and happened to meet Sager's eyes. Smiling with only one side of her lips only added to her dark mystique. Sager felt his stomach flip and tingle. He looked down and pretended to be reading the magazine that he had found on the table, but in no time, he peripherally saw the girl stand up and glide to where he was sitting.

He felt the blood rush to his face and feared looking up, just as when he had been a child, afraid to look under his bed for fear of what might have been there.

"Professor Miller?"

Sager's mouth and eyes opened wide.

"Um, hi. Sorry, do I know you?"

"Not well, Professor. I've seen you on campus." She looked only about fourteen years old now that he had a closer look. A student? "I'm Ophelia."

She held out her hand, and as he took it, his entire body tingled. Her hand felt cool, and the tingling was replaced by some sort of small revulsion, some sort of primal warning from his reptilian brain—a warning that lasted only a fraction of a second. She looked at his hand, and he realized that he had been holding hers too long for social propriety.

"Oh, sorry," he muttered. "I was just wondering… you look so young to be a university student."

"I am," she replied. "I'm still in high school, but my mother works at the university as a secretary in the Mathematics Department. Sometimes I go to visit her, and I see you walking across the quadrangle." She half-smiled again.

"Oh, oh, I see. I thought you looked a little young, but then I thought maybe you were a genius." She allowed a subdued laugh to pass her lips, and Sager felt stupid. "So, you and your mom live here in Ushaville, I guess?"

"Yes. Our family has been here for… for many years. You are an expert on pre-Colombian Meso-American cultures, right?" she prodded.

"Well, that's my field. Some might argue about whether I am any sort of expert," he replied and chuckled.

"I've read your papers. Your theories are really accurate."

"Oh, you're interested in that field? That's great! If you do decide to go to the university, let me know. I can help get you into the department and get you prepared in advance. We don't have too many students interested in our field, so I love to meet any young people who are interested in it!"

"Thank you, Professor. Nice to meet you. Welcome to Ushaville," she said. She picked up her coffee and exited the café.

Sager suddenly felt very guilty about the entire situation. First, he had a girlfriend, and although he could not help that other women were also beautiful, he should not have reacted so instinctively and passionately about merely seeing Ophelia. Second, she was a teenager, and while Sager was not old by any means, he felt terrible about having thought a girl that young was so attractive.

He heard a commotion outside and turned to look out of the blue-tinted window. Across the street was a small hotel, and in front of it stood four people loudly arguing— three young men and one young woman. They wore black mesh, black makeup, piercings, chains, Mohawks, and various other punk accouterments. The tall, thin one waved his arms and pointed at the café, while the girl stood with her arms folded and pouting. The other two guys seemed bored and uninterested. One yawned.

"What the…" muttered Sager as the group of punk rockers walked across the street, ignoring traffic and almost causing an accident, and entered The Fairie Realm. The tall, skinny one spoke out first.

"Oy! Anyone here?"

Titania sprung up from behind the counter, saw the group, and tried to contain a smirk, "Welcome to The Fairie Realm. You look like you could all use some coffee."

"Black," said the tall, skinny one.

"Cream and sugar," added the girl.

"Whatever. Doesn't matter," said the one with the sleepy face and yawned again.

"Latte, one hundred and eighty degrees, with steamed almond milk, please," said the last of the four, and the other three looked at him incredulously.

"What? I like my coffee, alright?"

Sager watched the group with great amusement instead of fear—he had seen his share of oddballs and weirdos in New Orleans, so this look was nothing new. Perhaps it was more the contrast between the outrageous, outlandish group, and the otherwise quiet and reserved nature of the townspeople.

They chose a table and sat, the skinny one choosing to sit with his chair backward, the back between his legs. Titania arrived with their orders.

"Say, love," began the skinny one, "we're stuck in your town for a day or two while our van gets fixed."

"Um, *my* van, Paul Junk," corrected the girl.

"Yeah, yeah, Scary Mary, your van, anyway, where's a good bar? Where can we get a good beer around here?"

Titania pursed her lips and thought for a moment. "Well, your hotel's on the west side of town, so you'll want to check out the Pallid Horse. It's, well, it's really *unique*, like no place you've ever drunk in, I am sure."

"You're a peach, darling," replied Paul, who then took a gulp of his coffee. "Damn, that's good coffee! Well fucking done!"

"Paul!" chided Mary. "This is a nice place. Don't act like an animal."

"Animal is as animal does, baby!" retorted Paul, and Mary tilted her brows, trying to understand what the hell he meant.

"Yeah," said the sleepy one to Titania, "what's with this east and west thing in this town? Why does everyone say not to cross sides?"

Titania bit her lip, paused, and replied, "Let's just say that this is a very old town, with many families who have been here for…well, for a very long time. Not everyone gets along very well, and the town is sort of split into the Eastside and the Westside."

"You mean that hillbilly Hatfield and McCoy feud?" asked Paul with a smirk.

28

"Well, that's part of it, but it's more complicated. You know how small towns are. Too many people know everyone else. This café is actually in the very center of town. It's the one place that people from each side come, and sort of ignore one another in an implied truce."

"Weird," said Mary, and the four sipped their coffee and ordered a second round.

CHAPTER 5

BEAST STALKER

Waking up the next morning, Sager remembered only flashes and incoherent scenes from his dreams. Titania, Ophelia, the punks, coffee, and some disturbing reference to blood—these were all he could see in his mind, but he could not piece them together into a dream-story.

He decided to take another walk around Ushaville, remembering his dinner date with Xiaoqing, his girlfriend. As he strolled farther down Unter den Linden Street, he almost could not believe his luck. This supposedly small, rural town offered boutiques, gourmet food shops, wine shops, and bookstores. How could this be in West Virginia? How had he never heard of this town before? Shouldn't it have been well known? He felt like he was back in Europe on holiday. He relished all of the luxurious possibilities available as he strolled and created a dinner menu in his mind. He had already passed The Fairie Realm Café, and since the main street divided the town vertically and not horizontally, he did not have to worry about crossing into the forbidden Eastside, although, knowing his innate anti-authoritarian streak, he knew he would eventually go, *just to see.*

A bookstore caused him to stop. Unlike the other buildings, which were neat row houses and shops done in a classical European brick style, this bookstore was made of wood. In fact, it was inside of the now finished and polished remains of a giant tree! This ancient arbor had surely been there longer than Ushaville itself.

He stepped inside and was welcomed with the luscious scent of incense. The decor emphasized natural wood, plants, and soft earth-tones. Rows and rows of books extended deep into the heart of the aged tree, and relaxing music subtly played in the background. Behind the solid, wooden sales counter stood a tall, solid man. His olive skin accented his almond eyes, and his long, straight, raven hair almost enshrouded his face. He wore traditional Cherokee clothing, and Sager was positive the guy was a Native American.

"Hello," spoke the man in a slow, deep, soothing voice. "Welcome to The Old Ways Bookstore and Ushaville museum," he said, and his voice sounded like the water in a curving river.

"Oh, thanks," replied Sager. "This store is amazing. So beautiful." The man only nodded. "What sort of books do you sell?"

"We have a variety, but I like to focus on the history and culture of the area. There's a small museum in the back, too. It has some artifacts from the people who lived here in the old times. You know, my people."

Sager nodded. "Cherokee?"

"Very good," answered the man with a small smile. "How did you know?"

"Oh, well, you could say that it's a bit of an interest of mine."

The man nodded, seeming pleased.

"You can call me Beast Stalker. It's my Indian name."

"Nice to meet you, Beast Stalker. I'm Sager Miller."

Beast Stalker slightly raised his eyebrows and said, "Not *the* Professor Sager Miller, expert on the pre-Colombian Americas?"

"Well," said Sager while blushing a bit, "I wouldn't say that. It's just my field of interest."

"I've read your books!" For the first time, Beast Stalker sounded excited. "You really understand the culture of the Old Ones, and also my people. You understand the importance of our connection to the land and nature. How did you come to be in my bookstore?"

"Oh, that's nice of you to say. Well, I teach at the university in Glenville, and I was able to find a house here that is larger and nicer than the one I had there, but also cheaper. This is quite a remarkable town, you know."

Beast Stalker allowed a minuscule, almost undetectable smirk to rise to his lips, then returned to his stone face. "That is one way to say it. Ushaville is unique in many ways. There has been human settlement here for twenty-thousand years, maybe more. We have evidence, as well as the oral traditions of my people. Before my people came up from the caves under the earth, there was the Dream Time—a time of the Great Spirit, the Elder Spirits, and the Old Ones. And, well, you know what happened when the Europeans arrived."

Sager rubbed the back of his neck and looked down awkwardly.

"I'm just messing with you," said Beast Stalker. "Sometimes, it's fun to make white people wince."

Sager laughed heartily. "You got me."

"I think you might enjoy the museum, Professor. Admission is free. You are the only one here right now, so come on. I'll show you."

He led Sager to the back of the store, where a giant knot in the tree acted as a passageway to a back room. The museum was small, but the walls and floorspace were crowded with interesting exhibits.

"Look around a bit, and then I'll show you some special items that might interest you," offered Beast Stalker.

Sager perused remarkably well-preserved pottery, clothing, weapons, and more, dating from various times in the history of the Americas.

"These are really nice Olmec pieces. And this Maya scroll fragment is just fantastic!" exclaimed Sager.

"I thought you might enjoy them. Come over here and look at this item."

Beast Stalker produced a large, sapphire amulet with writing that spiraled around it from top to bottom.

"Whoa! Sapphire? That must be worth a mint!" exclaimed Sager. "How safe is it to keep here in your bookstore?"

"In dollars, it is very valuable," explained Beast Stalker, "but as an ancient artifact of my people, it is priceless. As for its safekeeping, well, I will just say that I have a robust security system here. You can hold it and take a look."

Sager took the enormous jewel into his slightly-shaking hands and looked into it. The brilliant sparkles of a thousand universes danced inside of it as it reflected the lights, and it seemed almost to have a liquid core, so pure was it. There were no occlusions. He looked at the writing and frowned.

"Where did your people find this?" asked Sager.

"Well, the story from local elders is that a great warrior chief of old named Gigadanegisgi received this amulet from night spirits. These night spirits came upon the waters from afar and taught things to our people. Of course, this legend is local to us and not necessarily to other Cherokees around the country."

"But this language," argued Sager, "it's like no language I have ever seen. I have a fairly broad knowledge of linguistics and world languages, but this does not seem to fit into... unless... no, that's impossible."

"Do you know the language, Professor? No one yet has been able to identify or decipher it," said Beast Stalker while raising his eyebrows.

"No, I don't know it myself. I mean... it slightly resembles... no, I'm mistaken. Tell you what, Beast Stalker. I have a good friend down in New Orleans. We were childhood friends, and we've kept up all this time. He's a Catholic priest, and he is truly an expert in languages. He's probably fluent in more than twenty of them, but one of his specialties is ancient languages. I myself know, for example, Mayan, but he knows many more. Perhaps you would allow me to take pictures of the amulet and send them to him?"

"Yes, if only you promise me that no one else will see those pictures." Beast Stalker looked Sager in the eyes.

"I promise," agreed Sager. He snapped a few photos with his iPhone.

Beast Stalker nodded. "Would you like to browse my books?"

"I'd love to, but I need to do some grocery shopping. Any recommendations?" asked Sager.

"Four buildings down, The Ushaville Market. They have everything, and very fresh produce. They also have a nice wine selection if you are into that."

"Perfect, thanks! Well, it was truly a pleasure to meet you, Beast Stalker. I will definitely be back with the reply from my priest friend, and also just to browse. This place is really amazing."

Beast Stalker smiled and nodded.

After Sager found everything he needed in The Ushaville Market, he headed home and called Xiaoqing, who agreed to arrive early that evening. With a classical Asian face, wide cheekbones, straight black hair, and thin frame, she was beautiful. What attracted Sager to her, however, was her mind. In typical Chinese style, she was very practical, but also very creatively intelligent. She used her practical nature to solve most problems, even those of an intellectual nature, by inventing creative solutions that often did not fit the mold.

The couple enjoyed a dinner of roast pheasant, braised leeks, and roasted tomatoes, all accompanied by a rather indulgent bottle of Château Latour. Sager had winced at the $200 price tag, but he was so content with his decision to move, with his relationship, with his career, and with his life overall, that he felt it warranted one bit of decadence. Xiaoqing had scolded him for it, but she did not seem to mind sipping it with him.

As they were sitting on the sofa talking after dinner, with a documentary streaming on the iPad as background noise, three solid knocks hit the door.

"Who could that be?" asked Xiaoqing. "It's already nine o'clock."

Sager peeped through the hole, turned back to look at Xiaoqing with his eyebrows raised quizzically, then slowly opened the door an inch with the chain still attached. Outside stood a towering wraith of a man dressed all in black, with long black hair that fell from under a black fedora, and who wore sunglasses, which he removed when the door was opened.

"Yes? May I help you?" asked Sager. He felt a tiny, bitter seed of fear in his stomach's innermost parts, not unsimilar to what he had felt when he had touched Ophelia's hand.

"Professor Miller? I do apologize for disturbing you so late. I am Lorman McCoy, the mayor of Ushaville. I heard that you had moved in, and I just wanted to extend a welcome to our town."

"Mayor? Oh, well, that is very kind. Would you like to…"

"No, thank you; I must be on my way. I hope you will enjoy your life here. Please feel free to explore, but I should advise you to be careful when crossing into the Eastside. It's an area with some… well, some crime problems. We are in the process of rejuvenating it and making it safer. The Westside, on the other hand, has much to offer. Welcome, and please do not hesitate to contact me with any problems or concerns. My office is in the City Hall building on Under den Linden, our main street, which I believe you found today." He nodded, tipped his hat, replaced his sunglasses, and turned and walked away.

"Well, that was a little odd," said Xiaoqing.

"Yeah, it sort of was," agreed Sager.

"I mean, didn't he sound a little threatening, or at least controlling?" she asked.

"That's it. That's what I felt. And did you see him? He must be over seven feet tall, and so thin! In a way, he kind of looks like Joey Ramone."

Xiaoqing rolled her eyes. Sager laughed, picked her up, and carried her into the bedroom, where they made love all night long.

The next day, Sager picked up the phone: "Hello?"

"Sager? Hey, it's Jean-Pierre."

"Hey man! How have you been? Sorry I haven't called for a week or two. I moved to another town like I told you."

"How's the new place?" asked the priest.

"Surprisingly great. It's like a little European city in the middle of West Virginia. I really can't believe my luck. You ever heard of Ushaville?

"Never," answered Jean-Pierre.

"Yeah, me neither, which is odd. How could a town like this not be known and flooded with tourists? That part is really weird. Anyway, you should come visit when you have a chance, Padre."

"That's why I called," replied Jean-Pierre, "I got those pics you emailed me. Are you sure it's authentic, first of all?"

"Well, all I know is that it's real sapphire. Remember that internship I did one summer with the gemologist, Holly? I learned a lot about gems, and I can spot a fake sapphire pretty well. The size, too! This thing must be priceless. So, I figure, if it's real sapphire, then the chances are high that it is authentic otherwise."

"Amazing. Sager, here's the thing. I might be wrong about this, but the language on it... it's really, really out of place in North America. In fact, if my hunch is right, this could be one of the great archaeological discoveries of the ages. I was hoping I could pay you a visit and see it in person."

"The curator's a Cherokee guy named Beast Stalker. He seems nice enough. I bet he'd let you examine it if it led to deciphering," said Sager.

"Well, I'm due some vacation time, and I need a break from this place. You up for a few days' visit?"

"Buddy, I always have a spare room for my old friend. You can drive here from New Orleans in about fourteen hours. You might want to break it up into two days. Maybe stop on the way and check out Atlanta? The weekend's coming up, and I'm still on break from the uni."

"Alright man, see you in a couple of days. Email me directions. I'm not seeing this town on Google Maps. I'll call you from Atlanta."

"Sounds great, Padre! Look forward to it. And you can meet my newish girlfriend," said Sager.

"Oh, a new girl? Sounds exciting. See you soon, buddy."

Sager hung up and decided to take another look at the photos of the amulet that he had on his laptop.

CHAPTER 6

THE PUNKS GO EASTWARD

"That's the Pallid Horse bar? Fucking great!" yelled Paul Junk Roy, and the three other Gravediggers stared with their mouths agape.

"Right on for once, Junk," replied Gutter Gill LeBlanc.

The band looked at the edifice of the bar in punk amazement. It had obviously once been someone's home, wedged in among the brick row buildings like a splinter under a prisoner of war's fingernail. Built of wood rather than stone, it had been designed in the style of a New Orleans Garden District mansion, complete with verandas, columns, terraces, dormer windows, gables, and a wide porch that surrounded the entire structure on each of the three stories. The house had, without a doubt, once been a beautiful and extravagant palace for some wealthy pillar of the town, but over decades, maybe even centuries, no one seemed to have taken care of it, for it had become a ghastly monstrosity, a skeletal mockery of a Southern mansion.

The paint—perhaps once a bright, Caribbean color like you find on St. Charles Avenue in Uptown New Orleans—had peeled, warped, and sloughed off like so much burnt skin, leaving a namesake pallid color. Everywhere around the beast, warped wooden panels had sprouted and sprung out from their molds, and resembled pockmarks on a leper's face.

Windows were broken out here and there, and the entire three stories seemed to lean this way and slant that way, resulting in more of a structural lump than a fully-functioning residence. An ancient live oak, having managed to thrive in the front yard despite the evidently best efforts of the owners to kill it, had spewed out Spanish moss over the years like semen, drenching the house in trails of the stuff that blew in the wind like the beards of wizened old Chinese Kungfu masters.

But the crowning glory of the Pallid Horse bar was, in fact, the pallid horse. That is, someone at some point in history had thought it would be a great idea to place an enormous, pale, wooden horse on the roof right above the entrance. Perhaps they had meant it to look like the pallid horse of the Apocalypse, some sort of stark art piece to stun passersby, but one of the pallid hooves had pallidly broken in half, causing the gargantuan steed to lurch forward so that its horrific, apocalyptic face now stared down almost at the level of the door. Customers had to walk under the equine stare with only about one foot's gap. It was distinctly intimidating yet simultaneously comical.

"God, I love this place!" said Scary Mary. "It's freaking beautiful."

"Bloody gorgeous, it is," admitted Gutter Gill.

"Well, I'm thirsty," added Paul Junk, then proudly led the way under the horse's muzzle.

The inside decor did not disappoint. The grand staircase was now encircled with an oaken bar, and it looked like all of the mansion's rooms were open for customers to explore. Furniture covered in dusty sheets were like ghosts in the dark recesses of the chambers, half-broken chandeliers above their heads seemed ready to crash to the floor, and Fireplaces and mantles displayed curios from ages long gone. They even saw the occasional creepy doll.

"Did we just walk into a horror movie?" asked Scary.

"The only horror here's that I ain't had a drink today," said Junk. "Hey sweetheart, four beers, how about it?"

A girl around twenty years old with stunningly smooth, deep ebony skin and a large Afro smirked at him then produced four beers. She wore a black top with a black motorcycle leather jacket, and black shorts with black fishnet stockings. "I'm not your sweetheart. I started a tab for you, so don't run out on me."

Gutter Gill chuckled.

"This place is certainly, well, different."

The bartender nodded and answered, "Oh yeah. Best thing going for sure. I even hang out here when I'm not working."

Mucky Matt was walking through the various rooms, nodding at the other customers. He seemed glad to see that most people were dressed in rock, punk, or Goth attire. Not many normies. A few creepy old people were here and there, probably sad alcoholics. Mucky returned to the bar and asked, "So, what's your name?"

"Wouldn't you like to know?" snipped the bartender, causing Matt to start a bit and frown.

"Just kidding, man," she said and laughed. "I'm Nancy. I'm the manager here, and as you can see, also a bartender. Who are you guys?"

Mary responded before Paul could say something stupid or offensive, because Nancy seemed cool. "We're a punk band from New Orleans. Our name's The Gravediggers. I'm Mary, that's Paul, Matt, and Gill."

"So cool!" replied Nancy. "Like, real punk? Like eighties punk? Not this new crap that people call punk like Gwen Stefani?"

"Oh, hell yes," said Mary. "Our music may suck, but we're the real deal. Our idols are The Ramones, Dead Milkmen, Social Distortion, Sex Pistols, Misfits, The Damned, The Circle Jerks, shit like that."

"Hell yeah! I love that shit!" said Nancy. "You have a gig here or something? Never seen you around town."

"Well, there's the thing, Nance," interjected Paul, and Mary winced. "We've got a gig in Charleston. Well, we *had* a gig in Charleston. Looks like we won't make it in time. Scary Mary here doesn't keep her van in good shape, and it crapped out on us."

Mary gave him a frown.

"So, we ended up in the parking lot of this redneck store."

"Oh shit, you mean Red McCoy's place?" asked Nancy.

"Sounds right, yeah," affirmed Paul.

Nancy laughed and said, "He's a real moron. Him and his son Billy Mack and his hillbilly pack of hicks give this town a bad name. Let me guess: he told you to leave town and never come back."

"About right," said Matt. "Then this tall, thin dude in black shows up on a motorcycle. Red and his rednecks got all quiet and subservient all of a sudden."

"Oh, shit," said Nancy. "That had to be Lorman McCoy! He's like one of the town bosses."

"The mayor?" asked Matt.

"Something like that, yeah. He shares the power with Andy Hatfield."

Paul laughed.

"Yeah," acknowledged Nancy. "The Hatfield McCoy feud. Well, there's sort of an uneasy truce in this town. The McCoys live on the Westside and the Hatfields on the Eastside. Each says the other side is terrible, and theirs is great. Lorman and Andy keep the peace. They seem to get along alright I guess. Tons of people in Ushaville are Hatfields or McCoys. We have normal people too."

"Wait, are *you* a Hatfield or McCoy?" asked Mary.

"Oh, hell no! I just work for the Hatfields. The Pallid Horse is owned by some of them. I got no beef with either family, but I don't want anything to do with them either. They're all a bunch of hicks if you ask me." Nancy looked around. "Shit, I hope no one heard that."

The band found a dusty, antique table and sat there drinking for a couple of hours. Nancy wiped down the bar while another bartender, a guy in jeans and a white T-shirt, started prepping. She approached their table and took a seat.

"Mind if I hang out? I just got off my shift. You guys seem cool, at least compared to some of the people in this town," she said.

"Totally," answered Mary. "You're the first cool person we've met here."

"So, what's the story with your van?" asked Nancy.

"That Lorman guy who looks like Joey Ramone said he would take care of having it fixed for us, and then we can leave town tomorrow."

Nancy nodded.

"Say," asked Gill, "what exactly would happen if we went to the forbidden Eastside? Would we explode or something?"

Nancy chuckled. "Well, probably nothing would happen. Both sides know that if they do something stupid and set off another feud war, it will be bad for everyone. I mean, you could walk over there right now. People probably won't be very friendly, but no one's gonna actually mess with you, at least probably not. Hell, I'll go with you. They won't dare do anything if I am with you. I have protection." She turned around and pulled up her hair, revealing a small, red tattoo: it was a circle with a cross inside it.

"Protection? What the hell does that mean?" asked Paul.

"I know it sounds weird. So, the feud and everything. This town has three kinds of residents. First are the McCoys. You know they live on the Westside; they are mostly rich and well-to-do. Their side of town looks like something out of a European fairy tale. The second group is the Hatfields. They're poorer and, as you know, live on the Eastside. You'll see in a minute how their side is grungier and crappier. They tend to stay to themselves, hanging out in the shadows like creeps. The third group is just normal residents who have nothing to do with the feud, and probably don't know much about it anyway. But some of us longtime residents are given this tattoo as a mark of protection. It means we're immune from the feud. People without the mark are usually clueless, but also fair game if the feud resumes. It's fucked up. I know. Come on; I'll show you the Eastside. Just be cool and you'll be fine."

They left the Pallid Horse and headed off in the opposite direction whence they had come.

Almost as if there were an actual line painted in the middle of the road, things started to change. The buildings—no longer clean, tidy, German row houses and row shops—were now more haphazardly built in a variety of styles, some of them dingy European, others wooden and falling apart. Even the sunlight seemed to reach these streets less, and nature had become grave-silent. No birds chirped, and no squirrels climbed trees. In windows that were not already obscured with shades, they spotted movement and a sudden drawing of the curtains. Few people were on the streets, and those that were walked close against the buildings, in the shadows. Most of them wore black and eyed the group suspiciously.

They passed a cruddy building that made the Pallid Horse look like a golden palace. The sign above the door read *Lust Bar*.

"How's that bar?" asked a droopy-eyed Matt.

"You don't want to go in there. It's really tough, like a biker bar, and they don't like outsiders. They also check for your protection at the door." A gruff bouncer stood at the door and glared at them. Nancy waved to him, and the man grunted and nodded. A ruckus emanated from inside.

There were other grim, dingy businesses open, as well as some seriously bleak residences.

"Well, this sucks," said Matt, yawning. "I think I just got clinical depression."

"I told you guys. This is the dark side," Nancy said and laughed. "And it actually is getting dark. Best not to be on the Eastside after dark. You think it's scary now? Trust me; we need to go."

"Perhaps we should heed your wisdom," added Gill.

Mary chuckled nervously, and the group turned around and stared back toward the Westside's relative safety. Shadows were indeed growing long, and people began to come out of their houses. They crept along in the shadows, but as the last lashes of daylight's tongue licked ever softer, they became more daring and approached the streets.

"Shit," said Nancy under her breath.

"Uh, that's doesn't sound good, dear," said Paul. "In fact, it sounds fucking terrifying."

"Just... just walk faster, guys," urged Nancy.

They could see Unter den Linden Street a few blocks ahead of them; it was the street that divided the Eastside from the Westside.

"Just need to make it there. Come on, hurry," whispered Nancy.

Then, a towering, thin man all in black stepped from the shadows and directly into their path. Nancy gasped. Mary squealed. Paul shrieked like a girl.

"Wait, is that Lorman McCoy? Oh, never mind. This guy has a beard." asked Gill.

"Right. That's Andy Hatfield," replied Nancy.

"Indeed it is," answered Andy Hatfield. "Nancy, how nice to see you on this side of town. A rare event indeed. Won't you introduce me to your new friends?" He almost hissed the -s at the end of *friends*.

"Um, yes, Sir. This is Paul, Mary, Gill, and Matt."

The four punks were too scared to nod or smile or say anything.

"And what brings them to our fair city?" asked Andy.

"They... well, Sir, they're a band, and their van broke down, and Mister McCoy was kind enough to allow them to stay the night while their van is being repaired."

"I see. And you brought them to the Eastside?"

"Yes, Sir. They wanted to see the... the whole town, including your lovely neighborhood, Sir."

"Mhmm. Lovely, you say?" mocked Andy. "Then won't you stay a while longer? Perhaps I could have you all for dinner?"

"They, um, they need to get back, Sir, to work on their songs," improvised Nancy.

"Surely they have time for a drink? Say, at the Lust Bar?"

Paul stammered, "We... we must go, Sir, but thank you!" and then he ran as fast as he could around Andy and toward Unter den Linden. Andy Hatfield chuckled.

"I see that you all must indeed be in a hurry. What a shame. We Eastsiders are a hospitable lot. I am sure we would have enjoyed spending time with you all. Do come back soon!" said Andy, opening his black cape with his arm, stepping aside, and gesturing the way toward the Westside. They needed no prodding to quickly scoot past him and be on their way. As they passed him, he said, "And Nancy? Don't forget that you have protection. They don't. You know the rules, dear."

"Yes, Sir!" she said while speedwalking toward safety.

They made it to Under den Linden and paused, all gasping for breath. Matt did not yawn.

"What the bloody hell was that?" asked Paul.

"Yeah, Andy Hatfield is one scary mofo," said Nancy. "And you saw that side of town, right? Now you know why everyone warned you to avoid the Eastside."

"That was not even punk, not even cool," added Gill. "That was beyond even horror punk and the Misfits. That was downright terrifying, I must say!"

"Yeah, what did he say about your protection tattoo and the rules?" asked Mary in a shaking voice, producing a vibrato that would have made her a good singer if she did not suck so much.

"Um, well, there are other things you don't know about this town, and I can't tell you. I'm under oath to Andy, so you can understand why I will keep it. But I'll just say that the Eastsiders can be a little… well, violent and criminal. Anyone who goes there without the protection tattoo is fair game."

"Shit! You mean they can beat us and rob us and shit?" exclaimed Paul.

"And shit," answered Nancy. "And lots of shit. Now you know."

"Yeah, one visit was enough. Anyone for a nice beer?" asked Matt.

Everyone agreed, but Nancy did not want to return to the Pallid Horse, so she took them to another bar called Das Bierhaus. Unlike the Pallid Horse and the terrifying Lust Bar, the Bierhaus was designed like a German beer hall and was actually a little upscale. After the Eastside, the punks did not mind upscale for once. They all drank late into the night, then the punks returned to their hotel, and Nancy, to her house.

CHAPTER 7

DECIPHERMENT

"Sager! God, it's good to see you again," said Jean-Pierre, giving Sager a manly but affectionate hug. "And you must be Xiaoqing! Did I say that right? Sager's told me so much about you."

"Wow, your pronunciation is very good," replied Xiaoqing. "Wǒ shuō pǔtōnghuà. Wǒ zài zhōngguó zhù guò jǐ nián."

"Oh my God, Sager! Your friend speaks really good Chinese! He says he used to live there." remarked Xiaoqing.

"Gee, why isn't that a surprise," said Sager. "The man's a damn genius. He speaks like a hundred languages, and he's been all over the world."

"Oh now," said Jean-Pierre, his cheeks blushing a bit. "Who's the world's foremost expert on the ancient Maya?"

"Alright, enough bragging," said Xiaoqing. "Come on; I made dinner. You are probably hungry?"

"Chinese food?" asked Jean-Pierre.

"The real deal," she replied.

"Then, yes! I miss real Chinese food so much!"

They walked into the dining room and Jean-Pierre gasped. Sager's large, round table was covered in a dozen dishes or more, each full of some Chinese delicacy: meats, vegetables, noodles, tofu, dumplings, soups—it was a gastronomist's orgasm.

"I told you she can cook!" said Sager proudly.

"Where is your hometown, Xiaoqing?" asked the priest.

"It's called Shanwei. It's a small town on the South China Sea."

"I've heard the name. It's pretty close to Hong Kong, right?"

"Yes. It's also the only place on earth where our language, Shanweihua, is spoken," she replied. "It's close to Hokkien, but it's our own dialect."

"Fascinating! I love languages, as Sager mentioned. By the way, Sager, maybe I could take a look at the artifact after dinner?"

"Oh," answered Sager. "I don't have possession of it myself. It's still in Beast Stalker's museum."

"Alright. And what a name, Beast Stalker! You think he'll let us take a look tomorrow then?"

"I'm certain of it," replied Sager.

"So, can you drink as a priest?" asked Xiaoqing. "I'm sure you're familiar with our Chinese tradition of *baijiu*."

"Oh, God," chuckled Jean-Pierre. "I can drink, sure, and I do. And I could tell you many tales of *baijiu* in China!"

Xiaoqing laughed and produced a bottle of expensive *baijiu*.

"Oh, God. It's here," moaned Jean-Pierre, causing laughter at the table.

One enormous dinner and several rounds of the liquor later, Jean-Pierre patted his stomach.

"Xiaoqing, I have to say, that is one of the best meal's I've ever had in my life. You are an amazing cook," he said.

"Oh, it's nothing. I should have done better," she replied.

Jean-Pierre laughed a deep, belly laugh and said, "The classic Chinese humility! You know that, Sager? Compliment an American, and they'll say *thank you*. Compliment a Chinese person, and they'll demure and downplay it. It's a cultural trait. But seriously, Xiaoqing, that was just great." He reclined more on the chair before continuing. "So, you two, what do you think of this town? I took a little drive before I stopped here, and I'll be damned if you weren't right, Sager! It's like a little European town dropped out of the sky in the middle of the West Virginia wilderness. It's positively insane. How has no one ever heard of this town?"

"My grandmother thinks it's a cursed town," said Xiaoqing a little quietly.

"She's been here? And she's superstitious?" asked Jean-Pierre.

"She's never been here, but yeah, very superstitious. She moved to the US from China recently, and she lives with my mom in Los Angeles. I snapped a few pics today and sent them to my mom. She said grandma took one look at them and her eyes got big, and she said it's a cursed town. See, my grandma claims that she has the ability to see good and evil spirits in things and people and places. She swore that Ushaville's cursed. It kind of freaked me out."

The three sat in silence for a minute, then Jean-Pierre announced that he was exhausted and a little drunk, and excused himself to bed. Sager and Xiaoqing cleaned up.

The next morning, the three looked a bit worse for the wear.

"Hangover?" asked Sager. Jean-Pierre just chuckled and nodded.

"Me too," added Xiaoqing. She made them all strong Chinese tea and fed them bowls of rice noodles in a rich, spicy broth. It refreshed them quickly.

They decided to walk to The Old Ways Bookstore instead of driving so they could sweat out the hangover. As they approached Unter den Linden, Ophelia turned a corner and ran into Sager.

She was wearing a little black dress in the style of Chanel, and every exposed bit of her smooth, sallow flesh was covered with black lace. She wore black lace hose and a large-rimmed, black hat. Sager stared at her delicate face for a moment in silence, then seemed to snap back into reality.

"Oh, I'm sorry, Ophelia! Are you okay?"

"It's alright, Professor," she said with a smile, and placed her hand on his arm. "It was my fault. I should have looked. Are *you* alright?"

"I'm fine. Yeah, that was embarrassing. Sorry again. Ophelia, this is my girlfriend, Xiaoqing, and my good friend, Father Jean-Pierre de la Fresnière, from New Orleans."

"A pleasure to make both of your acquaintances," she replied. "I've been to New Orleans many times. My family has an ancestral home on Saint Charles Avenue."

"Oh, very nice!" said Jean-Pierre. "It's such a beautiful, grand old avenue."

Xiaoqing glared at Ophelia's hand, which was still on Sager's arm, but no one noticed.

"Ophelia is a local high school student who is also interested in pre-Colombian America. I believe you said your mom works at my university? Xiaoqing is a research assistant there, close to finishing her doctorate in European folklore."

Ophelia's lips, moist with blood-red lipstick, parted almost unnoticeably, a gossamer sigh escaping like a tiny breeze. "Oh? That is another of my interests. What sort of folklore is your specialty, Miss Xiaoqing?"

Xiaoqing lowered her eyebrows a bit and answered, "It's a little silly, but I'm interested in supernatural European folklore from the pre-Christian era and into the early Christian era."

Ophelia remained silent for a moment, then asked, "Are you an expert?"

"Oh, not really…"

"Yes, she is," answered Sager. "She's just too modest to admit it. She's already contributed several papers to academic journals, and her theory of vampirism is getting noticed in the right academic circles."

"Theory of vampirism?" prodded Ophelia.

"Basically, it's my belief that all of the legends of vampires around the world could possibly be explained through medical phenomena, but I think they're representative of a pre-Christian, pagan religion that focused on the earth and blood," explained Xiaoqing.

Ophelia nodded. "That sounds interesting and complicated. I'd love to hear more some time. Say, Professor, Father, Miss Xiaoqing, you should come over to our house for dinner soon. Since my mother works at the university, it's like you are colleagues, anyway. Mother would love to have you for dinner. Maybe this week?"

"Oh, Ophelia, that's very kind. I don't want to impose on your mom's hospitality, though," said Sager.

"It's alright, Professor. She already told me she wanted to meet you, now that we live in the same town. Would you give me your phone number, and I will text you when you should come, after I verify with my mother?" Ophelia had not removed her hand from Sager's arm. He could feel the coolness of her flesh against his own. His pulse accelerated slightly, and Ophelia looked down at her hand, then back up at him, and smiled."

"Um, sure, Ophelia. Here, I'll type it into your phone if that is okay."

She took her phone, smiled, and walked away, letting her hand slide along Sager's arm, down to the back of his hand, and then back to her side.

"What the *hell* was that about?" demanded Xiaoqing.

"Huh? What was what?"

"You know what I mean, Sager! She was hitting on you!"

"Oh, come on!" replied Sager incredulously.

"Sorry, Sager, but she's right," added Jean-Pierre. "That girl's hot for teacher."

"Ha! You two stop! She's only a teenager, for crying out loud!"

"I had a huge crush on my teacher in the third grade, Sager," admitted Jean-Pierre. "It's actually much more common than people want to admit."

"Well, that's ridiculous," said Sager, chuckling. "In any case, she's just being polite. Her mother works at the university, Xiaoqing. We should go to dinner, meet some locals. We can't be that weird, reclusive couple who never fit in, you know. You should come too, Jean-Pierre, if you're still in town. Come on, Beast Stalker's place is right up here."

Xiaoqing and Jean-Pierre expressed delight at the appearance of the bookstore and museum. They entered and found Beast Stalker checking out a customer. He looked at Sager and nodded. When the customer left, the three walked to the counter.

"Beast Stalker, this is Father Jean-Pierre de la Fresnière. He's the friend I told you about. He's an expert on languages," said Sager.

Beast Stalker nodded to each of them. "Thank you for coming. And thank you, Father, for coming such a long way, just to look at my people's artifact. It's very generous."

"Oh, it's my pleasure, Beast Stalker," replied Jean-Pierre. "I'm really interested in this sort of thing, and I needed an excuse to get away from New Orleans, and to see my old friend, Sager, and my new friend, Xiaoqing. So, not to be too forward, but I'd sure love to see your museum, and of course the artifact."

Beast Stalker smiled subtly. "Right this way. And no admission fee for my friends."

Jean-Pierre and Xiaoqing marveled over some of the excellent exhibits, while Beast Stalker went in the back to fetch the amulet. When he brought it out, Jean-Pierre instantly remarked, "It's as I thought. Impossible, but here it is. Beast Stalker, may I hold it in my hands? I will be very careful."

The Indian nodded and gently handed the priceless artifact to the priest, who then produced a jeweler's loupe.

"A loupe, Jean-Pierre? Are you an expert in yet another field?" joked Sager.

"It's just an interest." Jean-Pierre carefully examined the giant sapphire. The gemstone reflected a million points of light, as if the entire secret of life were hidden within its thalassic depths. The priest seemed almost enchanted, almost hypnotized by its brilliance. "I almost cannot believe it, but yes, it's a real sapphire. It's flawless. Not a single occlusion. Nothing. It's a treasure of humanity. Beast Stalker, before I tell you my theory on the writing, could you tell me everything you know about this gem and its provenance, every detail, every legend?"

"Hmm. I know only what I have conveyed to the professor. However, there is an elder of my people who knows very many things and has deep wisdom. Perhaps you would come with me to meet him tomorrow? If anyone in this world can tell you more about the amulet, it is Chief Cloud Mountain."

"Sager?" asked Jean-Pierre. "What do you say? It sounds like an amazing opportunity that we might never again have."

"I agree, Padre. Xiaoqing?"

"Oh, unfortunately, I have to work on my dissertation. Sorry, but I need to be back in my office in Glenville at the university. You two should go for sure."

"You sure? This is folklore, after all," said Sager.

"Oh, well, that's a good point. Maybe I will go then. Beast Stalker, is it alright if we all three go?"

The Indian nodded. "He will be happy to talk to you. We can meet here tomorrow at nine o'clock, if that is convenient."

They were all there the next morning, feeling refreshed due to their having abstained from more *baijiu*.

"Before we begin," said Beast Stalker, "I need to tell you just a few simple things about meeting a Cherokee elder. First, do not enter until he invites you in. Next, do not sit down until he sits down. Cherokees always remain standing while elders are standing. Third, let him choose his chair, and then let him suggest where you should sit. Finally, do not speak until he speaks. A Cherokee elder should be the one to speak first. And don't interrupt him while he's talking. We highly respect our elders, and Cloud Mountain is a chief on top of that. I spoke to him last night, and he welcomes you to his home. He is a good man, and he will not blame you if you break one of our cultural rules because he knows that you are from another culture, but if you do follow these rules I am giving you, it will impress him."

"Don't worry," said Xiaoqing. "We will respect your culture. And those rules are very similar to the way we are in the presence of elders in China." She looked toward Sager and Jean-Pierre and asked, "Can you two Western brats follow the rules?"

"Ha ha. Very funny," replied Sager. "We will show great respect. Don't worry, Beast Stalker."

They squeezed into Beast Stalker's old, beaten-up Toyota pickup truck. He drove for about forty-five minutes, and they entered the reservation. Beast Stalker followed a couple of side roads and then pulled his Toyota into the driveway of a depressing little wooden house. None of the three said anything, but Sager and Jean-Pierre felt pangs of guilt, both knowing exactly why so many Native Americans ended up living in such poor conditions.

"Come, friends," said Beast Stalker, and they followed him to the door. Before they reached the door, it opened, and a short, wrinkled old woman stepped onto the porch, her smile beaming out like sunshine.

Beast Stalker said something in Cherokee. She replied, looked at the three, then said in English, "Welcome! We're so happy you've come to visit us. Come in! Come in!"

They followed her into a worn, dingy living room filled with low-quality furniture. Even so, it was spotlessly clean and tidy.

"You can sit, please. I'm making some tea. Please, make yourselves at home!"

Beast Stalker sat first, and they all followed his lead. The old woman returned with some hot tea and began to serve them, but Beast Stalker said something in Cherokee, gestured for her to sit, and he served everyone their tea, beginning with the old woman.

"My husband, Chief Cloud Mountain, will be out in a moment," she said. "Beast Stalker told me that you are interested in our people's folklore. It is a long history, and there are many tales. Many of the young people don't listen or care anymore, but Beast Stalker is different. He's always been very interested in our people and very respectful to the old ways. Oh, here comes the chief now!"

Beast Stalker stood and gestured for the other three to stand. They watched as a man as old as a Redwood tree hobbled into the room. Wrinkles webbed across his thick, brown, leathery skin like ancient water channels on the Moon, long-forgotten but leaving traces of their time. From his scalp, hoary hair flowed like a cataract, like a dream hovering in the mists of the eyes after waking up. His joints seemed almost to creak as he walked. His eyes were deep pools of water, muddied by the passing of so much time.

He slowly made his way to his favorite chair as everyone stood in silence. His wife helped him to sit, and then he spoke, not in the crackling, weak tone of a reed instrument, as they expected, but in a voice as deep and rich and full as a mountain cave: "Welcome. Please, sit down."

As if his voice itself physically took hold of them all, they sat in unison and watched the chief in wonder. No one said a word.

The chief said something to Beast Stalker in Cherokee, then laughed.

"I just told Beast Stalker that it has been so long since outsiders have been to my home, that I almost forgot what they looked like. I am honored that you have asked to hear my words, young people. My wife and I welcome you to our land, to our people." There was something about his voice that entranced all of them, something powerful, with authority. "What you see around you is not how it always was. We were once a rich, strong, proud people. Now, we have been reduced to poverty, but we refuse to forget the old ways, the old times. Some day, probably soon, I will pass from this world, and someone else will rise to take my place. That's the way of the world. Everything is born, and lives, and dies, and is born again. What goes into the ground comes back up. That is the story of where our people come from. Did you know that? The ancients came out from caves in the ground into this world. They passed through a barrier, from earth to air. When we die, we then pass from air to spirit. There is no difference in the process, only in the material. But you have not come to listen to the ramblings of an old man. Beast Stalker told me that you wanted to learn about the Gatvdi, the Amulet that Beast Stalker has shown you."

He asked Beast Stalker something in Cherokee, and Beast Stalker pulled the amulet from his bag and carefully handed it to Chief Cloud Mountain.

"This amulet cannot be here long. It must return to the safety of Beast Stalker's museum. For now, I will tell you all I know of this amulet. What I tell you, my father told me, and his father told him, and a thousand fathers told a thousand sons through the ages; for this amulet is older than our people, older even than the old ones, the Ancients, older even than this land. This amulet was here before our people came up out of the caves," the chief said, and for what felt like an era but was actually only a couple of minutes, the old man stared at the sapphire before he continued with his tale."A very long time ago, the time before our people, this amulet was created far away, in another land, by another people. Those people were troubled by seven demons. No one, not even their greatest champion, could stop these seven demons from disturbing their people, destroying their crops, making their people sick unto death, and even stealing their little ones. Then, a very powerful sorcerer created this amulet from the earth, from the ground, and from his own blood. This sorcerer's name has been forgotten to time. When he came out of his workshop, the people saw that he could control the demons with the amulet, so the demons feared it greatly, and had to bend to the sorcerer's will. He finally used the amulet to drive the seven demons out of that land forever."

Chief Cloud Mountain paused once again, and Sager turned his head to his right to see Jean-Pierre's reaction to the tale. The priest was staring fixedly at the amulet, with an expression that Sager had seen on him many times before—wonderment. His eyes returned to the chief as soon as the man took up with the story.

"When the sorcerer died, he passed the amulet on to the elders of his people so that they could make sure the seven demons never returned. The amulet was passed down through the ages, until one day a wealthy king brought it to this side of the world, to what your people call the New World, to the ancient land of our people. That king met one of our ancient chiefs, Gigadanegisgi. He was a great warrior, and the king was so impressed by his greatness in battle that he gave him the amulet as a tribute gift. Since then, the amulet has been kept among our people, passed down from chief to chief, to protect our people from the demons around us. It truly does keep the demons away from our people, and it will always do so, as long as our people possess it."

Sager felt his entire body filled with goosebumps because of the chief's words. He didn't know why, but there was something ominous about them.

"And there *are* evil spirits here. They are everywhere, but this land has many. It is like an accursed land, but blessed because of the amulet. And the town you live in is especially accursed. It is home to many, many evil spirits, many demons. You must be very careful there. You must always trust Beast Stalker, whatever he tells you. He is a good man, and he has the amulet for the protection of our people, and the protection of your people, of everyone in Ushaville. If you get into trouble, go to Beast Stalker, and he will help you."

Beast Stalker nodded.

"Do you have any questions?" the chief asked.

After a moment of silence, Xiaoqing asked, "Chief, do you know anything about the writing on the amulet?"

The chief pursed his lips, thought for a moment, then answered, "Not too much. All I know is what the legends say: that the language was the language of the original people who created the amulet, a people from long ago and far away."

"Chief," asked Jean-Pierre, "do you know anyone who can read the language?"

"No, son, I do not. Our people would be very grateful to anyone who can decipher the writing."

"I might have an idea, Chief, but it is going to take a bit of study and work. Perhaps, with Beast Stalker's permission, I could spend a few days in his museum, examining the amulet," offered Jean-Pierre.

"That is fine," said Beast Stalker. "You can use the office I have in the back."

"And now that we have finished our talk," said the chief, "I invite you to have a meal with my wife and me. She has prepared some traditional Cherokee dishes. I hope you can join us.

The six enjoyed a veritable feast of corn, beans, squash, dear meat, bear meat, and fish, washed down with a special moonshine that Beast Stalker had made himself.

For the next few days, Jean-Pierre spent every hour, from morning to evening, studying the amulet, and one evening, he returned to Sager's house with the news: "I think I've cracked the code, guys!"

They ushered him in, Xiaoqing made everyone some tea, and they sat down in Sager's living room.

"Well?" prodded Sager.

"It seems impossible that this amulet would be discovered in rural West Virginia. It just can't be. Yet here it is," said Jean-Pierre.

"Just tell us already!" urged Xiaoqing, and the two men laughed.

"Fine, fine. Alright," he began, holding up some photos and drawings of the language, "see how the words are arranged. There are no spaces between letters or words, which was common in the ancient world, but this particular letter that you see here seems to indicate the beginning and end of words. I decided that it had to be alphabetic rather than glyphic because the letters are too abstract and patterned to be otherwise. Now, if this is the case, then these words are all based on a triliteral root."

"Meaning?" asked Xiaoqing.

"Meaning," he continued, "that the words are all either three letters in length or based on a three-letter root. I don't know the pronunciation, of course, but I did some analysis on the syntax and structure. Now, can I get a drumroll?"

Sager beat his fingers on the table.

"It fits the pattern of ancient Mesopotamian languages and languages related to those. My research shows that it is not a known language, but it's very obviously an ancient language from the Middle East, and it's related to Babylonian, Sumerian, Hebrew, Egyptian, and others. If the amulet is authentic, and I believe it is, then it clearly comes from the ancient Middle East, and is simply a dialect of a known language."

After several seconds of silence, Sager said, "Wow. Just wow. That is amazing. And it brings up two obvious questions, right? How did it get here, and what does it say?"

"Yep. Well, as to what it says, I have no idea. While it is clearly related to a couple of ancient languages I know, it is not exactly the same, so I can't translate it. As to how it got here? I mean, if it's authentic, and if it's been in the care of the Cherokees for as long as they can remember, then there's only one way. It had to have been brought here in ancient times," reasoned Jean-Pierre.

"It's not unheard of, padre. We know that Vikings made it to the New World, and possibly the Chinese and others, right? Is it such a stretch to imagine that some seafaring people took a northern route, hugged the coast, and arrived here?" asked Sager.

"It's not unreasonable, I agree. But then they made their way to West Virginia? That seems less likely, though not impossible."

"I want to know what it says," added Xiaoqing. "My grandma thinks this town is cursed. Chief Cloud Mountain thinks it's cursed; there has to be some truth to it."

"Xiaoqing, come on baby. You can't believe that. Spirits? Demons? Magical amulets? Are we back in the Middle Ages?" said Sager.

"Well, what about you, Jean-Pierre?" asked Xiaoqing. "You're a priest. That means you believe in God. And if you believe God can exist, then you also have to believe that angels exist, and demons, and other things like that."

"You know, Xiaoqing, the modern Catholic Church looks at lots of scripture as symbolic morality teachings."

"So, you don't believe in evil spirits?" prodded Xiaoqing.

Jean-Pierre closed his eyes for a moment. He could still vividly see the girl in Colombia while she writhed on the ground and burst from her chains with superhuman strength, while she leaped upon the priest and drank his blood, and while the man staked her.

"Well, I suppose I am not completely closed to it. I think there is indeed real evil in the world," he replied. "In any case, we need to get this information to Beast Stalker first thing tomorrow. Agree?" Sager and Xiaoqing nodded. They all moved to the dining room, and Xiaoqing served them the best handmade dumplings that they had ever tasted in their lives.

CHAPTER 8

COUNCIL MEETING

Midnight. Ushaville City Hall. It is a muted red, brick building on Under den Linden Street, and nothing about its architectural style differentiates it from all of its neighbors. They are all in a European style, mostly Nineteenth-Century German. However, there is something about City Hall that makes it unique—there are no windows. Like a mausoleum, it is a brick monolith, a square bully staring down at its neighbors without remorse. Like a coffin, its only interaction with the outside world is the front door, which is almost always closed and locked.

On this day, however, it is unlocked. A city council meeting is taking place.

The meeting room was on the third floor of the building—the second floor by European counting. It was ornately lavish. The walls were rich mahogany, and two of the four walls were covered in bookshelves stacked with leather-bound classics. The other two walls were artfully hung with rare, original paintings of some of the Dutch Masters. The room was lit, not by electric lights, but by antique oil lamps, and in the middle of it was a large, rectangular, antique, French table, around which were 10 Louis XIV chairs. Each place was set with a leather-bound notepad; an antique quill fountain pen; a bejeweled, golden goblet filled with what looked like a fine, vintage red wine; a handmade, cherry-wood, antique smoking pipe; an antique lighter; and a bowl of fine Virginia golden tobacco.

Sitting in each chair was a member of either the Hatfield clan or the McCoy clan: Hatfields on the east side of the tables, McCoys, the west. In one head chair sat Lorman McCoy, in the other, Andy Hatfield. As was the custom, there was cemetery silence, everyone waiting for either Elder to speak first.

Andy Hatfield took his goblet and enjoyed a long sip. Lorman then did the same, prompting everyone at the table to follow suit. Lorman picked up his pipe, loaded it, tamped the tobacco, and lit it. He gestured permission to the room, and everyone else also lit their pipes. Soon, the curling purple tendrils of smoke wisped to the ceiling, producing a brilliant, deep violet layer of smoke hanging in the air above them all. After several puffs and sips, Lorman spoke first.

"Ladies, gentlemen, friends, council, I wish you a warm welcome to this month's council meeting. As always, I trust that we shall all comport ourselves in the genteel ways of our ancestors, the Old Ones. Let us perpetuate our living together in harmony and stability, for in such a manner shall we ensure our continued existence in this world."

Andy smirked sarcastically but remained silent.

"Orders of business," continued Lorman. "Andy and I have agreed on a listed agenda, as usual. First, I have achieved no progress in identifying the mystic force that we discussed last month. We can all feel this force. It is very powerful, and it means us harm. I have attempted many times to track it down and locate it, but my attempts remain futile."

"We've got to find it. We can all sense its danger, whatever or whoever it is. We need to tear this town apart until we find it and destroy it, Asa." said Andy angrily.

"Andy, we will do no good by harming our own town. For so many centuries, we have worked hard to build this place and the careful balance that sustains it and us. Disrupting this balance will only harm us further," said Lorman. "And please, let us use our second names here as well as among the townspeople, so that we will not forget and give ourselves away."

"Asa Harmon McCoy!" shouted Andy. "I'm tired of hiding and lying and faking just so some humans won't know who we are. That's your name, and mine's Devil Anse Hatfield! That's been our names for over a hundred years. We're the rulers here, not the humans!"

"Andy, if you would just listen to…"

"To hell with that, Elder McCoy!" interjected Ida Hatfield, a young, pale woman with a smooth, attractive face. "Balance isn't working. All we're doing here is kowtowing to the humans! We're tired of living in the shadows, hiding away our true nature. We need to live, to feed, to thrive!"

"Now Ida," said Lorman, "we've provided perfectly fine animal blood for consumption. It is fresh, nutritious, and readily available. And while I do not like it, the fact is that you are allowed to feed upon humans without the mark of protection, after dark."

"It's not the same, Elder!" she said. "It's not what we're meant for!"

Lorman stood up to his full height. His human face transformed into a pale, monstrous, vampire face. He stared down at Ida: "You will obey the rules of order of this meeting!" His voice was like a growling, baritone voice from deep under the earth. Ida winced and shrank back down in her seat silently.

Lorman sat back down and said, this time more gently, "Order is necessary to preserve our vitality. If the world finds out that we exist, they will slaughter us, as they have done in various times and places throughout human history. They are the majority, and we are the minority."

Andy retorted, "But we have the clear advantage! We are stronger, faster, deadlier, and we can make them into us! We could turn the whole world into us and live in a huge empire that includes all humanity! We could make them our slaves!"

"Andy!" replied Lorman.

"That's Devil Anse to you, Asa Harmon!"

"Andy," repeated Lorman, "we have all of the examples of history to show that you are wrong. Ancient Sumeria, Medieval Transylvania, and many more—every time our kind has attempted to rise up and overthrow the human rule... they have stamped us out and driven us back to hiding in caves and dark places. Ushaville has been a success only because we are able, through careful behavior, to uphold this delicate balance. We allow humans to live here; we provide them an excellent life, and we protect them. In return, they do not even realize we are here."

"Pardon me, Elder McCoy," said Johnse Hatfield, noticeably humbler and quieter than how Ida had been. "But, Sir, only humans with the protection tattoo are protected. We have humans living in Ushaville without that protection, and the ones with the tattoo do not truly understand what it is protecting them for."

"And now," added Andy, "we even have new residents. There's that nosy professor and his girlfriend. They have a priest friend visiting. A priest! And there's that rock and roll band in town. What are they still doing here? The human population's getting bigger, and we can't just go on protecting them all. It just ain't natural, Asa! It's like a bunch of gazelles keeping lions in a zoo. One way or another, those lions are gonna eat!"

"And then what, Andy?" asked Lorman in an irritated voice. "And then what? You eat; you feed, people just disappear…what happens *then*? Have you ever even thought that far ahead? Professors have colleagues. Rock musicians have managers. Priests have…well, you know very well what they have. What about the Indians? They broker our truce with each other and with the humans. None of the Indians have the tattoo, but we sure as hell know to leave them alone. They have magic that we cannot control. You know I've been against the tattoo system from the beginning. I say we protect all of the humans. We only allow you, the Hatfields, certain… leniencies with the non-tattooed humans to appease you, but you've been in trouble before. Remember that real estate agent last year who wandered into the Eastside? What happened to her, Andy? Oh, we know well what happened to her, and then her agency came calling, and then her husband, and then the police from her hometown! They thought it suspicious that we have no police force, and it was only by my own glamour and reasoning that I convinced them to just leave." Lorman made a pause to let his words sink in. "So, Andy? What if we gave Hatfields free reign? What would happen then? I'll tell you exactly what would happen. Our little secret would be revealed to the world. This isn't the Middle Ages anymore, Andy, where bands of peasants with pitchforks were easy enough to dispatch with. Now we have powerful, unified governments with firearms and machines. They could eradicate our kind completely in a day if they wished!"

"Not if we turned them first, Asa! Not if we turned them first," yelled Andy, standing up to his thin, full height, his scraggly beard swaying in the air currents in the room. "I ain't saying we have to eat them all! We turn enough of them that we outnumber the humans, and then we turn those that come to fight us, and then they turn others. It'll be *our* world for a change, Asa! We've hidden in shadows long enough. Our time has come!"

At this, the Hatfield side of the table cheered and clapped. The McCoys hissed their disapproval.

"You're not the only of our kind here, you McCoys," continued Andy. "Half the town's ours, and you don't get to make all the rules!"

"And so, what are you going to do about it, Devil Anse Hatfield?" demanded Lorman, using his rival's real name for once. "Are you going to tear up the town? Kill and eat everyone? Destroy the only home you have in a world hostile to our kind?"

"You'll see what we'll do, Asa Harmon. You've held your money and class over us for long enough now. It's our turn to prosper. This meeting is adjourned!" shouted Asa, then turning and storming out of the room. His family members followed him.

The next morning, the *Ushaville Courier* ran the headline: *Double Murder in the Eastside!* The article was as follows:

The bodies of two murder victims were reported early this morning by residents of the Eastside. The bodies were discovered in Sultan Alley at approximately 7:30 am. The City Council is conducting an investigation into the crimes, and no details have yet been released. Several witnesses at the crime scene reported that the bodies were mangled, decapitated, and drained of blood. The *Ushaville Courier* will provide up to date information once we have obtained it.

CHAPTER 9

STRANDED PUNKS

Nancy had met up with the punks mid-morning at The Fairie Realm Café. They had fast become friends, and Nancy had agreed to show them where the mechanic's garage was so that they could check on their van's status. At a nearby table sat an average guy, a Chinese girl, a priest, and a Native American who conversed over some jewelry photos that they had laid out on the table. Titania, who had seemingly popped up out of nowhere, was polishing glasses behind the bar, occasionally looking toward the photos and squinting her eyes. She saw Nancy and the punks, and approached the table.

"Hi, Nancy. You guys want the same as last time?" asked Titania.

"You must have a good memory," said Gill.

"Oh, she does," answered Nancy. "It's almost like magic." Titania winked.

"Hey, Titania, the band here agreed to play a show at the Pallid Horse tomorrow night. You want to come? Mr. Hatfield agreed to pay them to play without even hearing them first."

"Oh, for sure!" answered Titania.

"Cool as shit!" said Paul too loudly.

"God, will you shut up?" retorted Mary. "You have no class!"

"Ah, Mary," interjected Gill, "that's one of the main foundations of the punk philosophy—societies should not be divided by social classes and class markers."

"Um, yeah, alright," replied Mary.

Nancy nodded her head sideways in the direction of the other table and whispered to Titania, "What's with the priest? Don't see many of them in this town."

Titania shrugged. "Not sure. That's the professor with him, and I think the Chinese girl is the professor's girlfriend. Kind of interesting. They've been looking at some pics of this weird looking writing on some sort of gemstone."

Matt yawned and added, "The intellectual types. Eggheads. Always looking at some boring or arcane bullshit."

"Well, on that intellectual note," smirked Nancy, "let's go check on your van, guys. Thanks, Titania. Tomorrow night, Pallid Horse, show starts at nine."

"Wouldn't miss it for the world," answered Titania with a wink to Paul.

"Oy! Did you wink at me, baby? Come to the show, and maybe I'll give you a little private show backstage."

"Paul!" yelled Mary, slapping him in the face. "You don't have to be such a pig!"

Paul chuckled and answered, "Christ! I'm just doing a little flirting, Mary."

Titania simply gave a sarcastic smirk and got back to work.

Nancy and The Gravediggers walked down a few blocks and reached the mechanic's shop. It was just on the side of the street that touched the Eastside, but it was not deep enough in to be frightening. It was next door to an Army surplus shop.

"What the...?" began Mary.

The brick building was bedecked with a large sign advertising *Hatfield Auto Repair*, and under it was a front door that had been boarded over. A handwritten note hung upon the boards, stating, in an elaborate handwriting script: *We are closed until further notice. We apologize for any inconvenience.* They peered through the gaps in a boarded-up window and saw the Microbus not ten feet from them, looking clean and in good repair.

"This can't be good," added Matt with a yawn. "They can't just steal our van, can they?"

"Um, don't you mean *my* van?" said Mary. "Who owns this crappy shop, anyway?"

"Titus Hatfield, I think," answered Mary. "He's just one of the Hatfields. They own businesses all over the town. Hatfields and McCoys are allowed to own a business anywhere, but they have to live on their side."

"Allowed?" asked Gill. "People are forced to live in certain places? Like a ghetto?"

"I mean, sort of, yeah. I told you it's a weird town," said Nancy and chuckled. "And I'm not supposed to tell anyone this, but you guys seem cool, so hell with it. There's also a system of underground tunnels under Ushaville that some of the Hatfields and McCoys use to get around."

"What?" shouted Paul. "Fucking tunnels? Is this some sort of weird movie we stepped into? Why the hell are there tunnels?"

"Not sure," replied Nancy. "I just know they've been here forever, and no one but Hatfields and McCoys are allowed to use them. Some of them get to their businesses that way. I've heard some people say that they're old Civil War tunnels, used to move guns and equipment without the enemy seeing. I've also heard that they're really ancient Indian tunnels that they used for religious rituals. No one really knows, I guess. Just know that we're not allowed in."

"Well, then you know what that means!" said Paul.

"No. No, Paul. Get the idea out of your head," said Mary. "You saw how scary that fucker the other night was. You want him catching you underground for fuck's sake?"

"Well, I want to see the tunnels," said Paul, crossing his arms and pouting.

"Criminy, Paul," added Gill, "you're like a damned child. Can we at least get through the concert tomorrow night before we run afoul of the rather frightening town elders?"

"Fine," said pouting Paul with a frown.

"Guys, if you go to the tunnels, I can't go with you. I mean, I won't. I've seen shit go down in this town before, and you really do not want to mess with it. But if you insist, then sorry, I will not go. It's too dangerous." A few moments of pensive silence elapsed, then Nancy continued, "Well, anyway, let's go get a drink at the Pallid Horse. I can show you where you'll set up your stuff. Isn't your equipment locked in the van?"

"Nah," said Mary. "We carried what we need to our hotel room. All we need is electricity."

"Oh, you'll be fine then. And Titus Hatfield's brother, Lucius, manages the Pallid Horse for Andy Hatfield. If he's there, I'll ask about the van, tell him you really need it."

61

The Pallid Horse was fuller than it had been the last time, with most tables occupied by shady-looking characters in dark clothing. The men Nancy said were Titus and Lucius Hatfield sat together at a small table in a shadowy corner. The punks watched as Nancy slowly walked over to their table, looking down the entire time. She said something to them that the punks could not hear over the general conversations throughout the bar. Titus Hatfield replied, and Nancy's eyes grew wide for a moment before she regained her composure. She nodded deeply, almost a curtsy, then walked back to the bar.

"So, we gonna get our van back?" asked Paul.

"Nancy, you look like the blood just drained from your face! What the hell did they say?" asked Mary.

"Well, they said that Ushaville is going to be closing down for a little while so that the Council can take care of some business. Until then, the repair shop is not accessible. They said your van can wait. This can't be good, guys; The Council has always tried to make this place normal and functioning. Why would they shut it down? What does that even mean? Are the McCoy's involved in this?"

"Is it not quite illegal to shut down a town? Will there be martial law?" asked Gill. "And to essentially steal our van? Can we talk to a lawyer?"

"Bloody right it is!" said Paul.

"Can I get a beer?" asked Matt.

"Well, guys, the concert tomorrow still needs to happen. It'll keep things normal until we figure out what is going on, alright? And Gill? No lawyer can do anything about the Council. They run this town. We're basically helpless against them."

"If we're going down, then I want to see those bloody tunnels!" said Paul.

"Shh! Christ, Paul, don't let people hear you. I'm starting to feel a little threatened here. Let's just try to fit in, alright?" said Mary.

"May I remind you, Mary, that the punk philosophy precludes the idea of conformity?"

"Bite me, Gill," she retorted.

CHAPTER 10

THE AMULET'S POWER

"Try this beverage," said Beast Stalker. "It is a special kind of tea made by my people from local fruits. Don't worry. No caffeine, no alcohol, nothing harmful. It's all good."

"Well, thank you, Beast Stalker," replied Sager. "I love trying new things." Beast Stalker nodded.

The now four friends sat in a circle in the back room of the bookstore, which had been made into an office, and also a social gathering place with soft, inviting chairs and sofas and warm, dim lighting. Beast Stalker had placed the amulet on a table with a lamp to make it easier to see.

"Father, you said you had made some progress on the language of the amulet?"

"Yep, Beast Stalker. Let me go over everything with you. I also have some exciting news that I've yet told no one." Jean-Pierre preceded to tell Beast Stalker everything he had already told Sager and Xiaoqing. "And now, I want to share something else with you all. Did you two notice that I was up very late last night?" he asked, and Sager and Xiaoqing nodded. "Well, that's because I was doing some more work on the language. I think I was able to come up with a basic translation!" announced Jean-Pierre.

"What?" gasped Xiaoqing. "How? It's an unknown language!"

Even the usually subdued Beast Stalker gasped.

63

"I told you he was a genius!" added Sager.

"Not a genius, I assure you, just a hard worker. Alright, so, I went on my premise that it is an ancient Near East language related to the Semitic and Hamitic language groups or something like that, right? So, I made a list of the top most commonly-used verbs in ancient Hebrew, ancient Arabic, Sumerian, Phoenician, and Middle Egyptian. Even though Sumerian is sort of an outlier and not really related to the others, it still influenced their vocabulary to some degree. So, I took these verbs, all of which are based on three consonants—triliteral roots, as I told you. I made some assumptions about the amulet language when it had a triliteral word in the verbal syntactical position. I then made some possible combinations that could fit as cognates of the other languages. I then did the same with nouns, and so forth. I assumed that the amulet language has the same syntax, word order, and grammar as the other languages in that general language family and that, like them, it reads right to left. I played with many combinations of words and sentences, and I stumbled upon one combination that is grammatically and syntactically correct, and makes a complete, sensible text. In fact, I have reconstructed the probable pronunciation."

"Well? Don't leave us hanging!" said Xiaoqing. "What does it say?"

"Here is how I think it approximately sounded in the original language," he said and showed them his notes.

Sager pronounced it slowly and deliberately—it sounded guttural and ancient, and certainly related to Middle Eastern languages. As he finished, the amulet began to glow with a blue hue.

"It is glowing!" said Beast Stalker excitedly. "Look!"

"What? What is it doing?" asked Sager.

"I don't know," said Jean-Pierre, "but the words seemed to have somehow activated its power! I guess I got them about right."

The amulet, to their amazement, then dimmed back to its natural color.

"Alright, if I am right, and I could be wrong, here is what it means in English: *Seven demons from the land, air, and sea. Seven demons come from below to trouble us above. They drink our blood. They steal our little ones. They take our life and they live forever. I, Asarial the wizard, have learned the secret of killing them. I, Asarial, have created this amulet to contain the power of their death.*"

"Holy crap, Jean-Pierre! That is brilliant!" said Sager. "It actually makes sense."

"The demons sound a lot like vampires," added Xiaoqing. "There are many folklores around the world that tell of dark creatures from below who rise up to drink our blood so that they can live forever. The European vampire concept, you know, like Dracula, is only one of them."

Beast Stalker said, "There are indeed old tales among our people of such creatures."

"Wendigos?" asked Xiaoqing.

"Yes, those, and also others. Wendigos eat human flesh, but other evil spirits drink human blood. You know, if you three are willing, I can arrange another kind of meeting with Chief Cloud Mountain. It is a tradition among our people to use certain plants and herbs to enter into the spirit world. With Chief as our guide, we can ask the spirits to reveal the meaning of the amulet writing. We can also ask the ancestor-spirits about the evil spirits that are in and around Ushaville."

"You mean hallucinogenics?" asked Sager.

"They are called that, yes," replied Beast Stalker. "Our people believe that they truly pierce the plane between the two worlds. Father, is this against your religion?"

"Hmm," answered Jean-Pierre. "Normally, I would not do hallucinogenics. But because this is done as a spiritual ritual, and in order to fight evil, I will do it. Sager? Xiaoqing? You in?"

Sager took Xiaoqing's hand and asked her, "Well, honey?"

"Yes, definitely. It will be a great cultural experience!"

"Just a brief note, Xiaoqing," said Beast Stalker. "It is a cultural experience, yes, but you must also take it seriously. We will be drinking the Black Drink, which will truly transport you to another realm. Whether you accept that realm as truly another dimension in existence is your choice, but believe me when I say that you will experience many great things you have never experienced before."

"Alright, I understand, Beast Stalker. I totally respect that," she replied.

Beast Stalker nodded, then said, "It is settled. I will speak to Chief Cloud Mountain and arrange a time. He has to approve of non-Cherokees taking part, of course, but I am sure he will, since it is about our people's amulet. He will be very pleased to know that Father has translated the writing." He took a pause and looked at them all directly in their eyes. "It is best to do this as soon as possible. Even tonight, with Chief's permission. His wife can make the drink. I have sensed an increase in the power of the spirits in Ushaville lately, and it is becoming stronger by the day. Like Chief, I believe that this amulet is a powerful weapon against whatever evil is here. However, we cannot fight that which we cannot know or see, or with a weapon that we do not know how to wield. I feel strongly that we must discover what the spirits want us to know immediately, or it will be too late to stop them."

"Normally," said Sager, "and I mean nothing against you personally, Beast Stalker, but normally, I would not put much stock in spirits and evil intentions and magical amulets. However, the amulet and Jean-Pierre's translation have opened my mind, at least to the possibility of something unusual happening here. I'm not saying that I believe in a spirit world, but I have faith in you and the Chief, Beast Stalker. You are solid, good men; I have a good sense of these things. And if you are inviting me to experience something very important to men like you, and to your people, then I'm willing to give it a try."

They reunited later in the afternoon after Beast Stalker informed them of the approval for their meeting with Chief Cloud Mountain. Before he drove them back, he spoke to them briefly about the coming experience: "When we arrive, Chief and his wife will be in a spiritual state of mind. There will likely be other Indians there too, who will also be mentally prepared. It is a very important and meaningful experience for our people. So, I will give you some practical advice now," he said. "First, please observe the rules of politeness that you were kind enough to observe last time we spoke to Chief. Second, the black drink will make you vomit before it ushers you into the spirit world—vomiting is a form of purification to prepare your body, mind, and spirit to go into the other world. Do not worry: it will not actually harm your body in any way."

Sager noticed that Xiaoqing's face lost a little of its color after Beast Stalker's words, so he grabbed her hand and squeezed it.

"Next, the experience that your people call hallucinating, and that my people call interacting with the spirits, will be very powerful—even if you believe it is only imagined, you will perceive it as very real, as real as this world is to you now. Again, do not worry. Your body will be in the same place, and there is no harm to your health in any way. Finally, your experiences will all be different and will be profoundly personal to you. Your experience will likely start with an animal appearing and guiding you down a path—we call this your spirit animal. That animal's own spirit and characteristics are tied to your own, and which animal appears to you will speak to who you are as a person. The entire experience will last throughout the night, and in the morning, you will return to this plane. There will be no hangover, no after-effects. It will be as if you found the path back into this world. After that, everyone will be expected to tell Chief what they saw, and he will interpret it for you. At that time, please simply listen carefully and do not interrupt him."

"This sounds pretty intense!" said Xiaoqing.

"It is, Xiaoqing," answered Beast Stalker. "That is why I caution you to be grounded in your body and in this world. It is your spirit, and not your body, that will be led by your spirit animal. There is no actual danger to you. Remember that, and do not fret, even if you see something disturbing, like evil spirits or things like that. Chief's wife will not be participating in the black drink. She will be there minding our bodies and making sure that everything goes well. She will also have some other young Cherokee women doing the same. Remember, our people have been doing this for thousands of years. We know what we are doing."

"Thank you, Beast Stalker," said Jean-Pierre. "That is very reassuring. I know this is a very sacred ritual for you, and I'm truly honored that you are allowing us to participate."

Beast Stalker allowed a rare smile to appear on his lips, and the group left for the reservation.

When Beast Stalker's pickup truck reached Chief Cloud Mountain's house, they noticed that his driveway, his yard, and the street were full of cars and motorcycles.

Beast Stalker led them around the house to the enormous backyard. The men had constructed a tall, immense tipi toward the back fence, and a large fire pit was ablaze, lighting the yard as it would have been lit a thousand years before. People were standing around chatting, and one man had a large barbecue pit in full action. They could smell rich venison cooking. Chief Cloud Mountain sat in a folding chair near the tipi, and he waved them over.

As per protocol, no one spoke until Chief began to talk. He said, "Welcome, my friends. We are so happy to have you with us tonight. I think you will find the experience richly rewarding. Please, go and enjoy some barbecue. We will not begin until later. Beast Stalker, would you please introduce the people to our three friends?"

Beast Stalker nodded and said in a loud voice to everyone, "Everyone, these are our three outside friends who will be joining us this evening. They have a deep respect for Chief, for our people, and our ways. Please welcome Professor Sager, Instructor Xiaoqing, and Father Jean-Pierre." All the people waved and welcomed them, and the man commandeering the barbecue pit called them over.

"I hope you folks like venison. Please enjoy! I'm Running Water."

"Thank you so much, Running Water," said Sager. "It smells delicious!"

Jean-Pierre had gone to speak with Chief privately to tell him the meaning of the amulet's writing. Chief was fascinated and said, "Perhaps we can consider the meaning after our spirit walk. Maybe it will be clearer then."

They ate and chatted with various people. The Cherokees all seemed fascinated that these three outsiders wanted to participate in the ritual, and everyone seemed impressed by their respect and humility. Beast Stalker pulled Sager aside and said in a muted voice, "The people like you; that is a good sign. They find that you are respectful of our ways, and they appreciate that. Good job, Professor. This will get you a long way in dealing with our people. I want you to know that we almost never let outsiders participate in the black drink ritual. It is in deep gratitude for Father's translation that Chief has decided to welcome you as friends. That is a very rare and very sincere thing."

"I am so honored, Beast Stalker. Truly. This is really an amazing night for me and for us three. When does the actual ritual begin?"

"It will begin in a while; Chief himself has to feel that the spirits are ready. We basically eat, drink, and socialize until Chief says otherwise. My guess is in about an hour; Chief is almost finished eating. One more thing, Professor. I do not mean this to sound racist or anything like that, but sometimes, you know, white people can tend to, well, have trouble letting themselves go."

Sager chuckled. "I hear you, Beast Stalker. We can be really uptight sometimes."

Beast Stalker smiled. "Glad you understand. Well, in this ritual, the more you resist the call of the spirits, the harder they will fight against you. The spirits have a message for you, for each of us. Just be ready to let yourself go completely, and the spirits will not guide you wrongly."

"Understood," agreed Sager. "I am trying to be as open-minded as possible. By the way, have you tried this venison? It's amazing!"

As predicted, about an hour later, Chief Cloud Mountain motioned to Beast Stalker with his hand, and Beast Stalker walked over. Chief said something in Cherokee, and the crowd became quiet. Everyone turned to face Chief as he stood up, and waited for him to speak.

He began by saying a few sentences in Cherokee, then switched to English, as everyone listened in complete silence: "For the benefit of our three honored guests, and for our young ones who are still learning their Cherokee, I will speak in English. Tonight friends, we are embarking on a journey to the spirit world. We will commune with the spirits of our ancestors and all other spirits who are willing to speak to us. Many of you have taken the black drink before. Some of you have not. If you have, then you know what to expect. If not, then open your ears and listen as I tell the tale of our ancestors."

Sager felt the excitement accumulate in the pit of his stomach, because even if he had a vast knowledge of the history of the Cherokee, to hear it from the lips of an Elder, of a Chief, was something he had never experienced before.

"A very long time ago, when the sun was still bright and clear upon the world, and when there were no men yet, our people lived in caves under the ground. We were not aware of anything else except the darkness and the earth. When the time came for a new age, a feathered serpent came down to our people and showed them the way out of the caves—he led them up into the light of this world. We became a people and established ourselves in this world. But we saw that people became old and then died, so we wondered where they went. They came to us in our dreams and taught us that, just as we came out of the cave world into this world, so had they gone out of this world into the spirit world. They are our ancestors, and they look into our world to guide us, instruct us, and discipline us when we do something that is not for the benefit of the people. We also learned that there are other spirits in the spirit world. Some are good, and some are dark and evil. Some mean us harm. For now, the Great Spirit allows them to attack us. One day, the feathered serpent will return to lead all of us out of this world and into the spirit world, and the evil spirits will have no more place to be."

Once again, an ominous feeling took control of Sager's mind, and when he turned to see Jean-Pierre, he was able to perceive that his long time friend was feeling something similar. The Father was frowning, and Sager saw how sweat had accumulated on his upper lip.

"The black drink was given to us by our ancestors. Using plants and herbs that nature gives us, we purify and purge our physical bodies so that our spirits can enter the spirit world, just for a time, and commune with the spirits and our ancestors. Tonight, we take this black drink, and we enter the world of the spirits. Our women will stay by our bodies as our spirits travel to ensure our well-being. To our three guests, I assure you that no harm will come to you. Open your eyes, ears, and spirits to the other world, and they will teach you. Now, let us gather in a circle by this tipi and partake of the black drink." Beast Stalker ushered the three into the large circle that the men had made, with Chief Cloud Mountain in the middle.

Chief sat down in his chair, and everyone else sat down on the grassy ground. Chief's wife and other women rolled a large pot into the circle and placed it in front of Chief. They then produced a large, wooden goblet of sorts and ladled the black, herbal contents of the black drink from the pot into the cup. Beginning with Chief, the women passed the cup around to everyone. The three guests all took a hearty draught just as the Indians were doing.

To Sager, it tasted bitter and herbal, with an almost astringent undertone. It was not exactly a pleasant beverage, but they managed to get it down.

As soon as everyone in the circle had partaken of the black drink, some drummers began playing from the outside of the circle—the drumbeats were rhythmic and slow at first. Some of the Indians had closed their eyes and had their heads raised to the heavens. Before long, one of them began to vomit, then another, until everyone was emitting, including Sager, Xiaoqing, and Jean-Pierre. It was not enjoyable, but it genuinely felt different than simply being sick with an upset stomach or a virus. It was as if the depths of the body, in contact with the base of the soul, was evoking and casting out all of the things that bind us to this world. Sager noted that they did not vomit up any of the food they had just eaten—only the black drink.

Sager waited and tried. He tried hard to experience something, but nothing happened; he was still there in the circle, in Chief's backyard. Some of the Cherokee men had fallen to the ground and were twitching, so the black drink had worked.

He looked at Xiaoqing and Jean-Pierre, but they were simply sitting with their legs crossed and eyes closed in a contemplative pose. Sager felt disappointed. He knew that hallucinogenics didn't always work on everyone and could have different effects depending on people's chemical tolerance. He remembered trying weed once in high school and being disappointed. While his other friends were having a great time stoned, he had merely sat and watched them, himself feeling no effects.

He heard a mew and felt something warm and furry brush past his legs. He picked up Chief's cat and stroked it while it purred. Perhaps, he thought, he could just be there for his friends, in case they freaked out. The Cherokee women were busy tending to the men, and no one was paying attention to Sager, rending him lonely and outcast. He had always felt like an outsider, useless and disconnected. His only

70

interests as a boy were on the academic side of things. He hated sports, despised the way that games turned friends into raging enemies at the slightest mistake. He raged inside at how the girls loved the boys who could kick and throw balls well, but mocked those who, like him, preferred to read books.

The cat jumped down from his lap and head-bumped his leg. He chuckled and petted it on the head. It wove through his legs and mewed, continually nipping his ankle and head-butting him. He knew cats well enough to recognize that the poor thing was probably hungry. Had Chief forgotten to feed it in preparation for the ritual? No one was really looking his way anyway, so he stood up to try to find some cat food. The cat purred and walked toward the trees at the far end of Chief's yard. Every few steps, it would turn, playfully nip his ankle, head-butt him, and then continue. As the cat led him closer to the trees and farther away from the large bonfire by the tipi, he caught his breath.

"Holy crap," he said to no one in particular, "that's not a cat. That's a damn lynx!" He was well-read enough to see that he had mistaken the rather large cat for a domestic. Still, he had handled Manxes and lynxes before, and he knew that they behaved very much like house cats. The poor thing, no matter the species, was hungry. It was urgently telling him to follow it into the forest, and as he considered this, he felt a warm wave of comfort fall onto and through him as if he had stepped into a waterfall.

The forest trees began to glow in a warm amber haze even though the sun had set. The lynx mewed and walked into the forest, and Sager followed. The cat led him down a path for what seemed like a long time, until they approached a large clearing where he saw fires burning and heard voices not speaking English. He thought he must have turned around somehow and ended up back at Chief's tipi. Still, he stepped into the clearing, and his head reeled.

"Impossible. Fucking impossible," he whispered.

In front of him was a gargantuan stone pyramid that must have towered two hundred feet into the air. At each stepped level of the monolith were dozens of torches held by sconces. Men were climbing the pyramid, and many people were around its base speaking—only a specialist like Sager could have recognized the language as ancient Aztec.

At the top of the pyramid stood a man that Sager knew was the high priest, with an empty altar in front of him, awaiting the sacrifice. The crowd began chanting, and drums began beating loud, urgent, bellicose. The high priest allowed the chanting and drumbeats to reach a piercing, intolerable crescendo, and then, with one motion of his right hand, it all instantly ceased, and the scene became gravely silent.

The countless crowd turned and looked at Sager, and he felt his throat drop to his stomach.

Two Aztec warriors grabbed his arms and pulled him roughly toward the pyramid. He looked down and saw that he was no longer wearing the jeans, polo shirt, and sneakers he had worn to Chief's house—now, he was naked except for a loincloth, and his chest was smeared with red paint while his arms were striped white. Professor Sager Miller, one of the world's top specialists in Pre-Colombian Meso-American studies, knew that this could mean only one thing: *he* was the sacrifice.

"Stop! Stop!" he screamed. "This is a mistake!"

The warriors looked at him quizzically, and Sager realized that he was still speaking English. He sighed in frustration, then, using all of the strength he could draw from his own survival instinct, struggled against the guards. It was useless—he was a professor, and they were Aztec warriors, so the men simply held on to him as if it were nothing. He let his body go limp, causing pure dead weight, but a third guard simply approached and helped to force him back upright. He realized that it was hopeless.

Because of his studies, he knew exactly what was about to happen—he had, with great enthusiasm and fervor, described the Aztec human sacrificial ritual to his students countless times. He had enjoyed their looks of repulsion, their *Oohs!* and *Ahhs!*, but his being present as the victim made Sager's lectures pale beside the horrific reality that he was about to face.

He found that the cliché of seeing your life pass before you at the point of near-death rang absolutely and shockingly true—he saw the face of his sainted mother, his loving father, his sister and brother. He saw his childhood friends, his teachers, his university, his professors, his graduation; he saw Xiaoqing and, with a piercing of his heart, watched her fade away. Last, as the warriors dragging him along approached the zenith of the pyramid, a strange vision of Ophelia appeared before him, less mental image than actual appearance, as if she were a specter of death bidding him to his fate. She dissolved as they reached the temple's pinnacle, her form replaced by the high priest.

He was a terrible, awesome sight, and Sager lamented that he could not have admired him in another context. The man stood at least six and a half feet tall, with brazen skin shining in the sun. His legs were wrapped with bright blue, green, and yellow leather; his loins were girded with a bright, multicolored dress of feathers. He wore an open serpent's head mask that revealed his face, which was painted white and which looked at Sager as if with the eyes of a god. His headdress was made of jade and vibrant green feathers.

Is he a god and not a man? he thought.

The warriors bowed their heads as they delivered Sager to him. There were other guards all around him with sharp spears, and thus he had no escape. He knew that, should he impossibly manage to slip out of their grasp, they would simply stab him and bring him back, only prolonging his horrible fate with torture.

A lesser priest signaled the guards, and they pulled him to a small cove behind the high priest, a cove hidden to the people below. The lesser priest said something to him in Aztec, then gave him a cup of dark liquid to drink. Sager knew from his studies that it was a painkiller and contained alcohol—a sort of good-luck drink from the Aztecs. He forgot the ingredients, but he remembered that it could help a little with pain, even though nothing could mask the level of pain that he was about to endure. Still, he took the cup, and said, "Oh, what the hell?" in English, and drank it. In a few minutes, he was slightly buzzed.

The guards pulled him back out, lay him onto the altar, and began to tie him down. Sager noticed, without much pleasure, the blood grooves and drain holes in the altar. He knew exactly what they were for. *How ironic*, he thought, *that all my decades of study would only make the anticipation worse for me.*

He was immobilized on the altar with thick ropes when the priest began to chant in Aztec, at first quietly, and then more and more loudly. The drums began again, matching his volume and fervency.

Sager became short of breath. He felt adrenaline rushing throughout his body, his veins. Poisonous, mortal fear gripped his bowels, and his mouth was filled with the acrid, metallic taste of adrenaline. The high priest produced a knife from his priestly garments a knife made of jade and bone, with a bejeweled handle. The drums beat frantically, and the priest shrieked his chant. The guards and lesser priests shouted in a bloodthirsty chorus, and then, the high priest raised the knife with both hands, holding it directly over Sager's heart. Sager looked around in the frenzied jerks of a berserker, the sort of last-second pleading with the universe for a way out, the mind's last-moment disbelief that death is coming.

The high priest plunged the knife into Sager's chest. A searing, internal, cancerous pain tore into his torso. It was the sort of pain that pain was designed for, a pain that was so encompassing that the mind could genuinely not think of anything else. There were no rational thoughts, no meta-analysis—it was raw, primal pain. Sager looked down just as the high priest ripped his still-beating heart from his chest cavity. The pain continued, but the world began to darken, then become brown, then black, then nothing.

Sager was still a being, somehow. Without a body, he was a spirit in the black void of death.

Death, death, and death.

He was not floating nor traveling down a tunnel of light. He saw no deceased loved ones, no heaven, no hell—there was just darkness, blackness.

Then he fell, fell so hard and fast that he wanted to flail his arms and legs to regain balance, but he knew that he no longer had arms or legs. He fell and fell for a minute? An hour? A year? A decade? A century? He fell and fell until he landed at the feet of a being. The being was a skeleton with bloody tissue on its bones—it had the face of a skull but also of a man, and it wore a multicolored headdress of feathers. Its chest had been splayed open, and a bloody heart hung down from the middle of the tissue. Sager immediately recognized the being as Mictlantecuhtli, the Aztec god of death. The god spoke to Sager in English.

"Death welcomes you, son. You have been granted a choice. Do you want to return to the world of the living and live a life of eventual aging, pain, loss, suffering, and a second death, or do you wish to join me now in Mictlan, to make the journey down, and to finally enjoy the blissful loss of all existence and sentience?"

Sager had almost forgotten who he had been. He was only a spirit without an identity, a part of the whole universe. He could remember little fragments of his life. Along with happy memories came memories of the sad suffering that comprises most people's lives. To simply accede to Mictlantecuhtli, to fall into his loving, bony embrace, to fade out into the nothingness of the universe, of God himself, felt warm and safe, like a womb.

He was ready to agree when one last shard of memory returned to the very last part of his personhood before it slipped away. It was a vision of desire, of longing, of love. It was not Xiaoqing; it was Ophelia. Her raven hair and porcelain skin beckoned him back into the world, to be reborn and to live again, perhaps to live forever? Her cold touch was like the warmth of a thousand fires to him. He knew then the answer that he had to give to Mictlantecuhtli.

"I want to live again."

At the very speed of thought, he was back in the forest behind Chief's house. The lynx was there, playfully pawing at his leg and nipping at his ankle; it gave a hearty mew, deeper than that of a house cat, and walked. Sager knew to follow it. It led him back to Chief's backyard, and when he arrived, he took his place again. The world began to spin, and a loud, rushing noise increased in volume inside of his head until he was jolted back into reality. Chief's wife was there beside him, offering him water.

"You had a vision, didn't you, Professor?" she asked. "I can tell. Just rest and drink some water. When the sun rises, everyone will be finished, and then Chief will tell you the meaning of what you saw."

Xiaoqing had watched as Sager and the others had fallen to the ground and had begun to move and twitch. She felt a bit groggy, and then the drums and flutes began to meld together in her mind to form a single, oscillating sound that became deeper and deeper in pitch until it sounded like an Australian Aboriginal didgeridoo.

She heard a bird calling from the forest, and it startled her.

She remembered growing up with her Chinese grandmother and mother in a small village in Guangdong. They had kept chickens in the small, dirt courtyard below their modern house—she had always feared the chickens and their cold, mindless aggression. They would chase her around the yard, trying to peck her legs, and for that reason, she had developed an intense fear of birds of all sorts. So, when a large falcon swooped out of the forest behind Chief's yard and landed not a foot away from her, she became paralyzed in terror.

The magnificent beast stood two feet high at least, with the arched beak and flat head that identify a Peregrine hunting falcon. It cocked its head to the side so that its steely, knowing eye stared directly into hers, and she felt warm calm. As if she could hear the bird's spirit talking to her, she simply *knew* that it would not harm her. It cawed to her in a shrill, piercing call and flew toward the forest. Instinctively, she knew to follow it.

As she entered the forest, the falcon would fly ahead for a distance of several trees, then alight on a branch and turn to watch her, and Xiaoqing was sure the bird did that to make sure she was following. After what seemed like hours of walking, she and the falcon came upon a large cave. She could see through the opening that the passageway led down at a slant, so the cave must have been subterranean.

The falcon perched on top of the entrance and cawed again—it waited and watched her with the clear message to enter. She looked the bird of prey in the eye and felt a sense of urgency. She entered the cave, and as it sloped gently downward, and as she continued, the faint moonlight from outside faded more and more, until she found herself in the blackest pitch of darkness that she had ever known. It was so black that it almost circled back around to purple.

Instinctively, she knew that a flashlight was in her back pocket, even though she had not taken one to Chief's gathering. She turned it on and was able to see that the passageway, just high enough for her to stand up straight, continued as far as she could see in the torch's circle of light. Down and down, deeper and deeper went she, until the air felt heavy and cold and motionless. There were no bats, no insects, no sightless fish in underground streams—there was only the darkness, hardly abated by her flashlight. Even so, she felt the need to continue.

Down, down, down, and then a faint light in the distance, and she pressed on as the light grew larger. Soon, she reached the cave's end, which led into a small forest clearing amid a copse of trees and brush. Outside of the ring of trees, nothing could be seen, and nothing was there except a pervasive sense of dread. She knew within that she could not venture outside of the clearing.

The moon above splashed a dull, yellow glow on her surroundings, just enough for her to see what was in the middle of the grove: a tombstone.

She remembered the day that her grandfather had died. As a child, she had delighted in the kind, old man. He would bounce her on his lap and sing songs in his native Cantonese dialect, which she could not understand, but it had not mattered—all that she had cared about was his smile and his laughter. When he would go to visit her, she would squeal with delight and run to the door to hug his legs. He must have been the kindest, sweetest, gentlest man on earth, which is why his death had punched her in the stomach as nothing else had in her life. Her mother had had trouble explaining it to her.

Grandpa's gone away? Where did he go, mommy? When will he come back? Will I see him again one day?

Xiaoqing's mother had taken her to her grandfather's funeral, which had been a traditional Chinese affair. She had walked to his body while holding her mother's hand. There had lain grandpa. She had not been able to understand why he was sleeping and pretending not to hear her.

Grandpa! Grandpa! Grandpa? Was he joking with her as he sometimes did? *Mommy, why won't he come and see me?* Her mother had simply broken down in tears.

Since that horrible event, Xiaoqing had suffered a fear, not only of birds but also of funerals, corpses, death, and tombstones. It was not unusual—many Chinese are superstitious. She, however, had a special hatred for death… and a dreadful terror of it. So, when she timidly approached the tombstone, she was shaking and felt like crying. Still, she instinctively knew that she had to look, just to see. *Just to see.* She faced the front of the grave marker and began to cry—on it was her name and birthday. There wasn't a date of death yet.

A soft voice wafted through the trees, "Xiaoqing? Baby? My dear? Come and see Grandpa!"

"Who's there? You are not my Grandpa! He died a long time ago!"

"And now it is your turn to join me, honey. Come and see Grandpa; I will sing to you again," rasped the voice.

She could not turn, could not look, could not process what was happening.

She felt terrorized, knowing that, if she looked toward the voice, she would not see her Grandpa but a living corpse. As it turned out, it did not matter. Hands burst through the earth under her—grey, stinking, sloughing corpse hands. They grabbed at her ankles and calves, their cold, slimy grip catching her here and there. She tried to kick them and run, but it was useless—their hold was icy and as firm as iron, and they hungrily, fervently pulled at her ankles, and then calves, and then thighs, as she sank into the grave. She was pulled down into a hole, a tunnel, and on both sides were grabbing corpse hands and rotting arms.

The acrid, sour stench of decay brought her to nausea, and she spewed vomit across the arms, hands, and dirt. The humid earth around her collapsed, and the corpse hands held her tightly as she began to suffocate. Skittering insects emerged from the dirt and crawled across her face and into her ears. As the soil started to fill in her nostrils and mouth, she gasped for air, and more insects crawled into her mouth and nose. She could feel them crunching, taste their bitter innards, and she involuntarily clenched and gaped her mouth like a fish. She panted and gasped, but only dirt and insects filled her lungs. The desperate panic of suffocation overcame her; the sharp, knifing pain in her chest was unbearable, and so she was finally happy when she felt death enter her.

Then blackness. Then nothing.

Like Caesar untimely ripped from the womb, she was instantly awake again, her lungs sucking up precious oxygen. She was in a hole, but there were no corpses, no hands, no insects, no crushing dirt. She used her feet and the sides of the hole to hoist herself up and onto the grassy surface. She was back in Chief's yard. An Indian woman stood above her prone form and said, "Welcome back. That looked intense. Here, drink some water."

Xiaoqing could only nod and gulp the water.

Jean-Pierre sat and watched as Sager and Xiaoqing, one and then the other, slumped to the ground and began to roll and twitch. He was not concerned because, before his vows, he had hung around many drug users. He had also researched the Cherokee black drink briefly before that night, and he was familiar enough with the hallucinogenic ingredients, so he knew what to look for. Therefore, he was not surprised when everything he saw began to sparkle and produce trails when he turned his head. It was frankly beautiful, and he felt a warm, pleasurable tingling in his stomach and chest.

This bliss was quickly interrupted, however, when Jean-Pierre heard the distinct, unmistakable clacking of a rattlesnake.

Not being an expert herpetologist, but being educated enough to possess some survival skills, he slowly looked down and saw the creature: a seven-foot band of dark and light brown, tapering to an oval rattle that oscillated at an unseeable speed. The snake raised his head into the air and looked at Jean-Pierre while flicking its tongue, and he instantly knew what to do. He began to very slowly back away from the beast, making no quick or sudden motions.

No matter how far he backed off, though, the snake followed. It remained about one foot in front of him. Then, the snake gently turned around and began to slither toward the woods behind Chief's house. It paused and looked back at Jean-Pierre, who was suddenly hit with the irresistible urge to follow it. It did not seem to intend to harm him, so under the influence of the black drink, he stood up and followed the rattlesnake into the woods. He walked for several minutes, then came upon some abandoned tipis and huts. It seemed like a tiny, abandoned Indian village.

"Fascinating!" he said aloud. "I wonder if Chief knows about this? Surely he does. How old are these?"

He walked toward a tipi to touch it, when he saw movement from his periphery. He jerked his head to the left and saw a humanoid shadow creeping around behind a hut.

"Who's there? Identify yourself!" he shouted.

To his amazement, Father Martin Peter, his friend and confessor, stepped out of the black shadows with a smile.

"Sorry, Jean-Pierre. I didn't mean to scare you!"

"Martin? What... what the hell? What are you doing here?"

"I just came for a visit, Jean-Pierre. You emailed me about the amulet, and it sounded fascinating, so I took a road trip of my own. This is certainly an interesting area. Very ancient. Very magical," said Father Peter.

"But Marty, how did you find me here? In Chief's backyard? Oh, also, I took the Cherokee black drink, so I'm tripping a bit. Excuse any weird behavior from me."

"I brought a friend too," said Father Peter, gesturing toward an empty building, and from behind it stepped the bishop himself.

"Bishop?" marveled Jean-Pierre. "Why... how are you here?"

"I've come to convert you, Father Jean-Pierre," answered the bishop.

"Convert me? Bishop, I'm already a Catholic priest. What do you mean?"

The bishop simply smiled, then began to approach Jean-Pierre along with Father Peter.

"Are you now, Father?" asked the bishop. "Haven't you been questioning your faith? Haven't you grown weary of religion? And what of a God who allows children to die of cancer? He is the god of flowers and birds, but also the God of Polio, and crippled children, and starving children dying of AIDS. How can you worship such a cruel God? When has he ever answered your prayers, Jean-Pierre?"

"What? Bishop, how can you say that?"

"Yes, Jean-Pierre, he is the God of cancer. He is the God who allows murder, like the one that happened right outside of your office. He is the very same God who allowed the little girl in Colombia to become a demon and die at the hands of a killer, isn't He?"

Jean-Pierre felt a cold tingling throughout his body.

"No, please, don't talk about that!" he pleaded.

"Why not, Father?" asked the bishop. "After all, God was watching over her, wasn't he? How old was she? Thirteen? Fourteen? Fifteen at the most? Yet your God allowed a demon to enter her body, allowed her innocent little soul to suffer the worst possible torture, and then to die. How do you think her parents felt? How can you worship such a wicked God?"

"You... this can't be real. It's the black drink, isn't it? Martin, Bishop, you're just hallucinations!" he cried.

"Are we, Jean-Pierre?" Father Peter reached out and touched Jean-Pierre's arm. It was as real and solid a touch as anything he had ever experienced. Father Peter gently pinched his arm, and he felt the sting.

"But... Marty! Bishop! Why are you blaspheming God?"

"Come on, Jean-Pierre," answered Father Peter. "What the bishop said about that girl, that's the real crux of your problems, isn't it? You saw something, experienced something that the Church has argued isn't real, is just metaphorical, ever since Vatican Two. But you saw it for real, didn't you, Jean-Pierre? You saw a real, innocent little girl taken over by a real demon; you saw her tortured; you saw her killed, never to live again. Her soul was never saved, Jean-Pierre. God did not even give her a chance at redemption. Do you know where she is right now, Jean-Pierre?"

"No!"

"Yes, *Father*. She's in hell right now. She's burning for eternity. She's being raped again and again by demons and horrible beasts. That's your God, priest. Your God. *YOUR GOD!*"

"No! What... He is the God of everything! Of heaven and hell! He is good!"

"Oh, Jean-Pierre, my old friend. He will let you grow old and die and rot some day. He doesn't care about you. But I can show you a way around it all; I can show you a loophole in his nefarious plan. Wouldn't you like to live forever, Jean-Pierre? Forever free from God and his punishment? Free from his endless suffering, from hell, from your decaying mortal flesh?"

"What are you talking about?"

"Just what I am saying, Jean-Pierre. Eternal life. No God. No right or wrong. No suffering. No obligations. Only pure bliss forever. Wouldn't you like that?"

Jean-Pierre paused. He could not honestly answer that in the negative.

"No, I... I can't. I made vows. I promised..."

"And he made you a promise, too, didn't he?" said the bishop. "He promised you joy and peace; faith, hope, and love. You know he did. Do you have those things, Jean-Pierre? Or is your life merely disbelief, hopelessness, and misery? We can show you another way, the way of eternal life, but without his intervention."

"A way? What way? What could you possibly offer me?" asked Jean-Pierre.

"A way of perfection, or eternity," answered Father Peter. "Watch this, my friend."

Father Peter pulled a knife from among his frock. He cut a long, deep line into his wrist, so deep that it severed tendons, ligaments, and nerves.

"What are you doing? Stop!" shouted Jean-Pierre.

"Just watch."

In a matter of seconds, the wound began to heal. The ligaments reattached, the inside healed, and the bleeding ceased. The skin joined back together, and it was as if there were never a wound at all.

"That's impossible. Impossible," said Jean-Pierre.

"And yet you just saw it. It's like the Colombian girl, Jean-Pierre. It was impossible, and yet it happened right before you."

"Alright," replied Jean-Pierre, "let's say you are right. What is your way? How would I achieve it?"

"I'll show you, Jean-Pierre. Just say the word. Just agree. Just say, 'Yes,' and I will make you live forever."

Jean-Pierre struggled against his very soul. If there really were a way to live forever outside of God's judgment and punishment, then what possible reason could he give not to accept it? But, if God were real, then would he not be sacrificing his own immortal soul? Wasn't it the greatest sin of all to reject God's mercy? Was God as cruel as they were telling him?

He thought about that Colombian girl, and his heart turned black. Yes, God was cruel. Any God who would allow that girl to suffer like that could not be good.

"I assent. Make me immortal."

Father Peter's face changed then. His eyes turned red, and his skin gained a deathly pallor. He growled like a beast and opened his mouth to reveal two long, sharp, canine fangs. In a nanosecond, he pounced upon Jean-Pierre and tore at his throat.

Jean-Pierre felt the agony of those two fangs ripping his skin back, piercing his tissue, settling upon his jugular artery—he felt his hot, thick blood spurt out in the rhythm of his panicking heart. He felt Father Peter sucking, guzzling, moaning in ecstasy as Jean-Pierre felt Death coming for him. The world became blurry, then brown, then black, and then he lost his sentience.

There was blackness. There was nothing. And then he became alive again.

He was under the earth and could feel the moist hummus filling his mouth. He struggled to breathe, but it did not hurt. He stopped struggling and realized that he was not breathing and had no urge to breathe. He clawed at the dirt above him and felt a new strength—it was effortless for him to push himself up through the layers of dirt and back into the crisp night air. He felt new, strong, indestructible. However, de did not feel perfect because he was overcome with a pang of ravenous hunger.

Before him, the rattlesnake appeared. It shook its rattle and slithered ahead of him. He knew that it intended for him to follow it. He pursued the snake as it continued through the forest until he found himself back in Chief's yard. Before he could find satiation for his terrible hunger, he felt faint. He fell to the ground and began to pass out.

Then he was startled awake by a loud rushing sound—he was back where he had begun his journey, and he was his own mortal self again.

Chief's wife gave the three guests large glasses of cool water, which they imbibed greedily. The edge of the sun was peeking over the horizon, painting nature in that rosy-azure hue that only appears in that magical, secret, first hour of *l'aube*. Beast Stalker looked worn out but refreshed inside—his eyes were bright and clear. He gestured for the three to follow him to Chief Cloud Mountain. As they approached Chief, he waved his hand to indicate that they should sit in front of him, on the ground, legs crossed. They obeyed.

"My three little friends, I can see that you each had a profound spiritual experience. I also can guess that you each met your spirit animal. I can see it in your eyes. Now, let's begin with Xiaoqing, please, and you can each tell me what you experienced. I will tell you the meaning as the spirits speak to me."

Xiaoqing, and then Sager, and then Jean-Pierre each recounted their experiences to Chief in all of the detail that they could remember. They told him which animal had guided them as well. Sager, of course, did not mention the part that Ophelia had played in his vision.

Chief waited patiently, silently listening to every word. When Jean-Pierre finished, he nodded, pursed his lips for a few moments, and then said, "Each of you had a frightening revelation. I am sorry that you had to experience that, but it is important. Vision quests are not always negative, but when they are frightening like yours, it only means that the spirits' message to you is extremely urgent. You encountered evil spirits as well, but these were kept in check by the ancestors and other good spirits. Now, the interpretation," Chief said, and Sager felt the anxiety fill his body. "Xiaoqing, your spirit animal is a falcon, which is a bold bird of prey. It represents not only passion and boldness but also significant changes and new beginnings. You are still bound to your past, Xiaoqing. Your family, your grandfather, your childhood fears—these are still holding you back from your true destiny. It is only when you die to them and bury them that you will rise from your grave anew and then fulfill your destiny. You have a great destiny ahead of you. I cannot tell you what it may be, but it is there. But you must first put to rest your past and your fears.

Sager automatically grabbed her hand and gave it a little squeeze; he knew how hard her grandfather's passing was to her and how much influence her family still had over her.

"Professor, your spirit animal is a lynx cat, an animal with complex meanings. A lynx represents someone who guides others, who protects secrets. This tells me that you will be entrusted with great power. The spirits will expect you to guard it and to use it only as appropriate. But they would not have chosen you for this if they had not thought that you were worthy. As to your vision, I am afraid that its meaning is not a happy one. You will become a sacrifice for the good of someone else, or of many people. This does not necessarily mean that your life will be sacrificed as in your vision, but that you will be expected to give up something that you cherish for the good of others. You have been chosen as an important part of this story, Professor, and you should consider it a great honor."

Chief's words gave him no rest, no understanding… just more questions.

"Father, your spirit animal is a rattlesnake. But don't worry because it is a good sign. The rattlesnake represents life and death at the same time. It is an animal of transformation, of change, but also of the power of life or death over others, as well as the power of eternal life. Your vision allowed you to choose life or death for yourself, but the rattlesnake tells me that you may soon have to choose life or death for someone else. The spirits have given you that power, and, like the Professor, they would not have chosen you if you had not been worthy. I will admit that your vision worries me somewhat. Your friends tried to convert you away from your life's calling. These spirits who were in the form of your friends were the sort of ancient spirits that our people have known for thousands of years. Your people call them vampires. We know them as eaters of blood, but they are basically the same evil spirits. They are eternal, but they must feed on the life force of the blood of mortals, or else they will desiccate and become dried out, withered bodies for eternity, alert and alive, but barely able to move. Father, you may have to make a very difficult choice in the future. I advise you to consider and assess your true spirit, your true self."

Chief stopped and looked at them, one by one, and when his brown eyes connected with Sager's blue ones, the ominous feeling that he had been having for some time returned tenfold.

"Those are my interpretations, my children. Now, let's address your bodies' needs. My wife and other Cherokee women have prepared breakfast for everyone. You are very welcome to stay and enjoy it with our people. You are like our adopted children now that you have gone through the black drink ceremony with us. We will always welcome you now as one of our own."

"That is a great honor," added Beast Stalker.

"Thank you, Chief, for such an honor. I am truly humbled," replied Sager. Xiaoqing and Jean-Pierre also added their humble thanks, and the three joined the breakfast. After eating and socializing, they felt much better. They spent the day at Chief's, talking to the Cherokee and genuinely feeling a part of the community. As the shadows just began to lengthen, they thanked Chief again and left for Ushaville in Beast Stalker's truck.

As they approached the town, they saw red and blue sirens flashing in the distance.

"Hmm. That doesn't look good," said Beast Stalker.

"I thought Ushaville didn't have a police force," mentioned Xiaoqing.

"We don't," answered Beast Stalker, "but the Council acts as law enforcement if needed. They have a few squad cars and some weapons. They very rarely ever have to use it, though. Most people in Ushaville don't commit crimes. If they've pulled out the squad cars, it could mean trouble. Let's see what it's about."

They approached the sirens and found a roadblock consisting of four squad cars. Several Hatfields stood in front of the cars with rifles pointed at the ground. They watched as one of the Hatfields walked up to the vehicle in front of them. They could hear the conversation.

"Good evening, Ma'am. Are you a resident of Ushaville?"

"Um, yes, Sir. I am."

"May I please see your identification?"

"Here you go."

The officer looked at it for a moment. "And do you have protection?"

The woman turned around and pulled down the neck of her blouse to reveal her tattoo.

"Alright, no problem then. You can go ahead. Have a good evening."

"Wait, officer? What's going on?"

"We're tightening down Ushaville temporarily. Only residents in and out, and only those with protection, and only for a reason. Hatfield businesses are closed for now, McCoy businesses are mostly still open. Neutral businesses are mostly closed, with a certain few allowed to operate."

"But why, officer? What happened?" asked the woman, incredulously.

"Just a little Council issue. No need to concern yourself with it. Now, have a good night."

She understood the sternness of his last comment and drove in without another word.

Beast Stalker rolled his pickup truck to the blockade, and the same officer approached.

"Roll down your window, please. Are you an Ushaville resident?"

Beast Stalker rolled down his window.

"Oh, Beast Stalker. Oh, sorry, Sir. Go right in. Have a good night."

"Now wait a minute," answered Beast Stalker. "What devilry are you Hatfields up to? What is this bullshit?"

Sager, Xiaoqing, and Jean-Pierre looked at each other with raised eyebrows.

"Now, Sir, please calm down. It's just a Council issue."

"You mean you two old families can't learn to get along after so many thousands..." Beast Stalker looked at the three in the rear-view mirror and continued, "...so many decades? Such bullshit. Please move and let us through. And before you do, see these three in my backseat? They are Professor Miller, his ladyfriend Xiaoqing Yan, and Father Jean-Pierre. They're all with me, under my protection, and I don't want anyone messing with them. Got it?"

"Yes, Sir, Mister Beast Stalker. Yes, Sir. Have a good night, Sir."

Beast Stalker scowled, rolled up his window, and drove past the squad cars.

"Alright, two questions, Beast Stalker," said Sager with a little chuckle. "First, what is going on with this feud? Are we in danger? And second, what the hell was that bit of intimidation?" Sager laughed. "I've never seen that side of you."

Beast Stalker smiled a rare smile and answered: "Don't worry about it. Those two families have been feuding since forever. Who knows what nonsense they've gotten into this time? It's like a bunch of damn children. No, you are not in danger. As to your second question, well, let's just say that the founders of Ushaville came to an understanding with my people, and we have a bit of authority and power around here. If I had been Chief, you would have seen that officer become downright subservient."

"Wow. They seem to fear you!" added Xiaoqing.

Beast Stalker smiled and said, "They know now that you are my friends. You will receive no trouble in Ushaville. You are under my people's...well, let's just say you have been made friends of my people, and that comes with certain benefits."

"Goodness," said Jean-Pierre. "I feel like I'm in *The Godfather*. But sure, thanks, Beast Stalker. I really appreciate that. You are our friend as well."

Beast Stalker nodded and said, "Now, let's get you three home. I don't know about you, but I could use a long sleep!"

CHAPTER 11

THE TUNNELS OF USHAVILLE

"**W**ell I don't know about you lot, but I'm gonna hit the tunnels before our show tonight," said Paul while combing and pomade-ing his Mohawk. "This town's weird as shit, and I'm gonna take advantage of it. Bloody hell!"

"Why do you speak with an affected Cockney accent?" asked Gill. "It's quite annoying, especially since you sound like a damn Victorian chimneys sweep."

Mary giggled.

"Oi! It's what punks do!" answered Paul.

"That makes no damn sense, Paul," added Matt while yawning. "Anyway, I'll go to the tunnels with you, as long as I can get a nap in before the show."

Nancy hushed them. "Dammit, guys, be cool, or you're not gonna like the consequences with the Council." Mary's face became pale. "Alright, listen," whispered Nancy. "I'll probably regret this, but if you four idiots insist on exploring the tunnels, then you'll be much safer with someone who has the protection. I'll go with you, alright? But you have to promise to listen to me." The four nodded, Paul with a puerile grin. His reaction made Nancy roll her eyes. "Why did I start hanging out with you guys? Remind me again?"

Mary giggled, and they went to prepare for their adventure.

Nancy led them down some streets just on the east side of Under den Linden, but not deep enough into the Eastside for things to really start to become dangerous—just dingy houses and sultry, suspicious businesses, most of them closed and locked up. A few faces peered from behind drawn curtains. On the street's left side, a crumbling old brick storefront with a gaping maw seemed to beckon them.

"Yeah, so, this is one of the entrances. It's the closest one to the Pallid Horse."

"Oh, Jesus," said Gill. "Isn't there a cheerier and inviting entrance somewhere?"

"It's all the same," answered Nancy. "The tunnels are the tunnels. The entrances all lead to the same place. Come on, chickens. You wanted to come. *Bok bok bok.*" She flapped her arms.

"Alright! Alright!" proclaimed Paul.

They entered the storefront's crumbling mouth and walked a few paces until some steps led downward into blackness. Nancy pulled out some flashlights.

"We'll need these. I also have some water and a few sandwiches if we need them."

"What if we get lost?" asked Mary. "You got a GPS?"

Nancy laughed. "No signal down here, dearie, but I know the tunnels pretty well. As kids, we would dare one another to come down and explore. But they're sort of like the Paris catacombs: lots of really old, unexplored parts, or parts that haven't been seen by human eyes in forever. The main rule is just to stick with me. And if you hear or see anything weird, for God's sake, just ignore it. Don't panic, don't run, don't try to fight. Just ignore it and keep walking, alright? Remember, Hatfields and McCoys use these tunnels all the time, so we may not be alone. I have the mark of protection, but you guys don't, so just please do not stray off, alright?"

The punks nodded nervously.

They descended the stairs and found themselves in a damp, dank, musty old earthen tunnel. Walking about a hundred feet, they saw that the tunnel began to be paved with black, sooty bricks. Torch sconces were on the walls every few feet, some holding extinguished torches, some empty. Every few minutes, a rat would squeal and carom across their path.

"Shit, I hate rats," said Mary. "Please, please let them just go on about their business and leave us alone."

Even Paul refrained from his pranks or sarcastic comments. The atmosphere was just too oppressive and terrifying.

"Alright, we turn left here. Everyone still good? The first place I'll show you is really cool. It's an underground pond."

They followed Nancy left, then right, and then the tunnel opened into an underground grotto the size of a small house. They could hear the liquid licking and lapping of water somewhere in the darkness. Nancy opened her bag, pulled out an electronic lantern, placed it on the floor, and turned it on. The cave lit up, revealing a large pond, a black and soulless reflection of what a pond would look like on the topside.

"Oh, shit!" exclaimed Paul. "Fucking cool! How did it form?"

"No idea," said Nancy. "The Hatfields and McCoys built most of these tunnels, but I think I told you guys, there were some tunnels and openings here way before the first white people showed up in the Americas. They built the newer tunnels on, and with, the ancient ones. Legends say that the first tunnels were built by the dark old gods, or maybe the Indians. No one knows."

Matt picked up a rock and tossed it into the pond. They heard the wet *bloip*. Matt said, "I wonder how deep it is?"

"Not sure I want to know," replied Mary.

"I knew someone would ask that," said Nancy," so I brought this. We used to do this as kids. You're not gonna believe this shit."

She took out a spool of string from her bag and tied a rock onto the end. She carefully approached the edge of the pond and dropped the rock in. *Plunk.*

"Here, Mary, you try."

Mary took the thick spool and began to allow it to turn in her hand and unravel it as the rock's weight took it down, down, down into the depths of the black water. The entire spool was exhausted, and the rock still had not reached the bottom.

"Fuck!" said Paul. How long was that string?

"Five hundred feet."

"Holy hell!"

"Yeah," said Nancy, "and as kids, our record was a thousand-foot spool. It still hadn't reached the bottom."

"A damned blue whale could live in there," said Gill. "Positively astounding. *Brava*, Nancy, for that experiment."

"Alright, everyone step back now. This one will freak you the hell out," said Nancy.

It took no encouraging for the punks to all give the shore a wide berth. Nancy pulled a Ziploc bag from her sack and pulled a whole, raw fish out of the bag. She stood in an action stance and threw the fish as hard as she could into the middle of the pond. *Ploink!* She quickly retreated back to the others. Within a few seconds, they heard a loud splashing as some dark, secret creature thrashed in the water and gobbled up the fish.

"Shit!" shouted Paul. "There's shit living in there!"

"Yep," laughed Nancy. "And I don't know about you, but I have no fucking desire to know what it is."

"Hell no!" added Mary. "What kind of horrible thing lives here? God!"

"I don't either," added Matt, who was most decidedly not yawning.

"Come on. There's more," said Nancy.

They traveled through more tunnels, made more turns, descended, ascended, and trekked on, until everyone but Nancy was thoroughly and hopelessly lost. The tunnel they were in widened a bit, and they saw crevices carved into the sides, one above the other. The fissures continued on the tunnel walls as far as they could see in the glow of their flashlights.

"This'll fuck you up," said Nancy. "Come."

She grabbed Matt's hand and led him to one of the crevices. She shone the torch, and they looked inside.

"Oh, God! Hell no!" exclaimed Matt. "Nancy, what the hell?"

Nancy chuckled as the other three inched closer to the opening. They dared to look inside, discovering a desiccated corpse, almost a mere skeleton, but with the thinnest of skin-bark remaining on the bones. The sunken, hollow face was crowned with long, grey hair.

"Oh shit!" yelled Mary. "What the fuck is this? Some sort of catacomb?" she asked.

"No one knows," answered Nancy. "No one. Not the Hatfields, not the McCoys, not the Indians. No one knows who these people were or where they came from. They've been buried here as long as the oldest townspeople can remember. And there are hundreds of them."

She led them down the tunnel, pausing, and looking into the spaces. Some of the bodies bore thin, papery remaining skin, while others were simply weathered, brown skeletons. A few of the burial places held nothing but piles of crumbling dust.

"Some of these are ancient. I mean really ancient, like thousands of years," said Gill. "Bones don't just turn to dust unless they've been lying there since fucking ancient Egypt. This surely must be the burial site of some of the earliest peoples of the Americas. I can't believe this is all under Ushaville."

"Yeah, it's fucking amazing," said Paul, whose intellectual interests usually involved women and their private parts. "What sort of secrets are in this damn town anyway?"

"Oh," said Nancy, "stick around and you'll be amazed. Now come on, there's more! Wait, anyone have the time?"

"Three," said Mary.

"Alright, we should leave soon, but I have one more thing to show you that I think is the fucking fuckingest of all."

They trod down and farther until the four punks became nervous that they had become lost, but Nancy, undaunted, led on. They made several turns, then ended up in a long, straight tunnel that was neatly masoned with thick stones on all four walls. Along the walls were thick, stone doors, each having a very small window toward the top. The doors were locked with thick, metal bars.

"What the living fuck is this?" asked Paul.

"What does it look like?" teased Nancy.

"Um... a jail?"

"Yep. At least that's what we think it is. We're not on the main tunnel route here, and most people have never seen this, but we made it this far as kids. I'm pretty sure these are jail cells of some kind."

"But who would be jailed here? And who put them here?" asked Matt.

"It's a literal dungeon," said Gill. "The worst sort of incarceration and torture. I would not be surprised if there were chains inside each cell. Nancy, is anyone in these cells?"

"Not since I have been coming down into the tunnels," she answered. "They've always been empty. We used to dare one another to peek inside the cells, and the brave ones always reported that they were empty. Just a stone floor and a small cell. No bed, but there's a small hole which is the toilet, I guess."

"Gross gross gross," said Mary. "Hey Matt, I dare you to go peek inside one."

"Not happening," he replied.

"Paul? You like to talk big. I dare you to go take a look inside one."

"Hell no," he insisted.

Nancy taunted him: "What, Paul? You like to dress like a punk, talk like a punk, but when it comes to doing something punk, you chicken out?"

Paul blushed.

"Oh, fuck it. I'll look."

He coughed, straightened himself up, and cautiously approached one of the cells. Beginning far back from the window, he squinted one eye and tried to see in, but it was pitch black inside. He held up his flashlight and took another look.

"Oh. Well, it's empty like Nancy said. It's definitely a jail cell," he reported.

Feeling more confident, they all went around peeking into the cells and discovering them empty. They were empty, that is, until Gill looked into the last one and froze. His face became yellow-pale, and he began to visibly shake. He carefully took a few steps back and whispered, "Guys? Guys?"

"Yeah, what Gill?" asked Paul. "You look like you saw a fucking ghost."

"It's—this one—not... it's not fucking empty!" Gill said.

"What?" said Nancy. "That's impossible. These've been here forever, and they've been locked forever. Let me see?"

She stood on her tiptoes and shone her torch into the cell.

"Holy shit!" she cried. "He's fucking right! There's a fucking corpse in there!"

"What?" shouted Mary and Paul in unison.

"Come look!" said Nancy. They each took a turn, and all saw the same thing: a human body, desiccated and long-since rotted, mostly a skeleton with some flesh still on it. The eye sockets stared at them accusingly.

"How the fuck is it still there?" asked Paul. That fucker must be a thousand fucking years old!"

"Let's get this door open," said Nancy.

"No! No fucking way, Nancy! Let's get the hell out of here!"

"Wait, guys. Calm down. It's just a body. It's barely even that. It's so old; it's not even gross anymore. It's just bones. You don't have to fucking touch it!" She laughed. "I just want a closer look."

"Shit," said Paul. "Just hurry up, alright? We need to set up for our show."

Gill approached the door and said, "Here. I'll do it. I guess I kind of want to see as well. I wonder how old it is? I wonder what the poor bastard's story was?"

He grabbed the iron bar blockading the door, but it wouldn't budge. It was almost molded to its metal bolts with the rust of the ages. Gill pulled as hard as he could, but he could not move it at all.

Paul laughed. "Alright, let me try. Fuck it. The fucker can't hurt us."

Paul pulled out the switchblade knife that he always kept and clicked it open. He poked at the rust and managed to pull away a little bit. He pulled on the bar, but it still would not move. He picked out more rust, and the blade slipped and poked his finger.

"Ow! Shit!"

He sucked on the small wound, and a little blood dripped onto his lip.

"Move," said Mary. She pulled on the bar and it lifted. "When you need to do a job right, get a woman to do it for you."

Nancy laughed and said, "Right on. Come on, guys. Let's just take a look."

They crowded into the cell's entrance. Bending down, they examined the body—Paul poked it with his knife a bit.

"Man, what's your story? What happened to you to end up in a jail cell in a subterranean tunnel?" asked Gill. "Who put you here? Why? What crime did you commit to receive such an awful fate? How did you die? Did you starve to death?"

"Don't think he can answer, mate."

"Paul, you idiot. I am asking rhetorical questions. Unlike some, I have intellectual curiosity and fascination with antiquities."

"Maybe you should've gotten a Ph.D. in archeology instead of becoming a fucking failed punk musician," said Paul.

"Yeah, yeah. Ha ha. Hilarious, Paul."

"Um, guys?" whispered Mary.

"It *is* funny, Gill," said Matt. "You have to admit, the idea of a punk rock musician being fascinated with ancient history and archeology is pretty fucking funny, you know?"

"Guys?" said Mary in a hoarse voice, a little louder.

"Fine," replied Gill. "I mean, there's no law against punks getting doctoral degrees, right?"

"Guys? Fucking guys?" said Mary a little louder.

"No law, dude," said Matt, "but it's a bit odd, don't ya think? I mean, why would…"

"Fucking guys!" yelled Mary. "It fucking moved!"

"What?" asked Nancy. "You're just scared, Mary. It's dark; it's a body, you know."

"Then explain that!" screamed Mary.

They all looked at the corpse's hand, where a tiny drop of blood from Paul's wound had fallen, splashing away centuries of dust. The bony fingers, almost imperceptibly but certainly, creaked as they curled a bit.

"Shit shit shit!" yelled Paul. "It's fucking alive!"

"It's impossible!" cried Mary. "What the hell is this?"

The five of them shrieked in horror and hustled and bustled to the door, almost becoming stuck as they tried to wedge their way through, each one wanting to be first. Nancy took one look back, and the thing was slowly standing up, testing each crepitating, ancient joint as bone scraped against bone. It worked its groaning jaws, desperately trying to speak but lacking the organs to do so.

"It's alive! Go! Go!" screamed Mary.

Like the Scooby-Doo gang, they ran down the tunnels, with the four punks trying not to lose Nancy since she knew the way out. She led them from turn to turn, tunnel to tunnel until they found themselves in the crypt again. Not being in the best of shape, they all stopped, put their hands on their knees, and sucked in wheezing breaths.

"Alright, alright, calm down," said Nancy. "Let's get our shit together. It can't move that fast. We're safe here for a while. What the *hell* did we just see?"

"I think it's obvious, Nancy," said Gill. "We found a corpse, and Paul's blood fell on it, and that brought it back to life. Now, it wants to eat us or something like that."

"Yeah," said Mary. "That's fucking impossible."

"And yet we just saw it," answered Gill. "Unless... Nancy, is this some sort of prank?"

"Prank? Hell no! I swear! You saw that shit. It was a corpse!"

"She's right," said Matt. "I saw it. We all saw it."

Paul was shaking silently.

Gill said, "By the way, Paul, you're not still bleeding, are you?"

Paul looked down at his finger. He had forgotten about the relatively minor wound in the chase, but now he saw that it was indeed bleeding, and the blood was falling, drop by drop, on the floor.

"Shit! I shouldn't have gotten so wasted last night. I'm fucking bleeding out."

"Yeah, that's not good," said Nancy. Because..."

She had no need to finish the sentence. They heard a rustling, and then a creaking, and then a shuffling, and then a chorus of groans, like some dark, psychotic symphony. From the crypts all around them—all down the tunnel walls, came movement. Then came skeletal, rotten fingers, arms, legs. From each tomb, the resident was climbing out, enlivened by the mere smell of Paul's blood.

"Um, fucking guys? Nancy? Get us the hell out of here!"

"Don't have to fucking tell me twice! This way!"

She ran ahead of them, and they all managed to keep up, despite years of smoking and drinking and drugs. The group ran through tunnels and made turns, all the while hearing the clicking of bones behind them as if they were being followed by horrid, skittering insects. They reached the pond and saw decomposing arms reaching out of the water, moving toward the shore.

"Shit! Hurry guys! Come on! I know a closer exit!"

Nancy led them through a different tunnel than the one they had entered from. Mary looked back and saw an army of the dead following them, walking much faster than living skeletons should have been able to. One of them swiped at her and she felt its cold fingers brush her hair. The tunnel filled with the acrid, sour, nauseating smell of death. They ran as fast as four out-of-shape rockers could, and they finally reached a staircase. Nancy fled up it and they followed, finally seeing glorious, blessed sunlight. They found themselves in a storage room. Crates, kitchen utensils, and miscellaneous supplies lined the walls.

"This way, guys!" said Titania, who had seemingly appeared from nowhere.

They climbed the steps behind her and found themselves in the Fairie Realm Café.

Titania led them to a table and quickly made their usual drinks, then sat down with them.

"Well, I guess you guys have discovered one of Ushaville's secrets," said Titania softly.

"You mean fucking zombies?" asked Paul in a wild voice.

Mary shushed him and said, "Let her talk."

"Yeah," said Nancy. "I grew up here, and I am not sure what the hell I just saw." Her hand shook as she lifted the coffee cup to her mouth.

"Alright, well, let's see how to go about this," said Titania. "All is not as it seems in Ushaville. We have, well, not sure how to tell you this, but we have things here that are supernatural. You know, paranormal."

"Kind of fucking figured that out just recently," answered Matt. "Welcome to Ushaville! Come for the coffee; stay for the undead hordes!"

Titania chuckled and continued: "Yes, well, that's a part of it. Only, those weren't zombies, guys."

"Not zombies?" replied Mary incredulously. "Dead people, skeletons, come to life, chase us, want to eat us. What am I missing here? It's like we're living out a fucking George Romero film."

"Zombies are not the only dead things that come back to life," said Titania. "Let me ask you this. When you found the old corpses, what happened that made them rise up?"

"Are we really having this conversation? Is this the same universe that I woke up in?" asked Gill.

"I know," said Paul. "I fucking know. It was my blood. My blood dripped on the ground, and I guess on the body. My blood made them come alive."

"Correct," said Titania. "And what sort of revenants crave blood?"

"Oh, fuck me," said Paul. "Fuck me. Are you saying those were fucking *vampires*?"

Titania raised her eyebrows.

Mary said, "Vampires? Oh, God. Oh, my God. I wouldn't believe it if they hadn't just chased me. I guess it makes sense. Zombies are supposed to be slow, right? I mean, vampires in Ushaville... it sort of explains lots of things. It sort of all makes sense now. Wait... your mark, your tattoo, Nancy? It lets you go around town safely, but not safe from muggers. *From being eaten by vampires*! Shit. Well, where does that leave us? We don't have the mark of protection, and the Hatfields said that the town is closing up temporarily. Guys, we're basically fish in a barrel. Open season on humans."

"Now that," said Titania, "is something you don't need to worry about. I have, let's say, an understanding with the vampires. You are all under my protection. I have natural intuition, and the first time I met you guys, I saw past the Mohawks and leather and metal dog collars. I can see the real you, and I immediately placed you under my protection."

"You gonna tattoo us then?" asked Paul.

Titania chuckled. "Not that. Let's just say that my protection is not visible, at least not to you. You need to trust me."

She placed a hand on Paul's arm, and he immediately felt a rush of warm peace and safety, like his own mother's womb.

"I trust you."

"My protection," explained Titania, "is strong, but not against everything. If you act aggressively against the vampires, well, my protection might fail."

"Titania," asked Nancy, "can you please just fill us in on everything? Growing up here, I guess I always sort of knew about the vampires; I mean, not really, not openly, but we all just kind of have that understanding. But can you just explain everything to us? Tell us everything about Ushaville?"

"There's way too much to tell you this afternoon, but here are the brass tacks of what you need to know. The Hatfields and McCoys are all vampires. Their feud is much older than you've read about. Regular Ushaville citizens are in two categories: under protection or not under protection. The McCoys mind their own business, but the Hatfields have no qualms about, well, attacking you for your blood and killing you. That's why everyone says to avoid the Eastside—not for the crime, but because the Hatfields are vicious. Based on an ancient treaty that even the Hatfields respect, they can't harm anyone with the mark of protection. Now, for those residents or visitors not under protection, if they go to the Eastside, especially at night, it won't end well. The good news, though, if I can call anything in Ushaville good news, is that the vampires do not mess with the Indians or with me. I can't go into why that is, but if you are friends of Beast Stalker or any Indian here, or with me, and we issue you protection, then you are out of range of the fangs."

"Alright, then why you, Titania? What's special about you?" asked Nancy.

Titania winked and giggled. "Maybe one day I'll tell you. For now, you need to know that you are relatively untouchable. But I will warn you, Paul, Mary, Gill, and Matt, if you go out of your way to provoke or attack the vampires, then even my protection can't save you. Understand?"

The four nodded in unison.

Titania placed her hands on all five of them, filling them with warm emotions of security and safety, then said, "Now, don't you have a show to play at the Pallid Horse?"

CHAPTER 12

DINNER WITH OPHELIA

"Thank you again for the invitation, Ophelia. And it's nice to finally meet you, Misses McCoy. Ophelia told me that you and I work at the same university!"

"A pleasure as well, Professor Miller," replied Mrs. McCoy, a slender, tall woman with Ophelia's Asianesque eyes and pale skin.

"Misses McCoy," said Xiaoqing, "are you sure you're not a student too? You look much too young to be Ophelia's mother."

"Oh, that is very kind of you to say. Trust me though, I'm older than I look," she replied, chuckling.

Ophelia took their jackets and hung them up for them. The girl and her mother lived right on Unter den Linden, and although they lived on the east side of the street, Unter den Linden itself was clean, beautiful, and, most importantly, neutral in the feud. They lived in a dark blue, brick row house of three stories with a facade that included castle-like structures at each corner.

"Your house is beautiful!" said Xiaoqing.

"Oh, thanks. We've had it in the family for a long time," answered Mrs. McCoy.

"Indeed," said Jean-Pierre. "Do you know how old the house is? I'm from New Orleans, and we have some very old buildings, so I always like to see other beautiful, old buildings wherever I go."

Ophelia half-smiled and said, "I think it's a few hundred years old, Father. We have family in New Orleans. I love your city."

She ushered the three guests into the parlor, which was populated with exquisite antique German furniture.

"Wow! That is some beautiful furniture," said Jean-Pierre. "It must be three hundred years old, and it is in mint condition. I've learned that Ushaville is special, but I would never have imagined such beauty in a small town. I do not mean to be intrusive, Ophelia, but do you have any other furniture around the house like this? It's sort of a minor hobby of mine."

"Of course, Father. You can all come if you want. I'll give you the grand tour."

She took them from sumptuous room to sumptuous room, all decadently adorned with the world's finest antique furniture. There were ornate paintings hung on the walls, and Sager recognized some of them as original French Impressionists' work. Knowing a bit about that sort of thing, Jean-Pierre ran up an informal tally in his head and estimated that the house and its contents must be worth at least five million dollars. When they returned to the living room, they all sat down as Ophelia served them rare, Chinese tea.

"This is *pu'er*, Ophelia. It's my favorite.

"Oh, that is good to hear, Professor. This particular one is over three hundred years old."

"This is very high quality," added Xiaoqing. "How did you get it?"

Ophelia paused while pouring tea, then answered, "My family has traveled extensively. We are very international. I know it might be hard to believe that, given the West Virginia setting, and the Hatfield and McCoy history."

Jean-Pierre laughed. "Not at all, Ophelia. People are often surprising in many ways."

She stood in front of the priest, pouring his cup. He noticed a beautiful, antique mirror on the wall across from himself, and his blood froze. In the mirror, he saw himself, as well as a teapot hanging mid-air, pouring tea into a cup. Ophelia was not there. He held his tongue but began shaking imperceptibly.

"I hope you all enjoy lamb. I've made a special roast tonight from an old family recipe," called Mrs. McCoy from the kitchen.

"Oh, we love lamb," said Xiaoqing. "You too, Jean-Pierre?"

"Hmm? Oh, lamb? Yes. I like lamb."

After thirty minutes of socializing and sipping tea, Ophelia led them to the dining room. A long, beautiful antique table was the centerpiece, and it rested on a thick, intricate Persian rug. Opulently textured wallpaper, in deep burgundy and gold, lined every wall, and the ceiling comprised rich, oaken panels. On the table was a burgundy silk runner, and two lit candelabras, one at each end. In the middle of the table, exuding steam that rose up to the ceiling, was a richly roasted, whole leg of lamb. Surrounding it were various vegetable dishes of every brilliant color and texture.

"My goodness, Misses McCoy!" exclaimed Sager. "This is a king's feast! You must be a professional chef?"

"Oh, no, not me. I just have years of experience. Please sit. I assume you all drink wine? Even you, Father? Are you allowed?"

"I, um, yes. I enjoy wine…" Jean-Pierre's voice was quiet and timid. Sager raised an eyebrow and looked at him quizzically.

"I've taken the liberty of decanting some wine from our cellar. It's 1961 Château Latour. I hope you like red?"

"1961 Château Latour? My God, Misses McCoy," declared Sager. "That's one of the best vintages they made. You really do not have to go to all of this trouble and expense for us, I assure you! I feel a bit guilty about all of this."

"Nonsense," she replied. "You are our guests, and Ophelia has spoken highly of you three. And to be honest, our family has collected wine for a very long time. If we don't drink it, then it's just going to eventually go bad."

"Well, then I am excited to try this vintage. I've dreamed all of my life about trying it, to be honest."

She smiled and poured a small splash in Sager's crystal glass. "Why don't you do us the honor of tasting it, Professor?"

"I must admit, I would love to. This is right up my alley," he replied.

"He's a wine snob!" said Xiaoqing with a grin, and everyone chuckled except Jean-Pierre, who seemed a bit withdrawn and quiet.

Sager rolled the wine around in the glass, then took a close, fast sniff, a close, slow sniff, and then two more sniffs from farther back. "I detect dark black currants, truffles, rich humus, and oak on the nose."

"Oh, Professor, you really do know wine!" said Ophelia excitedly while placing her hand on his arm.

He blushed and replied, "It's just a hobby. I have lots to learn."

He then looked at the glass in the light and said, "Deep amber garnet, which is to be expected at this age." He looked at the cork. "The cork is preserved remarkably well. Your family must really know how to store wine, Mrs. McCoy."

He then took a sip, sucking the red elixir over his tongue into the back of his throat, gargling a bit. "On the palate, I also detect dark black currants, truffles, earth, and oak, as well as Madagascar vanilla, raspberries, and medium-soft tannins as a mouthfeel."

Everyone except Jean-Pierre applauded.

"Wow, Professor," said Ophelia. "You sound like a wine expert! Do not be so unnecessarily humble. You truly know wine."

Xiaoqing glared at Ophelia's hand, which still rested coolly upon Sager's forearm, but Ophelia did not notice, or at least pretended not to notice.

Mrs. McCoy served their individual plates. The food was masterful, the work of a professional chef. As they all ate, drank, and chatted, Jean-Pierre observed carefully. He did not drink nearly as much as Sager and Xiaoqing because he wanted to remain sober. He watched as Ophelia and Mrs. McCoy pretended to eat. They were exceptionally good at it, also, as if they had practiced for a very long time. They would take a piece of food on their fork, take it to their mouths, then feign biting into it and chewing, using sleight of hand to bring the food back down to their plates. It was the same scheme with their wine. They pretended to take little sips, then to swallow them, but the volume of wine in their glasses never seemed to reduce, as they kept pouring Sager and Xiaoqing glass after glass of the expensive red.

Jean-Pierre was careful to act as if he were innocent of their ruse, but he also felt his stomach drop as he realized the import of what he was witnessing: these were not people, not humans. They were like the Colombian girl, somehow. He did not know precisely what they were, but he knew they were not human.

As he furtively, circumspectly regarded the two and their beguilement, he accidentally poked his thumb with the steak knife. A little blood dripped out onto his food, and he gasped. Ophelia and her mother froze and stared at his plate, then recomposed themselves.

"Oh, Father! Are you alright?" asked Mrs. McCoy in feigned concern. "Ophelia, please go get Father something to wrap his finger with."

"I am so clumsy," he said. "It looks like I have ruined my piece of lamb. I am so sorry, Misses McCoy. How daft of me."

"Not at all, Father. Just a slip of the knife."

"Father?" called Ophelia from another room. "Would you please come? Let me rinse your wound and then put a plaster around it."

He felt suspicious, but in order to avoid Mrs. McCoy's skepticism, he followed Ophelia's voice into a luxurious bathroom. The walls, floor, and ceiling were lined with expensive, blue, Italian tile, and the tub was antique and gilded. Ophelia smiled.

"May I have your hand, Father?"

He extended it, and she ran cold water over the small cut, dabbed the blood with a gauze, spread on some antibiotic ointment, then wrapped a Band-Aid around it.

"I'm sorry you hurt yourself, Father. Please do not be embarrassed. It was just an accident."

"Thank you, Ophelia," he said, returning to the dining room. As he took one last look back to admire the Italian tile, he spied Ophelia clandestinely licking the bloody gauze! He quickly turned away and sat back at his place.

The evening continued, Jean-Pierre suffering in disbelief and fear, Sager and Xiaoqing obliviously enjoying themselves, and Ophelia and her mother putting on a great act. After a couple of rounds of an absinthe *digestif*, Jean-Pierre affected a yawn.

"Oh, pardon me! I must be getting tired from not sleeping well last night. You have been such kind hosts, Misses McCoy and Ophelia. Perhaps we should not wear out our welcome," said Jean-Pierre.

"I am a bit sleepy as well," added Sager. "All that fabulous wine!" he said, and everyone chuckled. "I hope this is not intrusive, but your house and furniture are so beautiful and special. I was wondering if you had any other interesting pieces that I have not seen? Again, forgive me, but both Father Jean-Pierre and I share a love of antiques."

Ophelia stood up and said, "There are a few pieces that you did not see, Professor. Let me show you."

Jean-Pierre thought quickly. He did not want Ophelia or her mother to be alone at any time, as that gave them an opportunity to concoct a dangerous plot or to set a trap. He said, "Go on, Sager. I'll wait here with Xiaoqing and chat with Misses McCoy." He forced a smile. Sager nodded.

While Xiaoqing conversed with the other two, Ophelia took Sager's hand in hers and led him down a hallway. Frankly, he was rather intoxicated from the fine wine, so he held her cold hand and followed. As she interlocked her fingers into his, he did not resist—the fuzzy, anomalous haze of wine blinded him to the implications.

"Professor, I do not mean to insult your intelligence and knowledge, but do you know what a *lit clos* is?" she asked.

"No insult, Ophelia. Yes, it's a bed inside an ornate wooden box that the French slept inside of for warmth and privacy. They were common in the Middle Ages in France. Don't tell me you have a

Medieval antique?" he asked excitedly. Ophelia gave him a warm smile and led him into a bedroom.

"This is my bedroom, Professor. This *lit clos* is from the house of the valet of Philippe the Sixth."

"Are you serious?" he replied. "That is amazing! It must be from the Fourteenth Century and priceless!"

The *lit clos*, like a box constructed of rich, fine wood, was the size of a modern car and was ornately carved and painted on the outside.

"Ophelia, this is in perfect condition! How in the world did you come to possess it?"

"Well, Professor, as my mother mentioned, our family is very old. Here, have a look inside. It seems small to us today because people in the Middle Ages were shorter. They also slept in more of a sitting position than we do. Would you like to try it out?"

"Well," Sager replied, "I would not normally intrude like that, but how many other chances will I have to lie inside of the *lit clos* of Philippe the Sixth's valet? My God, it's a piece of history!"

Ophelia took her hand from his and placed it on his arm, guiding him inside the box bed.

"Careful! It's really small for a tall gentleman like you, Professor."

He was able to lie in a sitting position.

"This is truly amazing, Ophelia. Just think of the history that I am touching with my own hands here. This is a marvelous experience. Thank you so much."

She looked into his eyes and smiled. Through his inebriated haze, he saw her pale, delicate face, her gentle almond eyes, her raven, silken hair move closed as she climbed into the *lit clos* with him.

"Let me show you what it is like closed." She closed the box bed and lay down next to him; the side of her body pressed against his. Sager's heart beat more rapidly, but he condemned himself in his mind and tried to take slow breaths. He was unable to speak. Ophelia smelled like tannins and chrysanthemums, like an earthy musk with a soft undertone of roses. She leaned her head onto his shoulder.

"Professor, the other students at my high school always tell me that I am weird, that I act like an adult and speak too formally. What do you think?"

"Well," he answered in a shaking voice, "you are… certainly… I mean, you are mature for your age, which is what, by the way?"

"I'm three…I am fourteen years old."

"Oh, fourteen. When I was fourteen, I was called weird too, Ophelia. I liked literature, art, opera, music. The other kids were fascinated with basketball and soccer. Believe me, when you get older, you will be glad that you are different in a good way."

She rested her arm across Sager's waist. Tingling, almost unbearable tickling flowed through his veins and into his stomach. He did not resist. The wine... the damned wine!

"Professor, you really understand me. I am looking forward to being your student when I go to university. Maybe you could be my thesis director, too." She slid her leg over Sager's.

He hated himself, he despised himself, but he did not resist.

Instead, the warm ecstasy of the wine increased. Ophelia was a warm home, a soft womb in a cold world, a womb into which he could retreat his body and soul and finally be at one with his own soul. He felt her slide completely on top of him, felt her straddle him, felt the safety and security of her body. She was his warmth, though her body was cold.

Her cool pelvis slowly moved against his. He gasped as she looked into his eyes pleadingly, questioningly, begging him, pleading with his mind and body. She slowly ground her pelvis against his, increasing the speed and pressure with each stroke. She leaned into him and kissed him. He struggled with one strong effort to push her away, to defy his primal, bestial response, but he was too weak. *The spirit is willing, but the flesh is weak.* He was gone.

He kissed her back.

Her cold lips opened, and his tongue went inside of her mouth, exploring her hard teeth, her soft gums, rubbing against her own meaty tongue, their saliva mingling and lubricating the caresses of his lips and tongue. He longed to swallow her saliva, to take in all of her fluids and being. Inflamed with biological lust, he placed his hands on her thin, teenage thighs and ran them up her pale, cool skin. He reached her hips, and she moaned and gasped deeply.

Frantically, he reached up her skirt pulled down her panties, then reached his left hand up and pulled off her top and her bra. Her small breasts bounced down, her brown nipples becoming erect and long, hard and tight. He kissed them, then put them inside of his mouth, then gently bit them. She slid down and pulled his manhood out of his pants, putting it into her frigid mouth. Then, quickly, urgently, she mounted him. He felt her cool insides, the soft, moist, engorged tissues rubbing against his own. She thrust her pelvis fiercely, desperately, and quickly he felt the ephemeral euphoria ride up his entire body. He exploded inside of her as she came to a shuddering orgasm. She kept thrusting against him, slower and more gently, as her tissue and his pulsated less and less, and shrank back to normal size. She gently slid off of him, and he felt himself sliding out of her and flopping against his own stomach. Instantly, the pain of regret and shame punched him in the gut.

"Oh God, Ophelia... I'm sorry... I... what have I done? I'm so sorry... I..."

She placed her soft finger on his lips.

"Shh. Sager, be quiet, my dear. It is alright; we did this together. You must not feel guilty. I have felt this passion since the day I first met you in The Fairie Realm Café. I know you felt it, too. Do not deny it. You cannot stop this, Sager. I will not tell anyone. Please believe me, my darling."

"I can't be your darling, Ophelia! I am so sorry. The wine... I was drunk... I didn't know what I was doing..."

"Oh, you knew, Sager. There is no guilt, no shame. We did a beautiful thing together. I know you have to go home. I will not ask you to cuddle or stay with me. I understand the ways of the world. But know that we will be together again, my love. You are a part of me now, inside of me."

Sager felt nauseated and terribly guilty. He quickly pulled his pants back on, stepped out of the *lit clos*, and hurried back to the parlor. He, Xiaoqing, and Jean-Pierre took their leave and went back to Sager's house.

Sager and Xiaoqing were too drunk to talk to that night, so Jean-Pierre waited until the morning. He woke up early and cooked them omelets, New Orleans biscuits, bacon, and made some killer Bloody Marys. Distracted, he thought about the events of the night before. He had suffered torrid, tormented nightmares of dark spirits chasing and devouring him and had woken confused. Had he really seen what he thought he had seen at Ophelia's house, or had it been simply a part of the dream? The wound on his finger assured him that it had been quite real.

Sager and Xiaoqing plodded into the kitchen, both looking almost as pale as Ophelia.

"Oh God," said Xiaoqing. "Why did we drink so much?"

Sager chuckled and sat down to breakfast. "God, I don't know. Well, I do know. 1961 Château Latour. For regular people like us, it's a once-in-a-lifetime chance to taste one of the world's best bottles of wine. I regret nothing!"

Jean-Pierre noticed that Sager abruptly changed his demeanor. His long time friend had a sharp, painful stab look of regret and shame that almost made him double over in agony. What had he done? What had happened the night before that made his chuckling face changed into one of torrid agony? And apparently, Xiaoqing noticed the same.

"What? What is it, honey?" asked Xiaoqing.

"I..." sager coughed. "Nothing. Just the hangover. I just remembered how much we drank."

"Well, they kept pouring and opening more bottles!" said Xiaoqing. "They were like Chinese hosts: keep refilling until the guest refuses more."

"Eat and enjoy," said Jean-Pierre. And look, I know it sounds bad now, but a little hair of the dog that bit you will really make you feel better. I promise. Not to mention, I make the world's best Bloody Mary."

So, the three ate and drank. The salty, greasy food was perfect, and the small amount of vodka in the Bloody Marys indeed did the trick. They felt better, but for Sager, it helped nothing as his face looked still in torment. What had happened? He would have to tell them eventually, right? He was an honest man. But first, Jean-Pierre needed to open up about his experience.

"I have something to tell you, guys. It's pretty serious, so brace yourselves," said Jean-Pierre cautiously.

"Huh? What's the matter, J.P.?" replied Sager.

"Could we sit in the living room for this? We need some comfortable chairs since the discussion might take a while."

Xiaoqing and Sager looked at each other. Sager raised his shoulders, and they all went into the living room.

"Alright, I need to build up to this," began Jean-Pierre. "Now, we all experienced a journey into the spirit world with Chief and Beast Stalker, right?"

"I mean," said Sager, "yeah, but we know it was from hallucinogenics."

"Not me!" piped in Xiaoqing. "Sager, maybe it's my natural Chinese superstition, but there was more to it than that. I once did some acid in high school. That is one thing, but with Chief, it was so real, so tangible, so profound. I think we really did somehow encounter another world, whatever that might be. Sorry, Father, I know that's not Christian doctrine, but it's what I experienced."

"No need to apologize, Xiaoqing. Christian doctrine includes the existence of a spiritual realm filled with angels and demons, at least traditionally," responded Jean-Pierre. "In fact, I agree with you. Sager, as an academic, would you open your mind, just for now, just for the sake of argument, just as a hypothetical, to the possibility that there is another realm with things that we might call paranormal or supernatural in our world?"

"Alright, fine," replied Sager. "I can do that."

"Last night. At Ophelia's," began the priest. When he said the name, Jean-Pierre saw Sager look like a deer in headlights. *Did Sager see something too?* "I didn't get drunk. In fact, I only had one glass. I was completely sober, alright? Well, I saw some things. I saw some very disturbing things, and that, along with something I once experienced on a mission trip to Colombia, cause me to think, or rather to believe, that Ophelia and her mother are not what they seem."

"Not what they seem?" asked Xiaoqing. "In what way?"

"First, let me just tell you what I saw, and then you can draw your own conclusions," continued Jean-Pierre. "Fact number one: when Ophelia was pouring my tea, I happened to look in one of their antique mirrors. I saw myself, the teapot hanging in midair, but no Ophelia. She had no reflection."

"What? That's impossible!" interjected Sager.

"Sager, you promised to remain open."

"Alright, alright. Go on."

"Fact number two: Ophelia and her mother ate and drank nothing. They got you two drunk and full, but they were only feigning to eat and drink. They used sleight of hand to bring food and wine to their mouths, and then only to pretend to chew and swallow. Maybe you were too drunk to notice but think about it. At the end of the meal, your plates were just about empty. Theirs were still full, as well as their wine glasses."

"Now that you mention it," said Xiaoqing, "I actually did notice that! I thought it was weird, but since I had drunk so much wine, I just dismissed it without really thinking about it. Sager, it's true. They didn't eat or drink anything."

"Alright," said Sager, "so they're on a diet and teetotalers."

"There's more," persevered Jean-Pierre. "Remember when I accidentally poked myself with the steak knife? And then Ophelia took me to the bathroom to clean and dress it? She used some gauze to soak up the blood. When I was walking back to the dining room, I happened to look back to see if she was coming, and I very clearly saw her licking and sucking the blood from the gauze. She didn't see me."

"What the hell?" said Xiaoqing.

"Yes. Now, add to these incidents the fact that they are both very pale, that both of their hands were cool, almost cold when I shook them, and that their skin is flawless; even Misses McCoy's skin is like a child's, even though she must be approaching middle age by now."

"Jean-Pierre," said Sager, "you can't really be saying what I think you're building up to. Come on, man."

"What do you mean?" asked Xiaoqing.

"Well, let's assume that everything J.P. said was true. I've known him forever, and I believe he is very honest and would not lie. I believe that, at least in his mind, he experienced what he told us he did. Add it up, Xiaoqing. Pale and cold skin; no reflection, no eating or drinking of normal food and wine, drinking blood, being unnaturally young," said Sager. "What does all of that add up to?"

"You don't mean…"

"Yes," said Jean-Pierre. "Just say it. *Vampires*."

Xiaoqing, mouth agape, was silent. After several seconds, she said, "Jean-Pierre, I study folklore, as you know. All of those things are, in fact, traits of European vampire lore. But are you really arguing that vampires are real, and right here in Ushaville?"

"And what about Ushaville?" said Jean-Pierre. "It's an Old World European city in the middle of West Virginia. It is ancient, no one has really ever heard about it, and it has glowing amulets. Isn't Ushaville just a little suspicious to you?"

"Sure, it is," said Sager. "But it's a big leap from all of this to the real existence of undead vampires."

"I know, I know," said Jean-Pierre. "Look, just think about it, alright? I'm going back to New Orleans tomorrow morning, as we discussed. I know of someone there. He's an expert on the paranormal. Xiaoqing, I know you're an expert on folklore, so I don't mean that. I mean, he knows everything there is to know about the Occult. Vampires, ghosts, demons, werewolves, banshees—he is intimately familiar with it all. He's even written a book about his ghost hunting experiences, and he had a television show. I'll find him and ask him for help. Even if nothing comes of it, please at least consider it. It's no skin off your back. No one even has to know."

Sager and Xiaoqing nodded their assent.

CHAPTER 13

THE CONCERT

The Gravediggers had gotten themselves dressed and ready in their hotel room while Nancy went to the Pallid Horse to prepare for their concert. Paul Junk Roy spiked his black Mohawk into several individual towers and put in his nose ring. He wore a leather vest, torn black jeans, and combat boots. Gutter Gill Leblanc wore jeans and an olive drab Army jacket; his head was covered in a starburst pattern of foot-long spikes. Mucky Matt Moulin sported an afro, and a silk, purple, Jimi Hendrix jacket that contrasted against his shiny, ebony skin. Finally, Scary Mary Gambino sported a torn-up black *Siouxsie and the Banshees* T-shirt, black jeans with more holes than fabric; long, black dreadlocks; and black lipstick.

"Usual set tonight, alright?" said Paul. "I hope no one forgot the chords and shit."

"Nah," said Matt, yawning. "We remember. It's not like we're playing Beethoven or something. Three chords and a guitar. That's pretty much rock and roll, right?"

"Just make sure your shit's all in tune, at least close enough, alright?"

"Anyone having a little trouble staying focused on the music when we're about to play to a house of vampires?" asked Mary.

"I would argue," interjected Gill, "that tonight's show might possibly be the most *punk* event to occur in human history. A punk rock concert with an audience that includes vampires? This is the stuff of legend!"

"Woooooh!" yelled Paul. "Bloody right! Let's tear this joint up!"

They gathered up their gear and began the schlep down to the Pallid Horse. The sign outside read: *Tonight Only! Welcome The Gravediggers from New Orleans!* Nancy met them at the door and got some employees to help them carry everything in and set up on stage.

"Damn, you guys travel light," she said.

"Right," said Paul. "Bass, guitar, mic, a couple amps, and a few drums. Give us a plug, and we're good to go. Had to fit all this shit in a Microbus, which," and here he raised his voice, "*was stolen from us and is in lockdown!*"

"Shut up, Paul, unless you want this show to end really, really unfortunately," warned Nancy.

"Yeah, yeah," he said, in a noticeably quieter voice.

The bar was slowly filling up with people. Now that they knew Ushaville's big secret, it was not difficult to spot the differences between the vampires and the humans. Pale skin was the most noticeable feature, but the vampires also tended to find places in the dark shadows of the corners and nooks, while the humans tended to congregate near the bar, closer to the stage. The humans also seemed more excited and lively, while the vampires remained more still. Finally, the humans ordered all sorts of alcoholic drinks, while the vampires all drank goblets of *red wine* that looked suspiciously dark and viscous. Mary shuddered.

On the other hand, Paul wasted no time in plugging in his mic and then hitting the bar. He was easily three whiskeys ahead of the other three bandmates when they finally reached the bar. They all got drinks and began imbibing.

"Yeah, two questions," said Nancy. "First, don't you need to do a sound check or something like that? Second, aren't you gonna be too drunk to play?"

Paul answered, "Oh, Nancy, Nancy, my dear, we play hardcore punk rock. We'll do a quick sound check, but we're not prepping a fucking symphony or something. And too drunk to play? Frankly, I'm not sure we even *could* play sober. We write the songs drunk, practice the songs drunk, and perform the songs drunk. It's a tradition, and you wouldn't want to mess with tradition, would you?"

Nancy rolled her eyes and handed Paul another whiskey.

"And yeah, thanks for the open bar," added Mary. "Most places we play in are total dives and we're lucky to even get the fee, much less free drinks."

"Well, that's the rule at the Pallid Horse. All performers get free drinks all night. We really didn't discuss pay, but you'll each get a few hundred dollars at the end. Hatfields are many things, but they are not cheap or welchers."

"Shit!" said Matt. "A few hundred, plus free drinks? This is the best damn gig we've ever played. Maybe we should move to Ushaville."

Mary simply glared at him, and Nancy laughed.

"Anyway, guys, you alright to go on in about an hour?" They nodded while slurping down more alcohol. "God help us all," muttered Nancy as she went back to the stage to make sure everything was alright.

The four Gravediggers noticed that the place was becoming quite full, and a large number of customers were humans geared out in punk dress. From the back, the vampires glared and eyed them all suspiciously. Nancy noticed this and whimpered—vampires liked order in Ushaville above all, and punk rock was not known for being orderly. She guessed that many of the humans had been suppressing their wilder side for a long time. If they had not known overtly about the vampires, then they had sensed that something was controlling them, somehow. *Just please don't let the shit hit the fan tonight*, she thought. She looked over at the four punks at the bar, joking and laughing with slurred speech, and she shook her head hopelessly.

The hour passed, and she elbowed Mary. "Mary? You guys wanna go up now? It's about time."

"Oh, hell yeah!" said Paul loudly. "Let's do this shit!"

They staggered their way to the stage, managed to climb up on it, and grabbed their instruments. Nancy snatched the mic from Paul's hand and whispered, "Wait! I have to introduce you!"

Nancy stepped forward. Her beautiful, chocolatine skin matched her little black dress and leather jacket. Her glorious afro stretched upward and outward like the rays of the sun. With the stage lights on her, she looked like a goddess.

"Ladies and gentlemen, welcome to the Pallid Horse!"

Applause.

"The Pallid Horse brings you a very special treat tonight, a treat that is not often heard in Ushaville. That's right; we are proud to present, all the way from New Orleans, Louisiana, the Big Easy..." She paused for effect. "...the great punk rock of... The Gravediggers!"

Loud cheers.

Paul took the mic, looked at the others, then shouted quickly, "One, two, three, four!"

From Mary's Fender spewed out fast, distorted chords at a volume that caused even the vampires in the back to wince. The human crowd immediately rushed forward and formed a slam-dancing pit. Mary saw this and grinned—they still fucking had it! Gill joined her on his out-of-tune bass, while Matt pounded the drums in a 16/16 time that was close to rhythmic. It was a musical disaster. After a few bars, Paul began singing (shouting?).

> *Your conformity is disgusting!*
> *You all look the fucking same!*
> *Living corpses, zombies in shopping malls!*
> *You make me go fucking insane!*

> *Authority! Authority!*
> *Go lick your boots in the sun!*
> *Authority! Authority!*
> *Your day is coming! Your time is done!*

> *Your deformity is amazing!*
> *Your soul is like a monster!*
> *Looking just like everyone!*
> *You look just like a hipster!*

> *Authority! Authority!*
> *Go lick your boots in the sun!*
> *Authority! Authority!*
> *Your day is coming! Your time is done!*

> *Nazis! Nazis! Nazis!*
> *Following like stupid sheep!*
> *Whatever they say, you will do!*
> *A bunch of fucking creeps!*

> *Authority! Authority!*
> *Go lick your boots in the sun!*
> *Authority! Authority!*
> *Your day is coming! Your time is done!*

The song ended abruptly. The humans in the slam-dancing pit all cheered and yelled while the vampires in the back glared, seething. Nancy only shook her head and whispered to herself, "Well, shit."

The Gravediggers continued to run through their slaughterhouse of melody, song after song, outrageous lyric after outrageous lyric, driving the humans into a rock-and-roll frenzy. After an hour, Paul said into the mic, "Fuck yeah! You fuckers rock! We're gonna take a short break and get drunker, so hold tight!"

They descended the stage and headed toward the bar. Nancy trotted across the floor and stood behind the bar.

"Well, what you think, Nance?" asked Paul.

"Shit. I mean, it's definitely punk. You guys rock, in a sort of anarchist, destroying, unmusical way."

"Thanks!" said Paul.

"We aim to please, indeed," said Gill.

Nancy chuckled, shook her head, and refilled their drinks.

"Listen, guys; I need to talk to you about one thing. Come with me to the green room." She led them to an antechamber behind the bar. There were three red, velvet sofas.

"I know you're gonna hate me for saying this, but did you notice the reaction of the, er, well, the *non-humans* in the room?" asked Nancy.

"Uh, yeah. They were pissed!" answered Mary, laughing.

"Yeah, I know. And I know that's part of punk, shocking the audience. But, um, just remember who we're dealing with here. The *non-humans* are very, very dangerous people. Yeah, keep playing your music and shit, but maybe just keep being aware of their reaction. If they get too pissed off, the gig's over, and maybe our lives are over, got it?"

"You know, Nance," slurred Paul, "those fuckers can bite me." He laughed heartily at his own joke. Nancy gave up.

"Well, do what you want, but if you guys stir up shit too much, you need to find me. I have a secret way out of the Pallid Horse for emergencies. I think it's one of the oldest tunnels in town that everyone has forgotten about, even the vamps. I found it by accident. No one ever uses it. Pretty sure I'm the only one who knows it's there."

"Um, are the tunnels a great idea after what we saw?" asked Gill.

"This one is short and leads to an alley between two buildings on Unter den Linden. Nothing in there, I promise."

"That's a relief. What a fucked-up town. Sorry, Nancy, I know it's your town," said Matt.

"No apology dude. I know it's a messed-up place!"

After a couple of more rounds of drinks, the Gravediggers managed to stumble and stagger their way back to stage. Mary and Gill were so drunk that they each grabbed the other's instrument, and Nancy had to sort them out. She then took the mic, unraveling the cord that

Paul had managed to wrap around his torso and neck, and declared to the crowd: "Ladies and gentlemen! They're back to do the second half of the show! I present, once again, God help us all, the Gravediggers!"

The humans cheered as Paul counted in another song. They played their song list, each piece delving deeper and deeper into madness and running farther and farther away from what might be considered musicality, until they had descended into total chaotic, punk rock glory. The slam-dancing pit was spreading until most of the human audience was thrashing and bouncing around in a vast fit. The vampires in the back watched, glared, and began to whisper among themselves.

Paul looked at them.

"No, no, please no, Paul. No, you moron. No!" whispered Nancy. She could just see it in his eyes, the desire to say something. She edged toward the bar and the secret exit.

The band finished their song, and before they started the next one, Paul called out into the mic, "Hey! Hey, you in the back! What's the matter, mates? Not enjoying the show? You got a fucking problem with our music? Yeah, well, we gotta a problem with you! You fucking bloodsuckers! You fucking corpses! You fucking vampires! One two three four…"

Before the band could begin the song, a great din arose from the back of the crowd. Their faces had changed into something wicked, and their canine teeth had elongated into razor points. A symphony of hisses and growls accompanied them as several of them flew into the air and onto the stage.

"Oh shit!" said Paul. The humans in the audience looked confused, then terrified as complete tumult and pandemonium erupted from a volcano of entropy.

Screams, shouts, hisses, animalistic growls, bodies running, flying through the air, desperately seeking the exit.

Like a shark feeding frenzy, the vampires began pouncing upon the humans, ripping their throats out with their fangs, and gulping down their blood. Shadowy forms flew through the air faster than a bullet. The blood flowed, creating a slippery ocean on the floor so that humans trying to escape slipped and slid all over in a mockery of an ice-skating rink.

Paul bashed a vampire in the face with his mic, and as the blood and sweat hit the mic, it created a circuit that fried the vampire's face off—it shrieked and flew back. Mary and Gill were swinging their guitars around, knocking vampires in the head and chest, while Matt was using his drumsticks like stakes, thrusting them at the undead attackers, managing to even stake one that disintegrated into dust.

Nancy threw a beer bottle and hit Paul in the butt, which made him turn around angrily to see Nancy waving them toward her.

"Come on, guys!" he yelled, and the four punks managed to slide off of the stage and run through the chaos toward Nancy.

"This way! Hurry," she yelled as she led them down a hall, past a couple of offices, and into a bathroom. She pulled a radiator from next to the wall, revealing a hole. "In there! Go! Dive in!"

One-by-one, they climbed into the tunnel, which quickly opened large enough to allow them to stand. They ran in the darkness until Nancy slowed down and stopped.

"Wait, guys. Do you hear anyone following us?" she asked. They listened to thick silence.

"No," said Mary.

"Good. We don't need to run. It's too dark anyway."

They felt along the left wall as a guide and walked a few hundred feet until a faint, yellow glow appeared in the distance. It grew larger and brighter as they proceeded until they could see that it was a streetlight. The tunnel ended in a hole in an alley, just as Nancy had promised. The alley looked not to have been used in forever. They quickly climbed a wooden fence and found themselves on Unter den Linden, right at the punks' hotel. They heard screaming in the distance.

"Well, Nance," said Paul, "looks like you're staying with us tonight."

CHAPTER 14

HUNTING A GHOST HUNTER

Father Jean-Pierre de la Fresnière's first night back in his own bed in New Orleans should have felt luxurious and ecstatic, but how could he have possibly slept well, having experienced what he had in Ushaville?

After a fitful night of nightmarish flashes of monsters, he awoke early, brewed some strong coffee with chicory, and made a New Orleans *café au lait*. At about nine o'clock, he headed to the office, and several minutes later, there came a knocking on his door. He opened it cautiously, and standing outside was Detective Pace Barillo, whom he had met during the last murder investigation.

"Good morning, Father. Sorry to bother you, but do you have a few minutes?"

"Of course, Detective," replied Jean-Pierre. "How about some coffee?"

"That really sounds good. Thanks," replied the detective.

After serving, the two took a couple of sips before they began speaking.

"So, Father, I guess you heard the news?"

"News? I've been out of town for several days. What happened?"

"Oh, I see," said Detective Pace. "Well, there's been another murder."

"Oh, no. Oh, that's terrible. What happened?" asked Jean-Pierre.

"Well, it's the same MO. Neck almost completely severed, really torn up. No blood. No fingerprints or any other forensic evidence. This time, the body was found on Royal Street behind the cathedral."

"My God! It's savage, you know?"

"Father, it's the worst thing I've seen in my career for sure. This time, though, there was a little calling card left behind," said Pace. He reached into his trench-coat's interior pocket and pulled out a gilded calling card. "It's already been dusted by forensics. It's still evidence, though, so just be careful with it," said Pace as he handed the card to Jean-Pierre. It was real gold, upon which was etched the phrase *DIESNOXERIT.*

"That mean anything to you, Father?" asked Pace.

"First, please just call me Jean-Pierre; no need for formalities. And it's Latin. In ancient Rome, it was common to run all the letters together like that. Let's see; it means something like *day becomes night* or *day will be night.*"

"Alright, Jean-Pierre. You can call me Pace. Does that phrase mean anything to you?"

"Not really," answered Jean-Pierre. "I mean, there were and are some secret Catholic societies—some not so secret anymore—that use Latin phrases to designate themselves, such as *Deus Vult and Agnus Dei.* I wouldn't be surprised if this were something like that. You know, some modern secret cult or something."

"Interesting," said Pace. "But if they want to be secret, why leave the calling card?"

"That was my next question," said Jean-Pierre. "Also, why are so many bodies being found near the Catholic churches of New Orleans?"

"Thought I'd ask you the same."

"Well, they could be trying to make a point, something against religion, against Christianity?"

"Great minds think alike, Jean-Pierre," said Pace.

"Unfortunately, so do very mediocre minds," replied Jean-Pierre, and the two laughed.

"Alright, thanks for your time, Jean-Pierre; I just wanted to pick your brain. You've given me some leads to look into. Please call me if you think of anything else, alright?"

"Yes, of course."

Distracted by that sad news, Jean-Pierre spent his day in the office using the Internet doing some amateur research on Lâmié Chasseur.

The published author, considered one of the top experts on the Occult, lived and worked in New Orleans. He had starred in a local ghost hunting TV show for a few years, earning him local fame and interest. A year before, he had fallen off of the map, not releasing any more books or shows, and his whereabouts had become somewhat of a conspiracy topic among his fan base. Jean-Pierre had always enjoyed his shows. Unlike the more famous, national shows that went out of their way to fabricate evidence and over-hype every single creak of a board of fall of a leaf, Chasseur usually did not encounter anything paranormal. However, the few times that he did, the evidence was much more convincing: something moving, a shadow walking past, the sound of a word being whispered in the air. His production crew had all been interviewed more than once on TV and radio, and all of them insisted that it had all been real. Chasseur had insisted that they don't invent evidence, which was probably the reason he had not achieved national success. His books, moreover, were extremely well-written, philosophical, and almost scientific.

Jean-Pierre spent the better part of the day trying to track Chasseur down, but all of the websites seemed to be in the dark. Finally, on an obscure paranormal forum, he had found a clue in a single comment among hundreds: the poster mentioned that he had seen Chasseur at the French Quarter bar The Dungeon.

Jean-Pierre knew the bar—it had been an actual dungeon underneath a house that had been the setting of one of New Orleans' more bizarre stories, and that was saying a lot. The house had been bought by a man claiming to be a wealthy sheik from Arabia, who had imported luxurious furnishings and a harem of beautiful women, as well as a full household of servants. He had held lavish, excessive, orgiastic parties, until one morning, a passerby had seen blood leaking from under the front door. The police had found the remains of a slaughter inside—the sheik, his household, his harem, and several guests had been brutally murdered and dismembered. Furthermore, the police had found a secret underground tunnel that had led to a dungeon where the sheik had enjoyed kidnapping and torturing guests. This had really happened, and the dungeon's site had been converted into a popular New Orleans bar. Jean-Pierre could not imagine a likelier spot to find Chasseur.

At nine thirty that evening, Jean-Pierre doffed his priestly garbs and threw on some jeans and a T-shirt without his priest's collar. He combed his hair, shaved, and looked at himself in the mirror—he saw the dashing young man that he had been before taking his vows, but before the memories of his single life flooded into his mind and tempted him, he grabbed his wallet and walked outside. The French Quarter was characteristically hot and muggy, but a thick, soupy fog had rolled in off of the Mississippi River, coating the entire Quarter with a misty paint that brought to mind Victorian London and Jack the Ripper.

Jean-Pierre navigated his way through the foggy streets and narrow, cobblestone alleys, making his way from Pirates Alley to Toulouse Street, where it intersected with Dauphine. He knew where The Dungeon was, like most New Orleans residents, and he reached it right at ten o'clock, just as they were opening up the inner bar, the actual dungeon itself. He stepped inside and felt a tingling rush of pleasure. He felt like he had felt as a single man. Drinking, dancing, music, women—he tried to push these thoughts away as he considered the seriousness of his quest. He looked around the courtyard, furnished with torture cages where guests sat, drank, and talked. The Misfits, fittingly, blared on the speakers. He approached the bar and found a stool.

"What can I get you?" asked a young Asian girl behind the bar.

"Oh, let me think; It's been a long time. How about just a beer for now? You have Abita Amber?"

She smiled, reached under the bar, and placed the cold bottle in front of him.

"I'll start you a tab, Father," she said and winked.

"Wait, how did you…"

"I go to your church sometimes. It's no big deal; I know that Catholic priests can drink. It's one of the reasons I'm Catholic," she said, and they both laughed.

"What's your name then?" asked Jean-Pierre.

"Oh, I'm Kim.

"Now that you say it, I recognize you. You usually sit with your family on the left side, about halfway down?"

"That's me!" she said and smiled.

"How do you like working here?" he asked.

"It's a trip! But the money's good. Place is famous, you know? Lots of locals and tourists come here, and they tip really well."

"You probably make more than me!" said Jean-Pierre, and they chuckled. "Say, Kim, have you heard of Lâmié Chasseur?"

"The ghost dude? Sure, everyone has."

"Did you know he's rumored to be a regular here?" he asked.

"Yep. If you weren't you, Father, I wouldn't let you in on this, but since I know I can trust you, he comes here almost every night. In fact…" she trailed off and cocked her head to the side. Jean-Pierre looked, and there, at the end of the bar, was a man in his thirties. His black hair was oily and brushed back, but some long bangs hung across his forehead. He wore black jeans, a black shirt, and a black leather jacket. His face was sallow, and puffy black bags surrounded his eyes.

119

He had a glass of red wine in his hand and was talking to a cute young girl.

"That's him, Kim?"

"Don't tell him I told you. Good luck, and let me know if you need another drink. First round's on me."

He grabbed his beer, took a sip for courage, and casually drifted across the bar until he was near Lâmié. As fortune would have it, the girl sitting on the stool on the other side of Lâmié stood up and left. Jean-Pierre took a seat. He looked the other way, although he still could listen to how Lâmié flirted with another girl, but struck out. The second girl left, and Lâmié just looked down at his drink and took a large draught.

Jean-Pierre waited a minute or two, building up the courage to speak and thinking of what to say. He swigged the rest of his beer, caught Kim's eye, and she brought him another. He coughed, looked at Lâmié, and said, "Excuse me, but are you Lâmié Chasseur?"

The man slowly turned his head and replied, "Well, that all depends on what Lâmié Chasseur has coming to him."

Jean-Pierre chuckled. "I'm Jean-Pierre. Father Jean-Pierre."

"A priest? At this bar? I'm surprised you didn't burst into flames when you stepped inside. Well, hell, come drink with me. Next round's on me."

"Thank you."

"So, Father, what do you know about me?" asked Lâmié. "And why did you seek me out?"

"Well, I know you're an expert on the Occult."

Lâmié laughed sarcastically. "And what good has that done me, or anyone? Do you know the story of Faust, Father?"

"Sure," answered Jean-Pierre. "In fact, I read Goethe's version in German in grad school. Brilliant."

"Faust was one of the world's most educated men, you know? He had advanced degrees in science, the arts, medicine, law, theology... Do you remember the first lines of Goethe's *Faust*, Father?"

Jean-Pierre furrowed his brows, thought for a moment, then replied, "Habe nun, ach! Philosophie, Juristerei und Medizin, und leider auch Theologie! Durchaus studiert, mit heißem Bemühn. Da steh' ich nun, ich armer Tor! Und bin so klug als wie zuvor!"

"I'm impressed. Catholic education really is the best. Faust basically said that he had studied it all, Father. He had learned everything there was to learn. He had mastered every field. And at the end of it all, he was just as dumb and bored as before. This world has nothing to offer, really. That's the gist of the German."

"Yes, true," answered Jean-Pierre, "and so he turned to the Occult and to demons. They gave him an unimaginable life of wealth, satisfying every single need of his body and mind."

"Yep," said Lâmié. "And then they tore up his body and dragged his soul to hell. Call me Faust."

"How so?"

"You've seen my shows, right? You know I have a Master's degree from Harvard? I know more about the Occult than probably anyone else on earth. I've devoted my life to it. You could not mention a legend, a myth, a tale, a monster, a demon, a spell, a Medieval treatise, anything Occult, that I am not intimately familiar with."

"Yes, and it's quite impressive. Why did you quit your show? Why did you stop writing books?"

"Well, Father, after all of these years of study and fieldwork, you know what I came up with?"

"What?" asked Jean-Pierre.

"Nothing. Abso-fucking-lutely nothing. Oh, we had a chair move here and ghostly footsteps there, but so what? Anyone could fake that. It could be the wind. I devoted my life to bullshit, Father. It's all bullshit. There is no spirit, no soul, no afterlife. There are no angels, no demons, no God. No werewolves, no zombies, nothing. We are just lumps of mud with some electricity running through us for a few seconds, and then we die, and that's it. Nothing. It's all so fucking meaningless."

"It's tempting to believe so, I admit," replied Jean-Pierre. "Even as a priest, I've experienced major doubts and even a touch of Nihilism."

"Badass. But why have you come here, to me? Are you trying to convert me or something?"

Jean-Pierre laughed and ordered them both another round of drinks.

"Not in the slightest, Mister Chasseur. The fact is, I'm involved in a particular situation, and I would like your expert assistance."

"Yeah? What kind of help could I possibly give? You need me to translate Medieval Latin or something? Isn't that *your* gig?"

Jean-Pierre shook his head. "Listen, what if I told you that I'd found a real example of the Occult? The real deal."

"What? Like a ghost or something?" asked Lâmié, looking slightly more alert.

"Or something, yes. Listen, do you know that bartender?"

"You mean Kim? Yeah, I've known her for years."

"Alright. She can vouch that I am the priest at Saint Louis on Jackson Square," said Jean-Pierre.

121

"Fine. If she says it, I believe it."

"Thank you. Now, I'm willing to pay you for your services. I have a case, and I would like to hire your consulting expertise. What is your fee?"

"My fee? Father, I told you, I'm not interested. That part of my life is over—it was all a fraud, a sham. There is no supernatural, or, if there is, it's just a curtain moving in a breeze. I'm not going to charge you for bullshit, if you will pardon my language. I have no interest in that stuff anymore. Forget it."

"What if," said Jean-Pierre, "I could offer you something that you might find more valuable than money?"

"What, gold? Vintage wine? Cocaine?" Lâmié laughed sarcastically. "I have enough money, Father. I have savings, in addition to a wasted life. Now, if you don't mind, I would like to just sit here, drink my wine, and flirt with girls."

"A vampire."

"Huh? What do you mean?"

"A vampire. A real, undead, genuine vampire," replied Jean-Pierre. "I can show you a real vampire. Real deal Dracula. Undead creature of the night that survives by drinking human blood."

Lâmié stared at Jean-Pierre for a few seconds, then burst out in laughter. "Funny, Father. Very funny. Is this a setup or something? A practical joke?"

"I swear on my God that I am very serious," responded Jean-Pierre.

"A vampire? Come on, Father. Be serious here. Those are just old legends. In all of my hunts, I never found even a single ghost. Now you want me to believe that vampires are real? Do you also have a werewolf cousin you want to set me up with? She's cute, just a little hairy!"

"I'll make you a deal. Come with me to Ushaville, West Virginia. Investigate with me. If I am wrong, then you get a free vacation, and I'll throw in a case of red wine of your choice. But if I'm right, then you'll have discovered vampires."

"Wait, did you say Ushaville?" asked Lâmié.

"I did."

"Weird. Hmm."

"What's weird?" asked Jean-Pierre.

"Just the name. *Usha* means *death* in ancient Sumerian. Weird that a town in West Virginia would have that name. Maybe it comes from another source. Anyway, a road trip with a priest and free wine? You'll feed me well, too? I like to eat, Father."

Jean-Pierre smiled and replied, "Yes. We can stay with my good friend, Professor Sager Miller, who lives there."

"Sager Miller? That sounds familiar. Isn't he a Maya expert or something?"

"He is, and he has a spacious, inviting house."

"The priest at Saint Louis, a famous professor, free wine, free food, and a chance of seeing a vampire? Hell, I'm in," asserted Lâmié. "If nothing else, it'll be a great story to tell."

"Can you meet me at the church tomorrow at around seven in the morning?"

"You got it, Father."

Jean-Pierre walked home through the fog-stew.
Did he sense a shadow figure following him?

CHAPTER 15

ANOTHER SEDUCTION

Jean-Pierre had left for New Orleans, and Xiaoqing had returned to the university for some research in the library, leaving Sager alone with his thoughts. He had replayed the night with Ophelia time and time again, and each mental echo moved his emotions further from guilt and closer to lust. He remembered the feel of her cool, smooth skin, her pert breasts and hard nipples, her long thighs, her hairy womanhood, and then he had to shock himself back to the reality of the terrible impropriety of the act that he had committed.

He only saw two choices.

First, he could do nothing and try to pretend that nothing had happened, but this option depended on Ophelia's silence. The second option was to find her and talk to her openly about the danger to them both should she tell someone. Each time that he weighed these options, he recalled her delicate doe eyes, her wide, round cheeks, her elegant nose, her puffy, engorged lips, and he wanted nothing more than to see her. He knew already which choice he would make; like a Greek tragedy, it had already been ordained by the gods.

That afternoon, he waited outside of her high school—it was an ornate, Gothic Revival building in the western suburbs of Ushaville. He felt like a pervert. He heard a shrill bell ring out its call for the end of classes. The front doors swung open forcefully, and an ocean of students vomited out of the opening. Boys were dressed in shirts and vests with ties, and girls wore blouses and checkered skirts of dark green. He stood casually among the parents awaiting their children and wondered how he would find Ophelia and be alone with her enough to talk. Her lithe form exited the building, and he knew, even at a distance, the shape of her body and face. As if she had expected him, she smiled coyly and walked directly to him.

"Sager. I thought you might come," she softly said.

"Can we talk, please, Ophelia? Somewhere private?"

She only smiled, took his hand, and led him away from the school. They reached The Fairie Realm Café, and Ophelia chose a table. Titania glanced at them and did not smile.

She approached their table, "Hi Professor, Ophelia. The usual?" she asked.

"Yes, please," answered Ophelia. "We'll have the usual. How have you been, Titania?"

"Well, considering the lockdown, business is slow."

"Lockdown?" asked Sager.

"Yes, Professor. Some of the Hatfields," and here she paused and looked Ophelia in the eyes, "have decided to shut down certain aspects of the town temporarily due to a Council issue. It's not very convenient for the *other* residents."

"Oh," replied Ophelia, "I am sure it will be resolved soon. The Council, in its wisdom, will see to it."

"Hmm. As long as the Council remembers that it serves not only itself but also the other... sorts... of residents, I am sure it will be fine. I'll be right back with your drinks," said Titania.

Ophelia was sitting next to Sager rather than across the table, and she hooked her leg behind his while taking his hand in hers. Her cool, pale skin was so smooth against his. Normally, he would have been mortified and concerned about how it appeared to Titania, but now he simply felt warm and safe and secure—he wanted to be with Ophelia, next to her, inside of her, a part of her. Her body was warm and comfortable and secure. Ophelia's womb was the source of his being and the only place he desired to be. Inside of her was the wisdom and meaning of the universe.

Titania arrived with their drinks and cast a quick, concerned glance at Sager.

"Professor, come and see me at the counter when you're done. I have some really nice *Pu'er* for you to take home and try."

Sager grinned sleepily and nodded.

Ophelia asked softly, "What did you want to talk about, my dear?"

Sager thought for a moment, but he could not exactly remember what he had wanted to talk about. What did it matter, anyway? Being there with Ophelia was what mattered.

They drank their coffee and tea, Sager staring into Ophelia's dark eyes as if in a dream. While they drank, holding hands, the four punks and the girl called Nancy, who worked at the bar, walked into the café and sat down across the seating area. Titania took their drink orders.

The one he knew was named Paul nodded toward them and said in a not-too-low voice, "Oi, look at that nonce."

"Yeah, she looks a bit young for him, doesn't she?" added the girl named Mary. "Who is that guy?"

Sager felt a surge of shame assault him, but as soon as he looked into Ophelia's eyes, the shame disappeared

Nancy replied, "I think he's some hotshot professor who just moved here. He works at the university in Glenville. That girl, I've seen her around before. I think she's a McCoy, and her family is rich."

"Does that mean she's, you know, one of *them*?" asked Mary.

Them? What did they mean by it? *One of the McCoys?*

"Probably," Nancy said. "Could explain why he's so enamored of her. They can sway you like that."

"Oh! Hell, poor guy. Could ruin his career. And there they go."

Sager and Ophelia stood up and left, her leading him by the hand.

She took him back to her house, and this time, her mother was not there.

"Mom won't be home until late tonight," Ophelia said. "Come with me."

She led Sager back to her bedroom and lay him down in her bed. She slowly removed his clothes, and then hers. She mounted him and rocked back and forth with an increasing frenzy until they both climaxed together. She lay down beside Sager.

"How do you feel about me, Sager?"

"I... I don't think we should be doing this. It's probably not a great idea... I... I could get in real trouble, you know."

"Don't worry, silly; I won't tell anyone. But how do you feel about *me*?"

"I love you; I want you; I need you. I can only think about you all of the time," he said.

"I know," she replied and giggled. "And you will love me, and me alone. You must get rid of your girlfriend. She is nothing to you."

"I must... I must get rid of Xiaoqing; I feel nothing for her now. All I feel is you, Ophelia. I want to be in you, a part of you," he replied.

"Very good, Sager. Break up with her immediately. And your friend, the priest? He's coming back to Ushaville, isn't he? Yes, I thought so. You need to get rid of him as well; don't let him come. He's bringing a friend, and neither of them can be allowed to be here. Do you understand?"

Sager stared into her eyes, smiled, and nodded slowly. "Yes, I will do what you want, Ophelia. Just please don't leave me. Please, never leave me."

"I will not leave you, Sager. Now, you are friends with that Indian, Beast Stalker, yes? The one with the bookstore?"

"Yes. Beast Stalker," he affirmed.

"Does he have something, some book or object, that is very special or very old?" she asked.

Sager nodded, "Yes. He has an ancient amulet that seems magical and powerful."

Ophelia smiled slyly, "Excellent, Sager. You are doing well. Where does he keep that amulet?"

"In the museum at the back of his bookstore. You can go see it."

"Oh, Sager, I cannot go into that bookstore. Beast Stalker has a special kind of power, and I cannot enter. So, I need you to take the amulet for me. Can you do that, Sager?"

"I... isn't that bad? To steal something from Beast Stalker?"

"You will get the amulet and bring it to me," she said in a cold voice.

"Yes. I will bring the amulet to you, Ophelia."

"Very good, Sager. I believe that deserves a reward."

She mounted him again and again, and they made love into the early evening.

CHAPTER 16

![blood drip illustration]

EMERGENCY COUNCIL MEETING

"Calm down and have a seat! We can only resolve this through discussion. It has always been this way!" shouted Asa Harmon McCoy—or Lorman, as he liked to be called—at Devil Anse Hatfield—Andy. "And let us never forget who started this feud so long ago. It was you Hatfields who attacked me, and you would have killed me if you had not been... interrupted."

"The past! The past!" shouted Devil Anse back. "Enough of the past. Enough of your tradition. We're taking this town, and then we're taking the world. It is already in motion, and you cannot stop us."

"In motion? You mean your little roadblock stunt? Shutting the town down? All that will accomplish is an angry human population. Do not forget, Anse, that, while we may be stronger, they greatly outnumber us, both here and around the world."

"So what?" replied Devil Anse. "They don't even believe in us anymore. They've forgotten the old ways. They don't know how to hurt us or kill us anymore. They'll be like bleating lambs at the slaughter! And when we take over, then we'll use the humans as slaves and as food. We'll breed them for our purposes. We won't have to hide anymore, won't have to hold back our true nature."

"Do you forget, Devil Anse, that we were all once human too?"

"Well, we sure as hell ain't anymore!" shouted Anse. Everyone around the table began speaking at once.

"Order! Order!" shouted Asa Harmon. "I'm still the chair, and this is still the Council! Now, everyone, please sit down, and we shall follow our rules of order."

At that appeal to order, Devil Anse grumbled but sat down.

"Now, McCoys and Hatfields, we must first discuss a rather urgent matter. You are all aware by now of the incident last night at the Pallid Horse bar. Several vampires, from both families, may I add, were insulted by the singer of that punk rock band and revealed their true nature. They attacked the crowd and the band, killing several humans. I have managed to charm the survivors so that they do not remember what really happened. As you know, however, a vampire charm does not last forever. The memory will seep slowly back into their minds. This is precisely the sort of thing that bolsters my view of our future. The more we lose control and reveal ourselves, the more likely they are to discover and eliminate us. We have enjoyed this happy balance for centuries here in Ushaville. Both we and the humans depend on it." When he saw several members of the council preparing to talk, he continued, "Wait, wait. Before you protest, we need to address something very unfortunate. At the incident at the Pallid Horse, a few humans with the mark of protection were killed."

Gasps of shock came from the entire table.

"Even if you disagree with me on our future, you simply cannot disagree with this, that the system of protection marks was created by our ancestors as a sacred law. It has, indeed, been the glue that has held together the balance that has allowed us to survive. We are all allowed to drink from the humans without protection. The Hatfields on the Eastside have chosen to enjoy that license, while we McCoys on the Westside have restrained ourselves only to necessity. Either way, it is a rule without exception, and our ancestors laid out a cruel but necessary consequence of violating that law." At this, Asa nodded to a guard, who opened the door to the meeting room. Two other guards struggled with two vampires who had been bound and gagged. They screamed through their gags and thrashed about, but the guards outnumbered them and were able to bring them in.

As the Council members saw who they were, there were various gasps and moans.

"Guards, ungag their mouths."

As soon as the gags were removed, the two prisoners began protesting and complaining loudly.

"Silence!" shouted Asa in a booming, baritone, authoritative voice, and they became silent.

"Titus Hatfield and Red McCoy. You are hereby charged with attacking and killing humans who had the protection mark upon their necks. How do you answer this charge?" asked Asa Harmon.

"Bullshit! This is bullshit, Asa, and you know it! You can't do this to us! Tell him, Uncle Anse! Stop him from doing this!" shouted Titus, but Devil Anse only looked down and remained silent.

"Do you deny what you did, Titus and Red?"

Titus frowned in furious anger, but Red looked terrified and had begun to shake.

"Maybe, Sir, Councilman Asa, you could have mercy on us? We're kin, after all, and Titus here, he's kin to Councilman Anse. Please, uncle! We're sorry! We made a mistake!"

"I am sorry, Red, my nephew. I take no pleasure in carrying out the law of our ancestors, but it must be done. Let us do it quickly and as mercifully as possible. Guards, lay them down on the table, Red first," instructed Asa.

"No, please! Uncle Asa! Please! No! Oh, please don't do this!" pleaded Red, but the guards held him down firmly. Asa produced an intricately-carved wooden stake, its handle encrusted with rubies and emeralds. Without hesitation, Asa raised it as Red winced and closed his eyes. Asa brought the stake down, and it pierced Red's heart true and swift. With a final shriek of horror, Red's body immediately disintegrated into a pile of dust. Titus watched with wide eyes, now too terrified to speak.

"Guards, bring Titus." They held him down, and Asa raised the stake, then plunged it into Titus' heart. He was instantly a pile of dust. Everyone in the room was silent.

"Let this, the law of our ancestors, be an example of the consequences for breaking our sacred laws. Humans with the mark of protection are to remain unharmed and untouched," said Asa gravely. "In any case, I have no taste for politics anymore today. We shall reconvene in three days. For now, Anse, I plead with you to hold off on your plans until we can discuss this again."

The Council members filed out of the room silently, leaving the guards to clean up the two piles of dust.

As the members all walked toward their homes, Devil Anse passed a dark alley and heard his name whispered. He looked into the darkness, saw Ophelia, and Glancing around to make sure he was alone, Anse ducked into the alley.

The two spoke in hushed voices.

"Is Sager charmed?" asked Anse.

"Yes."

"And did you find out anything about Beast Stalker? I've thought for a long time that this powerful menace we all feel is connected to him somehow."

"I believe it is so," said Ophelia. "He has a powerful, magical, ancient amulet. I believe that the amulet is the source of his power and the secret behind why we cannot harm the Indians. The amulet must be very strong. You feel it. I feel it."

"Very good, Ophelia. You did well. The Indians've had power over us as long as anyone can remember. But we can't go inside the bookstore. There's powerful magic that keeps us out, but I bet you can get Sager to fetch the amulet."

"I already told him so, Anse. I should have it soon, maybe tomorrow," she said.

"Excellent. As soon as it's in your hands, bring it to me. We'll figure out how to use it, and then, with its power for us, instead of against us, we'll be unstoppable. As a reward for your good work, feel free to stop by my house and select one of my slaves to eat."

She giggled and curtsied.

CHAPTER 17

JEAN-PIERRE AND LÂMIÉ ARRIVE IN USHAVILLE

Jean-Pierre and Lâmié ended up getting along very well on their road trip. They both shared a loss of faith in what they had thought were their passions; they both saw a lack of evidence for the things that they had believed in. Moreover, both of their shattered faiths had dealt with things unseen, things in the spiritual realm.

As the sun crept below the horizon and night draped her gown upon the world, they were approaching the outskirts of Ushaville. They passed the *Ushaville General Store,* whose owner, Red, had apparently taken a vacation because the windows and door were boarded up. They continued until the flashing blue and red lights of sirens appeared.

"Oh, this again," muttered Jean-Pierre.

"What's going on?" asked Lâmié. "Do I need to worry?"

"Normally, yes, but I have connections. Don't worry."

Jean-Pierre pulled up to the uniformed officer and rolled down his window.

"Good evening, Sir. Do you have a tattoo on your neck?" he asked.

"No, but I'm with Beast Stalker," answered Jean-Pierre.

"Oh, oh, one moment, please."

The officer went and spoke to a few of the others, talked on the radio for a moment, then returned.

"My apologies for bothering you, Sir. You're all clear. Who's your passenger, please?"

"He's a friend from New Orleans, and he's with me," said the priest tersely.

"Very good, Sir. Welcome to Ushaville."

Lâmié looked back at the roadblock as Jean-Pierre pulled away and headed into the town proper.

"Um, Father? What the hell was that about? A tattoo? And what the hell is a beast stalker?"

Jean-Pierre chuckled and replied, "You wouldn't believe it if I told you. Just stick with me, alright? They can't lay a finger on you."

"You mean they would lay fingers on me without you around?"

"Not sure, but let's not chance it."

Jean-Pierre pulled up to Sager's house, and they knocked on the door. Sager opened it just a peep, with the security chain still attached inside.

"Hey, Sager. This is Lâmié, the guy I was telling you about," said Jean-Pierre.

Sager just looked at them.

"Well, can we come in? It's been a long drive."

"You had better not come in. My house is not in good condition for guests," said Sager.

"What do you mean? Sager, you knew we were coming. Is something the matter?" asked a concerned Jean-Pierre.

"No, nothing is the matter. You just can't stay here. There are hotels in town."

"What? Sager, you're not acting like yourself. Please, let me help you. Are you in danger? Is someone in there with you, threatening you?"

Jean-Pierre tried to peer into the house but saw nothing suspicious offhand.

"You must go. Goodbye," Sager said curtly and closed the door.

"What the hell?" said Jean-Pierre. "That is certainly not like the Sager I know. I spoke to him just yesterday, and he was happy to have us stay with him. Lâmié, I swear, he's a great guy. It's like he was hypnotized or something."

"Hmm. Well, vampires can charm people and exert some control over them, but you still haven't convinced me that they exist. Look, let's just go get a hotel room. He might feel more like himself in the daylight hours tomorrow."

Jean-Pierre shrugged, and they drove into town. They found the main hotel on Unter den Linden and checked in. While walking up the stairs to their room, they saw Paul, the rude punk from the band, coming down, his hair freshly washed so that his Mohawk flopped down into his face and made him look like a Lhasa Apso. Paul stopped short and looked at them.

"Hey, you're the dude I saw at the café with that nonce the other day. What are you doing here?" asked Paul.

"Yes, I remember you and your friends. Looks like we are hotel neighbors. What do you mean, nonce? Who's a nonce?" asked Jean-Pierre.

"Your friend, the professor. Saw him hanging out with this young teenage girl, holding hands, being all affectionate, you know? Pretty sick stuff, dude. Pedophilia is not punk at all. Anyway, welcome to Hotel Hell. Might want to be careful out there too. Shit's hitting the fan in Ushaville."

"Oh?"

"Yeah, like vampires and shit. You might think I'm crazy, but don't say I didn't warn you. By the way, the hotel bar is open twenty-four seven. Heading there now. See you around, mate."

Jean-Pierre and Lâmié headed into their room, which was spacious, clean, and furnished with lovely antique furniture and some very nice original paintings on the walls.

"Fancy," said Lâmié.

"Yeah, nice room. But wait, I need to tell you. Sager is the professor that punk guy was talking about, and he has an adult girlfriend who works at the university. I've known Sager most of my life. He is not the kind of guy to cheat on a girlfriend, and he is certainly not someone who would cavort with underage girls. I would stake my life on that claim. It really does seem like he's under some kind of influence. And didn't you just hear that punk talk about vampires?"

"Yeah, but trusting the words of a drunk punk doesn't seem like the sort of proof I was looking for."

"Alright, alright, I understand. Look, let's get some rest tonight, and tomorrow we'll go see Beast Stalker and ask him about all this. He's a Cherokee man who is my friend."

"Sounds good," answered Lâmié. "Want to go grab a drink at the bar before we hit the sack?"

"Sure. Why not?" They splashed some water on their faces, combed their hair, and headed down to the bar.

For a relatively small hotel, the bar was beautiful—it had an ornate Gothic theme and a long bar of oak and marble. It was populated with people here and there, and at a table in the back corner sat Paul with his band of misfits, if he remembered correctly, their names were Mary, Gill, Matt, and Nancy.

"Oi!" said Paul, a bit too loud for politeness. "Over here, mucker! Come have a drink with us!" He waved over Jean-Pierre and Lâmié, who could not help but comply. "Oi, waitress! Get our friends some beers, would ya?"

"God, Paul, you're so loud," said Mary. Paul just grinned and shrugged his shoulders.

The waitress brought their beers, and Paul began introductions. "I'm Paul Junk Roy. This is Scary Mary Gambino, Gutter Gill Leblanc, Mucky Matt Moulin, and Nancy."

"Just Nancy?" asked Lâmié. "The rest of you have such, well, unique names."

Mary laughed. "Those are just our stage names. Call us Paul, Mary, Gill, and Matt. We're a band: The Gravediggers!"

"Nice to meet y'all. I'm Lâmié, and this is Father Jean-Pierre."

"What? A priest? Wild shit!" said Paul.

"I'm just a regular guy. No worries," said Jean-Pierre. "I take it from the Mohawks, piercings, and leather that your genre is punk rock?"

"Right on, Pops!" said Paul. "We did a show last night that went to hell, that's for sure."

"Paul!" said Nancy. "No need to talk about that *show* to visitors to Ushaville, right? Let these people enjoy their stay."

"To be honest, Nancy," said Lâmié, "we're not here on pleasure." He looked at Jean-Pierre, who nodded, so he continued. "The Father and I here have heard some things about your town. Seems things here have a reputation for being a little, well, *out there*."

"Oh?" Nancy feigned innocence.

"Yes. In fact, things are supposed to be a little out of the normal here, as in *paranormal*."

"I knew I recognized you!" said Matt. "You're the ghost hunter from TV!"

"Lâmié Chasseur, at your service. And I prefer the title Paranormal Expert, although I've pretty much given up that life for now."

"Well, you might want to take a refresher course," said Matt, "No need hiding the secret, since it's pretty obvious, Lâmié. Yeah, it's got some serious paranormal shit, Ushaville does."

"Matt!" warned Nancy.

"No use hiding it, Nance," he replied. "Look around. Most of the town's boarded up, and you can't go into the Eastside, or you'll get eaten. Lâmié, some vampires attacked during our show. They killed a bunch of people. We barely made it back here alive, and I think the only reason the hotel's owner hasn't ratted us out is that she's either human too, or just unaware. Anyway, Nance, I thought Titania said we were safe?"

"I mean, we didn't get killed, I guess," said Nancy. "Whatever magic Titania's got might not be strong enough for a whole bar full of angry vamps, you know?"

"Whoa, wait, Titania? Magic? Could someone fill me in from the beginning?"

And so, they spend the night drinking and talking about Ushaville. Nancy told them everything she knew, including about the tunnels and the ancient vampires down there. Maybe it was the beer, but by the time she finished, Lâmié had begun to believe her.

"Alright, this is all pretty convincing," he said, "but I need to see a real vampire before I commit. And let me tell you, if this town really is infested with them, then you're gonna need my help to get rid of them, or even to make it out alive."

"For now," replied Jean-Pierre, I see two objectives. First, we need to call Xiaoqing—that's Sager's girlfriend—and get her here. Maybe she'll be able to snap him back to himself. Second, we need to talk to Sager. I'm not sure if that means entering his house with force or even kidnapping him, but I've known him almost my whole life. That's not Sager. That's a brainwashed version of my friend."

"Right, well, maybe we should team up," offered Nancy. "I've seen enough horror movies to know that rule number one is *don't split up*. We're all staying in this hotel, so let's get your professor friend and his girlfriend here tomorrow."

"A good move," added Lâmié. "*If* we're dealing with vamps—and again, I'm not convinced yet, but if we are—then their powers, even their power of glamour or charm, are much weaker while the sun is shining. Paul, you said that you saw the professor and a young girl in a café, right? Yes, well, how was she dressed? What did she look like?"

"Black hair, school uniform, and her skin was paler than a witch's butthole."

"What does that even... oh, never mind," said Mary. Gill just shook his head and sighed.

"I see," continued Lâmié. "Let's say, just hypothetically, that the girl is a vamp who's glamoured the professor. In order for her to be active during the day like that, she would have to be *extremely* powerful. Most vamps burn up in sunlight. And, to be that powerful, she would have to be *extremely* old."

"Talking Middle Ages, Lâmié?" asked Matt.

"More like ancient Sumeria, like thousands and thousands of years old."

"Holy hell," said Matt.

"Actually, Lâmié, why don't you give us a little refresher course on vampires, in case we need that knowledge?" asked Jean-Pierre. "Just how much of the traditional lore is true?"

"Happy to, after you buy us another round of drinks." Jean-Pierre complied, and Lâmié began: "So, it's believed that the very first vampire was a man who lived in ancient Mesopotamia, in one of the earliest civilizations that we know. Sumeria is a good guessing point. The story goes that demons were bothering the people, and a sorcerer who practiced black magic banished the demons and saved the land. But what that wizard *didn't* tell the people was that he banished them by sending them into someone else's body, his enemy. The sorcerer then murdered the man, hoping to eliminate the demons once and for all. The man was buried, but three days later, people started seeing him around town at night. He would come from the grave and drink people's blood. Some he killed, but some he turned into others of his kind."

"You mean, a vampire is basically a corpse that comes back to life because a demon is inside it?" asked Gill.

"Exactly," continued Lâmié. "Now, if a vampire attacks you and drinks your blood, it will most likely leave you for dead. But, if it thinks you're a good candidate, it will drink your blood, but not to death, then force you to drink some of its blood, and then it will drain you completely and kill you. Three days later, you come back as a vampire. There must be that exchange of blood for it to happen. The three-day timeline is thought to be a mockery of the burial and resurrection of Jesus, which, of course, was three days as well."

"Keep going!" said Mary. "This is fucking fascinating! Like, do vampires remember their human selves, or is it just the demon inside?"

"Supposedly, a part of their former humanity remains, which means it is tortured as it has to live out the life of a killer demon for eternity."

"Alright, what about garlic and all that shit?" she asked.

"Good question," replied Lâmié. "As to that legendary stuff. Garlic will not kill a vampire, but it will ward them off. It's not because they have bland palates; it's because garlic has traditionally been viewed as a medicinal food that thins and purifies the blood. Since vampires subsist on blood, anything that purifies it would go against their vile and impure nature. The metals iron and silver can also wound vampires and keep them at bay, but they cannot kill them. Silver is seen as a pure metal, so there's that, and iron is a metal associated with the earth.

Vampires are earth spirits, right? They come from the earth. So, iron wards them off. Holy water from the Catholic Church burns their skin and keeps them away. Christian crucifixes cause them deep revulsion and pain as well. Salt works too."

"Yeah, but how do you kill one?" asked Paul. "Stake the shit out of them like in *Buffy*?"

Lâmié chuckled. "Three things will kill a vampire. The first is sunlight. From the most ancient of times, the sun was considered a god, a god providing life to humanity. Vampires are dead, so the sun is the ultimate force of life against death. Second, you can stake them in the heart. It's the heart because, of course, it's the center of the circulatory system, and they are all about blood. But again, they're earth spirits, and by staking them, you are using wood from a tree, an earthen symbol, and you are, in a sense, driving them back into the earth. The wood has to be ash wood, though. Third, they can be killed with fire. Fire has always been seen as both a destructive and purifying agent, like with metal ore. Let's see, what else. Oh yeah, they're cold to the touch and have no pulse, just like the corpses that they are. And as the legends say, they cannot enter a home without invitation. Notice I said *home* and not *house*. They can enter a building, but if it is someone's home and hearth, so to speak, they cannot."

"What about mirrors?" asked Mary.

"Pretty sure I can answer this one," said Jean-Pierre. "The girl you saw Professor Sager with was Ophelia. We had dinner at her and her mother's house the other night. She had no reflection in the mirror, though I am confident that she didn't see me notice. No reflection."

"Right," said Lâmié. "It's because mirrors reflect light, and as I said, vampires are spirits of darkness, so that light cannot reflect them. Also, mirrors have been seen as mystical portals to the spirit world for millennia. If this town really has vampires, and I am partially convinced, then we need to prepare for the inevitable. Anywhere that vampires have been in the world, in any age, even if they have tried to restrain themselves, they have always ended up assaulting all of the humans in their area. So, first things first. Mobility. Do we have a vehicle available besides yours, Jean-Pierre? No offense, but a two-door hatchback is not ideal."

"We've got a bloody van, but its locked inside a repair shop by the vamps," said Paul.

"Perfect," replied Lâmié. "We'll break in if we have to. Now, is there anywhere in this town where we can find supplies, like camping gear or things like that?"

"Bloody Army surplus store right next to the repair shop," answered Paul.

"Perfect! We're gonna have to armor that van and dress it up a bit. Alright, so tomorrow we'll get in touch with the professor's girlfriend and try to nab him too. We can meet up here at the hotel."

At this, they all exchanged phone numbers, finished their drinks, and went back up to their rooms. Jean-Pierre went to the bar to pay the bill, and the bartender, a girl with black hair, puffy red lips, and pale skin herself, whispered, "Say, I couldn't help but overhear you all. I wasn't eavesdropping, I promise! It's just that something with the acoustics in here, you can hear lots from behind the bar. Anyway, I think I can help you." She turned around and walked in front of the mirror behind the liquor and said, "See? I have a reflection. I know I'm pale an all, but you can feel my pulse if you want."

Jean-Pierre took her wrist. It was warm, and a pulse beat beneath. "Alright, I believe you," he said. "Now, how can you help us?"

"I have to close up here tonight. Let me find you tomorrow. You'll be in the hotel in the late morning? Can you come to the bar?"

"Sure," he replied.

"By the way, I'm Janine. Nice to meet you." They shook hands, and then Jean-Pierre returned to his room.

CHAPTER 18

THE BIG REVEAL

The next morning, Jean-Pierre called Xiaoqing.

"Oh, hi Jean-Pierre. What's up? Did you have a good trip?"

"Yes, thanks for asking. Listen, Xiaoqing, I need to talk to you about something serious, and I need you to just trust me. It's about Sager."

"Oh, God, is he alright? What happened? Was there an accident?"

"He's okay, but he's in some trouble. Please, please, just trust me. I can't give you details over the phone because you just wouldn't believe me. Please, can you drive to Ushaville today?"

"I have a class, but if Sager's in trouble, I'll get a substitute. I can be there in less than two hours. Meet at Sager's?"

"Um, actually no. Meet my friend and me at that hotel on Unter den Linden. I think it's called the Summer Linden Hotel. Please just trust me. I promise I'll tell you everything when you get here."

"I'll hurry! Please take care of him in the meantime."

"I will, Xiaoqing. Don't worry."

Jean-Pierre knocked on the punks' hotel room doors and was greeted with a symphony of snores, grunts, farts, mumblings, and complaints. Finally, Nancy opened the door to her and Mary's room.

"Nancy, good morning. Sorry to bother you, but I need some help today."

"No problem, Father. I'll get everyone up. Meet in the bar downstairs in, say, an hour?"

"Perfect," said Jean-Pierre, thinking of the bartender's offer from the previous night.

He left Lâmié snoozing and sneaked downstairs, padding softly along the hall and stairs. Janine, the bartender, was polishing glasses and cutting garnish fruit behind the bar, which was otherwise empty.

"Oh, hi Father!" she said and smiled. "Good morning. Bloody Mary?"

"Well, hard to say no. And how'd you know I'm a priest?" he inquired.

She chuckled a little and answered: "First, I'm from New Orleans, and last night when I heard you talk, I knew your accent couldn't possibly be from anywhere else but NOLA. Second, my parents are strict Catholics, and when I heard one of your friends call you Father and then your name, I Googled you. Priest at the Saint Louis Cathedral? Not too shabby."

He laughed and said, "Now that I hear you talk, I can tell you're a fellow New Orleanian. And judging by your accent, I'll guess… Garden District?"

She rounded her eyes and mouth in surprise and replied, "Dang! How'd you know? My family goes way back in the Garden District."

"Accents are a hobby of mine," he said while she made his Bloody Mary and handed it to him. He took a seat at the bar.

"Janine, you mentioned last night that you heard our conversation and could help us. I don't mean to rush you, but could you fill me in a little? Everyone else will be here in about an hour, and I'm not sure if you wanted it to be a public discussion."

"Sure, Father."

"Please just call me Jean-Pierre. I haven't been feeling too priestly these days."

"Sure, Jean-Pierre," she said and winked. She looked around to make sure the bar was still empty, then said in a low voice, "You're right that Ushaville is full of vampires. The Hatfields and the McCoys are all vampires. Now, I need you to vow to keep this to yourself for now, please?" she said and waited for the priest to nod his agreement before continuing. "Okay, thanks. Well, Jean-Pierre, some of us human residents are very aware of the situation, and we've formed The Resistance."

"Oh?" he asked. "Like the French Resistance against the Nazis?"

"Yep, but even more is at stake here. Follow me."

She led Jean-Pierre behind the bar and pulled on a bottle of Bombay Sapphire Gin. Part of the liquor display—a secret panel—opened to reveal a passageway made of stone. They entered, and she pulled the hidden door closed. Electric lights were illuminating the tunnel, which ended in a set of stairs leading downward. She paused.

"So, this hotel's the headquarters. The owner and everyone who works here is a member of The Resistance. It's an absolute secret, and the only reason I'm telling you is that I know I can trust a priest from New Orleans. Down those stairs are a few rooms that we use. One of them is an armory. We keep all sorts of anti-vamp weapons down there."

"Well, if you'll pardon the expression, hell's bells!" Jean-Pierre said. "Are you planning a revolution or something?"

"Not quite. See, our intelligence officers have reason to believe the Hatfields are planning something. Traditionally, the McCoys have wanted to keep law and order, keep stability. They believe that humans will turn against them and kill them if we find out about them; after all, we outnumber them worldwide by far. Now, the Hatfields want something else entirely. They want to rise up against humans and turn the world into a sort of vampire's paradise, breeding us for food and as their slaves. In fact, Andy Hatfield, real name Devil Anse, already keeps human slaves at his mansion on the Eastside. We think something's going to happen real soon. They've already set up roadblocks and locked down the town," Janine said.

Jean-Pierre was impressed with the detailed information regarding the vampire's plans that Janine had.

"Something else you need to know. There are miles of tunnels beneath Ushaville. It's where the vamps travel during the day to avoid the sunlight, how they get around town, you know? It's also a prison for their members who break the code of the tattoo mark of protection." She pulled up her dark hair and showed him the mark on her neck. "Vampires who attack a human with the mark are put into prison down there and then executed. The tunnels are also where they put vampires who are so old that they can barely function anymore, their ancestors sort of. They keep them fed and alive, and sometimes they wake them up. We think the Hatfields are going to revive them for their attack."

Those must be the vampires from the guys' tale last night, he thought. Just the thought of hundreds of ancient vampires waiting to be awakened gave him chills.

"Jean-Pierre, you'd be an invaluable asset to The Resistance. I can tell you believe me, and it sounds like your friend, the professor, is already enchanted by Ophelia. Don't let her innocent schoolgirl look fool you. She's one of the oldest vampires here. Her family comes from ancient Sumeria and came to the New World to live among the Maya. She's several thousand years old and is one of the few vamps in town powerful and old enough to be able to move around in the sunlight, as long as she shades herself with dark clothing. There's no doubt that she has the power to control your professor friend. She's also extremely manipulative and plays the Hatfields and McCoys against one another without them even realizing it, and it's hard to fool a vampire. You really need to bust your friend out of his house during the day today. The vamps sleep in the day and come alive at night when they're the most powerful.

"Wait," said Jean-Pierre. "If she's thousands of years old, how is she a McCoy? That family's not that old!"

"She just assumes the name to fit in. Everything about her is deceptive. It's how she operates. It's all an illusion. Now, ff you can get the professor to the hotel today, and anyone else you think needs to be a part of your group, then we can protect you. The hotel is under powerful, ancient fairy magic, and the vampires cannot enter.'"Fairies are real, too?" asked Jean-Pierre in disbelief.

"Yep, and you've already met one. You know Titania, the owner of The Fairie Realm Café?"

"You're kidding!"

"Nope. Haven't you noticed how calm and safe you feel in the café? Doesn't she seem almost unnaturally slim and lithe and perky? Like the hotel, it's one of the places in town that the vamps can't enter because of her strong fairy magic."

"Normally, I would walk away and say you are full of it, but since I know vampires are real, it's not exactly a huge leap of logic to accept that fairies are, too. Alright, I have to ask. What about the Cherokee Indians around here?" He was thinking of Beast Stalker's glowing amulet.

"Very observant, Jean-Pierre. The Indians also have some sort of ancient magic that repels vampires. In fact, the vampires fear the Indians. The Resistance believes the Indians hold some sort of magical object somewhere that's the source of their power."

Jean-Pierre nodded. "Alright, this is a lot to take in at once, but I believe you. So, the fairies are sort of neutral, I take it, very protective of the forces of good. The Indians are true warriors against the vampires and also keep them at bay. And the human residents?"

"Those of us who grew up in Ushaville or have lived here for many years are given the tattoo mark of protection. The rest of the human population is blissfully unaware of any of this and are fair game for feeding. Ushaville has an unusually high number of *missing persons* every month, but since we have no official police force, no one is the wiser."

143

"I see. I see. Alright, so if the Hatfields plan an uprising, I'd be morally remiss not to join in the fight against evil."

"I knew I could count on you, Jean-Pierre. All of your friends can join in the fight, although I can't tell them about The Resistance just yet. Come, let me show you our armory."

They descended the steps and turned into a large chamber on the left. Jean-Pierre gasped.

Every wall was racked with weapons of all sorts. There were military rifles converted to shoot wooden stakes; real pistols that shot cartridges of holy water; fully-automatic machine guns that were loaded with wooden stakes as ammunition. There were real Army grenades that, as Janine explained to him, had been rigged to explode shrapnel of mini crucifixes, and others that exploded holy water; there were body armor sets and helmets covered in garlic and crucifixes; there was even a Bazooka that shot shells filled with holy water. He was maazed as Janine led him around and explained all of the weapons and armor to him.

"Oh. My. God," said Jean-Pierre. "This is better than the Army! Are all of these converted to hunt vampires?"

"Yep. The Resistance has been in Ushaville under this hotel since the vampires arrived here and set up the town. At first, this armory held stakes and vials of holy water, but as technology progressed, so did our weapons. Now we're pretty advanced, as you can see."

"I mean, how could any vampire possibly hope to stand against you with all of this?"

"Well, Jean-Pierre, you're forgetting something. Vampires have superhuman strength, speed, and agility. To even use these weapons against them, you have to catch them before they see you firing, or they can likely run out of the way. Enough of them, and we'd lose."

"I see. So, you need weapons, numbers, and a great strategy to stand a chance," Jean-Pierre reasoned.

"Short of dropping a nuclear bomb filled with holy water on Ushaville, yes."

"How many are in the Resistance?" he asked.

"Right now, about ten, including me. Our numbers have waxed and waned over the years. Even humans who know about all of this and have the mark of protection are scared to fight back or to even be discovered. If Devil Anse or Asa Harmon found out about us, there's no doubt that they would execute us immediately."

"So, I guess it's only fairy magic that keeps this a secret?"

"Correct. Like I said, fairy magic and Indian magic are potent against the bloodsuckers."

"Thank you for opening up to me. I don't know how this situation with my professor friend will go, but I have to imagine that Ophelia will find out about us. If that happens, then what's to stop the Hatfields from beginning their uprising?"

"Nothing. That's why I wanted you to know that we have your back. Now let's go back upstairs before your friends get here."

Once Paul, Mary, Gill, Matt, Nancy, Jean-Pierre, and Lâmié gathered at a table, Jean-Pierre began speaking. "Alright, so here's the plan. I have insider information that the vampires are planning an uprising very, very soon. I can't say how, but trust me. I suggest that Lâmié and I go get Sager, the professor. We'll use force if we have to. His girlfriend Xiaoqing is coming to meet us here at the hotel after a while; I just talked to her, and she'll be here in another hour or so. While we do that, why don't you guys try to get your van out? Even if it means smashing the window, you have to do it. Remember, the vast majority of vampires can't go out in sunlight. I doubt anyone will stop you, and you said that the repair shop is not on a main street. Just try not to garner too much attention. Drive the van back to the hotel's underground parking. It will be safe here; trust me. But before you come back, you should break into the Army surplus store and get, pardon my language, as much shit as the van can hold. Think things that we can armor the van with, things that will keep the vamps away, things that will allow the van to bust through barriers and that sort of thing."

"Fucking A-Team! Bloody right!" said Paul, causing Mary to roll her eyes and facepalm herself. Matt yawned. "Can we get that dude who looks like Joey Ramone?"

Lâmié chuckled and said, "Paul, remember what we're dealing with here. These are ancient creatures, reanimated corpses filled with demons. It only sounds fun until they fight back. They are super-fast and strong. They could probably lift that van and toss it into the air, so please try to get some heavy-duty things. You might also check the repair shop for spare metal parts, and definitely get a gas welder! I already have some ideas about what to do. I mean, Mary, I assume you are alright with your van being modified?"

"Hell, vampires are real. What do I care about vans anymore?" she said. "Guys, we can do this. Nance, you coming along?"

"I'm with you guys now. After all this is over, you might need a roadie," said Nancy, causing Mary to laugh.

"If we survive this shit town, hell, you can be our manager," said Mary.

"Everyone has their task?" asked Jean-Pierre. Everyone looked around at one another and nodded, then they all left the hotel and entered the town.

CHAPTER 19

TEAMING UP

"**O**pen up, Sager! It's your friend, Jean-Pierre. Come on, buddy. Talk to me."

Lâmié, holding a pair of heavy steel-cutters, stood to the side of Jean-Pierre so as not to spook Sager, and to be hidden from Sager's view. They could hear footsteps approaching the door from inside the house, and Jean-Pierre nodded to Lâmié.

As the day before, Sager opened the door and kept the security chain attached so that the door could only open a small bit. Jean-Pierre quickly wedged the door open with his shoe, and Lâmié leaped onto the scene. He deftly used the steel-cutters to make quick work of the chain, which snapped in half and fell to the floor. As gentle as possible, Jean-Pierre forced the door open, and they both stepped inside.

"What are you doing?" yelled Sager. "You can't be in here! She— not… you must go!"

Jean-Pierre covered his nose with his hand. The house stank of rotting food and filth. Sager had grown stubble, and his hair had become wild and unkempt. He wore a white T-shirt and some ragged jean shorts and was barefoot. Used dishes and bowls sat unwashed on the furniture, and dirty laundry carpeted the floor. A roach frantically skittered across the living room.

"Sager, are you alright? Do you need help? You've fallen apart pretty quickly, man" asked Jean-Pierre.

"Help? No! Do not need. All I need is her. Leave me alone! She will come later tonight! Go away!" he shrieked.

"Sager, please come with us to the hotel. You are among friends there, and Xiaoqing will be there," said Jean-Pierre warmly.

"No! No friends! Leave! I want to be alone until she gets here!"

Jean-Pierre frowned, looked at Lâmié, and nodded. He said, "Sager, I apologize in advance for this. It's for your own good, buddy."

Like a Scooby-Doo cartoon, Lâmié threw a piece of netting over Sager, and Jean-Pierre, against Sager's thrashing and screaming, tied him up with a rope. He picked up Sager's torso, and Lâmié grabbed his legs. They carried him out of the front door, then threw him in the trunk of Jean-Pierre's car. Quickly glancing about to make sure no one saw, they zoomed off to the hotel.

Across town, the punks and Nancy had slinked down the sidewalk, sticking to the shadows and cover or storefront awnings. Fully aware of the probability that the vampires were looking for them in particular, after the debacle at the Pallid Horse, they remained silent and moved stealthily. Nancy tapped Mary on the shoulder and pointed down the street. They all stopped and looked—the repair shop's front gate was open, and someone was walking around, picking up tools and arranging things. Given it was daylight, and the man was the opposite of thin and pale, they assumed he was a human.

"What the hell are we gonna do?" asked Mary.

"We have to get in there," answered Nancy. "We can wait him out, but he could be in there all damn day. The shop's too small to sneak around in without him seeing us."

"I've got a bloody good idea," Paul chimed in. "Let's knock him on the head with a wrench and get our damn van back. Fuckers stole it."

"To be quite serious, if I may," added Gill, "Paul's plan, as primitive as it may seem, might be our only chance. We absolutely have to get the van and our supplies and get back to the hotel quickly. I'm pretty sure we're wanted people in this town, and if we are even spotted, it's the end of us. We don't have to kill the bloke. He looks human. Maybe just a little knock on the head to put him out, then tie him up, get supplies, then get the hell back. We can split up. How about Paul and I take the van, and you three break into the Army surplus shop and stock up. We'll back the van in; you load up all the crap, and then we speed off to the hotel."

Everyone looked at everyone else, then nodded.

"It's a plan, then," continued Gill. "Wait until we knock him out, then just break the store's windows. There is likely an alarm, so we need to do this quickly. Think of it as our first heist!"

"Pretty exciting, to be honest," added Matt. "I need the exercise anyway. I'm tired as shit."

"You got, like, twelve hours of sleep last night, Matt! What more do you need?" said Nancy.

"Wait, wait," said Paul with a mischievous grin. "How do you know about Matt's sleep last night? Is that where you snuck off to, Matt? You dog!"

Nancy blushed, and Matt said, "Bite me. Mind your own. Let's do this before we're all drained of blood."

They hugged the brick wall of the shop, then stopped just short of the gate. They peaked inside and noticed that the man was bent over a cash register, counting money and making entries into the accounting books. Matt, Mary, and Nancy tiptoed across the opening and toward the Army surplus store next door. Matt picked up a heavy stone and nodded at Gill, who then nodded at Paul.

Gill and Paul quietly crept across the garage's cement floor. Paul found a heavy torque wrench and silently picked it up. They padded softly to the man. Paul raised the wrench and said, "Good morning, bastard!" the man started and turned around, but it was too late: Paul brought the wrench crashing across the side of the man's head, who immediately crumpled to the ground.

"Jesus, Paul! We're not trying to kill the poor bastard!" said Gill.

"He'll be fine. Hurry and tie his ass up before he comes to!" Gill found some rope, and they tied the man up tight then stuffed an oily rag into his mouth as a gag.

"Matt, now!" shouted Gill as he ran to the keyboard and found the keys to the Microbus.

Matt heaved the rock through the window of the Army surplus store, shattering it to bits. Instantly, a loud siren blasted their eardrums.

"Shit!" cried Matt. "Hurry, girls! Take anything you can!"

They rushed into the store and ran around, quickly taking in the layout of the merchandise. Suddenly the siren stopped.

"What's the hurry?" boomed a voice from the back of the store. All three of them froze.

"Come now," said the deep voice. "Why rush? Let's have some tea. It would be quite rude of me not to be hospitable, would it not?"

149

Matt, Nancy, and Mary huddled together in an aisle, and they saw a dark shadow moving down the cross-aisle. When the shadow's maker appeared, it was a short but muscular vampire. His skin was blue-pale, and his fangs had extended and were borne.

"Oh, uh… we were just leaving," said Matt in a shaking voice.

"No, you were not," said the vampire. The three felt an invisible force rooting them to the spot they stood on. "What you were doing was breaking into my store and robbing me. Add to that the fact that you are those musicians—and I use that term charitably—who caused the ruckus at the Pallid Horse the other night, and I'd say you were in some serious trouble."

"That wasn't us," said Matt. "Those were… um, other punk musicians."

"It's true!" said Nancy.

"Nancy? Oh, my," said the vampire. "What will your Hatfield employers say when they learn that you were helping fugitives rob my store? Oh, dear, this will not end well."

"And who the hell are you?" demanded Matt in a voice much braver than he was feeling.

"I thought you would never ask. I'm Joseph McCoy, at your service. I own this business and two others about town. I was here doing some inventory when, to my surprise, I heard the shattering of glass and the footsteps of three filthy thieves. Back in my day, you know what happened to thieves? They were hanged publicly if that made it that far. Usually, they were beaten to death by street mobs. You moderns have so much privilege."

"Um, is there something we could give you, Sir, or do for you, so you would let us go?" asked Mary. "We're very sorry, you see. We thought we saw someone in your store, and, well, we…"

"Silence," interrupted Joseph. "Don't embarrass yourselves with lies. I will tell you what is going to happen. First, I am going to enjoy a lovely taste of your blood, each of you, and then I'm going to call one of Asa McCoy's associates to fetch you and take you to him. Then you are at his mercy, and I can assure you that he has no mercy for human thieves, even those with the mark." He glared at Nancy. "If Asa does not kill and drain you on the spot, then he will throw you into his dungeon and use you for food for as long as he pleases. Either way, only death awaits you."

"Feed on us?" asked Gill. "You mean… drink our blood?"

"What else would I mean? I try to keep a balance in this town, you see. You've tipped that scale. Even I understand the principle of justice."

"Won't that turn us into vampires, or kill us or something? That's gotta be illegal."

"You are turned into a vampire only by drinking our blood and then being drained to death. I just want a little taste as my reward for catching you. After all, beneath my civility and stability, I'm still a vampire at heart. Asa will not even realize it. And if I drink a bit too deeply and one or two of you end up dying, he'll be none the wiser."

Gill, Matt, and Nancy tried to move but could not. His powers were great, and he smirked as he strolled up to them.

"Let's see, which one shall I taste first? Nancy, it would be poetic to do you first, given you have the mark. Then again, it might be tastier to watch you squirm as I drink the precious life from one of your friends. You," he said to Matt. "Has anyone told you you look just like Jimi Hendrix? Anyway, what does it matter? And you," he said to Gill, "look like you might not have bathed in a few days. You certainly smell that way. It's decided, then. Jimi Hendrix it is."

"No, please!" pleaded Matt, but he was supernaturally frozen in his place. Joseph took Matt's head in his hand, and effortlessly turned it to expose his jugular artery.

"Don't do it, you shit!" said Gill. "Fuck! Nancy, do something!"

"I can't!" she said. "I can't move!"

"And I thought the McCoys were supposed to be the nice ones!"

To Matt, it felt like slow motion as Joseph McCoy opened his mouth fully and exposed inch-long fangs as sharp as a tiger's. They were pearl-white and coated with saliva. Joseph lowered his mouth, paused for a microsecond, and then plunged his fangs deep into Matt's artery. Matt felt the sharp sting as they entered, then the uncanny agony of having such long, rigid things inside of him. He felt every nerve burning as the tip of the fangs poked against his vertebrae. He felt his hot, irony blood spew out in thick bursts with every fast heartbeat. He felt the suction as Joseph greedily slurped and guzzled it down while Nancy and Gill screamed. Then… he felt bliss. He felt happy and warm and safe. He felt tingling ecstasy in every cell of his being and wished only one thing: that Joseph would never stop, that he would drink him dry and let him fall into vampiric elation and euphoria.

When Joseph slid his fangs out after a few seconds of drinking, the feelings instantly disappeared, leaving him with a headache, nauseated, and dizzy.

"Not bad at all, Jimi Hendrix. In fact, it was rather tasty. I suppose I can sacrifice one of you and take the other two to Asa. After all, only two of you broke in here, right?" He chuckled wickedly and grabbed Matt's head again, but was interrupted by a roaring crash as the

Microbus burst through the window, sending exploding glass and metal bits everywhere and running right over Joseph the vampire, who had tossed Matt aside once he had seen the van approaching.

"Get in you fucks!" yelled Paul. They did not hesitate but leaped into the still-moving van. Paul turned the wheel and floored the gas pedal, sending the old four-banger into a circling series of donuts and knocking down the shelves. Joseph was slowly trying to push himself back up, so Paul hit the brakes, opened the door, quickly got out, grabbed a few supplies, got back in, and then floored it through the window, out of the store, and back toward the hotel.

"Holy shit!" exclaimed Nancy. "Did we kill the fucker?"

"No," said Paul. "I saw him moving. Remember? Only sunlight and stakes and fire."

"Well, if we weren't wanted before, we sure as hell are now!" added Mary. "Christ, Matt! Are you alright? Are you a vampire now? He bit him!"

"I don't think so," said Matt. "I feel like shit, but I'm still breathing. I think I just lost a good bit of blood. Remember? You have to drink their blood then die to become one."

"Well, we need to get you some first aid," said Nancy. "I'm sure the hotel has some."

Paul screeched the van into the driveway that led to the underground parking lot, sending the van a little into the air as it hit the speed bump. He slammed the brakes, and the van slid to a stop.

"Don't ever drive for Uber, dude! You'll get shit ratings!" said Nancy as they all climbed out and took the stairs to the ground floor.

They found the hotel bar empty of regular customers, leaving Jean-Pierre, Lâmié, Xiaoqing, Janine, and Sager, who was then tied to a chair with ropes and with a gag in his mouth. His pupils were large, and he was just staring into space. Xiaoqing was beside him dabbing his forehead with a cool, wet cloth.

"Well, what the hell happened here?" asked Paul eyeing Sager.

Janine saw Matt's pale face and asked, "Is he alright? What happened?"

"We need first aid, babe," said Paul. "He lost lots of blood."

"You don't mean…" she asked

"Yeah, he was bitten, but not turned into a vampire," replied Paul.

"Sit him down! I'll get him some water, an iron supplement pill, and a candy bar. It'll help his condition. How much did you lose, Matt?"

"Not sure, but he sucked for about ten seconds."

"Alright, then probably not fatal," Janine said.

"Gee, thanks," said Matt.

They took care of Matt, and then Paul asked again, "Yeah, so what's going on here?"

"Long story, but if Janine's alright with it, I'll fill you in," suggested Jean-Pierre.

Janine nodded. Jean-Pierre told them all about The Resistance, fairy magic, Indian magic, and kidnapping Sager. He left out the Ophelia part for now, to spare Xiaoqing's feelings, but he knew that he had to tell her soon. It was only fair, and it was an integral part of their situation. Paul and Nancy told them about their experience.

"Well, that settles it," said Janine. "So far, you've staked one vamp at your show, and now you've run over a pretty prominent McCoy. The vamps will be after you, and not just the Hatfields. You have to stay inside this hotel. You're safe here."

"We need to get to Beast Stalker, though," said Jean-Pierre. "It's the amulet. It has to be. It must be the source of their strength against the vampires."

"Too late!" said Sager, giggling like a madman. "No amulet! I stole it! Heehee! Ophelia has it! Heehee!"

"Shit!" said Janine. "Are you serious? Then we need to get Beast Stalker to this hotel fast. He doesn't realize that he's no longer safe in his bookstore! We have to do a recon mission and save him. I think Titania should come to the hotel, too. She's powerful, but her magic has its limits, even in her café. And after what happened at the concert and today, this can only end one way: the vamps will attack us. I'll get the other members of The Resistance here, too. Can we accomplish all of this today?"

Everyone looked around, and Lâmié said, "Yeah, or we'll die trying!" He was animated and excited. "Jean-Pierre and I will go fetch Beast Stalker."

"And I'll get Titania," added Nancy. I know a tunnel that leads to her café from here. It's pretty old, and I think it's abandoned or forgotten by the vamps."

"Be careful," said Matt. "Remember what happened last time in the tunnels."

"How could I forget?"

"I'll stay here and take care of Matt," said Mary, earning a subtle glance from Nancy.

"Xiaoqing, can you stay here and take care of Sager?" asked Jean-Pierre. She nodded.

"And I'll go prep the armory and pull out some weapons and armor," said Janine.

"Wait, were you able to get some supplies from the garage or the Army store?" asked Jean-Pierre, and Paul grinned boyishly.

"Did we!" Paul said. "Wait'll you see the shit we got!"

"Alright, everyone has their mission. Let's do this." They joined hands in the middle of the table, and impulsively, Nancy said, "Here's to the Resistance! One, two, three, kill the bloodsuckers!" They all cheered and then went about their tasks.

CHAPTER 20

MISSIONS

Jean-Pierre and Lâmié wove through several unpopulated back streets and then into the alley beside the tree that was The Old Ways Bookstore. Unter den Linden was full of pedestrians as always, but they didn't see any apparent vampires, so they quickly walked to the front door and opened it.

Fortunately, the bookstore was mostly empty, with maybe one or two customers browsing the aisles and stacks. Beast Stalker, behind the sales counter, as usual, looked at them and pursed his lips grimly.

"Father, hello," he said, then turning to Lâmié and introducing himself. "Lâmié Chasseur? I've seen your shows. I always enjoyed them. I am sorry you decided to stop filming."

"Heck, after this trip, I think I'll be starting again!"

"He knows then, Father," asked Beast Stalker, "about this town's quirks?"

"Yes. In fact, if you have a moment, Beast Stalker, could we speak in private, the three of us? It's quite urgent."

Beast Stalker nodded, then said loudly, "Dear customers, I'll be back in a few moments. Please ring the bell if you need assistance." He motioned for Jean-Pierre and Lâmié to follow him back into the museum, which was empty.

"Beast Stalker," began Jean-Pierre, "let's be completely open now. Lâmié and I know that this town is full of vampires and other supernatural creatures."

"I thought you would catch on," said Beast Stalker.

"There's something else. Brace yourself. Professor Miller has been charmed by the vampiress Ophelia, and he claims to have stolen your amulet!"

Beast Stalker's eyes grew round, and he immediately ducked behind the counter to the secret safe where he kept the amulet. The safe was open and empty.

"Oh, no! Oh, God! This is terrible! Chief must be told immediately."

"It's more than that, Beast Stalker," said Jean-Pierre. "I'm sure you knew or at least suspected this, but the amulet is the source of your people's power, and also the power that keeps the vampires away. Without the amulet, you're unprotected. And now that the town's in lockdown and the vampires are looking for us, you need to come with us to the Summer Linden Hotel. It's protected by fairy magic."

"I knew that the amulet was the main power keeping this town from total chaos. If it's in the vampires' hands, it means they have all the power. Yes, let's get to the hotel quickly. Who's there?" asked Beast Stalker.

"I'll fill you in on the way," said Jean-Pierre.

"And I'll call Chief on the way," replied Beast Stalker. He apologized to his two customers that something had come up and ushered them out, locked the doors, and then the three stealthily used alleys and back streets to reach the hotel safely.

Meanwhile, Nancy had descended into the tunnel that led to the Fairie Realm Café. The moment she began walking, the air felt oppressive and heavy, almost humid. The hairs on her arms were erect like nipples in snow, and the faint foul odor of rotten eggs slithered into her nostrils like a noxious gas—she instantly regretted taking the tunnel. She hadn't used it in years, but it had always been empty and neglected.

She stopped and thought about returning, but it would be too risky on the streets for her. Every vampire in town would be looking to get their fangs in her; moreover, the thick stench was coming from all directions, including behind her. She remained perfectly still. In the pure silence, somewhere down the tunnel, she heard a single drop of water fall. Then, she heard dragging footsteps, sliding across the tunnel's stone floor, like two feet thickly bandaged. The steps were uneven and labored. Something was in that tunnel with Nancy.

With a shaking hand, she turned her flashlight toward the sound, took a deep breath, then turned on the torch. She saw nothing in the flashlight's powerful cone of illumination but thought she saw a part of the wall move, and then she realized that it was not the wall—the *thing* there with her was the same pallid grey as the stone walls. It moved, and, like a chameleon coming out of hiding, it revealed its true colors. It was a withered, sinewy, ancient thing, full of death and dust and bones, staggering towards her. The thing was one of the ancient vampire ancestors that had been stashed away down there in some long-forgotten time in Ushaville's history.

She looked at her hands and saw that a small, insignificant cut had exposed blood to the air, and that had enlivened the hideous undead corpse. Frozen this time—not by vampiric magic, but by raw terror—she watched as if through someone else's eyes as the archaic vampire dragged its misshapen feet toward her, one tortured step at a time. She stared in terror as its bony hand reached out and clasped her forearm with its cold, dusty, bony digits.

"Leave her alone!" shouted a voice from behind her. The thing creaked its head up and looked, then released her arm and cowered backward. Nancy spun on her heels and shone the flashlight at the source of the voice to reveal none other than Lorman McCoy.

"Come with me immediately, Nancy," he said, and with such authority and power that she had no choice but to comply. She followed him down the tunnel and then up the stairs into the Fairie Realm Café, where Titania was bound to a chair with thick ropes, her mouth gagged. She glared at Lorman hatefully.

"Now, Nancy, why don't you have a seat? I would order us some tea, but I'm afraid Miss Titania is a little tied up at the moment."

Nancy sat silently.

"Well, Nancy," continued Asa. "I've heard some rumors, and I would like to know if they are true. A little crow told me that you and your punk musician friends started a riot at the Pallid Horse and ended up killing one of us. Then, I heard that you broke into Joseph McCoy's place of business and tried to rob him, ultimately running him over with an automobile. What do you say to these, Nancy?"

"I…" she stammered.

"There's honestly no need to say anything, as I know quite well that these things are true… Nancy, Nancy, Nancy. Has Ushaville been unkind to you? Has the Council not given you every privilege that we bestow upon humans? We gave you the mark of protection. We took care of your family when your father passed away. We even gave you employment and made you the manager of a Hatfield establishment. Is this how you repay us?"

"Sir, you don't understand. The show was an accident. And the rest… well…" Lorman nodded then sat in silence for a few moments. "Sir," continued Nancy, "could you please consider untying Titania? She's just a small girl. What danger could she possibly pose?"

Asa chuckled. "You think I don't know about Titania and her wee Fée magic? The only way I was able to enter this place was by convincing her to invite me inside. Now, here's what's going to happen, my dear Nancy. I shall take you tow to my residence and place you under incarceration. I shall invite your friends to turn themselves in in exchange for your release. Both of you are longtime residents of Ushaville, and while you deserve death for your insolence and opposition to the Council and my kind, I am willing to allow you to live in exchange for the lives of those newcomers. From the day that they arrived, there has been nothing but chaos and entropy and destruction."

"They won't turn themselves in!" said Nancy with slightly more confidence. "They're punks. It's against their nature!"

"Oh," said Asa, "they will believe that they are coming to rescue you, but I will have a trap laid, waiting to spring upon them. Now, a car is going to pull up to the front. You will enter it willingly, or I shall make you do so forcefully. The choice is yours. Either way, you will get into the car. It shall transport you to my residence, and I will handle you once you are there. In the meantime, I have a bit of sleuthing to do around town before night falls." Nancy just hung her head low. There was no resisting.

"What's keeping Nancy?" asked Mary to no one in particular. "It's not that far to Titania's place, and she's been gone half an hour already. I hope nothing happened to her."

"What could've possibly happened?" replied Xiaoqing. "It's just a tunnel there and back, right? And Titania's place is safe, she said."

Janine poked her head out from behind the hidden door and said, "I don't like the sound of it. There's no reason Nancy and Titania shouldn't be here by now." Mary nodded.

"By the way," asked Matt, "did you call your Resistance friends?"

"Yep," said Janine. "I got ahold of three of them. The rest are probably busy or out. Lee, Nikki, and Aurore will be here soon. When they get here, we can start bringing all the weapons up and check on the Paul and Gill's van status."

CHAPTER 21

AMULET IN THE WRONG HANDS

In the dark depths of an Eastside residential neighborhood sat a colossal mammoth of a mansion in the style of a Southern plantation house. Grimy columns held up a sloping, deteriorating roof, and several broken windows dotted the face of the sad walls. Shabby, former decadence decked the walls and halls of the black monstrosity, and so it fit the Eastside perfectly.

Ophelia stood at the front door and gave it several raps. It opened, and a human with a chain collar and in a butler's uniform opened it.

"Lady Ophelia, please come in. Master Anse is expecting you."

She shoved him aside like so much meat and stepped inside. She continued around the grand staircase into the parlor on the right and took a seat on one of the antique chairs. A puff of dust splashed up from the cushions. After a minute or two, Devil Anse walked down the stairs and noticed her.

"Ophelia. Welcome. May I assume that you have something for me?" he asked.

"Just as you requested, Anse. May I also assume that you will keep your part of the bargain?" She handed Anse the amulet, and he turned it over in his hand, looking at every aspect.

"Yes, yes, of course. This writing, what does it say?"

"No idea," she replied. "I don't think the Indians even know."

"How exactly do they wield its power? How do I use it?"

Ophelia just laughed mockingly. "No idea, old man. You should go ask Beast Stalker. I'm sure he'll welcome you to his shop. Now, I did what you asked. Do I get my pick?"

Anse was staring at the amulet, then after a second, said, "Hmm? What are you talking about?"

"Your slaves. You said I could have one."

"Oh, that? Yes, yes, go choose one. Anyone you want, but just one. You can use the third spare bedroom upstairs to feed if you want," he said while looking over the amulet intently.

"How delicious," said Ophelia. "I think I want a boy this time. Your butler is too old and ugly. Do you have something much younger and more beautiful, a male in good health?"

"Think so. Check the dungeon; there are a few new ones there still in training."

Ophelia skipped off to the basement stairs like an excited schoolgirl. She alighted in the basement, which, already made of stone, had been converted into a series of small iron cells, in which were incarcerated various humans who had either committed some offense against a vampire, or who had been without the mark of protection and merely unlucky. Ophelia slowly walked between the cells and examined each prisoner.

"Here! Over here! Help! Please help us! He kidnapped us, and I think he's going to kill us!" whispered a voice from the end of the row. Ophelia smiled and approached the cell. Inside was a man in his early twenties. He had blonde hair and blue eyes, and, like all of the prisoners, wore only a tunic so that Ophelia could see his rippling, developed muscles.

"Oh, no!" she said. "Who did this to you? What's going on?"

"The owner of this house! He kidnapped me off the street and put me in here. Same thing happened to all of us. Please, the keys are on the wall right behind you. Please let us go. I think if we work together, we can overpower him and escape!"

"How awful!" said Ophelia. "Oh God, of course I'll save you, you poor man!"

She grabbed the large, iron key off of its wall hook, then opened his cage.

"Thank you! Oh, God, thank you! I'm Adam. What's your name?"

"I'm Ophelia. Follow me. I know a secret escape passageway. I'll distract the man while you escape and go for help!"

He paused, a little confused, the very slightest bit unsure, but he finally said, "Alright. Everyone? I'll go get help! Hang tight. I'll hurry!" Ophelia grabbed his hand and led him up out of the dungeon. She feigned looking around carefully to make sure that no one noticed them and then led him upstairs into the third spare bedroom.

"In here! There a secret panel that leads to the trellis. You can climb down and then climb over the backyard fence for help. I'll go start opening everyone else's cages."

"Oh, thank you!"

They entered the bedroom, and Ophelia closed and locked the door.

"What are you doing?" he asked. "Where's the panel?"

"Oh, surely you can have a moment for a little fun before you go?" she said as she slid out of her dress and stood before him in all of her pale glory.

"I… what are you doing? I really should hurry…"

She approached him and slid her hand into his pants, grasping his manhood firmly as he moaned in surprise and pleasure. She pushed him back onto the bed and aggressively pulled off his clothes. It did not take long for him to lose interest in escape as she mounted him and rode him to an explosive finale.

"Wow. Just, wow. Who are you anyway, Ophelia?"

"I am death personified," she said, hissing and revealing her long, ancient fangs. Her smooth skin became wrinkled and rough, and her eyes turned red.

"What? No! Help! Help!" he cried, but to no avail.

When Ophelia walked out of the bedroom, fully dressed again and licking blood off of her fingers, she left behind a gory mess. Blood, flesh, organs, brains—these were scattered and smeared about the bedroom. Another human slave was standing in the hall, a young girl in a maid's outfit and a metal collar. She stared in terror.

"Clean that up, will you?" said Ophelia, continuing down the stairs. Devil Anse was still in the parlor, trying to discover the secret of the amulet.

"Still nothing? Well, thanks for the boy, at least. He was scrumptious."

"Wait, Ophelia. Listen. This amulet holds the key to human controlling us, or us controlling humans. If I can figure out how to use it, then it can give us strength and power as we have never imagined. But if it is in the hands of the humans like it was for so long, and if they figure out all of its power, they can use it to destroy us."

"Well, what do you expect me to do about it? I do not recognize the language on the amulet. When I was human, so very long ago, we spoke Sumerian, but our writing did not look like that. I believe that the amulet must be ancient, but as to how to use it or control it? How could I possibly know? If you simply keep it safe and apart from the humans, then they cannot use it."

"Unless…"

"Unless what, Anse?" she asked.

"Unless we get Beast Stalker here to tell us how to use it."

Ophelia cackled. "How do you propose to do that? And why do you assume that he will tell you how to use the amulet?"

"Humans tend to talk under torture. That's what I'll do. I'll send a squad to kidnap Beast Stalker and torture him until he tells us."

"Anse, I've lived a long, long time. Indians like Beast Stalker are powerful and proud warriors. He will likely let himself die before telling you."

"I'll make him wish he was dead, for sure," swore Anse. "And thanks for the amulet. You did well."

"My pleasure, and I do mean that literally," she said with a sly smile and then walked out of the front door.

CHAPTER 22

BEAST STALKER KIDNAPPED

"**L**âmié," said Beast Stalker, "I have some items at the bookstore, some Cherokee magical items. They're not as powerful as the amulet, but they are designed to keep away bad spirits, and I imagine that they'll work on some level against vampires. Would those help?"

"Probably," said Lâmié. "Indian magic's not a part of the traditional European lore, for the obvious reason, but we know that there are vampire legends and stories in almost every culture, as well as individual magical protections."

"I've seen them work against bad spirits before," said Beast Stalker. "Maybe I should go get them."

"It's too dangerous!" objected Janine. "It's almost nightfall, and once night comes, you can be sure that this town will be teeming with vampires, all of them looking for us."

"I can be very fast and silent when I need to be," said Beast Stalker. "It's an Indian thing." He smiled and winked.

"Well, I can't stop you. Please just be careful!"

"Should I go with you, Beast Stalker?" asked Jean-Pierre. "You know, the buddy system?"

"I mean no offense, Jean-Pierre, but I can travel faster and more quietly alone. I'll be back in under ten minutes," he said as he slipped out of the hotel and into the streets.

Beast Stalker removed his shoes and silently padded barefoot. He blended in with the shadows cast by the afternoon sun, scanning his surroundings carefully. If he were lucky, he would not even encounter another person on the way to the bookstore.

He had advanced all the way to the front door of The Old Ways when he heard the rumbling roar of a large automobile engine being raced to its limits. Instantly, a black Cadillac XTS with dark black tint on the windows screeched to a halt right in front of him. Out of it leaped three burly, muscular vampires wrapped in black clothing with black hats and dark, black sunglasses.

Beast Stalker was no slight man himself, and though he fought back with all of his might, he had no chance of winning a fistfight or a wrestling match against vampires. They shoved him into the backseat and held him down effortlessly as the car sped off to Devil Anse Hatfield's dark mansion.

He soon found himself tied to a chair in a side room off of the main dungeon. The room was made of bare stone with no furniture save his wooden chair and a rather disturbing table topped with several classic, metal instruments of torture. There were pokes, prods, blades, scissors, drills, and more. Beast Stalker felt nauseated when he saw this because he knew it could only mean one thing. Soon enough, Devil Anse and one of his thugs entered the room. Anse's long, gaunt frame contrasted with the other brawny, burly vampire goon.

"Hello, Beast Stalker," said Anse.

"Devil Anse Hatfield. You've really stooped low this time; I thought you couldn't be lower, but you continue to surprise me," replied Beast Stalker.

"That's some strong back talk for a man in your current position, Beast Stalker."

"I already know why I am here and what you want, but you won't get it from me. Once Chief and the others get here, you'll regret this."

"What?" asked Anse in mock surprise. "You need backup? What happened to all of that power and authority you had? It's almost like you lost your power."

"I know you have the amulet. I know you plan to torture me to make me tell you how to use it, but you can't use it. It was made to be used *against* your kind, not *by* your kind. It was made by a very ancient wizard to destroy vampires. What do you expect to do with it, even if you do get it to work?"

"Isn't it obvious? I'll be the most powerful vampire in the world. All humans, and all other vampires, will have to do my bidding. I'll be the emperor of the world."

"Devil Anse, you fool," replied Beast Stalker. "Day and night cannot dwell together. The amulet will not serve you as it serves my people."

"So you think. It will serve me, and I will be a god among men and vampires!" boasted Devil Anse.

"Dogs cannot become men, however much they try."

Anse spat in Beast Stalker's face. "It's easy to boast before torture. How's that for a proverb, you fool?" He turned to his thug and said, "Make him talk. I want the secret of the amulet. I'll be back in half an hour."

Anse walked out of the room. The thug grinned wickedly and approached Beast Stalker, who only stared the vampire in the eyes without expression.

"How should I start? Alright, let's do a classic. So simple, but so effective," said the brute. He took his shirt off, revealing a bodybuilder's physique covered in tattoos.

"I didn't know your kind took tattoos," said Beast Stalker. "I'd think you would bleed out."

"You're so funny," said the goon. "Let's see how you laugh after this." He picked up a long, steel poke from the table. "This little one's been known to bring the toughest warriors to their knees, and it's so elegantly simple."

Beast Stalker's arms were tightly roped at the wrist, and the circulation had been disrupted, so his hands were already tingling. The torturer grasped his index finger and slowly slid the metal rod underneath his fingernail, all the way to the bed. His entire body shook from the sharp, unbearable pain, and he screamed out involuntarily. The thug let the steel remain in place as he reached for a second one.

"All you have to do is tell me how to use the amulet, and I'll stop. The pain will go away in one second."

Beast Stalker glared at him but said nothing.

"Fine. Your choice."

He grabbed the middle finger and slowly slid the metal rod underneath the fingernail, tearing into the quick. Beast Stalker shrieked in pain and torment but refused to talk. One by one, finger by finger, the torturer slid the metal rods under each fingernail until Beast Stalker's hands, gushing with blood, looked like some sort of demented metal bird's claws. Still, he did not break down. With gritted teeth and shaking jaw, Beast Stalker hissed, "I'll never tell you, you son of a bitch! You'll be sorry for this!"

The torturer chuckled. "Pretty impressive, but they always talk tough at first. Let's see how you like round two."

He picked up a pair of steel cutter sheers. Beast Stalker winced, then pursed his lips and remained silent.

"I supposed you don't care that much about your fingernails. After all, they do grow back after a month or two. But you know, fingers don't grow back." He positioned the open sheers around Beast Stalker's index finger. "Now's your chance, fool. If you merely *agree* to tell Mister Anse the secret of the amulet, I'll leave your finger alone. After all, Mister Anse's goal is not to take your fingers. All he wants is to know how to use the amulet. Just say you agree, and I'll stop."

Beast Stalker only glared at the thug silently. The vampire sighed and closed the sheers ever so slightly, so that the sharp blades just barely cut into the skin, causing a few droplets of blood to fall.

"Boy, it's going to be hard to resist that blood. I can't say I've ever tasted Cherokee blood, but it's considered a delicacy in some circles. The more blood that comes out, the more likely I might lose control and just suck you dry. Now, let's try this again. Just say the word. Agree to tell Mister Anse, and I'll immediately stop."

Beast Stalker remained silent, mentally resigning himself to the most exquisitely intolerable pain, the sort of pain that takes all thoughts out of your brain, so that the reptilian brain stem takes over. The vampire squeezed the sheers a little more so that the blades passed through all three layers of the dermis, causing a stream of blood to hit the floor and begin to pool. Beast Stalker shook in agony but did not talk.

"Don't mind if I do," said the vampire, lapping the blood off of the floor. "Oh, yes. Oh, oh, yes. It's true. Your blood is delicious. It is blood for a gourmet. It is without equal."

"What the hell are you doing?" shouted Devil Anse as he walked back into the room.

"Mister Anse! Please don't be mad, Sir. I just wanted to taste a little Cherokee blood," pleaded the goon.

"Well? Is he ready to talk?" asked Anse. "Are you, Beast Stalker?"

Beast Stalker merely stared Anse in the eyes and refused to open his mouth.

"Ah, well, your choice. We can keep this up all night until you plead for the sweet release of death. You! Get up, you fool, and keep torturing him until he talks. Drag it out all damn night if you have to. And *do not* kill him. Is that clear?"

"Yes, Sir, Mister Anse, Sir!" said the torturer, and Anse stormed out of the room. "You heard him, Beast Stalker," said the vampire. "Well, I guess we continue." He pressed the sheers only a little further until Beast Stalker felt the blades clamp onto his finger bone. The horrible agony was beyond anything Beast Stalker had ever known. He could not think, talk, blink, breathe—anything. His entire being focused only on the pain.

"Talk! Tell me you'll talk, and I'll stop, you fool."

Beast Stalker just screamed and stared at the ground. The torturer shrugged and clamped the sheers down fully. Beast Stalker heard the crunch of the bone shattering and the soft thud of his finger hitting the ground. The blood was pouring out, and the vampire produced a small gas welding torch.

"Oh, that won't do. You'll pass out from blood loss. I guess we'd better cauterize the wound."

"No! Please! Stop!" screamed Beast Stalker, but the vampire turned the dial until the hissing of gas was heard, then clicked the spark, and a searing blue flame appeared. He swiftly pointed the flame at the stub of Beast Stalker's missing finger. The air filled with the smell of charred meat, and the Native American shook as the raw, exposed flesh, bone, and nerves burned and withered. He shrieked in unfathomable agony.

"Well, that'll take care of the bleeding! Let's see, only nine more fingers to go. I gotta say, Beast Stalker, I'm fucking impressed. No one has ever lasted this long. Now, come on, you really don't want to endure that nine more times, do you? Just talk. It's that simple. Just say the word, and I'll stop."

Beast Stalker spat in the vampire's face.

CHAPTER 23

DETECTIVE PACE BARILLO ARRIVES

Detective Pace Barillo pulled up to the Ushaville roadblock around noon. He squinted his eyes as the uniformed Council offer approached his car.

"Good day, Sir. Do you have the mark?"

"What? What mark?" asked Barillo.

"Oh, nothing, Sir. I apologize, but Ushaville is currently closed to the general public because of a gas leak. No one is allowed in or out at the moment. We hope to resolve the situation soon," said the officer.

"Hmm. I see. Would this help?" asked Barillo, pulling out and displaying his New Orleans Police Department badge.

The officer took it, studied it, and said, "Just a moment, please, Detective." He walked over to the group of fellow officers and showed it to them. They commenced a lively debate, waving arms and raising voices, although Barillo was too far away to really hear what they were saying. One of them spoke into a walkie-talkie and had a conversation with someone. The officer returned to Barillo's car and asked, "Detective, may I please inquire as to why you are in Ushaville?"

"It's official police business," answered Barillo. "I'm here on the request of the New Orleans Police Department for a murder investigation."

"One moment, please, Detective," said the officer, handing Barillo back his badge. The officer went once again to his colleagues, and there was a repeat of last time. The officer returned to Barillo. "So, the NOPD knows you're here, Detective?" asked the officer.

Barillo was smart and knew what to say: "Yes, they do, and they are expecting me to check in with them in a few minutes, and then daily."

"Very well, Detective. Good luck," said the officer, waving him through the barricade. Barillo thought it was odd that the officer had not offered assistance or asked questions about the investigation. He shrugged and drove into town, marveling at the Old-World, European charm. "This is in West Virginia?" He found Unter den Linden and happened upon the Summer Linden Hotel since it was the first one to appear when entering the town from the south. He parked on the side of the street, took his suitcase out of the trunk, and entered the lobby. Janine greeted him.

"Oh, hello, Sir. Did you need a room?"

"Single, please."

She checked him in and handed him his keys. "I apologize that the bar is currently closed due to renovations. Please let me know if you need anything."

"Shame," said Barillo. "I sure could use a drink."

"Detective Barillo?" asked a voice incredulously from within the hotel bar. Jean-Pierre walked into the lobby. "What in the world are you doing here?"

"Father? Oh, man. This is a coincidence," said Barillo, awkwardly scratching his forehead.

"It's alright, Janine," said Jean-Pierre. "I know him from New Orleans."

"Yeah, well, Father, could we sit down and talk, please, after I get myself unpacked?" asked Barillo.

Janine and Jean-Pierre looked at each other. "Sure, Detective, we can. Janine, he's trustworthy. And given the current situation, we need all the allies on our side that we can get."

Half an hour later, Detective Barillo joined Jean-Pierre in the hotel bar. Barillo looked around, especially at the punks, and raised his eyebrows, but said nothing.

"Detective," began Jean-Pierre, "this is Lâmié Chasseur. He's from New Orleans, too."

"Lâmié Chasseur? Wow, nice to meet you! I'm a fan, believe it or not. Not that I believe in that stuff, but your shows are really entertaining, and you explore some interesting historical places in New Orleans that I find fascinating."

"Thanks," replied Lâmié.

"Alright, Detective…"

"Remember? Just call me Pace."

"Ah, yes," continued Jean-Pierre. "Pace, how the heck did you end up in Ushaville? It's not exactly well known."

"No need lying about it. I'll confess. I followed you here, Jean-Pierre," said Barillo.

"Oh. I see. May I ask why?" asked Jean-Pierre.

"Alright, yeah. I wanted to see if you were connected in any way to the murders in New Orleans."

"What? You think I did it?" asked Jean-Pierre incredulously.

"No, no, not like that. But I did wonder if you had information that you hadn't told me. First, that one murder happened right outside your office door. Second, you left town pretty quickly after that. Granted, you came back, but I trailed you walking through the French Quarter in the shadow of the night. Then I saw that you were with Mr. Chasseur, and then you left town again. Gotta say, it's not that it's suspicious *per se*, but it's curious. I'm determined to solve those murders, so I thought I'd see what you were up to. There, Jean-Pierre. I fessed up. Are you angry with me?"

"No, not angry," replied Jean-Pierre. "A bit baffled, but I do see it from your point of view. You're doing your job. Well, Pace, I can tell you that, if it's information you want, you came to the right place. And I bet those New Orleans murders are related to Ushaville somehow."

"Oh?"

"How about a drink, Pace? You might need one when you hear what I'm going to tell you."

"What's your poison?" asked Janine.

"Whiskey, neat," said Barillo.

"A true detective's drink," said Janine with a wink as she trotted off to pour it.

After he had taken a nice, big sip, he said, "Alright, Jean-Pierre. Why don't you start from the beginning?"

Jean-Pierre told him about Sager, the amulet, Ushaville, and finally built his way up to talking about vampires.

"Vampires. Vampires. You mean, like the bloodsucking monsters?" asked Barillo.

"The very ones," replied Jean-Pierre.

"Why are you wasting my time, Jean-Pierre? You expect me to believe that?"

"I do not, not any more than I believed it at first. I'm telling you, though, they're real. They run this town, and I bet they're all over New Orleans. It's the perfect city for vampires, you know?"

Barillo sighed, pursed his lips in thought, then said, "Look, I know you're a priest, and I'm pretty sure it's a sin to lie. I dunno; maybe you're just mentally ill. I want to believe you, but... *vampires*?"

"If you can't accept that, Pace, then at least know that this town is in a big turf war, and things are going to get nasty soon," said Jean-Pierre.

"Oh, hell. What did I get myself into? Maybe I should head on back to New Orleans. Nice to meet you all."

"I wouldn't do that, Detective," said Janine. "They know you're here. They followed you here, no doubt about it. Once you're associated with this hotel and us, you're their enemy. Your safest bet is to stick with us."

As Barillo was about to respond, the shriek of tires pierced through the night, and one of the hotel windows shattered as a brick flew through it, nearly hitting Barillo in the head.

"Whoa! What the hell?" he shouted.

"There's a message attached to it!" said Janine, picking it up.

"That's some Mafia-style shit, if you pardon my language!" exclaimed Barillo. "What does it say?"

Janine read the note aloud: "Humans, we have Nancy and Titania at Asa Harmon McCoy's mansion. You have until first light tomorrow morning to surrender yourselves to us, or we will kill them. If you do surrender, we will not kill them or you, but we will exile you from Ushaville forever. Those are your only choices." A bloody fingerprint served as a signature.

"They have Nancy! Shit!" cried Matt.

"Bloody hell," said Mary. "What are we gonna do?"

"We're going to call the local police," said Barillo. "You shouldn't negotiate with people holding hostages. Let the experts do it."

"There's no local police force," said Jean-Pierre. "There's only a Council of vampires who run the town like the Mafia."

"They said tomorrow morning because that means we'll have to go at night. Nighttime's their time. They want the home-field advantage," said Janine. "Well, shit. That explains Nancy's absence. Where's Beast Stalker? He should have been back by now. I hope they didn't take him, too! He has no magical protection."

171

As if on cue, in an act of absurdity, a *second* car screeched down the street and threw a *second* brick into another window.

"Hell's bells!" screamed Mary.

"Oh God, oh no!" said Janine. "It's a note, but there's also… a *finger*. Oh please, no, don't let it be…"

She read the second note aloud: "I have the amulet and Beast Stalker. He's a brave man. Send a party to my mansion with the secret of how to use the amulet, or I will send more and more of Beast Stalker. He's still alive for now. Signed, Devil Anse McCoy."

"Oh, for fuck's sake," said Mary. "This is getting ridiculous."

"God, poor Beast Stalker," lamented Jean-Pierre.

"Not sure I believe you about the vampires, but I definitely believe you about the gang war," said Barillo. "What are we going to do?"

"I'll tell you what we'll bloody well do," said Paul as he walked into the room from downstairs, followed closely by Gill. "We drive the van right up to those bastards and take them out!"

"You finished rigging it?" asked Janine. "I hope the stuff I gave you helped."

"That," said Gill, "and the shit we stole from the mechanic and the Army surplus store. Yeah. It kicks ass! Everyone, come see it."

While Xiaoqing remained with Sager, everyone else followed Paul and Gill to the underground parking lot, and as they turned a corner and saw what was formerly the humble Volkswagen Microbus, gasps and exclamations echoed in the cement garage.

The van had been transformed into a vampire death machine. All of the windows were covered in metal bars, and a metal slatted ballistic shield protected the windshield. Armored skirts covered the wheels and tires, which were themselves adorned with thick snow chains. The roof had dozens of iron and wooden stakes bolted to it, pointing upwards. On the front bumper was a thick, metal bull bar, also with forward-pointing iron and wooden stakes. The side and back panels were covered with ballistic armor, all with the same iron and wooden stakes pointing outward. Every square inch of every surface was hung with metal crucifixes, and hundreds of cloves of garlic were wrapped around all spikes. They had also modified a cargo carried on top of the van. It had high, metal guards and was capable of holding a few people as gunners, like a howdah on an elephant, only heavily armored with little murder holes for shooting.

"Holy. Shit." Exclaimed Mary.

Janine laughed loudly. "My God! It's perfect! Holy hell!"

"Engine's armored too," said Gill.

"I… I don't know what to say," said Janine. "Well, at least we can get through the town without problems. I think this thing could survive a zombie apocalypse. Alright, the sun's starting to set, and we have to move soon. Everyone follow me to the armory. We need to get everyone kitted out. The other Resistance members should be here any minute, and then we can pack into the van and roll."

"Wait!" said Lâmié. "We have to name it first! The van!"

Paul chuckled. "Any suggestions, fuckers?"

They thought for a few moments.

"How about the A-Team van?" said Barillo. Paul gave him a Bronx Cheer with a thumbs down.

"The Vampswagen?" said Mary, and they all laughed.

Gill spoke: "How about… the Microbite?"

"Ha! Not bad, mate!" said Paul, and everyone agreed. "The Microbite it is!"

The other members of The Resistance never arrived, and Janine knew that it was probably because they were slaughtered on the streets of Ushaville.

While the others descended into the armory to kit out, Jean-Pierre stayed behind with Xiaoqing and Sager.

"Xiaoqing, I need to tell you something. I know we've been telling you that Sager is sick and feverish, but that's not the real reason he is acting so strangely. He's acting this way because he's controlled by vampire magic."

"I would never have believed that before, but now, everything I know, I believe it. Poor Sager," she said.

"There's something else you need to know. I'm sorry, but this might hurt," said Jean-Pierre.

"Oh, God. What is it?" she said.

"Well, you remember that girl, Ophelia?"

"Oh, shit. What? What did he do?" she asked frantically.

"Well, keep in mind that she's not really a teenage girl. She's a vampire thousands of years old. She's also very powerful and devious. Well, look, she seduced Sager."

"You mean they had sex?" she screamed.

"Wait, wait. He had no choice. He had no will, no volition," reasoned Jean-Pierre.

"Sager! How could you!" she screamed and burst into tears. He seemed unfazed and kept staring into space, muttering about the amulet. "Oh God, this hurts so bad!" She quickly walked out of the bar crying.

"Well, that didn't go well," said Jean-Pierre to the air. "Sager, sit tight. I'll take care of you, but man, we're going to have to contain you somehow when we go. We can't have you just wandering around Ushaville."

The rest of the group came back out of the secret door. They were adorned with ballistic armor and helmets, iron and wooden spikes, garlic, and crucifixes. They carried all manner of assault weapons that shot stakes, holy water, and salt and iron shot. They looked absurd, but every piece of armor, every weapon, had been honed to perfection for one purpose only: to kill vampires.

"We can't sit around and wait for the rest of your Resistance friends, Janine," said Paul, who had brought up some gear for Jean-Pierre, Sager, and Xiaoqing.

"Yeah, he has a point, Janine," said Jean-Pierre. "Also, we need to figure out what to do with Sager. He's useless in a fight while he's enchanted by Ophelia. And Xiaoqing's furious at him. We have to convince her to come with us."

"You don't have to convince me," said Xiaoqing, who had come back into the bar. "I don't want to deal with Sager, but I'm with you for the fight."

"We have to take Sager with us," said Jean-Pierre. "If we leave him here, he's vulnerable, and he might invite vampires into the hotel. He might also wander off into the town, and he's a sitting duck."

"Fine," said Xiaoqing. "You tie him up and deal with him. He's dead to me."

"Tie him up," said Janine. "Sorry to be cruel, but I know what we're dealing with. We need to put some armor on him, but don't give him a weapon. While he's charmed, he might use it against us. We'll put him in the van with us for his protection."

And so, they all managed to pack into the van. Everyone took a window if they could, and Paul insisted on driving, God help them all. On the roof station were Janine, Lâmié, and Gill. Matt stayed in the middle down below, still recovering from his blood loss.

The van squeaked on its light suspension, and it looked like a Toyota pickup filled with freedom fighters in the Middle East, but damned if that little Volkswagen four-banger didn't hold its own and power them up the ramp and onto the streets of Ushaville.

CHAPTER 24

RESCUE AND ABSCONDING

W here to?" asked Paul as he revved the engine.

"I vote Beast Stalker first, then Nancy," said Jean-Pierre. "We know for a fact that they are torturing Beast Stalker, and while Nancy is just as important, Beast Stalker could die soon if they keep that up. Everyone agree?"

Everyone nodded, gave a thumbs up, or simply said *yes*.

"How to get there, Janine babe?" asked Paul, and Mary grimaced.

"Alright, so Anse lives on the Eastside. It's gonna be *très* dangerous, especially since we're all wanted by the Council. Hell, every vamp in Ushaville probably wants to eat us now."

"Oh, gee, great boost of confidence there, Janine," said Barillo, and he winced.

Paul slowly started the trip, at Janine's direction, to Devil Anse's dark mansion. The streets were quickly filling with vampires, more than any of the team had ever seen before at one time. Dark figures—short and tall, thin and fat, men, women, and children—and pale faces that reflected the moon stared at the Microbite as it slowly rolled by. The length of their exposed fangs matched the height of hatred in their red eyes as they hissed. Several of them approached the van as if to attack, but the garlic and crucifixes worked, slapping them back with a flurry of flailing arms, hisses, and growls.

"Holy shit!" exclaimed Paul loudly. "The Microbite works! It really fucking works!"

"Alright, I believe you now," said Barillo with wide eyes.

"It works, but it also draws attention. Christ," said Mary. The vampires were formed into hordes of roving night creatures, becoming more and more agitated as the van rolled slowly down the streets and into the Eastside. The worn, sagging buildings, adorned with cobwebs and mold, no longer hid peeking eyes from behind torn, yellowed curtains. Instead, the inhabitants had come out to stare murderously as the Microbite continued toward Devil Anse's mansion. Several charged at it at superhuman speed, but the armor always repelled them.

They rolled up to the curb in front of Anse's mansion, and the van was instantly surrounded by a throng of vampires, staying just far enough away to not be harmed by the garlic and crucifixes.

"Well, what now? We can't exactly walk through them," said Mary. Soon, however, the mob parted like the Red Sea as Devil Anse Hatfield approached the van.

"Let them through!" he commanded, and the vampires, though hissing their antagonism, obeyed.

"Come out," Anse called to them. "You have my word of honor that none will harm you as you enter my house."

"I think it's alright, guys," said Janine. "When a vampire swears by their word, especially a very old one like Anse, they mean it. They take oaths seriously."

"Wait, let's think this out for a moment," replied Lâmié. "Alright, let's say we get inside his house. Then what? He has Beast Stalker in there somewhere, weak and injured after all that torture. What's our plan then? I'm sure there are more vamps inside. Are we going just to fight our way through, find Beast Stalker, then fight our way back out to the van? I'm pretty sure we won't survive that."

"True, true," said Jean-Pierre, "which means that our only hope is to negotiate. He took Beast Stalker for bargaining power, so he's not going to actually kill him for now. We know what he wants: the instructions for operating the amulet. Since I was the one who figured out how, I'll be in the most danger. So, I think what we need to do is distract him with some clever talk, maybe give him the wrong instructions, and while he tries to use it, we make a flank attack. Before any of that, though, we need to find out where Beast Stalker is. Remember, Anse has bargaining power in Beast Stalker, but we also have some pretty tremendous bargaining power in the secret of the amulet. He lusts after it. He's not going to kill us all and risk losing the secret of the amulet forever. So, let's go in armored, but try to find a point in time to rescue Beast Stalker and fight back. As for reaching the van, I disagree with Lâmié, no offense, buddy. But with these armored suits, we may not be able to destroy them in battle, but we will be able to at least stave off their attacks long enough to get back into the van. Someone has to stay in here with Matt and the Professor, though. They're in no state to come with us," said Jean-Pierre.

"I'm fine," interjected Matt. "I feel fine. I'll go."

"I'll stay in the van with Sager," offered Xiaoqing. "I'm pissed at him right now, but I don't want him to die."

"Father, I mean... your plan is as good as any, I guess," said Janine. "We have to do something."

"Are you coming, friends? It'd be really rude to refuse an invitation to my home," called out Anse mockingly.

"We're coming, Anse," shouted Janine. "You just make sure your bloodsucking friends stand down, or you'll be sorry!"

Anse chuckled, then simply bowed and waved his hand in the manner of a servant ushering his betters in a specific direction.

"Hell's bells, let's do this," said Paul, as he carefully opened the driver's door, exited, then stood up. The vampire mob stayed back for the moment. "Um, guys? Don't make me stand out here alone!"

The others followed suit, cautiously exiting the van and then standing in a group on the sidewalk. Moving together, like a Roman military tortoise-shell formation, and all in armor and carrying their weapons, they proceeded step by step up the path leading to the front door, where Devil Anse Hatfield stood with a smug smile that barely covered his extended fangs. He ushered them inside of his mansion of morbidity and gruesomeness, and into the grand parlor.

"Set a spell, as we say in West Virginia. You are my guests," said Anse.

"We're not here for parlor games, Anse. You have Beast Stalker, and we want him," said Jean-Pierre.

"Well, Beast Stalker's a little tied up at the moment," he said, chuckling.

"Where is he, Anse?" asked Janine.

"Janine? Oh, dear. You've bitten the hand that feeds you. I won't forget your betrayal. When we take over, and we will, I'll make sure you suffer especially long before death."

"Don't care, not scared," she replied. "Take us to Beast Stalker."

"Oh? Such a demanding voice. What've you got to offer me for his release?" demanded Anse.

"How about we'll agree not to kill you?" said Janine. Anse only laughed heartily.

"If you think you can even lay a finger on me or my household, you're very mistaken. I can think of something I want, though," replied Anse. They heard a scream of pain coming from the basement.

"Beast Stalker!" cried out Jean-Pierre. "We're coming for you!"

"Alright, so now you know where he is," said Anse. "Tell you what. I'll make a deal with you. You tell me how to use the amulet, and I'll let Beast Stalker go, and I'll let you live."

"Not gonna happen," said Janine. "Why would we give you all that power?"

"Hmm. Well, maybe after you take a look at Beast Stalker, you'll change your minds. Follow me," said Anse as he led them down the stairs and into his basement dungeon. They all gasped when they saw Beast Stalker.

Still bound to his torture chair, the Cherokee was missing three fingers, slathered in blood and vomit, with bright-red lash marks all over his back and stomach, and all fingernails and toenails were missing.

"Beast Stalker! What did they do to you? You sons of bitches!" yelled Jean-Pierre. "Let him go, you wicked creatures of the night! I command it in the name of Jesus Christ!"

At that name, the torturer and Devil Anse hissed and turned their heads away.

"Say that name again, and I'll personally rip your guts out right here," said the torturer.

"Stop torturing him! He's on death's door!" said Jean-Pierre.

Beast Stalker, blood dripping from his mouth, managed to utter, "I'll... never... give... In. Kill me... I'll never talk!"

"Torturer," instructed Anse, "stop for a while. Give him some water and food, and dress his wounds. Now that they've seen him, they might be ready to make a deal. Everyone, back upstairs."

Back in the grand parlor, Anse said, "Now, let's talk. My torturer's a real pro. He can keep Beast Stalker alive for several more days, so it's simple. Tell me how to use the amulet, and I'll let you and him go right now. Keep on not telling me, and I'll make him scream for you some more."

"Enough!" said Jean-Pierre. "I'll tell you. I'll tell you! Bring Beast Stalker up right now. Dress his wounds, and then I'll tell you."

"Good choice, priest," said Anse. "And I'll do you one better. My kind can speed up the healing process. Torturer! Bring him up now!"

The muscular man lifted Beast Stalker over his shoulder as if he were a feather, walked up the stairs, and laid him down on the dusty

Victorian sofa. Anse used a sharp fingernail to cut his own wrist, then held his wrist over Beast Stalker's mouth.

"Wait!" shouted Janine. "What the hell are you doing?"

"Our blood heals," answered Anse.

"You're going to turn him into a vampire!" she replied.

"Actually," said Lâmié, "it won't. Remember? He has to drink the vampire's blood, then die and rise again, and the vampire has to drink his blood before all that. There *is* evidence that a vampire's blood can speed up the healing process, according to my research."

Beast Stalker groaned, nearing unconsciousness.

"Fine, but if this is a trick, you're dead, Devil Anse," warned Janine.

Anse held his wrist back over Beast Stalker's mouth and let three drops of blood fall onto his tongue. The Native American's swallowing reflex took them down his throat, and in a matter of seconds, Beast Stalker opened his eyes. His wounds had already begun to close and heal, and his severed fingers began to grow back.

"It's true! I'd always heard about it, but it's true! Fascinating," muttered Lâmié.

"I can keep taking him to death's door, then healing him, then torturing again for years if I have to. Now, priest, what's the secret of the amulet?"

"Don't tell him, Jean-Pierre... I'd rather die..." said Beast Stalker weakly.

"Beast Stalker, I can't possibly let you continue to suffer like this. Devil Anse is right that he can repeat this cycle indefinitely. It will drive you mad with pain and torment and false hope." Beast Stalker, too weak to reply, said nothing. "Just a moment, Anse, just a moment," said Jean-Pierre. He turned to his friends, and they huddled like a football team while Jean-Pierre quietly consulted them. He turned back around and said, "Fine. Very well. I'll tell you the secret of the amulet, Anse, but you have to let Beast Stalker go first. You have to let him come to us right now."

"Sure thing," said Anse. "After all, I can reach you all in less than a second if I want to. Go on, Beast Stalker. You, help him up," he said to one of his human slaves, who assisted Beast Stalker in standing up and hobbling over to the group. "There. I kept my word. Now, priest, how do I use the amulet?" asked Anse.

"You have to rub it between your hands," answered Jean-Pierre.

"Don't treat me like I'm stupid, priest. I've been handling for hours. Now, you will either tell me the truth, or I will kill you now."

Jean-Pierre sighed and replied, "The language on it. You have to read it aloud."

"Oh? And what language is it?"

"It's an ancient lost language. No one knows the name of it."

"Then how am I supposed to read it? Don't you lie to me, priest, or I'll kill you all right now!"

"I translated it. I used my knowledge of similar ancient languages to translate it," said Jean-Pierre.

"Then what's it mean in English?" asked Anse.

Jean-Pierre recited his translation: "Seven demons from the land, air, and sea. Seven demons come from below to trouble us above. They drink our blood. They steal our little ones. They take our life, and they live forever. I, Asarial the wizard, have learned the secret of killing them. I, Asarial, have created this amulet to contain the power of their death."

"Contain the power of death..." mused Anse. "If I control the power of life and death, then I am a god! How do I say it, priest? Tell me now!"

Jean-Pierre uttered the pronunciation of the ancient language, word for word, as Anse held the amulet and repeated. As Anse spoke the last syllable, the amulet began to glow, this time not the deep, rich blue that it had emanated when Beast Stalker had held it the first time, but rather a dense, smoky black, like factory pollution.

"Yes! It worked! It's working! I hold the power of life and death in my hand!" boasted Anse.

Having been hiding in the kitchen, listening to the conversation, Ophelia burst into the room at vampiric speed, snatched the amulet from Anse's shocked hands before he could even move, and shouted, "Not for long! Thanks for the instructions!" as she bolted out of the back window and into the night. Her ancient vampiric powers and speed were unmatchable by Anse, and he knew it, so he declined to even attempt to pursue her.

"Now!" shouted Janine, and Paul and Gill fired rounds of holy water from their automatic weapons, blasting Anse in the face. He shrieked as his skin began smoking and charring. Jean-Pierre let Beast Stalker lean against him, and Mary fired stakes at the vampire torturer as he rushed them. One of the stakes pierced him in the chest, much to his surprise, and he exploded into a cloud of black dust. They backed toward the mansion's front door, shooting holy water at a hissing Devil Anse Hatfield, who remained just out of range but could get no closer.

"They're coming out! Kill them! Kill them, my children!" shouted Devil Anse, and as they exited the house, the enormous crowd of vampires outside, who had been waiting, surrounded them.

"Wait!" shouted Janine. "Cease fire! They outnumber us twenty to one. Save your ammo. Your armor will protect you. The van's only a few feet away. Everyone, circle up, backs together, and move slowly toward the van. Only fire if they attack first."

Painfully slowly, the group moved through the angry mob of vampires until they reached the Microbite. Paul carefully opened the main van doors, and they inched in, one by one until only Gill was left. He was backing into the van when several vampires rushed him. Though it burned their skin, they ripped off his armor. All he had was his holy water cannon.

"Gill!" shouted Mary. "Someone save him!" But the vampires had surrounded him, cutting him off from the van. Gill turned to them.

"Go on, guys. Go on. Find the amulet and get it back. Give the vamps hell. You can't save me. Plus, going out in a crowd of vampires is punk as fuck!" said Gill. He turned back to face the vampires then shouted, "Fuck you, bloodsuckers! I hope you rot in hell!" as he opened up his weapon and sprayed holy water into the crowd. Vampires hissed, screamed, burned, smoked, but there were too many of them. He eventually ran out of ammunition, and as the gun clicked empty, his friends watched in nauseating horror as the vampires closed in and tore him apart.

CHAPTER 25

REGROUPING

In silence, Paul drove the Microbite back to the Summer Linden Hotel's underground parking. They exited and helped Beast Stalker up the stairs. Though his cuts were healed, he was still physically exhausted and in pain. Janine fetched more first-aid supplies from the Resistance armory, and they all took a seat in silence. Janine spoke first.

"I'm so, so sorry guys. Gill was a good guy."

Mary replied, "He was amazing and funny and—and…"

"He sacrificed himself for us," said Paul. "That fucker died so we could escape. He's right: nothing could be more punk. This really sucks. I swear it, I'll get revenge on those fucking bloodsuckers. Gill and me grew up together. I knew him since I was a kid. I'll kill all of those motherfuckers."

"I'm so sorry, Paul," said Jean-Pierre. "So sorry. You are right that Gill died a hero. We'll never forget him or his sacrifice. I'm with you; I vow to fight the vampires until they are eliminated. Please let me know if I can help you in your grief in any way." Matt simply sat in the corner with his head between his hands, staring silently at the table. "I hate to bring this up right now, Janine," said Jean-Pierre, "but what happened to your fellow Resistance members?"

"I think I know what happened to them," she answered, "and it's not good. If they tried to get here after sunset, well, we all saw the streets. And Nancy and Titania are still captive in Asa McCoy's mansion. We still need to rescue them, guys."

Lâmié joined the conversation: "I also hate to bring this up right now, but that vampire girl, Ophelia. She took the amulet, and she heard the instructions on how to use it. It's just a matter of time until she controls life and death. She'll take over the world."

"Not if we stake her fucking heart first!" said Paul.

"Yeah, I agree, but how do we find her?" asked Lâmié.

They sat in silence for a few moments, then Jean-Pierre looked at Sager and Xiaoqing. Sager was still in a stupor.

"Xiaoqing?" said Jean-Pierre. "I know this is a sensitive subject, and I am really sorry to have to discuss it, but as you know, it's a life-and-death situation. So, Ophelia used her powerful vampire magic to enchant Sager, make him her servant, and do her will. Well, I bet he still has a connection to her. I bet he senses where she went. Maybe he can even see through her eyes on some level. We could try to, well, interrogate him."

Xiaoqing just nodded sadly.

"That's a great idea, Father," said Janine. "But we need to rescue Nancy and Titania first. It's more urgent. Plus, Titania's fairy magic can help us to get that information from the professor."

"Alright, that sounds good," said Jean-Pierre. "Are there other fairy folks in town?"

"There are," said Janine. "The thing is, though, they're really good at hiding, even in plain sight. It's part of their magic. And their magic is centered around protection, defense, and charms; it's not violent or aggressive magic. I imagine that the fairies of Ushaville right now are hiding and terrified. And they can sense one another, sort of like a network of magic, so they definitely know that Titania's in trouble. Maybe if we can rescue her and get her back here, they'll come out of hiding, and they can pool their magic together to help us. The way I see it, we have two main goals. First, we need to figure out how to rescue Nancy and Titania. Asa's obviously trying to lure us to his mansion so he can capture us for what we did to the Army surplus store owner and from the concert. He'll either execute us or keep us in his dungeons as slaves, maybe ever put us down in the tunnel jail cells."

"Oh, fuck that!" said Paul. "I'll die before I go back there again!"

"Alright," said Janine. "I agree. Second, we need to find where Ophelia is, track her down, and get the amulet back. It needs to be back in its rightful place among the Cherokees. They are the sacred keepers of the magic that keeps the vampires at bay. Beast Stalker, we'll get that amulet back. This time, we can make it impossible for anyone to get the amulet. We can use the amulet's magic and the fairies' magic, and add in a good dose of good old human booby traps and defensive measures."

Beast Stalker, becoming stronger by the minute, nodded and replied, "When we get it back, we'll also use some ancient Cherokee magic to guard it. Chief Cloud Mountain is powerful in his own right, even if he looks old and frail. You'll see."

"I noticed some things at Devil Anse's mansion," said Lâmié. "First of all, none of the vamps could get through the Microbite's armor system. That's good news. It means we basically have safe transportation anywhere in Ushaville. Next, our personal armor seems to work as well, as long as we stay together. They managed to overpower poor Gill's armor by the sheer number of them and because some of them were willing to be burned so that they could all get to him as a group. But all of us in a group seems to be too much for them to outnumber. Third, these weapons work pretty damn well. Though, the bad thing is that I think the oldest and most powerful vampires are stronger and hurt less by our armor. I mean, we can still stake them, but the holy water had less of an effect on Devil Anse than on the crowd of younger vamps outside his house. Janine, do you have refills and more stuff in the armory?" Janine nodded. "Good. This time, I think we need to have as much armor and as much firepower as humanly possible, if you'll pardon the pun. Of course, we need to reserve some of it to defend the hotel once we get back, and eventually, we'll need to try to get out of town, I guess. But yeah, let's really stock up this time."

"Can do," said Janine as she descended back down into the armory.

Jean-Pierre said, "Xiaoqing? Did you want to stay and take care of Sager again this time? We sort of need someone to. We can't risk leaving him alone."

Xiaoqing nodded her agreement.

"Beast Stalker, maybe you should stay here as well? You're still recovering. You went through so much."

"I don't mind fighting, Father," responded Beast Stalker. "I'm a warrior. But I did manage to keep some of the magical ingredients from my bookstore. I hid them in my pants, and the torturer never really checked for anything like that. If you need me, I am there with you. But I could also stay here and do some Indian magical spells and activate some of my magical items. I'd do it now before we go, but it might take a little while."

"Then yes, I think you should stay here and do that," said Jean-Pierre. "Does everyone agree?" Everyone nodded and muttered their agreement.

"That settles it," said Jean-Pierre. "Paul, could you give the van a once over and make sure it's still roadworthy?"

"Well, Gill was really the mechanic, but I helped him, so yeah, I'll see if anything obvious is broken."

As Paul went down to the van, and as Janine came up with more armor and weapons, everyone was mostly silent, realizing that the burden of saving the world from a vampire rule had been unceremoniously dumped upon their motley shoulders.

CHAPTER 26

RESCUING NANCY AND TITANIA

After everyone except Xiaoqing, Sager, and Beast Stalker were armed, armored, and squeezed into the van an on its top turret-cage, Paul started it and eased toward the parking's exit.

"Oh, shit," he said.

They saw that the street was packed with throngs and throngs of vampires, thick, dense mobs that surrounded the entire hotel. Any humans in Ushaville were either hiding or had already met their untimely vampiric fate. That place was no longer a town but a vampire citadel.

As the Microbite neared the exit gate, the vampires in the street turned and looked at them, instantly becoming agitated. Thin frames, bony fingers, pale faces, feline fangs—a sea of undead demons faced them, challenging them to dare to exit.

"Yeah, guys?" said Mary. "This doesn't look too good. What the hell are we gonna do?"

For once in his life alert, Matt replied, "Well, looks like we got two choices, guys. One, we stay here and wait until morning. They'll have to clear out then. Two, we bust through that gate in a blaze of glory, give 'em hell, and use brute force. But, if we wait 'til morning, then Asa might kill Nancy and Titania, and I'll be damned if I'm gonna lose another friend."

"I must agree," said Jean-Pierre. "Paul, I say you just gun it through the gate and the crowd. As soon as we hit that gate, everyone needs to start shooting. You three on the roof, we're depending on you the most. Start firing into the crowd. Everything—holy water, iron shot, stakes. Everything. Those of you at windows, do the same. I hope the van's armor will hold out while we drive through them. This is our moment. We'll rescue our friends or die trying! Are you with me?"

Everyone shouted. Paul revved the engine just for fun. He shifted into first gear, hit the accelerator, and popped the clutch.

With a shriek of rubber on cement, the Microbite lurched forward right through the parking gate, causing it to explode into splinters and sparks. The van plowed into the crowd of vampires, who were shocked and angry. Pale bodies flew and smoked as the van's weight and spiked, iron armor pummeled them into the air, and the cross-and-garlic armor burned their skin. The three on the top turret, and everyone at a window, opened fire.

As holy water spewed out, smoke arose from the screaming crowd like a bonfire. Iron buckshot pierced vampires' chests, making them howl in agony, and fully-automatic wooden stake rounds pierced dozens of hearts, turning some of the crowd into smoking carbon dust. The Microbite was like Moses, parting a pale sea as it made its way toward Asa Harmon McCoy's mansion.

Paul kept the accelerator floored as the van's little four-cylinder engine, in its top, fourth gear, roared and whined in protest. However, the narrow stock tires held their own even while the engine heated up dangerously close to failure. Like an icebreaker ship in the Arctic Ocean, the van's iron bull bar not only pushed vampires to the side but also burned their skin as it touched them, and as more vampires in front noticed what was happening, they began to part a little to avoid the wrath of the Microbite. Asa's mansion came into view at the end of the street, causing the friends to cheer.

"Keep going, Paul!" shouted Mary. "Just plow the fuck through his front door!"

Paul laughed and cackled maniacally.

The door of the mansion opened, and Asa's tall, lank, grim figure stepped out, surveying the scene to try to discover what all the commotion was about. As the van lurched and accelerated toward the mansion, it was almost comical to see Asa's facial expression change from curiosity to realization, to shock, and then to fear, and then to see him mouth the words, "Oh, shit!"

The Microbite hit the curb and flew into the air like a ballistic missile aimed right at Asa Harmon McCoy. As it came down and hit him square in the chest, he flew back into his mansion through three rooms, landing on the floor of the back servants' kitchen.

"Fuck right!" screamed Paul. "Everyone out! Stay in a group! Find Nancy and Titania!"

They all jumped out, formed a back-to-back circle, and proceeded, step by step, into the front parlor, where Nancy and Titania sat bound and gagged, their eyes wide in surprise as Mary ran to them and untied them.

"Into the van, now! No questions! Hurry!" shouted Mary, looking past them into the kitchen, where Asa had already recovered, stood up, and was walking briskly toward them.

They all jumped into the van, slid the door shut, and Paul gunned it backward, the tires' snow chains squealing on Asa's polished, wooden floors and tearing them up. Lâmié, who was on the roof turret, opened his holy water cannon and shouted, "Take this, bitch!" he screamed as he soaked Asa in holy water. The vampire shrieked in a furious, inhuman pitch as the Microbite burst through the wall and back outside, over the sidewalk, and into the street. Paul turned it around, put it into gear, and floored it. He drove at top speed, hitting the occasional vampire, sending it flying into the air as they made their way back to the hotel.

Volkswagen made an excellent van, a great van, to be sure. The Microbus endured the abuse of countless hippies and cross-country treks, puffing on as its simple, air-cooled, four-cylinder boxer engine suffered like a champ. Like all things man-made, however, nothing lasts forever without problems, and the Microbite picked a hell of an inconvenient time for a tire to explode and the engine to overheat. As it rolled to a quiet stop, everyone inside froze in silence, finally broken by Paul.

"Um, what now, guys?"

Nancy replied, "Over there! There's an unused tunnel that goes near the hotel. It's our only hope."

"The tunnels? We have no chance there!" said Mary. "The vamps can go down there too!"

"I'm pretty sure they don't know about this one. I think it's been unused for hundreds of years. The entrance is hidden. Come on; we have to try! Otherwise, the vampires will surround us. The van is amazing, by the way, but there's no way we could stand a siege. There are tens of thousands of vampires in this town. Once they find our location, we're sitting ducks. We have to move. We can't just run down the street, either. After what you did at Asa's, they'll all be on high alert.

They outnumber us. We'll never last. Our weapons will run out of ammo eventually, and it won't be dawn for a few more hours."

"I hate to say it," said Jean-Pierre, "but she's right. We have to move quickly. If the vamps don't destroy it, we can come back for the van tomorrow in daylight. Nancy, take us to the tunnel."

Not everyone agreed, but once they began pouring out of the van, the remainers had no choice but to follow. Nancy ran in front of them toward an alley between two abandoned row houses. She moved aside a metal drainage grate, revealing a hole with a ladder that led down into the blackness. She took a deep breath, then began climbing down. The rest followed as they descended into the dark underworld of Ushaville.

CHAPTER 27

THE TUNNEL NIGHTMARE

Janine had brought a flashlight, but it was barely a pinprick of light in the vast, inky well of the Ushaville underground. The air was cold and dank, very unlike the warm humidity above them. This must have been one of the most ancient tunnels because the walls were only roughly hewn from the natural bedrock, and the floor was uneven natural stone. It lacked the refinement and masonry of the other tunnels, as if it had been clawed out by some rough monster with no thought of smoothness or form. They had to proceed slowly to avoid stumbling.

"Anyone else have a torch?" asked Paul.

"I think we all left them in the van. All I cared about was my armor and weapon, and making it to the tunnel in time," said Jean-Pierre.

"Ditto," said Mary. "Shit. How much battery you got in that, Janine?"

"Should be fresh batteries, but you never know in this batshit crazy town," she replied.

The wet plunking of drops of water resounded in the distance, not a subterranean lake, but probably just water naturally leeching from the bedrock. The air was stifling, making it a little difficult to breathe. There were no air currents or natural breezes. It was as if theirs were the first lungs to inhale that air in thousands of years. The acrid, musty smell of fungus and mold assailed them.

"Nance?" asked Paul. "You sure about this? It seems like no one's used this tunnel in forever."

"And they haven't," she replied. "It's probably as old as the Indians or older, and we discovered it on accident when I was a kid. I'm positive that even the vamps have forgotten about it. It only has three or four branches, and all of them are just dead ends, except the one that leads to an alley near the hotel. Just look at the walls. You can tell it's ancient—no stonework, no groundwork, no masonry... just rough rocks. I'm not even sure that humans or vampires even made it. Maybe something much older."

"Something? Like what?" asked Paul.

"Not sure I wanna know," answered Mary.

"Nancy and Titania, how are you feeling?" asked Jean-Pierre.

Titania replied, "We're okay. Asa didn't hurt us or anything like that. In fact, he gave us food and water, and was pretty polite. I can't believe I'm saying that. He only tied us up and gagged us right before you showed up. He mainly wanted to use us to lure you in."

"Yep," said Nancy. "He used us as human bait, but he was nice about it." She laughed sarcastically.

They walked for almost an hour, not saying much, but weighed down under the tunnel's oppressive atmosphere. They reached a stopping point—their path traversed into distinct directions.

"Oh. Hmm," mused Janine.

"Which way, Nancy? Door number one, two, or three?" asked Jean-Pierre.

"Behind door one is... death!" said Paul. "Door two? Death! And door three, death!" He chuckled.

"Christ, Paul, don't be so morbid," said Mary. "But yeah, Nancy, which way?"

"Well, I'm thinking."

"That doesn't sound good," said Matt, then yawned.

"I mean, I haven't been down here since I was a kid. Let me try to remember for a moment."

However, that moment was interrupted as the flashlight's beam dimmed, flickered, and then blackened out. Janine shook it and tried to flick the switch with no luck.

"Shit!" said Paul. "Now we're blind to boot!"

"Hold on, everyone," said Titania in a gentle voice. They heard her mutter something in a language that sounded nothing like any they had ever heard, and then Titania herself began to glow, casting the area in a soft, green light. "Fairy magic!"

"Oh, wow!" exclaimed Lâmié. "It's real! It really is! It's amazing!"

"Fucking brilliant," added Paul, "but it still leaves us with choosing the right path. Nancy, whaddya say?"

"Shit. I just don't remember."

"Hold on," said Jean-Pierre. "The tunnel has been mostly straight, yeah?"

Everyone agreed.

"When we came into the tunnel, we were generally facing the hotel. So, the middle path seems the most likely."

"Sounds good to me," said Paul. No one else had a strong argument against it, so they carefully entered the middle tunnel.

"We might want to go a little faster," said Titania. "I cannot glow forever. I can do this for maybe an hour, but then I become too tired, and I have to turn it off for a while to regenerate my strength."

As they sped up, being careful not to trip on the uneven floor, the tunnel around them became even more primitive—the walls had not even a semblance of having been smoothened. Large rocks jutted out at sharp angles randomly. The ceiling was just as rocky, and mineral stalactites hung down, occasionally brushing against their hair, causing them all to walk with a slight stoop. They had not walked more than a couple hundred yards when they reached a dead end.

"Shit!" cursed Janine. "It's a dead-end, guys. We chose the wrong tunnel!"

"I'm sorry!" said Jean-Pierre. "I just thought…"

"It's alright, Father," said Mary. "Your guess was logical, and none of us knew better. Hell, we better turn around and get back quickly before the light wears off. How you holding up, Titania?"

"Fine for now," answered the fairy, "but let's do try to hurry!"

They turned around and carefully made their way back toward the entrance to the middle tunnel when they heard a voice that made their blood chill—it was Devil Anse Hatfield.

"Wrong way, little mice!" he taunted. "You're not going to like what you find in that tunnel!" He chuckled wickedly, and they watched helplessly as, in the distance, Devil Anse's figure rolled a massive boulder in front of the entrance, effectively sealing them in a tomb.

"Shit!" said Paul. "We're fucked! What the hell are we gonna do? And what did he mean about what we find in this tunnel?"

"I'm going to cut off the light for a little while, friends," said Titania. "We know we're in a closed tunnel, so we really do not need light to explore, and I can save the energy in case we need it later."

"Titania," asked Jean-Pierre, "can your magic move that boulder?"

"Oh, I am not sure," she replied. "Fairy magic, although powerful, is subtle and usually comes in the form of influencing people, not moving boulders. Let me rest, and I can try, though. It is worth a shot. Give me half an hour to rest."

They squatted, sat on the floor, or leaned against the rough tunnel walls as they silently and individually thought about what to do in the worst-case scenario. In the inky blackness, every sound was magnified as the other senses attempted to compensate for the blindness. Every breath, every shift of a foot or hand sounded like explosions and screeching metal against metal to their delicate ears. Thus, they all gasped and jumped when the distinct sound of dragging footsteps approached them from the dead-end of the tunnel.

"Oh, not this shit again," whispered Paul as more slow, loping footsteps joined the first.

"This can't be good," said Mary. "Why can't we just be left alone?"

"Not in their nature," answered Janine. More and more footsteps joined the invisible herd. "Titania, dear? Do you have enough energy to light up and show us what horror is coming toward us?"

"Yep," said Titania, muttering the magical fairy spell and glowing again. About fifty yards away, and approaching them slowly, was a nest of the Ancient Ones, the millennia-old vampires that preceded Ushaville, that the modern vampires revered as elders. All desiccated and withered and bony, with dried strips of forgotten flesh hanging in spots, these living corpses dragged, plodded, and slid toward them with lust in their eyes. Their delicate, sharp fangs were extended.

"Oh, fuck me!" said Nancy.

"What the hell are those?" screamed Barillo. "I think you neglected to tell me about these, Father!"

Nancy answered, "They're the most ancient of vampires, thousands and thousands of years old. They came here from the Old World almost certainly. They haven't tasted blood in maybe a thousand years. That's why they look like dried out corpses. I'm not sure, but I suspect that, if they get their fill, they will become more like they were in life. And if you think Asa and Anse are powerful, well, a vampire's power only increases with age. These'll be like a super breed!"

"Well, they ain't getting any farther away," said Paul. "What the hell do we do?"

"Come on," said Titania. "I'll try to move the boulder now. It's our only hope." She lifted off of the ground and literally flew to the boulder that blocked the exit.

"Damn, she really is a fairy!" exclaimed Lâmié.

With everyone crowded around her, and with the Ancient Ones moaning and limping ever closer, Titania closed her eyes and said, "I have to go dark to do this. Just hang tight, guys." She extinguished herself, and the sounds of the approaching arcane vampires became all the more horrifying since they could not see how close they were. Titania began to speak, this time confidently and loudly, in her fairy language. As she spoke, and as the intensity and volume of her words increased, she began to glow again, this time not in a soft haze, but in a pure, bright, emerald light that exuded from her being all over the cave. For a brief moment, the vampires hissed and hesitated, but then began moving again. As Titania repeated the spell repeatedly, each time using more and more energy, the boulder began to tremble ever so slightly.

"Look! It's working!" shouted Mary.

Titania continued, and the boulder proceeded from trembling, to shaking, to moving. It slowly rolled to the left about three feet and then stopped.

"That's all I can do!" said Titania. "I need a recharge. Can you squeeze through?"

"We have to try," said Jean-Pierre. "Ladies first. How about Mary, then Janine, then Nancy, then Titania?"

"I'm going last. I brought you all down here, and I'll make sure you make it out," insisted Nancy.

"No! You didn't know, Nancy," replied Jean-Pierre. "We can't leave you here…"

"There's no argument," Nancy said. "I'm going out last. I'll stay and fight them off. Father, leave your weapon with me, so I'll have backup when mine runs out. With a little luck, I can hold them back until everyone gets out, blast them back with some holy water, then slip through myself. Go! Don't argue, just go!"

"Good idea! I hope no one has claustrophobia!" said Mary, who had already begun to crawl through the small gap. She made it.

As the primordial vampires steadily gained distance on them, they slid through, one by one: Mary, then Janine, then Titania, then Matt, then Paul, then Lâmié, then Barillo. As they each wriggled through the impossibly small space, Nancy fired holy water at the vampires. They hissed and smoked, and for a moment, they held back, buying the gang more precious time. As the holy water stores ran out, she picked up Jean-Pierre's sawed-off shotgun and began letting iron buckshot fly into the risen corpses. As the shot splattered into their parched and arid papyrus-skin and clang against their bones, they were weakened. A few of them fell down and struggled to stand back up.

"Woohoo! Kickin' ass!" screamed Nancy.

After the iron shot was depleted, Nancy took hold of the last weapon in her arsenal: a fully-automatic, bullpup gun loaded with a magazine of wooden stakes. *Pop pop pop!* The rifle rang out as stakes sped from the muzzle. Some of them connected with their targets, who exploded into a stunning dust cloud.

"Take that, you walking dust fuckers!" screamed Nancy, but then the gun jammed. "Fuck! No, no, no! Not now!" she cursed.

Barillo had just wormed his portly frame through the hole so that only Nancy was left. The remaining vampires were no more than ten feet from Nancy and steadily progressing. They seemed to gain speed as they became closer to their prey, as if their fossilized nasal passages detected the living, pumping blood inside of her.

"Come on, Nancy! You got this!" shouted Jean-Pierre as he peered through the hole. "Give me your hand! I'll pull you through!"

Nancy tossed the gun aside and began climbing through the hole. The bare skin of her ankles could feel the breeze as withered arms and hands swiped at them.

"Almost there, Nancy! You're just about there!" shouted Jean-Pierre, his own heart palpitating and racing in anxiety.

"I'm here! She said as her hips passed into the hole. An icy claw of a hand grasped her ankle.

"Shit! They have me! Pull, Father! Pull!" she cried.

Jean-Pierre pulled with all of his might as Matt crouched behind him and grasped him around the chest to anchor him.

"Ah! It hurts! I can't keep being pulled in two different directions!"

"Kick!" shouted Jean-Pierre. "Kick their faces in!"

She kicked as hard as she could, connecting with one of them. She heard the crunch as her boot broke through the old skull, and the vampire screamed in pain. There were just too many of them. More and more blisteringly-cold hands clutched her ankles and calves. Jean-Pierre's strength was no match for that of ancient vampires, even weakened ones, and he watched as Nancy was pulled back into the tunnel by the things. A tear fell from his eye as he saw Nancy rolled over, and the vampires begin feeding on her.

In macabre wonderment, he watched as the dried-out old corpses started to become fuller as they drank Nancy's blood. Flesh expanded and became thick. Facial features appeared. Hair grew. The heap of vampires blocked his view from a screaming Nancy as the boulder, victim of gravity, rolled back and re-sealed the tunnel.

"Nancy! No! Do something!" shouted Matt.

Jean-Pierre only shook his head. "There's nothing we can do. They have her. I'm so sorry."

Matt started to weep quietly, and everyone looked at the ground in silence.

"She gave herself so we could escape," said Matt. "Nancy, you beautiful, amazing idiot. She knew what would happen. She did. She only held them off long enough for us to escape. She knew that. She gave herself for us."

"Right she did, mate," said Paul in a soft voice for once. "We'll never forget her or Gill."

"I hate to be the one to bring it up too soon, but we need to get back to the hotel," said Lâmié quietly, "or else we'll all die, and that'll be no use to anyone. We need to decide which of the other tunnels to take." He looked at his watch while Titania's green light still burned. "It's not daybreak yet. We can't go back the way we came in. Anse will be waiting for us, along with who knows how many others. We have to find the right tunnel and get to the hotel."

"He's right," said Titania. "There's no point in all of us dying. I'm almost out of juice here, but I'm going to try one more thing. I need to turn off the light for a minute, and then I'm going to try a locater spell. It's not normally a spell we fairies use, but I might be able to bend another spell a little bit, and it just might tell us which tunnel to take to get back. After all, the Summer Linden Hotel is under the protection of strong fairy magic, so I might be able to make a connection. Be still for a minute or two while I recharge."

The tunnel went dark again, and this time, everyone tried to be as quiet as possible to avoid a repeat of what had just taken Nancy from them. Fortunately, this time, nothing happened while Titania recharged.

"Alright, let me try this," said Titania. She chanted again in her language, this time not as frantically and loudly, but steadily. She chanted for several minutes. Nothing. Titania sighed.

"Well, it looks like the spell I tried to create didn't work."

"It's alright, Titania," said Janine. "You tried. Thank you. Guys, how are we going to choose the right tunnel? We don't know that Devil Anse isn't still watching us. If we choose the wrong tunnel again, well…"

"Look!" said Mary. "Look, everyone!"

They all turned their heads and beheld a green glow coming from the tunnel to the right.

"Oh, my!" said Titania. "It worked! Green is the color of fairy magic. It's trying to show us the way to take! I can feel it. The spell worked!"

"Well, Hallelujah!" said Jean-Pierre. "Let's not waste time. Come on!" He led the way into the green tunnel, which became more and more refined as they proceeded. Rough-hewn, rocky surfaces transformed into masonry, and the floor became smooth and tiled. The tunnel tilted upward slightly, and after a hundred yards, they reached a hatch. Jean-Pierre opened it and climbed through, finding himself in the alley right next to the hotel. They all exited, and it was an easy feat to slip into the hotel just as the first yellow fingers of the sun began to caress Ushaville.

CHAPTER 28

CHEROKEE MAGIC

A s they rested, ate, and drank at the hotel bar, no one was really saying much. The heavy pale of the loss of Gill and Nancy hung over their heads like a black anvil. Thus, when Mary gasped and yipped, everyone immediately snapped their heads in the direction she was looking. As if they had been perfectly camouflaged into the wall, three young adults—one man and two women—seemed to materialize right in front of them. Barillo instinctively drew his wooden-stake-shooting pistol and pointed it at them. "Freeze!" he shouted.

"It's alright, Detective!" said Titania. "They're my friends." Barillo slowly lowered the gun; his arm was slightly shaking.

"Everyone, these three are my friends, Alwin, Breen, and Lylia."

Alwin was a lithe young man with smooth, pale skin with eyes like those painted on ancient Egyptian tombs. Breen was a delicate young lady with curly blonde hair and blue eyes and long, curly eyelashes. Lylia was a fragile and exquisite Asian girl with black hair that shimmered, and skin like the smooth surface of fresh cream. As Titania introduced them, they bowed and curtsied in turn.

"Um, Titania? I'm going to ask the obvious," said Mary.

Titania giggled. "Yes, they're fairies like me. They tell me that the other fairies in town have fled in fear, but they have stayed behind to help us out if we will accept it."

"Wait, they told you?" asked Mary.

"Oh, yes, I supposed I never mentioned that fairies can communicate without words. Trust me, friends, we'll be glad to have these three on our side: they are some of the most powerful fairies alive. With their fairy magic and mine, by the power of four, we'll have a very potent magical tool at our use."

"I have something to show you, also," said Beast Stalker. He raised up a bowl filled with a wet, muddy, green-and-brown substance.

"Boy, that looks delicious," mocked Paul.

Beast Stalker nodded and continued, "It does not taste good, I can assure you, Paul. What I have in my hands is a special Cherokee magical salve. It is a magical recipe from the most ancient of times, and very few people outside of my tribe know about it. Like the amulet, it is a sacred secret that I am entrusting you with, so please keep it so. Anyone who rubs this all over their body will become invisible to evil spirits and evil creatures. They will not be able to see, hear, touch, smell, or harm you. It does not last forever, though. After just a few minutes, it wears off, and you are exposed again. I made the most I could with the ingredients I had. There is enough here for one person to use when necessary."

"Invisible?" said Paul. "Badass! Can I use it to creep around and prank people?"

"Paul, shut up, you idiot," chided Mary.

Beast Stalker replied, "It does not make you invisible to people or good spirits or magical creatures, only to evil ones. I suggest that we carry this with us and use it in an emergency. Remember, there is only a single dose for one person. We must use it judiciously."

"Excellent, Beast Stalker!" exclaimed Titania. "Cherokee magic, like fairy magic, can be potent against evil spirits when applied properly. Also, like fairy magic, Cherokee magic doesn't last forever. It requires strength and concentration." Beast Stalker nodded.

"Hey, Titania," said Matt. "I just lost two people I really liked today, but I feel warm and happy. Is that something to do with you?"

"Yes," she replied. "Feeling happy, warm, and secure is one benefit of being around fairies."

"Are there bad fairies, too?" he asked.

Titania paused, looked at the floor, then at Alwin, Breen, and Lylia, then looked up, and said, "Unfortunately, there are. Half of the fairy kingdom turned to the darkness and are very evil and powerful. Luckily, there are none in Ushaville that I know of. They tend to stay in and around New Orleans."

"Man, I never knew our city was so damn magical. Vampires, fairies, spirits—hell," commented Lâmié. "I think I need to revive my career!"

"So, what's next?" asked Jean-Pierre. "It's daytime now, but night will come again sooner than we want. Are we going to fight here in Ushaville or try to find Ophelia? Speaking of..." He looked at Xiaoqing and Sager. "Xiaoqing, can we try to talk to Sager?"

"Sure. Why not?" she answered.

Jean-Pierre sat next to his old friend and took his hand. "Sager, it's me, J.P., your friend. How are you feeling?"

"She left!" said Sager in a high-pitched voice. "The Mistress has left! I must go to her! She has the power now!"

"The Mistress is Ophelia, right?"

"Yes! Mistress! I must be near her!"

"Where did she go, Sager?" asked Jean-Pierre.

"She's gone! I must find her!"

"Yes, and where did she go, Sager?"

"She has all the power! The Mistress! Hee hee!"

"Father," interjected Titania, "we might be able to help. We can use our magic to try to see inside of Sager's heart and see if there is any connection to Ophelia."

Xiaoqing bitterly turned her head and looked at the floor.

"Good idea," said Jean-Pierre.

The four fairies seemed almost to float as they gracefully crossed the room and surrounded Sager, who was still staring into the distance as if he were somewhere else. They each placed a hand on Sager. Titania began to chant softly in the fairy language, and the other three joined her, and as they chanted the spell, all four of them began to softly glow green. Sager did not seem to react, but everyone in the room felt the warm buzz of fairy magic tickling their arms and hands.

After several minutes, while still touching Sager and glowing, Titania spoke: "I see... I see her. Oh, such darkness there! She is so dark! I see... I see a sort of alley, beside a large church... it is a narrow alley, with cobblestone, the church is white... now I see flashes of old streets with old houses on each side... narrow streets, so many people, people dancing and eating and drinking... now... now it is night...I am back in the alley, I am following someone, a young girl, she does not hear me... I get close to her... no one else is around... oh, no, no... such darkness... I see the young girl attacked, screaming into the night, no one coming to help, the girl's neck..." Titania began to shake violently, and her aura changed from green to dark red, an angry, bloody red, and electrical sparks began to shoot from Titania's skin into the air.

"Titania!" shouted Alwin as he grabbed her hand and pulled it from Sager, causing his own hand to sizzle and smoke. Titania fell to the ground, unconscious.

"Titania!" shouted Mary. "Help her!'"

"I can help her," said Lylia and she appeared by Titania's side so quickly that it seemed that she had teleported. She held her hands over Titania, and her hands began glowing a strong, emerald green. After several seconds, Titania opened her eyes, then gently sat up.

"Thank you, Lylia. I feel better," said Titania.

"What was it, Titania?" asked Jean-Pierre. "What happened?"

"Oh, it was terrible. Sager can see through Ophelia's eyes. She's so evil, so ancient, so powerful," answered Titania.

"Where is she?" asked Jean-Pierre.

"I don't know. All I saw, I told you."

"Father?" asked Lâmié, "it has to be New Orleans. It sounded like the French Quarter, like Pirate's Alley, in fact, right next to your church."

"That would explain some things," said Barillo. "The murders in New Orleans; they're the work of vampires. It makes sense. Victims drained of blood, attacked at the neck. It's gotta be."

"If you think Ushaville is overrun with vampires, imagine New Orleans once Ophelia takes charge of the amulet's power," said Jean-Pierre. "There must be ten times more vampires in New Orleans, or maybe more. If society breaks down as it did here, then it will spread to other large cities once the word gets out. There's nothing stopping vampires from taking over the world, just like Devil Anse Hatfield wanted to do originally. It could truly mean the end of humanity, or maybe an existence where we are enslaved to vampires and treated as labor and food. We absolutely must find Ophelia and take the amulet or destroy her, or both. Then, we need to return the amulet to its rightful keepers, the Cherokees. Once they have it again, then we can use the amulet, Cherokee magic, and fairy magic to bring Ushaville back to order and balance."

"Summary: we have to save the fucking world," said Paul.

"Sounds like it," replied Mary. "What makes us the ones to do that?"

Paul said, "Well, we've done pretty fucking well so far! Anyone up for a road trip to New Orleans? I miss the food. Plus, you can legally walk around outside with booze, and maybe we can save the world to boot!"

CHAPTER 29

ROAD TRIP!

"**Y**ou have a spare for this thing?" asked Lâmié.
They had managed to access the broken-down Microbite in the daylight easily. No vampires were out, likely tired from hunting them the night before.

"Yeah, underneath," said Mary.

As Lâmié began to change the tire, Paul and Matt looked over the van to see the damage.

"Too bad Gill's not here," said Paul. "He was good with engines." Mary looked sad. They opened the rear engine access panel.

"Anyone know engines?" asked Paul.

"Yeah, I can take a look," answered Lâmié. "I used to rebuild motorcycle engines. Let me finish up the tire."

The fairies were keeping a lookout for vampires, and everyone else was sort of mulling about. Lâmié finished up the tire then squatted down to look at the engine. He poked and prodded a bit, tugged on a few wires and cables, and ran his hand underneath the engine block.

"I don't see anything fundamentally wrong with it," he said. "It probably just overheated. These things are air-cooled, and you were gunning it pretty hard. Mary, why don't you start it up and see what happens?"

She sat in the driver's seat, inserted the key, paused a second, then turned it. The engine hummed to life.

"Fuck yes!" shouted Paul. "Now it moves again. We need to redo the armor, though. Looks like we hit enough vamps to knock off most of it. Without the armor, we're fucked. Oi, Janine, you got more stuff in the armory?"

"Shit," said Janine. "I mean, we're a little depleted, but I think I can scrape up enough for a couple more rounds. I think we can refresh our weapons and body armor and the van's armor and then make it to New Orleans. Assuming we get the amulet, then we won't need this armor and shit anymore, but... well, let's just cross our fingers, yeah?"

"We'll need some food and supplies," said Matt. "I'm guessing that Red McCoy's general store and gas station isn't open anymore. We can raid it, though, if it's not being guarded."

"Pretty sure it won't be," said Janine. "Those hicks are on the low end of the vamp pecking order in Ushaville. The Council won't waste any resources on them. I bet it's open for the taking. Come on, drive us back to the hotel. We'll stock up on weapons and armor, then hit Red's and stock up on food and other shit, and then head to New Orleans. I probably don't need to say it, but it's essential that we get the hell out of Ushaville today while it's still daylight."

As Janine had predicted, they could replenish their weapons, body armor, and the van's armor from the armory. They reached Red's store without any trouble, and it was unguarded but closed up with boards nailed across the windows and door. However, they were no match for the group's tools, and they soon found themselves inside a fully-stocked general store. After filling up the van outside, they helped themselves to food, snacks, tools, cigarettes, lots of booze, and sundry other items, so that the van sank beneath the weight of all of the people and gear.

"Damn, they meant business when they made these vans," said Lâmié.

The road trip took all day and into the evening, and by the time they arrived in New Orleans, they all wanted to rip one another's hair out. Between Paul cursing and farting, Mary telling him to shut up, Sager ranting about Ophelia, Xiaoqing fussing at him and slapping him, and Matt snoring, it was not a very pleasant trip. They were relieved when they pulled into Jean-Pierre's rectory—a three-level, luxurious apartment in the historic Pontalba building, right on Jackson Square and next to the St. Louis Cathedral. Multiple bedrooms and bathrooms allowed everyone some comfort and privacy.

"Shit, I should've become a priest," said Paul, whistling. "Sweet gig, Father."

"Well, free room and board are a couple of perks of the priesthood, yeah," replied Jean-Pierre.

"Vow of poverty, eh Father?"

"Oh hush, Paul," said Jean-Pierre, chuckling. "You're welcome to sleep on the curb downstairs."

"Humph."

After everyone had showered and rested a while, they gathered in the grand parlor to discuss their strategy.

"First thing," said Janine, "we need to know where to look for Ophelia. I think we should split up; after all, this is a pretty big city."

"Haven't horror movies and Scooby-Doo taught you anything?" asked Mary. "I told you, you *never* split up."

"I think Janine's right," said Lâmié. "Ophelia could act at any time, and this city has countless hidey holes for vampires. I mean, there must be thousands of vampires in New Orleans, and I'm sure they have a network. If we split up into groups, we could hit the obvious places first—the cemeteries, the French Quarter bars and alleys, Saint Charles Avenue, the Garden District, you know. She's a vampire after all, and they seem to like spooky places like that."

Beast Stalker spoke next: "I am sorry, Lâmié, but I must disagree. I believe that Mary is correct. Splitting up is dangerous. If she and the vampires corner two of us somewhere, it's very dangerous, and then they will have hostages as leverage. If we go down, we should all go down together, fighting."

"I think I agree with Beast Stalker and Mary," added Titania. "Plus, I believe Alwin, Breen, Lylia, and I can put together a fairy magic spell that might help us locate Ophelia. That way, we don't have to waste time looking. Also, we should strike during the day. It's when vampires are at their weakest, right Lâmié? It's evening already, so we'll have to start first thing tomorrow."

"Fine," said Janine. "That all makes sense. As for tonight, is anyone else still hungry and interested in seeing New Orleans? Not all of us have been here before."

"Sure, sure," said Jean-Pierre. "I'll show you some stuff. Let me see, what's a good restaurant where we can eat, drink, and be merry for a night? After all, tomorrow we may die."

"Grim, Father," said Paul. "I especially like that *drinking* part."

"I know just the place," offered Lâmié. Get ready, and I'll take us!"

They got on a streetcar and rode it across Poydras Street, around the Lee Traffic Circle, and onto St. Charles Avenue. The neutral ground, as they call the median in New Orleans, was grassy with planted flowers. Magnificent ancient oak trees reached their arms across the avenue, forming a canopy of green. The avenue was flanked with grand old mansions, many of them representing old money and important families that had lived there for centuries and now shared them with the ghosts of their ancestors. The restaurants and cafés lining the extravagant place were filled with people enjoying themselves and spilling out onto the sidewalks.

At the next stop, they descended from the streetcar. They stood in front of a pub that had been a lovely residential house at one time. Inside, the rich, oaken wall panels and ceiling made it feel cozy and warm. They enjoyed gumbo, jambalaya, crawfish étouffée, raw oysters, and boiled crawfish, as well as countless rounds of Abita ale until they were ready to explode.

They returned to the rectory and slept the deep, dreamless sleep of travelers.

The next morning, they walked across Jackson Square to Café du Monde. The square was already full of artists hawking to people to have their portraits painted; fortune tellers in Eastern garb, promising to reveal the future; mimes escaping invisible cages; jazz horn bands piping out old New Orleans standards like *Saint James Infirmary*; as well as the other, less festive side of New Orleans—grizzled homeless people sleeping on the cement; hopeless alcoholics staggering around already; heroin-addled teenagers begging desperately for money; and the ever-present scammers. New Orleans, the city of darkness and light, never failed its promise to amaze and wonder. At Café du Monde, they enjoyed yeasty beignets dusted with powdered sugar and the famous café au lait with chicory.

"Alright, where to first?" asked Titania. "Father, should we look in the crypts under your church?"

"No crypts in New Orleans," said Jean-Pierre, chuckling. "The entire city is below sea level. They would flood with water. That's the same reason we have to bury our dead above ground in vaults, instead of in traditional graves."

"Oh God, that sounds terrifying already."

Lâmié furrowed his brows, pursed his lips, rubbed his chin, then spoke, "That makes me think. We should start in the cemeteries, and the oldest ones at that. Saint Louis Number One. It's the oldest, the creepiest, and the one that the Voodoo queen Marie Laveau is buried at. Ophelia seems like the type to dig sleeping in an ancient tomb during the day. I mean, it's sort of the stereotypical vampire lore, right? If she's not there, we'll go to the other Saint Louis cemeteries, to Lafayette Cemetery, and Metairie Cemetery. After the cemeteries, I think we should hit the oldest houses in the French Quarter, and then the Garden District. We'll have to send someone in to pretend they're with the city utility company or something."

"No need," said Titania. "I can enchant people to let us into their houses."

"Ooh, sneaky fairy magic!" said Paul.

"Alright, it's settled. To the cemeteries!" said Jean-Pierre.

They hopped back into a streetcar and made their way over to the St. Louis Cemetery No. 1.

The city of the dead, it was called, and for a good reason. Ancient family crypts lined narrow pathways laid out like city blocks. Some of the tombs were extravagant and luxurious marble towers of Gothic beauty, adorned with statues of angels, gargoyles, and children. They held the remains of generations of families from the beginning of New Orleans. Others were simpler—white stone vaults that held their family secrets well. Still, others were unkempt and decrepit: broken stone crypts with gaps and holes through which you could see the pale, grisly sheen of human bones. The tomb of the great Voodoo Queen herself, Marie Laveau, was simple but decorated with her followers' gifts and wishes. Sets of three XXXs covered it, a symbol of asking her for luck. Around it were trinkets and tokens and magical items and spells on paper, candles burned, Voodoo dolls, piles of ash, and other mysteries.

"This cemetery is creepy as hell," noted Paul.

"Haunted as hell, too," said Lâmié. "It's notorious not only for lots of Voodoo, Hoodoo, and Santeria, but people see ghosts all the time here. The people who live around it swear they see old Marie Laveau herself rising from her tomb on a regular basis. They swear to it."

"Maybe we should not linger here until nighttime," said Mary. "Ghosts and zombies on top of vampires… geez."

They walked the narrow, stone lanes of the city of the dead, looking at crypts in interest, but more importantly, looking for crypts that seemed to show a recent disturbance or opening. There were several partially-open vaults, the neglected ones, and they could see skeletons, but nothing stood out as being particularly suited to a vampiress or recently opened.

"Say, Titania," said Jean-Pierre, "what are your feelings?"

She replied, "I can sense many, many spirits here in this cemetery, but nothing particularly evil stands out to me. Maybe I could do the spell on Sager again?"

"No, no, it hurt you last time."

"I can try it again tonight, maybe, and see if we can deduce where Ophelia is. She's just sleeping right now."

Sager himself was subdued, glassy-eyed, and silent.

"Alright, gang, let's head to the other cemeteries," suggested Lâmié. They spend half the day in Saint Louis Numbers Two and Three, and Lafayette Cemetery. In each of these ancient burial grounds, they inspected above-ground vault after vault, and, besides a funeral or two in progress, they saw no clues that any of them had been opened or disturbed recently.

"I guess she isn't in a cemetery," said Jean-Pierre, exasperated.

"There's one more possibility," said Lâmié. "Metairie Cemetery is huge. It's like an entire town of corpses. It's where rich people are entombed."

"Well," said Janine, "she is wealthy and prissy. It might be just her style."

"It's getting late," continued Lâmié, "but we should be able to canvas it before nightfall. How about it?"

They all agreed and hired taxis to take them there as quickly as possible in the slow old city.

When they arrived, the non-natives gasped in awe. Metairie Road, which winds through a suburb of New Orleans, contained exceptionally wealthy neighborhoods. Metairie Cemetery was the final home for some of New Orleans' wealthiest deceased families. Not only was the cemetery vast, but the crypts were opulent. Mammoth vaults of Italian marble were lined with intricate flourishes and expert statues of angels. Many of the vaults looked like tiny mansions, completed with marble columns and ornamented doors and refined gates of the finest ironwork. Like the whitewashed tombs of Jesus' Pharisaical wrath, these gorgeous buildings, showcasing some of the finest craftsmanship and money the world has to offer, were also full of rotting flesh and crumbling bones and all manner of unclean things.

The guard at the gate questioned them, but Jean-Pierre was wearing his priest's collar and made up something about leading a prayer group, so the guard let them in.

"Well, hell," said Paul. "Even in death, the rich screw the poor."

"Let's start at this end," suggested Jean-Pierre. "Remember, we're looking for any sign of recent disturbance: divots in the grass, scrape marks under the doors, broken seals, unlocked gates, and things like that. He glanced at the sky. "And it's late afternoon. Try not to be too slow. After all, if she is here, we really don't want to be caught after dark."

They began walking the lanes and avenues of the morbid complex, scanning every detail for signs of disturbance. They all noticed that Sager was becoming more and more agitated and started rambling about the Mistress again. They thought it a foreboding omen.

"How can we possibly cover the entire place?" asked Titania. "This is incredible. I've never seen anything like it."

"We're making good progress," said Jean-Pierre. "Anyone has seen anything yet?"

They all answered in the negative. They pressed on until they heard Matt call to them, "Everyone, come here. Look at this shit!"

Matt stood in front of a sophisticated, imposing family vault. Over the door was a marble placard, carved to look like a banner fluttering in the wind. On it was the family name *McCoy*.

"Well? What are the fucking chances?" asked Matt. "It's definitely not a local French name, is it? Now, look at this."

He pointed toward the iron gate protecting the vault. A combination lock had been smashed and broken, and the iron gate was partially open. The heavy marble door to the crypt itself was closed, but a half-circle scrape mark led from it. Moreover, there was some dark, black dirt scattered here and there.

Lâmié said, "Well, someone, or something, has definitely been in and out of this tomb recently. Could it be her? What do we do now?"

"We didn't really think that far ahead, did we?" asked Jean-Pierre. "I brought stakes, but, what? Do we walk right in and do the deed?"

"Um, guys?" said Mary. "Guys? Look!"

They all turned in the direction she was facing. As the burning, yellow globe of the sun visibly descended beneath the horizon, bit by bit, a figure walked toward them with the sun behind it. From their perspective, it was a diminutive figure all in black, and the heat waves from the sun behind it caressed it in undulating arms of haze. As it approached them from across the cemetery grounds, it became taller the nearer it went, until they could see that it was a petite, delicate old lady with brown skin, wearing a black robe.

"Hola! What are you doing?" she called out in a raspy voice with a distinctly Puerto Rican accent.

"Oh, we're just conducting a prayer service for the souls of the departed. May I ask who you are?" answered Jean-Pierre.

"I'm Yarielis. And Yarielis knows you're conducting no prayer service of any kind. You're here for this tomb and what's inside it."

Surprised, Jean-Pierre replied, "Uh, what do you mean?"

"Oh, you know what Yarielis means, Padre. We all know what lies in that tomb. And unless we're quick about it, it's gonna come out tonight. Look at the sun! It's setting! And you think she's the only one in this whole, big cemetery? No, no, Yarielis is tellin' you, there's more here. Tonight's the Summer Solstice, and they'll be out in crowds tonight. You shouldn't be here, and when the sun sets, they lock the gates. Probably too late."

"Yarielis," said Lâmié, "are we talking about the same thing?"

"Vampires, child! Vampires! I know, and you know they're here. Now you're locked in with them. They'll be rising soon. But don't you worry. Yarielis is a Voodoo priestess. Yarielis knows how to handle them, keep them away."

"I'll be honest, Yarielis," said Jean-Pierre. "Yes, you're right. We're here for vampires, but for one in particular, named Ophelia. She looks like a teenage girl, but she's really thousands of years old. She has something we need desperately. Can you help us get it?"

"Padre, we're all locked in here all night with them together. Yarielis can help you stay alive, Yarielis can, but if you need to steal something from a vampire, that's on you. I ain't getting anywhere near them. Come with me, and hurry. I have a special vault that I use for protection. Strong, strong Voodoo magic. We hole up in there." She looked at Titania, Alwin, Breen, and Lylia. "And old Yarielis knows what you four are, too. Magical beings, fairies." She looked at Beast Stalker. "You got magic too, Indian man. All this magic, we gonna be safe from them vampires. Hurry, this way!"

They all looked at one another, shrugged, and followed Yarielis, who, for an old woman, moved remarkably swiftly and with dexterity. In fact, they had trouble keeping up with her.

Near the center of the cemetery, which was the oldest part, they came upon an enormous tomb. The family name *Dauterive* was etched into a marble banner above the door.

"Come, come, don't be scared. Ain't nothing in here but dusty old bones, dead for too long to remember. Nothing gonna harm you in here. Yarielis gives you her word."

One by one, they all ducked into the vault and beheld a scene of morbid beauty. Smooth, Corinthian columns supported a room the size of a small house. In the walls of the room were countless crypts, and unlike the ones in the tunnels of Ushaville, these were sealed completely so that they could not see inside them. At the back of the room was a door leading presumably to yet another room. It was clearly the tomb of a wealthy, powerful old New Orleans family that had simply been neglected and abandoned. Perhaps the bloodline had died off after a child had never married? It would remain a mystery.

Yarielis had drawn in chalk a large magical circle in the center marble floor of the room. On the five points, and also at various places around the room, were both black and white candles. In the middle of the circle was the bloody carcass of a chicken. The blood had not congealed yet, so it must have been recently sacrificed.

"You stay here with Yarielis," she said, "and you'll be safe. I conjured Papa Legba and offered him a sacrifice, and he promised to keep the vampires away, as long as we remain in this tomb."

"A couple of months ago, I'd have called bullshit," said Mary, "but hell, why not? Vampires, fairies, magic… why not fucking Papa Legba too?"

The disconcerting sound of stone scraping against stone then seemed to come from all parts of the cemetery.

"You see? Yarielis told you. Vampires coming out now, all of them," she said.

"Holy hell," said Paul. "That's a shitload of vamps. We don't even have our armor and weapons. What the hell are we gonna do?"

"First thing I'm gonna do is not look outside," said Mary.

Lâmié disagreed, "Are you kidding me, Mary? I've been waiting my entire life to see this stuff, a cemetery full of risen vampires. Yarielis, I'm just going to peek out."

"Look if you will, but don't you leave this tomb, child! They'll tear you up!" she chided.

He walked to the door and opened it only a tiny crack, then peered through the gap. The cemetery was teeming with the undead beasts. Crypt doors opened as pale, spindly fingers grabbed the outside and pushed them fully open. Vampires, some in black, and others in their burial shrouds and clothes exited the vaults and began to congregate and talk. Several of them sniffed the air and looked in Lâmié's direction, forcing him to jump back and close the crypt's door again.

"Oh, they can smell you, child," said Yarielis. "They know we're here, somewhere. Papa Legba's magic hides us for now, but they can tell something's amiss!"

"Did you see Ophelia?" asked Xiaoqing.

"No, not offhand, but…"

Just then, Sager began to rock back and forth agitatedly, and to babble: "The Mistress! She's here! I must go to her! I'm coming, Mistress!"

"Well, that answers that," said Matt. "She's here alright. How the hell are we supposed to find her with all those others, and when we do find her, how the hell are we supposed to get past the others?"

"I guess we can't get the amulet tonight. We'll have to wait until we can get her alone," said Mary.

"We can't!" urged Janine. "She has the amulet. All it takes is her using it to begin the new vampire world order. She obviously has vampire friends here in New Orleans, and it wouldn't take much to convince them to join her in her power over humans. We have to strike immediately. We don't know when she plans to use it. We have to get it from her tonight."

"I'm afraid Janine is right," said Jean-Pierre.

"I have a crazy idea," said Paul.

"Oh God, here we go," answered Mary.

Paul chuckled and said, "Just fucking let me say it, and then you can shoot me down. The problem? A cemetery full of fucking vampires that want to eat us for breakfast. The mission? To steal an amulet from a powerful vampire girl. I know a thing or two about stealing, mates. Let's say you want to shoplift. You don't walk into the store, acting all suspicious and try to sneak something into your jacket. You'll get caught that way. That's what they expect. No, you gotta create a diversion. Knock some stock onto the floor, and when they go to clean it up, nab something from another aisle. Something like that. Do something they won't expect and create a distraction. Alright, right here, we have three, fucking *three*, kinds of magic. We got the Indian, the fairies, and the Voodoo lady. The Indian has invisibility cream. The fairies seem to be able to do anything they fucking want. And if there's one thing I know about Voodoo, it's *zombies*. So, we make zombies, distract the vamps, and send someone invisible over to Ophelia to snatch the amulet, then we get our asses back in this tomb and wait for sunrise."

"Zombies? What the fuck, Paul?" said Mary.

Lâmié added, "It's so beyond insane and messed up that it just might work. Anyone have a better idea? The other option is hiding in here until Ophelia takes over the world. Miss Yarielis? Can you make some zombies?"

"Oh, you don't know what you're asking!" she replied. "That's dark magic, very dark. It's the blackest magic you can imagine. It takes a terrible toll on the ones doing it!"

"Yarielis, let me explain to you, if you don't mind, why this is so urgent," said Jean-Pierre. "One of those vampires out there, named Ophelia, is a very powerful and ancient one. She took a magical amulet that was entrusted to our Cherokee friend here. It is a very powerful magic that protects against vampires. Now that Ophelia has the amulet and has learned how to use it, she can and will take over the world and create a vampire kingdom that either kills all humans or enslaves us."

"Oh, the evil!" said Yarielis. "I knew! I knew! I sensed something very powerful and terrible in this cemetery. It drew me here. Now I know for sure what it means. I will conjure your zombies, yes. You must know that it will take a toll on me and all of you! You can't upset the balance of life and death without the universe requiring something very heavy of you. What is it? We don't know until it comes. To make zombies, I need corpses. The ones in this crypt will do."

"But they're just old bones by now," said Jean-Pierre.

"That's okay. It will work. Now, I'll have to use the very blackest of Voodoo to do this. It takes a blood sacrifice for sure, the blood of a person. Maybe many people. You all willing to give blood? You won't die, but you'll give lots of blood!"

"I guess we are," said Matt. "Who's gonna be the one that uses Beast Stalker's salve to become invisible, sneak up to Ophelia, and snatch the necklace?"

They all looked around at one another. After a few seconds, Jean-Pierre spoke. "I'll do it. I need redemption in God's eyes, and the protection of the Church will help me. It may not be like magic, but of all of us, I'm the best choice."

"Thank you, Father," said Janine. "You are very brave."

"Fine line between bravery and foolishness," he said and grinned. "So, here's what I imagine we'll do, if everyone agrees. Yarielis will raise some zombies from the bodies here. We'll send them out against the vampires. I'm not sure a zombie can put up much of a fight against a vampire, but at least it will create a distraction, as Paul said. Beast Stalker will put the salve on me, and I'll be invisible to evil spirits. Titania and the fairies, you'll give me extra magical protection against the vampires. With luck and with God's help, I'll be able to get to Ophelia and grab the amulet from around her neck, then get back here fast enough, where Papa Legba's magic will keep us safe until morning.

When the sun rises, the vampires will have to return to their tombs. Then tomorrow during the day, we start back to Ushaville to return the amulet to Chief Cloud Mountain and the Cherokees, and balance is restored."

"What could possibly go wrong?" asked Paul sarcastically.

"Well, how do we find Ophelia out there among the others?" asked Janine.

"Titania, can you work some sort of magic on Sager to help him home in on her and tell us where she is?"

"I think so," she said while looking at Alwin, Breen, and Lylia.

"Oh, you're doing that ESP shit," said Paul.

"Alright," said Titania. "We think we know a spell that can do this. No time like the present, right? Beast Stalker, how long does your salve take to work?"

"It begins immediately when you rub it on," he answered.

Titania nodded, then she and her three fairy friends moved over near Sager. The four fairies joined hands, encircled Sager, and began to chant in the fairy language softly. Before long, a gentle green aura surrounded them all, including Sager. In an instant, Sager's eyes rolled back in his head, revealing only the whites. He rocked back and forth, and Titania became silent and focused on Sager. After about a minute, Sager's eyes rolled back in place, the fairies stopped chanting, and the green glow subsided.

"I saw her through his eyes," said Titania. "There's a large oak tree behind us, about three hundred feet away. She's there holding council with vampires. Father, if you just go directly to the back of this tomb and look ahead, you will see the tree. You can't miss it. Run directly toward the tree, and you will see Ophelia sitting at its base, on its roots. She has the amulet hanging around her neck. You should be able to yank it off, then run as fast as you can back to us."

Beast Stalker added, "The salve will make you invisible to the vampires, but they will still be able to tell that an enemy is there among them. You must be brave and run fast, Father. I believe in you."

"God is with me," Jean-Pierre replied.

CHAPTER 30

THE FATHER'S SACRIFICE

Yarielis added some symbols to the magic circle in the middle of the vault, then said, "Alright? Who's gonna give the blood?"

"I guess I will," answered Matt. "I haven't done too much to help, so why the hell not?"

Yarielis explained, "First thing, we need to get one of them bodies over to here in the magic circle."

"Yeah, blood is where I draw the line. I'm not touching a corpse," said Matt.

"I don't mind," said Paul. "It's either this, or *we'll* be the corpses. Which one, Voodoo lady?"

"It don't matter."

Paul went to one of the burial slots and pulled open the stone door that had sealed it off. Nothing emerged, but some dust and a musty smell. He looked in carefully and saw a skeleton, so old that no flesh or clothes were attached to it. Paul took a big gulp, then pulled the bones together into a pile and carried them to the middle of the magic circle.

"Well, that was fucking gross," he said.

Yarielis uttered a spell in Haitian Creole, then took Matt's hand. "Ready, child?"

"I guess so," Matt replied.

She ran her ceremonial knife across his palm, and a stream of blood spilled onto the bones.

"Fucking ouch," said Matt. "I hope you sterilized that knife first."

Yarielis guided Matt out of the magic circle, and Mary pulled a bandanna from her pocket and wrapped his wound. Yarielis lit a black candle, cupped it in her hands, and helped it over the bones while uttering more Creole. She began to shake, and her head began to bob violently, and her voice rose louder and more frantic.

In shock and wonder, they all watched as the bones began to stir, first in tiny quivers and then actually moving against one another to re-attach to their proper calcified mates. Once the skeleton had arranged itself into a human form, bloody flesh and connective tissue began to blossom and grow across the bones. Once the creature reached a point of a semi-decomposed corpse, it began to groan and attempt to stand up. Yarielis reached down, grabbed its arm, and helped it to stand.

"Don't worry, children. I control it. It won't hurt you. Let's send it out and create a distraction! Maybe we only need to make one."

Like a Romero film, the created zombie stumbled and staggered out of the tomb, moaning mindlessly. It staggered and lurched its way for a few hundred feet before the first vampire noticed it. They watched as the vampire tapped his friend on the arm and pointed. Before long, the zombie had attracted a crowd of vampires, giving Jean-Pierre the perfect opportunity.

Beast Stalker opened the lid of the jar holding his magical ointment, and Jean-Pierre stripped to his boxers.

"Sorry, folks," he said. "I know a pale, flabby priest is not what you wanted to see tonight, but Beast Stalker said it has to be over most of my skin to be invisible."

Mary and Janine snickered.

"Remember, Father," said Janine, "you only have a few minutes. You need to run. Nothing evil will be able to see you, so be as fast and quiet as you can. Titania said that the amulet is on a chain around Ophelia's neck. Grab that amulet and pull with all of the strength you can muster. Sorry to say this, but the fate of the world rests upon your shoulders. You were made for this, Father. Bring that amulet back in here, and then you'll be safe until morning."

"That's the plan," Jean-Pierre responded. "I just wished I'd exercised more over the past year!"

"I got your back," said Detective Barillo, brandishing a 9mm Walther pistol. "I grabbed some silver bullets out of the Resistance armory back in Ushaville. I know it won't kill them, but if I can plant some silver in their chest, it'll at least buy you some time. Right, Lâmié?"

"Yeah. It will burn them intensely and set them back, but it won't kill them. It might make the difference of several seconds, though, and that matters. Remember, guys; vampires run at superhuman speed. If they figure out what is happening and manage to guess where Father Jean-Pierre is, and they run as fast as they can, they'll catch him in a second. Detective, I think you're right. I think you should stand by the door and blast as many vamps as you can. Just don't accidentally shoot Father."

"Yes, please don't," said Jean-Pierre, chuckling despite the hopelessness of it all. "The last thing I need is silver shrapnel in my butt."

Everyone laughed, releasing some tension.

"Holy-man," said Paul, "I'm not exactly the most religious fucker around, but if there is a God, I hope he protects you. The world depends on you. No pressure though."

Everyone encouraged Jean-Pierre and gave him parting words of luck. Beast Stalker applied the magical salve all over Jean-Pierre's nearly-naked body. He was still visible to everyone in the crypt, as Beast Stalker had mentioned.

"Well, this is going to take a step of faith," said Jean-Pierre. "You say they can't see me, but you can see me, and I can see myself. God help me, I'm going in. Pace, back me up."

Jean-Pierre closed his eyes, uttered a brief prayer, and took a step out into the cemetery proper. There were vampires near the crypt, but none seemed to notice him. He sighed in relief. He crept around them to the back of the crypt and squinted in the darkness, lit by dim security lights only here and there. He saw that giant oak that Titania had mentioned. At its base, a group of vampires stood talking, and seated against the tree itself, in the center of the group, was Ophelia. She was unmistakable: her thin, pale form; her straight, raven hair; her almond eyes; her youthful beauty; it was her. The other vampires watched her and listened to her speaking, their body language implying deference. She was thousands of years old, remembered Jean-Pierre, and thus most likely the most powerful vampire in the cemetery, if not in New Orleans.

Jean-Pierre stopped and lowered himself into a race starter's stance. He whispered a quick prayer of protection, then took off at a sprint. He passed many vampires who were mulling about, and as he passed, they sniffed the air but remained impassive. The salve was working! Thanking God, Jean-Pierre aimed straight for Ophelia, determined to retrieve the amulet or die trying. As he approached the oak, he gritted his teeth and gave a final effort to speed up. He burst through the crowd of vampires around her, sending some reeling to the ground by a force that, to them, was invisible.

Ophelia quickly jerked her head up and reached for the amulet, but it was too late: in a glorious gesture, Jean-Pierre thrust his hand against her sternum, grabbed the amulet in a death-vice-grip, and pulled as hard as he could. Michael the Archangel himself must have aided Jean-Pierre because the metal chain around her neck burst into pieces as he clutched the amulet, turned around on a dime, and began the sprint back to the safe crypt. The others inside it cheered him on, clapping and shouting for him to hurry.

He made the mistake of glancing back behind himself. The vampires in the cemetery were sniffing the air and looking around in confusion, but not Ophelia. Ophelia was looking directly at him. Whether she could see him or her ancient sense of smell was so developed that she could use it like echolocation, he did not know, but he saw her lower herself into a sprinter's stance. He remembered Lâmié's words: *vampires run at superhuman speed*. He knew that once she started, he would not be able to outrun her. The crypt was looking ever closer as he pounded his legs, the lactic acid building up and burning them worse than fire. He felt a tingling all over his skin, and he instinctively knew that Beast Stalker's ointment was wearing off. Vampires all over the cemetery turned toward him and began walking toward him, then running, just as Ophelia began her sprint. The vault's door was only about ten feet in front of him, and with his lungs about to malfunction, he pushed every ounce of willpower in himself to run faster.

It was futile. No human can outrun a vampire.

As he was only five feet away from his cheering and screaming friends, he felt Ophelia's burning-icy hand grasp his ankle. He fell to the ground.

"Give me my amulet, priest!" she screamed in a deep, rough, demonic voice.

"Jean-Pierre!" screamed Lâmié as he began to run out of the crypt to help, but Beast Stalker held him back.

"You cannot overpower them," Beast Stalker said as Lâmié struggled fruitlessly in his arms. Barillo took a shot or two at some vampires. They tumbled to the ground in pain, but he did not have nearly enough rounds of silver bullets to shoot them all.

Ophelia was pulling Jean-Pierre toward herself by his leg, and dozens of other vampires surrounded him. He strained with all of his soul, but it was no more than an ant struggling against an elephant. He knew what was happening. It was his final moment in this world. Unexpectedly, the words of Chief Cloud Mountain came back to him:

Father, your spirit animal is a rattlesnake... the rattlesnake represents life and death at the same time. It is an animal of transformation, of change, but also of the power of life or death over others, as well as the power of eternal life. Your vision allowed you to choose life or death for yourself, but the rattlesnake tells me that you may soon have to choose life or death for someone else. The spirits have given you that power, and, like the Professor, they would not have chosen you if you had not been worthy. Father, you may have to make a very difficult choice in the future. I advise you to consider and assess your true spirit, your true self.

Jean-Pierre knew what he had to do, so he looked at Beast Stalker, and in the Indian's eyes, he saw understanding and approval. Beast Stalker smiled, then nodded. Jean-Pierre could feel the vampires tearing at his flesh. He felt the sharp shock of their talons ripping into his skin. Some had already begun to feed on him, to suck at his wounds so that the blood drained from him quickly. The world began to dim, but in his last, dying moment—and perhaps with the help of God—he managed to throw the amulet as hard as he could.

As it sailed toward the crypt, everyone, even the vampires and Ophelia, watched, and as if in slow motion, it arced over the iron gate, through the door, and into Beast Stalker's capable hand.

"Never forget me..." said Jean-Pierre as the world turned black. As the vampires ripped him apart and fed on his body, the very last thing he saw in this world was the glorious, warming light of God shining before him, and as Father Jean-Pierre de la Fresnière died, he realized, finally, that he had regained his faith.

CHAPTER 31

FLY BY DAY

Everyone in the crypt was silent as they sat on the floor and looked down. No one was in much of a mood for conversing, and the somber emotions pervaded the thick atmosphere of the ancient family vault. Vampires had gathered around the outside of the tomb. They hissed and scratched their claws against the stone exterior, but true to Yarielis' promise, the Voodoo magic of Papa Legba protected them.

The vampires called them, begging them to come out, but even their greatest magic and charms affected no one. As the sun began to rise, the vampires returned to their own tombs, including Ophelia, but she vowed to regain her amulet and kill them all and drink their blood before she left them. No one was comforted.

Regrouping at Jean-Pierre's rectory, they discussed their plans. Yarielis had declined to return with them but had performed a Voodoo spell of protection from evil spirits.

"First, we need to keep the amulet safe," said Beast Stalker. "I should keep it on me, on a silver chain around my neck. The silver will help to repel vampires if they try to take it."

"Good idea," said Janine. "Our goal is to get to Ushaville in one piece."

"And then? What do we do when we get there?" asked Matt.

"Then," said Paul, "it's an all-out, bloody war, and I mean bloody in both ways. We use the amulet, fairy magic, and weapons and armor to wipe out the vamps. We kill Ophelia."

"Pretty much," said Janine. "Now that Ushaville's secret's out, and I bet vamps around the world know what's happening, they'll flood there. Even with the amulet's restraining power, we can't return Ushaville to the balance that it once had. The vamps will constantly be killing humans and trying to steal the amulet. It'll be hell on Earth, so I agree with Paul. Our only hope is to destroy them, including Ophelia and the town Council. With the amulet, we have a fighting chance, but they'll outnumber us. Who knows how many vamps from around the country are already there, ready to help them in the fight? We can still use the hotel as a home base, right, Titania?"

Titania looked at Alwin, Breen, and Lylia, and they communicated silently for a moment, then she replied, "Yes, we all agree that the hotel's protective fairy magic is so ancient and powerful that it will hold against the onslaught. And we might be able to convince some more fairies from around the country to come. Alwin has agreed to travel to the heart of the fairy world and recruit them."

"Where's the heart?" asked Paul.

"Oh, you know we fairies like to keep our secrets. No human can know where it is. Sorry."

"So, um, when do we leave?" asked Xiaoqing. Sager had ceased from babbling and simply stared off into space quietly. "We should travel by day, right?"

"I don't think we have *any* time to waste," offered Lâmié. "Every minute that we hesitate could mean countless more vampires piling into Ushaville or attempting to steal the amulet back. We can't defend ourselves forever. We can't fend off innumerable hordes of vampires. The quicker we get that amulet back into the hands of the Cherokees and Beast Stalker's protection, the better chance we have of, well frankly, saving the world."

"I agree with Lâmié," said Xiaoqing. "And maybe when we kill Ophelia, Sager can return to normal."

"Anyone disagree?" asked Janine, but everyone remained silent. "Alright, then let's pack up and get ready to go today. It means we'll get into Ushaville at night, though. We'll have to play it by ear."

They packed all of the armor and weapons back into the van and took all of the food they could fit from the rectory. They had decided not to report Jean-Pierre's death to the police or the church—what was left of him would eventually be discovered by the cemetery crew, and they did not want to be linked to the death. It would only cause more trouble and take time from their mission. However, they had done the best they could to gather Jean-Pierre's remains and respectfully place them in the vault that they had hidden in. None of them were particularly religious, but Lâmié had insisted, as a matter of respect, to form a crude cross out of wood and place it above his remains.

As they fueled up the Microbite, they drew stares of astonishment from the people around them. This was quite a feat in New Orleans, which is a strange and shocking city, to begin with.

The drive to West Virginia took all day, and as the sun began to bow its head underneath the horizon, they saw the sirens of a roadblock in the far distance.

"Shit!" said Paul as he pulled the van off to the side of the highway and slightly into the forest for cover.

"What do we do?" he asked. "It's almost night, and there's a roadblock. We can't possibly get through that."

"Well, we can't sleep here!" said Mary. "We're sitting ducks. Eventually, another car's gonna pass, and if it's vamps, they'll be onto us. We can't go back and find a motel because it'll waste time. Titania, can you use some magic to get us in? Beast Stalker? Does Yarielis' Voodoo spell still work?"

Titania said, "I can do a protection spell. It might keep them away from the van until we can get into the hotel's parking lot. The hotel shouldn't be a problem because of the strong magic there."

Beast Stalker spoke, "Remember the power of the amulet. I can use it as well, and…" He paused. "I just remembered something. Father Jean-Pierre was the one who knew how to speak the words on the amulet. Without him, how can we activate it?"

"Lâmié to the rescue! I remember it. I have an excellent memory when it comes to language. I remember how to say it."

"Good, Lâmié!" said Mary. "So, do we do this?"

Everyone agreed. Titania chanted some words in her fairy language and began glowing green again. Lâmié recited the words on the amulet, and it began to give off a dark blue hue.

"Well, that's about the best we have," said Janine. "Paul, can you just floor it and bust through the roadblock? Make that four-banger sing!"

"I sure the fuck can!" he replied. "I'll bust through the barrier and then just floor it all the way back to the hotel. I just fucking hope it doesn't overheat again. If it does, we're screwed."

"Then let's do this!" proclaimed Matt.

"Wait, one last thing," said Paul, who then popped an old tape into the antiquated cassette player. The Misfits *Last Caress* began, and just as Glenn Danzig began to scream, *I got something to say!* Paul pulled the Microbite back onto the highway and smashed the accelerator pedal to the floor. Though not exactly a Ferrari, the tough little engine began to scream as they picked up speed. The red and blue sirens of the roadblock flashed closer and closer until they could see the officers manning it.

One officer stepped out in front of the wooden barricades and casually held up the palm of his hand, indicating that they should stop. However, as they did not stop but accelerated faster and faster, a look of surprise came onto the officer's face. He began to shout things to his colleagues. They looked up and began to run to him, but it was too late. The little Volkswagen blasted through the barricade at eighty miles per hour, sending wooden shrapnel flying into the air, along with one officer.

"Woohoo! Fuck yeah!" screamed Paul. "Punk as fuck!"

The streets were packed like Mardi Gras with vampires. The friends winced as they saw that the vampires had created a party-like atmosphere, with unfortunate humans splayed out on tables for feeding upon, impaled on spikes rising above the crowds, and in cages being tortured. In other spots, vampires were roasting humans alive on a spit, and each shriek of agony and torment produced great laughter from the creatures.

"Holy crap. This is what they want. This is why they want to take over the world," said Janine. "They want to use us for breeding and feeding. And that's the lucky ones. The unlucky ones will simply be slaughtered. Just keep driving, Paul. The magic seems to be working!"

As they flew down the street, vampires growled and hissed at them and screamed threats, but as the Microbite glowed green from Titania and blue from the amulet, none of the vampires could approach it. Paul screeched around the corner and onto Unter den Linden, hitting and running over dozens of vampires before they reached the Summer Linden Hotel. He turned and sped into the underground parking, almost rolling the van over as it made the curve, but they made it—the parking gate closed, and the vampires were kept at bay by the ancient fairy magic.

"We made it! We fucking made it!" cheered Paul.

"My suggestion, everyone," said Lâmié, "is that we get some sleep tonight. There's no use fighting them on the streets with their sheer numbers, and they can't get into the hotel anyway. The amulet is safe with us here. Tomorrow when the sun rises, we can hunt them on our terms. We'll go to the houses of the leaders and find Ophelia. We'll stake them while they sleep, Dracula style."

"Have to agree," said Mary. "Plus, I'm tired as hell. Did you see how many of them are out there? It'd be a deathwish to try to fight them at night."

No one argued, and they all splayed out on the exquisite Oriental rugs that covered the bar's wooden floor, not even bothering to go up to the hotel rooms, so exhausted were they. A few of them had a nightcap before going to sleep, but after an hour or so, the room was filled with snores.

CHAPTER 32

THE TURNING

The hotel bar. Darkness. Deep slumber. The still, quiet night. Outside, crickets chirp, but then they stop. At a window, two shadowy figures creep through the silence. One of them noiselessly, stealthily lifts the window open. Underneath the window sleeps Professor Sager Miller. As he stumbles through oppressive, confusing nightmares, a whispering voice, sweet as honey, calls to him.

"Sager. Sager. Wake up, Sager. Come to me, Sager."

He stirs slightly, but the voice continues.

"Sager. Wake up. Open the front door, Sager. Come to me. Come to me in the night, my lover."

Sager's eyes open and he hears the voice. Seemingly still in slumber, he stands and slowly walks to the front door. He reaches for the doorknob, unlocks the deadbolt, and opens the door. In the darkness, just beyond his vision, the voice persists.

"Come to me, darling. Come to me!"

He knows the voice instinctively.

"Mistress!" he calls out. "Ophelia! Mistress!" He steps out into the warm, humid night. He sees Ophelia and Nancy, although something about Nancy has changed. Her chocolatine skin has become much paler, much more livid. Her eyes are penetrating and red. She smiles at Sager, and two sharp canine fangs protrude from her ruby lips.

"Nancy…"

"Come to me, lover!" says Ophelia, and Sager falls into her cold arms.

Ophelia whispers in Sager's ear, and Nancy suppresses a cruel laugh.

Back in the hotel bar, Xiaoqing is fast asleep. She is dreaming about Sager, how he was before the change. In her dream, it is a sunny day and they are on the university campus. They are holding hands and walking toward their offices. Sager stops and looks at her, calling her name. "Xiaoqing! Xiaoqing!" The voice persists, and she awakens. The voice is still there, in the waking world. "Xiaoqing!" It is Sager's voice, and it is coming from outside. The front door of the hotel is open, allowing the deep darkness inside.

She walks to the door and peers outside.

"Sager?" Are you out there? What are you doing? It's dangerous! Get back inside!"

"Xiaoqing! Come out with me! I need help!"

"Sager? What's the matter?"

"I fell down and hurt myself! I must have been sleepwalking. I think I hurt my ankle."

"You are talking again? Oh honey, are you finally back to normal? I'm coming!"

"Wait, no!" screams Janine from behind Xiaoqing. "It's a trap!"

It is, however, too late. Xiaoqing goes outside of the hotel's protection, and Janine watches in horror as the new Nancy rushes to her, bends her head to the side, and pierces her jugular vein with the new fangs. Janine is paralyzed in terror as Nancy takes deep, bloody draughts of Xiaoqing's lifeblood. As Xiaoqing falls to the ground, Nancy slices her own arm with a sharp claw, letting the blood flow into Xiaoqing's mouth and down her throat. Nancy looks up at Janine and smiles.

Janine slams the door shut and locks it.

"Wake up, everyone! Up! Up!"

"What the fuck..." says Paul as they all awaken and look around in confusion.

"It's the vampires!" Janine tells them. "They tricked Sager and Xiaoqing into going outside. Bad news: Nancy is back and she's a vampire now."

"Oh no!" cries Matt. "Poor Nancy...those vamps in the tunnel must have changed her. Oh, Nancy!"

"More bad news," says Janine. "I just watched Nancy bite Xiaoqing and make her drink her blood. You know what that means."

"Shit," said Lâmié. "It means that now Nancy's a vampire, and Xiaoqing will be one in three days. What are we going to do? We have to rescue Sager before they make him one, too."

"I don't think that'll happen," says Janine. "They need him as bait. Let's think of a strategy."

No one can sleep any more this night.

CHAPTER 33

INCUBATION

J anine gathered everyone around a table as if they were King Arthur's knights and brought a chalkboard up from the basement to write as she spoke.

"Alright guys, here's the situation. Gill and the Father died, and Nancy and Xiaoqing became vampires. Sager is captive. Ushaville is flush with vampires, and more are arriving daily, I am sure. Any remaining humans in Ushaville have either been killed or enslaved. Obviously, the situation is dire. Our goals? One: to rescue Sager. Two: to kill Ophelia and as many bloodsuckers as possible. Three: to get the amulet to Chief Cloud Mountain and seek his counsel. Four: to use the amulet's power to restore order to Ushaville and prevent the infestation from spreading around the country and around the globe. That's how I see it. To accomplish this, we need the Microbite, weapons and armor, and some magic. We have Cherokee magic, fairy magic, and, of course, the amulet itself. The problem is that the vamps can outnumber us. Even with the amulet activated, there's no reason a throng of hundreds of vamps couldn't simply overwhelm us and snatch it away, or even destroy it. So, we need a good strategy to accomplish all this."

"I got an idea," said Paul. "I think we forgot something in our last attack. Lâmié, you said there are three ways to kill a vamp, right? Stake through the heart, sunlight, and *fire*. We need to come up with some sort of flamethrower as a weapon."

"That would burn down Ushaville!" answered Janine.

"Then let's fucking burn down the town!" said Paul. "It needs a reboot anyway. It didn't exactly do well this time around."

"You know," said Lâmié, "he's got a point. In supernatural lore, fire is usually seen as a purifier, a way to start anew, life from death. Think of the phoenix as an example. The bird dies in the fire, but it is reborn gloriously anew. Maybe we really should burn the town down. We have the weapons and magic, but Janine makes a good point. There must be tens of thousands of vamps out there. They could definitely just overwhelm us with numbers. But if we shoot them with fire, well hell, there's not much they can do. My suggestion: we build a flamethrower, then push through the crowds to Anse's and Asa's mansions and burn them to the ground. I mean, just totally fuck them off the face of the earth. I'll bet Ophelia is living with one of them, and Sager will be there. We find him, rescue him, burn the mansions, then kill Ophelia. With fire, we can blast through the crowds and make our way to Chief Cloud Mountain."

Janine said, "I see your point. Alright, what does everyone else have to say?"

She went around the table to give everyone a chance to talk.

Matt: "Agree."

Mary: "I guess."

Beast Stalker: "It is a good idea. I will go along with it."

Titania: "Agree. I'll work on the magical part."

Detective Barillo: "Sure. I mean, what other options do we have?"

Breen and Lylia in unison: "Yes."

"Well, that settles it," said Janine. "Now, how to make a flamethrower?"

Paul replied, "I know how. Don't ask. Do you have any…"

Paul was interrupted by a tinkling sound in the air, and a bright, green glow engulfed the entire hotel bar.

"Oh!" said Titania, giggling.

Out of the nothing but air, Alwin the fairy appeared, with ten other fairies behind him.

"Shit! Fuck! What the bloody hell?" shouted Paul.

"I found backup," announced Alwin. "These fairies have agreed to come and fight with us. Allow me to introduce them: Blinky, Corky, Dalliance, Ghent, Harpy, Rose, Puck, Senfus, Phoebe, and Limerick." The ten fairies bowed and curtsied melodramatically.

"Shit. I'll never remember all that," said Paul.

Titania laughed. "It's alright. We understand."

"Now, on to that flamethrower!" said Janine.

"I don't suppose you have some napalm lying around?" asked Paul, grinning.

They all helped pull everything up out of the Resistance armory into the hotel bar to see what they had to work with. Since they already had used many of the weapons and most of the armor, there was not too much left, but there were two promising things—a rocket-propelled-grenade launcher with ten rockets and a gasoline-powered leaf-blower.

"I have an idea!" said Paul. "There's a few gas cans in the parking garage." He ran downstairs while the others looked at the remaining equipment. Paul returned with two huge plastic cans. They heard the gasoline sloshing around inside of them as he moved.

"Let's try not to burn down the hotel for fuck's sake, Paul," said Mary.

Paul explained: "Alright, mates, hear me out. First, the rocket launcher thingy. Those rockets have sockets up front to screw in grenades. Instead of grenades, we fill up some sort of small container with gasoline and some sort of propellant to ignite it when it hits something. It'll be a giant fucking fireball! Second, the leaf blower. We make a reserve tank of gasoline and attach a lighter or something to the front of the blower tube. We turn it on, and it blows out gasoline into the air. We light the gas and watch a bunch of vampires burn the fuck into the next world!"

Matt replied, "Well damn, Paul, I hate to admit it, but those are two fucking great ideas. They just might work too. Maybe you should become an inventor."

Janine laughed and said, "He's right! Paul dammit, you continue to surprise me. I think we can find everything we need around the hotel. There's a pretty big maintenance room downstairs with tons of tools and parts and gadgets. You and Matt want to get on that right away?"

"Hell yeah!" said Paul, pulling Matt by his black, leather sleeve downstairs to see what they had to work with.

"After they make the fire weapons, they'll need to refurbish and refresh the Microbite," said Janine. "In fact, all of us should check out our weapons and armor, clean them, make sure they function, stock up on ammo, and all of that. Titania, do you and your fairy friends need time to come up with magic?"

"Yes," said Titania. "I think we'll go take a quiet corner and talk about how we will proceed."

Everyone took to his or her task, spending most of the day working. Paul and Matt remained coy about their creations downstairs and also descended to the parking garage to work on the van. Around nightfall, they gathered into the hotel bar to discuss plans.

"First things first," said Janine. "We need to eat. Let me go into the kitchen and cook something. Everyone alright with pasta and steak?"

"More than alright!" said Lâmié. "Got any good red wine to go with it?"

"I see no reason not to empty out the hotel's reserve wine cellar," Janine answered. "It feels like the apocalypse. I can't imagine the hotel going back to business as usual any time soon. So yeah, why not? We have some really good stuff down there."

Janine cooked them dinner, and the others helped her out. When they finished, the bar's largest table was covered in mouthwatering steaks and pasta with several different authentic Italian sauces. Janine had pulled out ten or so bottles of high-end Bordeaux. They feasted like kings and drank like fools. While the town around them was again filled with dark, vampiric shades on every street, they feasted as if it were a Plague Banquet. After dinner, when everyone was quite drunk— including the fairies, mind you—Janine turned on some '80s music, and they all danced around like idiots, but like happy idiots. An implied agreement not to start fighting that night meant that they all understood that they would sleep richly and deeply that night, then get ready to go to war on the morrow.

"Before we all pass out, guys," said Janine, "we need to decide when to attack. I think they'll be expecting us to pounce quickly, especially since they have Sager. But I think he's safe as long as they're using him as bate."

"I hate to bring it up, but another question is whether we wait until Xiaoqing turns fully into a vamp. That takes three days.," said Detective Barillo. "I'm going to give my advice as a detective. I've had three serial killer cases in my career so far. I've learned that you have to be very strategic with an intelligent killer, which is what the vampires are, right? You need to strike when they least expect it. Sometimes that means waiting and making them sweat it out. It often forces their move, and that's when they make a mistake, and we nab 'em. The vamps expect us to go tomorrow, as Janine said. If we wait a couple of days, it'll throw them off guard, so I vote to wait the three days. That's tomorrow, the next day, and the next day. We strike on the fourth day. We have more than enough food and drinks to make it, and we know the hotel's protected. They'll get confident. Even now, they're throwing a dark party out there. They'll get drunk on blood. They'll celebrate. They'll think we're cowering in fear, but on the fourth day, we go out with guns blazing. We start mid-morning when most of them'll be sleeping. With so many vamps in town, they can't all stay hidden.

They'll be sleeping inside of businesses, under awnings, in houses. We'll have almost free reign. While we wait here for three days, we can train and make plans. Most importantly, we stick together. What d'ya say?"

Everyone agreed that it was a good plan. That night, they each found a place on the floor with blankets and pillows taken from the rooms above them and had disturbing dreams of vampires and battle.

CHAPTER 34

THE BATTLE BEGINS

T he three days were spent in a sort of haze—the sort of illusionary denial that must have existed in the high days of the Bubonic Plague in Europe. The group trained and sparred; they cleaned and upgraded their weapons, the flamethrowers, and the van; they ate, drank, danced, sang, laughed, and enjoyed the hell out of themselves.

But nothing was quite as sweet as a drop of honey in a sea of vinegar, as precious as a moment of love in a time of death. The night before the fourth day, an ascetic seriousness descended upon the hotel, and they abstained from food and drink together, having decided to go to sleep early to prepare for the battle the next day.

Everyone naturally awoke at sunrise on the fourth day, as if Nature herself had ordained it. No one spoke much, and the butterflies in all of their stomachs flapped their wings frantically. There was an implied understanding: they might all die that day. In fact, the chances that they would die were much greater than the chances that they would prevail against innumerable dark creatures of the night and save the world. They all felt that, ate it, drank it, breathed it.

"Friends," said Beast Stalker, "and I can truly call you all friends now, take heart. In the culture of my people, when two people fight the enemy together, they become brothers and sisters. In our past days of glory, before the Europeans destroyed us, our great warriors would go out on the morning of the battle and say, *Today is a good day to die.*

We fight today, not for selfish reasons of land, gold, influence, or empire. No, we fight today, my brothers and sisters, for the sake of good against evil. We fight to save the world from such a great darkness that we cannot even imagine it. May we fight true, and hard, and fast. May we attack like the eagle, who descends upon its prey, striking quickly and surely. May our weapons find their marks, and may our armor fend off the weapons of the enemy. Say it with me, friends: *Today is a good day to die.*"

"Today is a good day to die," repeated everyone in unison.

"Thank you, Beast Stalker. That is very inspiring," said Janine. "Now, everyone, let's go over our plans. The sun is just rising, meaning that the vampires have all found a place to sleep for the day. We've improved our weapons, stocked up on ammo, and strengthened our armor for the past three days. Paul and Matt, do the flamethrowers work?"

"We think so," answered Matt. "We don't have enough gasoline to test them. It would waste the fuel. They work in theory, but if we shoot them off now, there'll hardly be any fuel left for the outside world."

"Alright," continued Janine. "That'll have to do. We'll just hope they work when the time comes. And the Microbite?"

"Fucking brilliant!" said Paul. "All armored up, gassed up, weaponed up, tuned up, and ready to fucking go! Crosses, holy water, garlic, silver, iron, armor everywhere, a gun turret, fortified tires with armored shields, a bull bar…it kicks ass, it does!"

"Excellent. So, where do you guys think Ophelia is holed up with Sager?"

"Gotta be Devil Anse's mansion," said Detective Barillo. "Think about it. We destroyed a wall in Asa's mansion last time. He couldn't have had time to rebuild it in just a few days. She probably knows we'll go there, and what she wants is to draw us in. Plus, it's on the Eastside, so there are more vampires all around to protect her."

"Makes sense," said Janine. "So, we agree to go to Anse's mansion first? Since it's daylight, we shouldn't have any trouble getting to it. But once we go inside, it's a crapshoot. The vamps'll be sleeping most likely, but since inside the mansion will be dark, there's nothing stopping them from waking up. We have to be quiet and ready to fight. Our goal is to find and rescue Professor Sager and to kill Ophelia. In the meantime, we'll kill as many vamps as possible. Let's save the fire until we absolutely need it. Titania and the fairies, were you able to come up with a spell?"

"Yes," said Titania, her voice sounding like tinkering glass. "We've created a potent spell of protection. We believe that it will hold off vampires for as long as we can maintain it, which depends on how many of them there are."

"Great!" said Janine. "Beast Stalker and Lâmié? Are you ready to activate the amulet when we need it?"

They both nodded.

"Okay, good. Well, there's no time like the present. Everyone bring it in!"

She extended her arm with her hand palm-up like a football huddle.

"Oh God, that's so hokey," said Paul.

"Shut up and do it, Paul, or I swear I'll slap you!" warned Mary.

"Fine. Geez. Shit."

Everyone gathered in and made a pile with their hands. Janine counted to three, and everyone shouted, "Today is a good day to die!"

"And fuck the vamps!" added Paul, causing them all to laugh.

They ate breakfast, then loaded the Microbite with all of their weapons and armor. Paul would drive; Matt, Barillo, and Mary took the roof turret. Paul and Matt had welded the fire-bombing rocket-propelled-grenade launcher on a rotating mount on the roof as if it were a tank; the flame-throwing leaf blower was mounted on the hood, facing forward. While the van's windows were guarded with iron bars, they had drilled murder holes underneath each window, allowing them to stick the barrels of their weapons outside in all directions.

"Well, shit!" exclaimed Janine. "This is genuinely badass! It's like a tank! Alright, everyone get in. Take a window if you are near it. Let's go rescue Sager and kill that bitch, Ophelia!"

Paul turned on the engine, and it hummed smoothly. He shifted the transmission into gear, and hit the accelerator. The van responded deftly as they exited the parking garage and entered Ushaville proper. The streets were empty of vampires but replete with the unfortunate humans who had been in Ushaville. There were corpses everywhere, as well as blood smears, severed limbs and heads, piles of internal organs, and the remains of the poor souls who had been roasted alive on the spits.

They all remained silent in outraged shock, but Paul kept driving. He kept their speed low, both to save fuel and reduce their noise so they would not awaken all vampires. They could see through the windows of all of the businesses that they passed, and they noticed each store's floor covered in sleeping vampires, their arms folded over their chests like in movies.

"So, it's true. They really do sleep like that," whispered Lâmié. "Fascinating."

As they entered the Eastside, the curtained windows of the grim houses blocked their view inside, but they knew that the places were brimming with sleeping vampires like fish in a stocked pond. After a few minutes, they approached Devil Anse's grimy mansion, and Paul cut off the ignition and coasted the van to the curb to maintain silence. They all got out of the van stealthily, using hand signals to communicate.

Janine tried the front door and found it unlocked. She cautiously opened it and stepped inside, signaling the others to follow. The floor was filled end-to-end with sleeping vampires. Only a small cleared pathway through the middle allowed them to proceed without stepping on the creatures. They quietly, gingerly made their way to the main parlor, looking into every room on the way and finding them all also replete with sleeping vampires. Slowly, room-by-room, they searched the floors for Ophelia, but she was not on the first floor. Janine pointed upwards, and they proceeded up the stairs, which were free of sleeping vampires.

Laboriously, they quietly searched the bedrooms, beginning with one end of the main hall. The master bedroom found Devil Anse himself sleeping on the bed alone. The other bedrooms were shared with various vampires, male and female, in various stages of undress. Their pallid, sallow bodies were sickly and emaciated. Finally, in the last bedroom of the hall, they discovered Ophelia's gravely-beautiful, sleeping form. And on the floor next to the bed, like a dog, was Sager. A spiked, metal collar was around his neck, furthering his humiliation and emasculation.

As Paul stepped into the room, his lamentable foot managed to find a loose floorboard, causing a loud *creeeaaak*. Everyone froze, but it was too late. Sager woke up, rubbed his sleepy eyes, and looked at them. Then he screamed.

"Mistress! They are here! The intruders!"

Ophelia opened her bloodshot eyes. Her torso rose up from her waist, and she looked at them with a wicked smile.

"I see my bait worked, you fools. Drawing you here was like training monkeys. Oh, how I'll enjoy feasting on your blood!"

Ophelia opened her gaping maw and issued a shriek like that of a banshee.

"Shit!" said Paul. "Fuck it; I'm doing this." He rushed to Sager, yanked him up by Sager's arm, and tossed him over his shoulder like a potato sack. "Go! Go! Go! Downstairs and outside!"

They ran out of the bedroom as Ophelia growled and began to get out of the bed. Speeding down the hall, they reached the staircase and started to go down. They heard the vampires in every room stirring, the rustling of their clothes, their hisses and growls as they realize something was amiss, their audible sniffing of the air to detect the fresh, living blood that was among them.

"Fucking go!" shouted Paul, no longer caring about being quiet. The gig was up, after all.

As they reached the bottom of the staircase, their way was blocked by many vampires stumbling out of the side rooms like zombies. Paul stopped and turned around, but Ophelia was at the top of the staircase, smirking at them.

"Shit! What do we do now?" asked Paul frantically.

"Alright, guys, it's time to fight! We'll blast our way out!" cried Janine. "Open fire!"

They let forth a barrage of holy water, stakes, silver bullets, and iron buckshot into the crowd of vampires. As the creatures were hit, they howled, whimpered, and hissed while the smoke from their skin created a foggy cloud that was difficult to see through.

Vampires assaulted them from all directions.

Their armor fended most of them off, but some of the vampires could rip off some pieces and scratch some of them with their razor claws. Paul held on to Sager with a vice-grip through it all, determined to save him or die trying. As they burst through the front door of the mansion, they heard Ophelia's angry, surprised cry, almost piercing their eardrums. They piled into the Microbite and backed it up so that the front faced the mansion.

"About ready to test out that fire bomber?" shouted Janine to Matt on the roof.

"Fucking right I am!" shouted back Matt. Vampires were pouring out of the front door of the mansion, and Matt aimed at the door itself. Taking one last breath of hope, he pulled the trigger. The cannon did not disappoint—a rocket flew out of the barrel, its small rocket engine propelling the attached firebomb at the door at lightning speed. It hit the floor of the mansion just inside of the door, and a fireball exploded, reaching even its roof. Vampires screamed in confusion as the vast, fiery explosion began to engulf the mansion's old wood structure in a raging inferno. The vampires trapped inside were being burned alive, and those who had made it outside had backed away from the van, expecting a second firebomb at any moment.

"Fuck yeah!" shouted Matt, laughing as loud as his lungs were able. "Paul, gun it! Let's get the fuck out of here!"

"Don't have to tell me twice, mate!" shouted Paul as the van careened backward, the tires screeching on the pavement. Paul managed to turn it around, and they sped off from the mansion and out of the

Eastside onto Unter den Linden. Sager had been strapped into the rear seat, and his face bore an expression of fear and worry.

"Did we kill Ophelia?" asked Barillo.

"Look at Sager. I don't think so. He's still under her power. That's not good, because it probably means she can track us wherever we go," answered Janine.

"Speaking of, where *do* we go now?" asked Paul.

"I think we should still go to Asa Harmon's mansion and torch it. We don't even need to go inside," replied Janine.

Paul nodded and pointed the Microbite toward Asa's manor.

As they arrived, there was no resistance. The Westside streets were still empty.

It was a simple matter of shooting the second rocket right into the center of the front of the mansion. It exploded and set the place ablaze. They heard shrieks of pain from the inside as the vampires were roasted alive.

Matt cackled maniacally as the mansion burned like a torch. A small number of vampires managed to break out of the windows into the front yard. Some of them were hit by the sunlight and caught fire, burning up in a deathly clamor, while others were smart enough to stay in the shadows of the giant oak trees. Among them was Nancy.

"Oh, shit," said Matt. "It's Nancy!"

"Shoot her, Matt," said Mary. "It's not her anymore. Don't make her suffer inside of that body. Release her soul, Matt."

Matt hesitated and said, "You know, Mary, Nancy and I had something. We slept together, but I think there was more. I think we really could have fallen in love with each other if she hadn't been turned."

"I suspected that," said Mary. "Then do one, last, loving thing, Matt. I know it must hurt to see her like this, and I know how hard it must be to kill the person you love. But remember what Lâmié said? He said a small part of the former human remains inside of the vampire, suffering torment. Put her out of her misery, Matt."

Matt stood up in the turret and pointed his wooden-stake-loaded, automatic rifle at Nancy's heart.

"Matt!" she screamed. "Matt, don't kill me! Come, be with me! We can be together forever! Please, Matt, I love you. Please come be with me."

Matt hesitated only for three or four seconds before taking a deep breath and replying, "I'm so sorry, Nancy. I know a part of you is still in there. I'm setting you free because I love you. I'll see you in the next life."

A tear ran down Matt's cheek as he pulled the trigger, sending several wooden stakes flying through the air toward her. As the wood penetrated her heart, did he see the look of shock and anger on her face change briefly to one of peace and relief? She exploded in a cloud of ashes.

CHAPTER 35

THE LAST SHOWDOWN

Paul threw the Microbus into reverse and gunned it away from Anse's former mansion, now a towering inferno. He turned the corner and sped out of the Eastside back onto Unter den Linden. It was still daylight, so he pulled over to the side of the street and cut off the engine.

"Alright, mates, what now?" he asked.

"We can't take the amulet to Chief Cloud Mountain until we kill Ophelia. If we give it to him now, we're that much weaker, and I have a feeling that we're gonna need it in the final showdown. And like we said, we have to kill her to save Sager, and especially to make sure she never gets the amulet again," said Janine.

"Well, we know she's on the Eastside somewhere near the former Anse mansion. There are a million places for her to hide during the day on the Eastside. We can't possibly case every single house and business. And look at the sun, guys. It'll be sundown before too long."

"We can't go back to the hotel another night," said Matt. "We have to finish this, or we'll be in hiding forever. We kill Ophelia tonight."

"Gotta agree, Mucky," said Mary. "I'm tired of waiting, of hiding, of wondering. We kill her now, or we die trying." No one else argued.

"Titania," asked Janine, "can you do the Ophelia locater thing again with Sager?"

"I'll try," Titania replied. She touched Sager on the shoulder and began chanting. After a brief moment, she was slammed back by the audible buzzing of electricity.

"Titania! Are you alright?"

"I... I think so. Ophelia's onto me. She was waiting for me to do the locater spell. She used her vampire powers back against me."

"Did you get a glance of where she was?" asked Janine.

"I saw a dark bar, under a giant oak tree, then she zapped me."

"Gotta be the Lust Bar on the Eastside. Any of you know it?" asked Janine.

"Yeah," said Paul, "we passed it with... with Nancy... when we went to the Eastside for the first time. We wanted to go in, you know. It looked pretty punk, but Nancy told us that they check for the mark of protection, and we wouldn't be safe."

"Yeah, that's normally how it works," said Janine, pulling up her hair to reveal her own tattooed mark of protection, the same small, red circle with a cross inside of it. "Now that's Ushaville's gone to shit, I don't think that matters anymore. If she's at the Lust Bar, then she must feel safe there. She's using it as headquarters, which means she'll have plenty of backup. And this time, they'll be expecting us. Shit."

Janine nodded, then turned to Paul: "Paul, how much fuel do we have in the flamethrower-leafblower thingy?"

"Not sure," Paul answered. "A gas can full. Don't know the rate of fire, 'cuz we couldn't waste the gas testing it. I'd guess we have several minutes of continuous flame."

"Well, that's enough to do some serious damage. But I don't think we can just drive up to the Lust Bar and firebomb it. We need Ophelia herself, and she's very cunning: she'll have an escape route."

"If I can butt in," began Detective Barillo, "if she's clever like a good criminal, she'll try to bait us into using all of our resources against the Lust Bar, and then she'll flank us. We have to wait until we have her on sight before using fire, in my opinion."

"Yeah, good point," said Janine. "So, then let's go there. We'll case it out carefully, then go inside if we have to. Just remember that it's definitely an ambush or a trap. She knows we're coming, and she'll be ready. This is when we'll have to use every resource we have, alright gang?"

Everyone nodded and agreed.

"Here we go!" said Paul as he aimed the Microbite back to the Eastside.

They cautiously approached the Lust Bar. Since the sun had not yet set, the front doors were closed, and no one was outside. In another context, it would have looked like a lazy summer late-afternoon, but the knowledge of the vampires inside soured any pleasant feelings.

All was quiet on the Eastern Front, so they carefully stepped out of the Microbite, forming a circle around Sager, whom they had encased with body armor. Like a roman phalanx, they joined their shields together to form a sort of barrier, and marched slowly toward the bar. They listened carefully but heard nothing inside. Janine gave a nod and tried the door, but it was locked, so she formed a fist and pushed it into the palm of her other hand, indicating that she would force it open. She took a step back, then gave a strong, forward kick. The door flew open. They hustled inside, ready for action, but the bar was quiet and empty.

There were cages around the bar where Janine knew that human slaves would usually be forced to dance for the vampire customers. They checked out all of the areas of the bar: the main room, behind the bar, the bathrooms, the office—no one was there, human or vampire. Then they heard footsteps by the front door.

"Oh, shit," said Janine—a crowd of vampires had sneaked inside the bar behind them, at the front of which was Ophelia.

"Well, that was easy," said Ophelia. "Like trapping rats in a cage. Now, I'll make this simple. I have power over Sager. He is my slave. All I have to do is twist my hand, and his head will twist off. It is that easy and fast. Give me the amulet, right now, and I will not only spare Sager, but I give you my word as a vampire that I will let you all walk out of here alive and leave Ushaville, never to come back."

"And let you take over the world and enslave mankind?" asked Paul. "Not likely, bitch."

"Well, now, you did not allow me to offer you the other option. If you do not give me the amulet right now, then my friends here and I will tear you to bits, drink your blood, and take the amulet anyway," said Ophelia with a sly grin.

Detective Barillo, accustomed to spotting weaknesses in criminals, replied, "If it were that easy for you to kill us all and just take the amulet, you'd have done it already." Ophelia became furious and hissed. "I thought so," continued Barillo. "See, here's what I think. I think you're a very old and powerful vampire, sure, Ophelia. I'll give you that. But I think you also know just how powerful the amulet is. You know that it was designed long, long ago to fight your kind, to defeat vampires;

you know that it's not as easy as just snatching it from us. I think it has to be given to you voluntarily, like when Sager gave it to you to give to Devil Anse the time before, or you can't use it. That's what I think. Otherwise, why wouldn't you just come over here right now, kill us all, and take it? After all, it'd be easy enough, like you said."

In a growling, gravelly, demonic voice, Ophelia replied: "Well, Detective, aren't you clever? So, you figured out the secret of the amulet. Yes, it has to be given to a vampire voluntarily. But I have ways of making you do that."

She clapped three times loudly and shrieked a piercing cry that hurt their ears. They heard rumbling from underneath the bar, and then a hidden trapdoor in the floor burst open. The trapdoor led down to the tunnels, and like the very mouth of hell, the dried out, creaking old skeletal vampires began to stumble and stagger out of it.

"Shit! The ancient ones!" said Janine. "We're cornered!"

"You're surrounded," said Ophelia, having recomposed her voice into the deceptively seductive one she normally used. "You have no chance of escape. None. I am very ancient and powerful, and the ones from below are almost as ancient as I. These here in with me are the strongest vampires in Ushaville. You cannot win. Your only choice now is this: do you want to lose voluntarily and with honor, or do I have to torture you until you give up the amulet while begging for your life like so many dogs?"

"We'll go down fighting, Ophelia! Fucking believe that, bitch!" shouted Paul, shouldering and aiming his holy water rifle.

The air was tense and terrifying.

Like a Wild West shootout, each side waited for the other to act. Before anyone could begin, however, the undead Xiaoqing entered the front door of the bar.

"Xiaoqing!" shouted Janine. "Oh, God! You poor thing! Ophelia, you bitch! You made her into a vampire!"

"No need to be angry at Ophelia," said Xiaoqing. "I like it. In fact, I love it. I am so powerful, so deadly, so free, so eternal. You can be like me, too. All it takes is a little bite, a little sting, and you can be free of all of the sickness, aging, and misery of humankind."

"Xiaoqing?" asked Sager. "Is that you?"

"Don't mind her," shouted Ophelia. "You're mine forever!"

"Ophelia," said Xiaoqing, "I think I should get to turn him. He's my boyfriend, after all."

"He *was* yours, Xiaoqing!" countered Ophelia. "He left you! He made love to me! He's my slave, and he always will be. And you had better watch your tongue. I am ancient. You are a new vampire. You owe me honor and obedience."

"Honor to the whore who tricked my love away from me? Do you think he would have anything to do with you if you hadn't used vampire magic to enslave him?" shouted Xiaoqing assertively.

"You *will* honor and obey me, young vampiress!" shouted Ophelia. "Do it, or I will destroy you!"

"You couldn't destroy me, you slut!"

While the two screamed threats, Paul decided to take action into his own hands. He had attached a 1980s-style boom box to his backpack and had loaded it with an old *Misfits* tape. He carefully and slowly punched the play button, quietly aimed his holy water rifle at Ophelia's face, and, just as the opening of *Don't Open 'Til Doomsday* blasted their eardrums, causing everyone to jump, Paul pulled his trigger. Chaos erupted.

The water shot through the air and hit Ophelia right in the face.

As her skin burned and smoked, she hissed and shrieked, grabbed her face, and twisted around in agony. This set off the vampires around her, who began to attack the group of friends. The Ancient Ones behind them began to move, moaning in agony, longing for their first drop of human blood in centuries. Everyone in the group opened fire into the vampires in front of them and behind them. Holy water, silver bullets, iron buckshot, and wooden ash stakes flew through the air in all directions. Screams, shouts, and hisses filled the bar as vampires dropped.

Janine fought valiantly, and when three vampires jumped onto her, they felt the sting of her silver and iron armor and fell back. She had pulled out a silver sword, and she swang it through the air, slicing the head off of one of them. Paul, Matt, and Mary had formed a punk fighting unit. As Michale Graves screamed the lyrics, *Don't open 'til doomsday! Destruction's not far away!* The punks screamed and shot their stake guns wildly. Several of the stakes met their targets, turning vampires to puffs of carbon, startling the other vampires near them.

Detective Barillo had turned to face the Ancient Ones. He had two semi-automatic pistols—one in each hand, one shooting holy water, the other shooting small wooden stakes—and he blasted them both against the hoary creatures. Slow as they were, he picked off a dozen of them in a few seconds. "Woohoo!" he screamed. A younger vampire grabbed his right arm and knocked the pistol to the ground. The vampire leaped upon him, opened his fanged mouth, and brought his mouth down toward Barillo's jugular, but right as the fangs were going to penetrate his skin, the vampire burst into a cloud of dust.

"You're welcome!" screamed Mary and Barillo grinned. She had staked the vampire from behind.

Beast Stalker stood like an oak, not budging one inch as he fired his stakes into the vampire crowd approaching him. He had fashioned a bow and arrow with ash stake arrows, and with it, he made quick work of them.

The ground was becoming covered in a layer of carbon ash as they killed vampire after vampire.

A fresh wave entered the bar and ran toward the group. But suddenly, from out of nowhere, Titania, Alwin, Breen, Lylia, and their ten fairy friends—who had magically camouflaged themselves against the walls—appeared. They hovered above the ground, each of them having opened a magnificent, stunning set of golden, gossamer wings. They shouted a spell in their fairy language, and a bright, green light burst outward from them, knocking dozens of vampires to the ground and stunning them. The punks ran to the downed group and staked them all into powder.

After half an hour of the deadly battle, the humans had lost no one, but the vampires were down to Ophelia, Xiaoqing, and only five or six others.

"Stop!" cried Ophelia in a booming, devilish voice of authority. Everyone immediately stopped fighting and stared at her in surprise.

"Enough!" she continued. "There's no need to kill everyone. Give me the amulet now, or Sager dies!" She held out her hand, muttered something in an ancient, forgotten, guttural vampire language, and then made a fist. Sager howled in agony.

"Stop! Leave him alone, bitch!" shouted Paul. Ophelia smiled, knowing that she had found their weak point. She moved her hand around in the air, and Sager's body followed the movements like a limp scarecrow. He cried out in torment as his bones and ligaments were stretched to their limits. She continued for a few more seconds, then stopped, causing Sager to fall to the floor.

"Now, I can continue, or you can give me the amulet. I can torture him for hours, or I can snap his neck at any time. I will unless you give me the amulet."

The pain, however, had managed to snap Sager out of his vampiric enchantment to Ophelia. He struggled to stand up.

"Sager!" shouted Xiaoqing. "We're meant to be together, forever! Come to me, my love, come to my dark embrace, and I'll make you eternal, just like me!"

"No!" shouted Ophelia. "I command you to come to me!"

Sager staggered to a spot between them both. He looked at Xiaoqing and Ophelia.

"Come here, my darling!" said Xiaoqing. "Come be with me forever!"

"Do not!" commanded Ophelia. "Come to me, lover, and we shall rule the world together! I'll make you a mighty vampire. We shall enslave the human race, and together rule an empire of darkness!"

Sager felt the power of Ophelia's vampire magic creeping again into his heart, but this time, he resisted it. He looked at Xiaoqing, and the words of Chief's prophecy came to him:

Professor, your spirit animal is a lynx cat. This is an animal with complex meanings. A lynx represents someone who guides others, who protects secrets. This tells me that you will be entrusted with great power. The spirits will expect you to guard it and to use it only as appropriate. But they would not have chosen you for this if they had not thought that you were worthy. As to your vision, I am afraid that its meaning is not a happy one. You will become a sacrifice for the good of someone else, or of many people.

He remembered what Lâmié had said as well: *...a part of their former humanity remains, which means it is tortured as it has to live out the life of a killer demon.* He looked deeply into Xiaoqing's eyes. There was a demonic hatred and wickedness in their blackness, but for just the briefest instant, he saw something else, something that flickered like television static, and then disappeared—it was a plea for help, for release, from the real Xiaoqing that was inside of the monster. He knew that it was her; he knew her eyes, her glances of love. He then knew what he had to do. Sager walked toward Xiaoqing.

"Yes, yes! Come to me, my love!"

"No! Come to me!" shouted Ophelia, but Sager continued to Xiaoqing. When he reached her, she opened her arms and embraced him; then, she opened her mouth, revealing white, glistening fangs. She placed the tips of the fangs against his skin, and as she was ready to pierce, she gave a look of shock and betrayal—Sager had taken a wooden stake from his armor and had thrust it into her heart. Her head fell back, and as she fell into a pile of dust, Sager heard her whisper, "Thank you."

Ophelia started toward Sager with venom in her eyes.

He turned and put his hands up in defense, but it was too late— Ophelia tore him apart in seconds as his friends watched in terror and anger. She turned back toward the group and began walking in their direction, Sager's blood dripping out of her mouth.

But Lâmié was able to recite the amulet's words aloud very quickly. Beast Stalker held out the amulet, and a stunning, blazing blue fire emanated from it throughout the room. The few remaining vampires, except Ophelia, were hit by the light, and as they shrieked in shame and agony, they caught fire and burnt up into the dirt from which they had arisen. Only Ophelia remained.

She gasped as the brilliant, blue clarion burst reached her. She screamed in pain and backed up. "It's... it's so powerful!" she cried. They walked toward her, forcing her back and outside of the bar. She fell to her knees and whimpered.

"I'll kill the bloody bitch!" shouted Paul as he ran at her with a stake. However, before he could reach her, she crawled backward, just out of the blue light's circle, then turned and ran at superhuman speed. She reached the end of the street, shot up into the air, and vanished.

"Holy hell," said Matt. "Is she... is she dead?"

"I don't think so," said Lâmié. "She's definitely weakened, though. That's why she ran away and escaped. She knew that we had power over her. I didn't suspect that vampires could fly like that. Lore says they can levitate, but that was all-out flying!"

"Where'd she go?" asked Mary.

"Who knows?" answered Janine. "New Orleans? Paris? Prague? Plenty of places around the world for a vampire to hide and recover its power. The important part, though, is that the most powerful vampires of Ushaville have been stopped for now. We need to get that amulet to Chief Cloud Mountain."

"Wait. We need to do one more thing first," said Paul. "Burn Ushaville to the fucking ground."

"He's right," added Lâmié. "This place must be accursed. The ancient vampires in the tunnels show that the evil has been here for a very long time. It could be that the land itself is cursed, so it needs to be purified. The evil must be banished once and for all."

Beast Stalker agreed, "This land is indeed cursed. There are still ancient vampires in the tunnels below and vampires on the streets above. It is infested beyond redemption. Please let me just retrieve some of my people's history from my museum, and then we should burn down Ushaville once and for all."

No one argued.

CHAPTER 36

F ire. It purifies metal ore; it removes the slag from the gold; it eliminates all impurities, leaving only the untainted essence; it burns away the wicked and allows the good to remain; it separates the temporal from the immortal. Fire burns, and it purifies. Like Lord Shiva, it is a destroyer, and a creator, of worlds.

The sun rose on Ushaville once more while Paul drove the Microbite to the Ushaville Council building.

"Fire at will, Mucky Matt!" he shouted.

Matt aimed at the center of the building and fired off a rocket. It hit the building's side and exploded, knocking a hole in the wall and burning the insides. They heard vampires screaming as the building caught fire.

Paul drove the van around Ushaville, using the front-mounted leafblower-flamethrower to torch building after building, one spurt at a time. Soon, entire streets were set aflame, and thousands and thousands of vampires were burnt up to carbon inside the buildings. The fires leaped from house to house, from business to business, from Westside to Eastside. Beast Stalker wept silently as his Old Ways Bookstore caught fire, and the grand old tree returned to its elements.

The entire town of Ushaville—from Red McCoy's general store to the last reaches of the dark Eastside—was roaring in flames as they left town to head to Chief's house. The agonized and excruciating shrieks and screams of the countless vampires burning up inside of all the buildings was like a grotesque, hellish chorus of demons. Paul looked in the rear-view mirror and saw a wall of flame in the distance.

They reached Chief Cloud Mountain's house, and his wife served them all coffee. The fairies, all except Titania, bade their farewells and returned to their homes, disappearing into the glittering, green air as they had never been there in the first place.

"The ancestors have spoken to me," said Chief. "You all have destroyed the evil in Ushaville. You have done well. No town must ever again be built on that ancient, cursed land. Once the fire goes away and the ground cools off, I'll have my tribe salt the earth to assure that nothing again grows there. Do you have the amulet?"

Beast Stalker carefully and respectfully handed the amulet to Chief, who took it into his arms as if cradling a baby. The amulet glowed a soft hue of light blue.

Lâmié wrote down the pronunciation of the amulet's words and gave them to Chief, in case they ever again needed to use the magic. Chief spoke again.

"I will put the amulet in a secret, sacred place. No evil thing will ever be able to find it. If evil ever returns to Ushaville, it shall be accessible to my people. Now, I have something else to announce."

Everyone looked at him quietly and expectantly.

"As you can see," began Chief, "I am not getting any younger. I am well advanced in my years. I hope to live as long as possible, but I will return to my ancestors one day, and so shall my wife. It is the way of nature, the way of man. When a Cherokee chief becomes my age, he has the duty and the sacred honor of appointing a male Cherokee to take his place as chief when he passes into the next world. You may see where this is going. Beast Stalker, you have proven in all of this that you are a great warrior. You have stood up against the greatest forces of evil; you have withstood torture without revealing the secret of the amulet; you have fought alongside your friends bravely, without a single complaint. You have been a leader and a great Cherokee warrior. You have proven more than enough that you are the man who will be our next chief."

"Wait, Chief Cloud Mountain, I can't... who am I to..."

Chief Cloud Mountain simply interrupted him, "Beast Stalker, it is appointed. The ancestors have confirmed it to me in a vision; you will be the next Chief of our tribe. On the day that I join my ancestors, you will be the chief. Chief Beast Stalker. It is a noble name that has a good ring to it. Don't you all agree?"

Everyone applauded, causing Beast Stalker's face to blush a bright red as he looked down humbly at the floor.

"Then Chief," he said, "I most humbly accept this sacred duty and honor. I will lead our people well. I will not fail you."

"I know," said Chief. "You will be a great leader. The ancestors have also given me another vision, but they have kept it vague. They told me that you, as chief, will face another great evil and that you shall have to fight it and defeat it. I do not know what this means, but it will come to pass."

"Say, Beast Stalker?" asked Mary. "What's your spirit animal anyway?"

"It is a bear," he answered.

"The bear," explained Chief, "symbolizes great power and sovereignty. The bear is a guardian with great power and strength, very courageous, but also speculative and careful. It is the perfect spirit animal for Chief Beast Stalker!"

They all spent the night at Chief's house, everyone finding a spot on the floor. Some Cherokee men stopped by and barbecued a large feast for everyone. They ate, drank, and talked late into the night. After all they had been through, no one opposed a little celebration.

The next day, as they sat and talked, Paul asked, "Well? What now? Where do we go? Can't live in Ushaville anymore. Do we go look for Ophelia?"

"We probably should," replied Janine. "As long as she's out there, and those like her, humans are in danger. Plus, vampires aren't the only monsters out there, you know."

"Wait, what?" said Mary nervously. "There's other shit too?"

Janine laughed and nodded. "Yep. All sorts of nasty. I think we did pretty well against the vampires. Maybe… I dunno, maybe we could do some good another way? Just a thought."

"Well, fuck it, why not? We need to find a replacement for Gill for the band, but until then, I'm game for anything."

"Adventure," said a hungover Matt, yawning and slurring his words.

"Then let's go back to New Orleans," suggested Janine. "I could sure go for some more gumbo and beer!"

Printed in Great Britain
by Amazon

54317318R00151